Praise for
POLITICAL SUICIDE

"When you open the pages of a Michael Palmer novel, you know you are in the hands of a pro. This author knows how to weave a plot and keep the action coming, and the readers know it won't all fall apart at the end. Such is definitely the case with *Political Suicide*. Each page adds a new dimension to the characters and a new revelation to the plot. It is action/mystery reading at its best. Palmer just keeps delivering good stories, one right after the other."

—*Huffington Post*

"This book goes from great to outstanding . . . a definite keeper!"　　　　　　　—*Suspense* magazine

"Plenty of chills and spills."　　　　　—*Kirkus Reviews*

"Palmer writes terrific medical suspense, and he has thrown political intrigue into the mix . . . fans won't be disappointed."　　　　　　　—Associated Press

"Michael Palmer once again delivers an adrenaline-pumped political and medical action thriller . . . Palmer fans will not be disappointed in this suspenseful and realistic, fast-paced whodunit."　　　　—*Jewish Journal*

"A must-read for fans of political intrigue."

—*Fort-Worth Star Telegram*

"The military conspiracy is frightening, while Lou's interactions with his daughter and his blossoming romantic interest in a tough attorney provide some breaks from the merciless pace of the investigation. Suspend disbelief that an ER doctor can, or should, attempt some of these actions and enjoy the ride."

—*RT Book Reviews*

"Michael Palmer mixes politics, medical science, and the military to create another suspenseful medical thriller." —Examiner.com

OATH OF OFFICE

"One of the most exciting thrillers of the year."

—*Huffington Post*

"A shocker." —Associated Press

"This is Palmer at his most terrifying, most plausible and, worst of all, most realistic."

—*RT Book Reviews* (4.5 stars)

"Suspenseful . . . Palmer's easy mix of science and individual courage should please his many fans."

—*Publishers Weekly*

"Compelling." —*Kirkus Reviews*

"Michael Palmer anchors his thrillers in high concept and steeps them in medicine. *A Heartbeat Away* opens with a prologue, and from the opening line, the reader knows things are not going to go well . . . This is the book for readers who wholeheartedly believe politicians are capable of anything."

—*Boston Globe*

THE LAST SURGEON

"Prepare to burn some serious midnight oil."

—*Boston Herald*

"Highly suspenseful and compelling." —*Booklist*

"Palmer has always been a good writer but he has never crafted a story as suspenseful as this one . . . This is the kind of book you read with a bright light on and all the doors locked . . . Franz Koller is one of the most deadly villains to grace the pages of a novel since the introduction of Hannibal Lecter."

—*Huffington Post*

"Should please . . . all those who enjoy their suspense mixed with medical characters and settings."

—*Library Journal*

"The thrill of the non-kill . . . [is] chilling."

—*North Shore Sunday*

"More twists and turns than a sociopath's psyche . . . inventive and effective, an entertaining and engaging read." —*California Literary Review*

THE SECOND OPINION

"A heart-pounding medical thriller . . . satisfying, expertly paced [with] enough suspense to keep readers happily turning the pages." —*Boston Globe*

"The novel is not merely a thriller but also an exploration of its central character's unique gifts and her determination to communicate with her comatose father despite overwhelming odds. Another winner from a consistently fine writer." —*Booklist*

"A splendid novel." —*Globe and Mail* (Canada)

THE FIRST PATIENT

"An exciting thriller that is full of surprises and captures the intense atmosphere of the White House, how the medical system works, and how the 25th Amendment could be brought into play. I thoroughly enjoyed it." —President Bill Clinton

"An incredibly realistic, frightening thriller that is every White House doctor's nightmare."
—Dr. E. Connie Mariano,
White House physician 1992–2001

Also by Michael Palmer

POLITICAL SUICIDE

MICHAEL PALMER

St. Martin's Paperbacks

This is a work of fiction. All of the characters, organizations, and events portrayed in this novel are either products of the author's imagination or are used fictitiously.

POLITICAL SUICIDE

For information address St. Martin's Press, 175 Fifth Avenue, New York, NY 10010.

ISBN: 978-0-312-58756-7

Printed in the United States of America

St. Martin's Press hardcover edition / January 2013
St. Martin's Paperbacks edition / April 2014

St. Martin's Paperbacks are published by St. Martin's Press, 175 Fifth Avenue, New York, NY 10010.

10 9 8 7 6 5 4 3 2 1

With my thanks and deepest respect to Dr. Lloyd Axelrod and Dr. Michael Fifer of Massachusetts General Hospital

ACKNOWLEDGMENTS

Much energy and thought have gone into this novel, not all of it mine. This is my chance to thank those who have been with me during this journey, and I do so gratefully:

My brilliant editor, Jennifer Enderlin, has a gift for story that few possess.

The gang at the Jane Rotrosen Agency, especially my agent Meg Ruley, who continues to be incredible fun to work with.

Experts Dr. Lisa Sanders, Dr. Geoffrey Sherwood, Dr. Kate Isselbacher, author Cilla McCain, attorney William J. Bladd, ballistics guru Steve Ostrowski, Dr. Rock Grass, and Dr. Ethan Prince.

Others without whom I could never have completed *Political Suicide* include:

The Palmer brothers, Daniel, Matthew, and Luke.

Robin Broady, Donna Prince, and Susan P. Terry.

And the many, many friends of Bill Wilson and Dr. Bob Smith.

PROLOGUE

MAY 3, 2003

The three men, members of Mantis Company, slipped out the open hatch of the C-130 transport as it flew thirty thousand feet above the world. They had trained for this jump countless times. Their gear, ballistic helmets, oxygen masks, Airox O_2 regulators, bailout bottles—all fastidiously maintained—assured them a successful landing. Altimeters marked their belly-to-earth rate of descent at 115 miles per hour. Minutes of free fall were spent in an effortless dive, with the men dropping in formation, still and straight. Automatic activation devices engaged the parachutes eight hundred feet before impact, the lowest altitude allowed for combat high altitude–low opening jumps.

They descended through the low cloud covering like missiles, emerging out of nothingness beneath a starless predawn sky. Their landings, each completed with a puma's grace, would have made their instructors back at Quantico proud. Perfection. Mantis demanded nothing less. In silence, the three exchanged their polypropylene undergarments, vital to protect against frostbite at high altitudes, for white cotton robes and the traditional head coverings of Taliban fighters. Then they zippered shut their fifty-pound combat packs.

Wearing their dusty garments, the men anticipated they would not immediately rouse any suspicion. Each of the three had a tanning booth tan supplemented by professionally applied makeup, as well as a closely trimmed mustache and a fully grown beard. Moving stealthily, the trio blended in with their surroundings—a mountainous, rocky region in southern Afghanistan, barren as a moonscape.

"Any injuries?"

"No, Sergeant," the two men replied in unison.

"Miller, how many klicks to the target?"

Miller checked his handheld GPS. "Five kilometers south-southwest of the target, Sergeant."

"Gibson, ditch the gear."

Gibson knew not to look long for a suitable location in which to hide their parachutes and other equipment. By the time any Afghani stumbled upon the array of high-tech military paraphernalia hidden behind a jagged boulder, it hopefully would be too late.

They walked in single file, moving silently across the rock-strewn terrain, with Miller and his GPS taking the lead. Behind them, dawn rose in streaks of brilliant pinks, yellows, and blues—giant fingers extending skyward, beckoning the new day. If anyone had checked the men's pulses at that moment, none would be above fifty beats per minute.

Miller found the road, a rutted stretch of dirt that

would carry them to the outskirts of Khewa, a town of twenty thousand that would look the same today as it did a century and a half ago. Young women wearing chadors stopped farming the fields of wheat, rice, and vegetables lining the roadside to give the trio a cursory glance before quickly resuming their duties. The marines' disguises were good enough so that none of the women bothered with a closer inspection. They had estimated that unless their luck was extremely bad, they could survive twelve hours or so before they were identified by soldiers or one of the villagers.

Way more than enough time.

The men of Mantis Company reached the crumbling clay brick walls of Khewa's borders without incident. The town was defined by its absences—no cars, no electricity, no running water. Evidence of twenty years of war was seen everywhere. Craters left by bombs and land mines made what limited roads there were treacherous to pass even on foot. Bombed-out buildings and homes were in greater number than habitable ones.

The smells of the market guided the men toward their destination. They wandered about casually through shabby stalls built of boards, sheets, and mud and bunched together on each side of a single-lane dirt road. The central market was already bustling despite the newness of the day. In some stalls, slabs of fly-covered meat dangled like macabre wind chimes, while blood-stained butchers called out the day's prices in Pashto. Persian music blasted from cheap radios as the marines continued their stroll past stalls selling fruit, breads, and rudimentary household supplies.

Two hours had brought a sweltering midmorning before they caught the attention of a town elder.

"Don't look now," Gibson said, his voice hushed, "but it looks like we've been noticed."

The Afghani, with a white beard descending to his chest, carrying a Kalashnikov assault rifle, approached the men the way he might a poisonous snake.

The three marines turned their backs to the man and moved well away from the women and children in the crowded market. To the extent they could control it, this operation was going to be soldiers only. When they finally stopped, the Afghani took two cautious steps toward them . . . then a third. His dark eyes narrowed. Then he began to shout and point frantically.

His shrill voice rose above the market's din, catching the attention of more men dressed in dirty gray or white robes, each, it seemed, carrying a weapon different in make and age from the others. The commotion rapidly crescendoed, with more Afghani men—some armed, some not—racing up from all directions to surround the intruders. They were screaming, shouting in Pashto, and pointing long, dirt-encrusted fingernails at the three men now trapped inside the rapidly expanding circle.

"How do you like the show so far, Miller?" the sergeant asked, barely moving his lips.

"Just what you told us, Sarge," Miller said without a waver in his voice. "Provided they go and get Mr. Big." He moistened his lips with his tongue.

The Taliban fighters were ten deep now, 150 of them at least, many with weapons leveled—PK machine guns, ancient Lee-Enfields, plus a variety of handguns. They were pushing and shoving to get a closer look at the men who had so brazenly strolled into the center of their city.

"Just keep your hands raised," the sergeant said to both his men, "and keep scanning the crowd for Al-Basheer. If our intelligence is correct, none of them will make a move until he gets here."

The closest men in the milling circle were a smothering five or six feet away.

Miller spotted Al-Basheer first. His orange beard and bulbous nose were distinct giveaways.

"That's him, Sergeant," Miller said as the crowd parted to admit their leader, one of the most powerful and influential fighters in the region.

Al-Basheer strode through the ranks. The sergeant smiled and nodded, and immediately the three marines formed a tight triangle, facing outward with their shoulders touching. The sudden movement caused some of those surrounding them to step back.

But not Al-Basheer.

"Whatever it takes," the sergeant said.

"Whatever it takes," Miller and Gibson echoed.

In a singular motion, the three men threw off their robes.

The crowd began screaming again.

Strapped to each intruder's chest were bricks of explosive—three on the right side and three on the left—with wires connected to a battery hinged to their waists.

"Whatever it takes," the sergeant said again.

The push of a button, a faint click, and in an instant, every man in the warrior circle was vaporized within a white hot ball of carefully concentrated light.

CHAPTER 1

Dr. Louis Francis Welcome could do a lot of things well, but doing nothing was not one of them. His desk at the Washington, D.C., Physician Wellness Office, one of four cubicle work areas jammed inside 850 square feet had never been so uncluttered. On a typical midafternoon, the voice mail light on Lou's Nortel telephone would be blinking red—a harbinger that one or more of his doctor clients needed advice and support in their recovery from mental illness, behavioral problems, or drug and alcohol abuse. At the moment, that light was dark, as it had been for much of the past several days.

Lou got paid to manage cases and monitor the progress of his assigned physicians, with the express goals of guiding them into recovery and eventually getting surrendered licenses reinstated. The holiday season inevitably brought an influx of new docs, often ordered to the PWO by the D.C. board of medicine.

But not recently.

He strongly suspected the lack of clients did not

indicate a dwindling need for PWO services. On the contrary, as with the general population, the stress accompanying the last six weeks of the year unmasked plenty of physicians in trouble for a variety of reasons. So why in the hell, he mused, absently constructing a chain from the contents of his inlaid mother-of-pearl paper clip box, was he not getting any new cases?

There was, he knew, only one logical explanation for the paucity of referrals—Dr. Walter Filstrup, the director of the program.

Rhythmically compressing a rubber relaxation ball imprinted with PFIZER PHARMACEUTICALS, Lou sauntered over to the reception desk, where Babs Peterbee seemed to be quite busy.

"Hi, there, Dr. Welcome," she said, her round, matronly face radiating a typical mix of caring and concern. "I didn't see you come in."

"Ninja Doctor," Lou said, striking a pose. "Any calls?"

"A man who said he wanted to talk to you about the head of his department drinking too much. I referred him to Dr. Filstrup's voice mail."

"Did you get his name?"

Peterbee forced a smile. "Not my job."

The woman's favorite phrase. Lou said the words in unison with her. The woman definitely knew how to make it through her day unscathed. *Not my job.*

"BP, is Walter in?" Lou asked. "His door's been closed since I got here."

"He's having a telephone meeting right now," Peterbee said, cocking her head to the right, toward the only door in the suite except for the one to the small conference room across from her. The door was also the only one with a name placard, this one bronze and elegantly embossed with Filstrup's name and degree.

"Is this a real meeting, or a Filstrup meeting?"

Again, Peterbee strained to smile. "How's your daughter?" she asked.

"Emily's doing great, thank you," Lou said, shifting his six-foot frame from one foot to the other and switching the Pfizer ball to his left hand. "She's closing in on fourteen-going-on-thirty, and is far more skilled than even our esteemed boss at skirting issues she doesn't want to deal with. So I'll ask again, is Walter *really* busy?"

This time Peterbee glanced down at her phone bank and shook her head, as though she was no longer betraying whatever promise she had made to Filstrup. "Looks like he's off now."

"When the Employee of the Year awards come up, BP, I'm nominating you. Such loyalty."

"You mean poverty."

"That, too. His overall mood?"

"I would say, maybe Cat Two."

The small staff at the PWO measured the volatile director's demeanor on the Saffir–Simpson scale used by meteorologists to rate the power of hurricanes.

"Cat Two isn't so bad," Lou said, mostly to himself. "Blustery but not life threatening."

"It won't stay that way if you go barging in there, Dr. Welcome," Peterbee admonished.

Lou blew her a kiss. "Never fear," he said. "I've got a Kevlar life preserver on under my shirt."

Lou knocked once on Filstrup's door and opened it. The director's office, filled with neatly arranged medical textbooks and bound psychiatric journals, was even less cluttered than Lou's cubicle, a reflection not of the man's thin calendar, but of his overriding need for order.

Fit and trim, wearing his invariable dark blue suit, wrinkle-free white dress shirt, and solid-colored tie—this day some shade of gray—Filstrup shot to his feet, his face reddening by the nanosecond. "Leave immediately, Welcome, then knock and wait."

"And you'll beckon me in?"

"No, I'll tell you I'm expecting an important call, and you should come back in an hour."

Lou pulled back the Aeron chair opposite Filstrup and sat. On the desk to his right was an orderly pile of dictations to review, alongside a stack of client charts. No one could accuse the man of not running a sphincter-tight ship.

"I haven't seen you for most of the week, boss, so I thought I'd stop by and find out how business was."

"Snideness was never one of your most endearing qualities, Welcome, although I'll have to admit that it's not one of your worst, either."

"Who's monitoring all these cases?" Lou asked, gesturing toward the stacks. "Certainly not me."

Filstrup looked down, favoring Lou with an unobstructed view of his bald spot, and theatrically signed a form that Lou suspected might be the equivalent in importance of a follow-up survey from the census bureau.

"The board of trustees keeps renewing your contract," Filstrup said, "but they don't say how I'm supposed to use you."

"How about some work?" Lou asked, his tone not quite pleading, but close. "I'm champing at the bit."

"You *have* cases to monitor," Filstrup said.

"What I have is a handful of doctors who are in terrific, solid recovery," Lou said. "I'm here to be helpful. I like doing this job, and I've never gone this long without getting a new case to monitor. What gives, Walter?"

"What gives is we have a new hire who's working full-time, and I've got to get him up to speed on what we do around here and the way that we're supposed do it. You know yourself that the best way to indoctrinate somebody new is to get them huffing and puffing in the field."

"Huffing and puffing," Lou said. "I like the image. Colorful. Asthmatic even."

"Wiseass," Filstrup grumbled.

"So I'm being punished because I'm not full-time, even though I've done more than my share of huffing and puffing?"

Lou had been part-time with the PWO for five years. Five years before that, he was one of their clients, being monitored for amphetamine and alcohol dependence— the former used to cope with a killer moonlighting schedule, and the latter to come down from the speed. It was Lou's belief that having battled his own addiction benefited the docs assigned to him. Filstrup, who was hired by the board well after Lou, would not concur.

"That's not it at all," Filstrup said. "You're working almost full-time in the Eisenhower Memorial emergency room, and twenty hours a week here."

"Can you spell 'alimony'? Listen, Walter, I enjoy both my jobs and I need the income, so I put in a little extra time. Have there been complaints?"

"Since you got moved from the hospital annex back to the big ER, you've seemed stressed."

"Only by my reduced caseload. There should be enough work for both Oliver and me."

"I told you," Filstrup said. "Oliver needs to get up to speed."

"This wouldn't have anything to do with him being a psychiatrist like yourself? Would it?"

"Of course not," Filstrup replied, dismissing the statement with a wave.

Lou knew better. He and Filstrup had been at odds since day one, in large measure over their disagreement as to whether addiction was an illness or a moral issue.

"Does Oliver think every monitoring client should go through extensive psychotherapy?"

"It doesn't always have to be extensive," Filstrup said.

Don't drink, go to meetings, and ask a higher power for help.

Lou knew that the terse, three-pronged instruction manual was all that the majority of addicts and alcoholics involved with AA ever needed. Psychotherapy had its place with some of them, but protracted, expensive treatment was often over the top.

He could sense their exchange was getting out of hand, and kept quiet by reminding himself, as he did from time to time for nearly every one of his docs, that whether the stone hit the vase, or the vase hit the stone, it was going to be bad for the vase.

Filstrup removed his glasses and cleaned the lenses with a cloth from his desk drawer. Lou thought the gray tie would have done just as well.

"Just because you were once a drug addict," Filstrup went on, "doesn't give your opinions greater authority here."

"I can't believe we're going at it like this because I came in here to ask for more work."

The phone rang before Filstrup could retort. He flashed an annoyed look and pushed the intercom button. "I thought I told you to hold all my calls, Mrs. Peterbee," Filstrup said.

I thought you were expecting one, Lou mused.

"I'm sorry, Dr. Filstrup," the receptionist said. "Actually, this is for Dr. Welcome. I have the caller on hold."

Lou gave Filstrup a bewildered look. "Who is it, Mrs. P?" Lou asked.

"Our client, Dr. Gary McHugh," Peterbee said. "He said it's urgent."

Filstrup reflexively straightened up. "McHugh, the society doc?" he said. "Put him through." Filstrup allowed the call to click over, then said in an cheery voice, "Gary, it's Walter Filstrup. How are you doing?"

The director's conciliatory tone churned Lou's stomach, but it was not an unexpected reaction, given who was on the other line. Gary McHugh tended to the D.C.

carriage trade and probably numbered among his patients a significant portion of all three branches of the government. He was renowned for his acumen, loyalty, and discretion, as well as for making house calls. What he was not known for, at least within the confines of the D.C. Physician Wellness Office, was for being one of Lou Welcome's closest friends since their undergraduate days together at Georgetown.

Several years before, McHugh had lost his driver's license for operating under the influence and refusing to take a field sobriety test. The board of medicine's knee-jerk policy was to refer such physician offenders to the PWO, and in the absence of another associate director, Lou was placed in charge of his case.

Although McHugh adhered to the letter of his monitoring contract, he regarded the whole business as something of a joke. Lou could not help but enjoy the man's spirit, intelligence, and panache, even though he never had much trust in the strength of McHugh's recovery—too much ego and way too few AA meetings. Still, McHugh, a sportsman and pilot with his own pressurized Cessna, had always been irrepressible, and Lou looked forward to their required monthly progress meetings, as well as to any other chance they had to get together.

"Am I on speakerphone?" McHugh barked.

"I was just finishing a meeting with Lou Welcome," Filstrup said, as if the appointment had been on his calendar for weeks.

"Dr. Filstrup, I need to speak with him."

"I'm here," Lou said.

"Dr. Welcome, get me off speaker, please."

Lou stifled a grin at Filstrup's discomfort, and with a *what can you do?* expression, took the receiver. "Hey, Gary," he said, pressing the phone to his ear to seal off as much sound as possible, "what gives?"

"Welcome, thank God you're there. I'm in trouble— really, really big trouble. I need to see you right away."

"Talk to me."

"I can't. Not from where I am."

"Where, then?"

"My house. You have the address?"

"Of course," Lou said.

"When can you get there?"

Filstrup kept quiet and still. Lou forced any urgency from his voice, and pressed the receiver even tighter against his ear. He checked his Mickey Mouse watch, a Father's Day gift from Emily. Nearly four—eight hours before he was due at the ER for the graveyard shift. McHugh lived in a tony neighborhood, midway between the Capitol and Annapolis.

"I can be there in about forty-five minutes," Lou said.

"Get here in thirty," McHugh urged. "Before too much longer, the police are going to show up here to arrest me."

"For what?"

"For murder." He hung up without saying good-bye.

CHAPTER 2

Murder.

The word reverberated through Lou's mind as he left the city and headed east.

Gary McHugh, suave, adventurous, almost painfully popular, believed he was about to be arrested for killing someone—not killing, but murdering.

Who? How? For the moment, the questions far outstripped their answers. One thing that did make sense was that McHugh's first move would be to call Lou. Their history together was a colorful and at times wildly adventurous one that included parachuting with two magnums of champagne onto a remote field, where two bewildered women were waiting with their picnic baskets for their double blind dates to arrive. If Lou were in mortal trouble, there were few people he would turn to before calling McHugh.

The December afternoon was already dark, and the wipers on Lou's ten-year-old Camry were working to keep up with a fine, windblown snow. He pulled off of Route 50 and onto a secondary road lined with McMansions, many of which were already decorated for Christmas. White bulb country, Lou had once heard someone describe upscale neighborhoods such as this one—understated holiday decor featuring small white lights on the front shrubs and electric candles in every window. Nice enough, but he was still partial to the tangled strings of blinking colored bulbs outlining Dimitri's Pizza shop, just below his apartment in D.C.

It was one of Walter Filstrup's few sensible rules that clients be identified only by their assigned numbers, and that no doctor's name could be removed from the office. In a totally out-of-character concession to the man, Lou kept his client numbers next to their initials on a card in his wallet, and their contact information locked in his smartphone, which, at that moment, was resting on the worn passenger seat of the Toyota. McHugh's cell phone number was in it, but if he had wanted Lou to call, he would have said so.

Murder.

What in the hell is the man talking about?

The two of them had met once or twice a month since McHugh's monitoring contract became active, sometimes at the PWO, sometimes at McHugh's home or D.C. office, and less frequently at a restaurant. Filstrup insisted that Lou include a credit card validation that he paid for his own meal. Lou never reacted maturely to being told what to do, and he resented the implication that he or the other associate director could be bought—certainly not for the price of a dinner. So, even though Filstrup's policy made some sense, Lou had taken trips in McHugh's plane, and gone to a couple of Redskins games thanks to his friend's season tickets.

As things evolved between them, McHugh did test Lou once by claiming he never had the time to see a doctor, and had ordered some Percocets from an Internet pharmacy in Canada to deal with a chronically balky back. His reasoning was that alcohol was the substance that had gotten him a PWO contract, not painkillers. Lou made little attempt to point out the foolishness of that belief, or the quickness with which a positive random urine test for Percocet or any such drug would get his license pulled. McHugh's denial was as thick as a glacier, but he still knew what was at stake, so Lou extracted a promise that, when the Percocet bottles arrived in the promised plain brown wrapper, they would be opened in his presence and the pills dumped in the toilet.

After the pills had been disposed of, Lou sat beside the phone as McHugh made an appointment with his orthopedist. The final steps would be the assurance that the orthopedist had been informed of McHugh's status with the PWO, and would provide the program a copy of any prescription he wrote.

"No thanks necessary," Lou had said as the last of the Percocets swirled down the toilet.

"None given," McHugh had replied testily.

Not long after that exchange, when Lou mentioned in passing that Emily was assigned to do a school report on a new piece of environmental legislation, McHugh arranged for the congressman sponsoring the actual bill to speak at Emily's school. Case closed. Friendship preserved.

Lou cruised through the gated entrance of McHugh's elegant Tudor-style home. The electric candles in each window looked as if they had been included in the design when the house was built, but there were no bulbs on the shrubs. Lou observed only one car parked in the circular driveway—a Lexus, which he assumed belonged to Missy, McHugh's wife. McHugh prided himself on his high-end black Jaguar. Lou wondered if the car had somehow been involved in the man's current plight—a fatal accident of some sort, perhaps. Then he reminded himself that McHugh had very specifically said *murder*.

He braked the Toyota to a stop in front of the roofed entranceway. McHugh—graying red hair, broadshouldered, dense five o'clock shadow—stood waiting. He wore a green collared sweater, but no jacket. His face was distorted by a huge bruise involving the area between his left cheek and hairline. His left eye was swollen shut.

"Hey, thanks for getting here so quickly," McHugh said grimly, "I forgot it was rush hour."

"No problem. Gary, let's get inside. It's freezing out here."

Limping slightly, McHugh set Lou's peacoat on a hook in the foyer, and shook his hand. His wrestler's grip had not been diminished by whatever had battered his face. His one open eye was bloodshot, and Lou almost immediately smelled alcohol—more, it seemed from the man's pores than from his breath. Whatever had happened today, booze was almost certainly part of it. Lou's recurrent warning that he did not feel McHugh could ever drink in safety had gone unheeded and was now apparently extracting a heavy toll.

"What's going on, Gary?"

"Let's go my study," McHugh said. "I just lit a fire to take the chill out."

The temperature in the cherry-paneled room had already responded to the neatly laid blaze. The space was perhaps a third the size of Lou's entire apartment. A forty-inch plasma TV mounted above the stone fireplace was tuned to CNN. The walls were decorated with pictures and souvenirs that defined the man—his travels to exotic locales, his plane, skydiving certification, skiing with a skill and grace that showed even in a photograph, black-tie parties featuring A-list notables, testimonials and letters of thanks, at least two from recent presidents.

McHugh motioned Lou to one of two red leather armchairs, while he remained standing, glancing from time to time at the TV.

"Talk to me, Gary," Lou said.

McHugh, now watching CNN steadily, had his back turned. Despite the odor of alcohol, there was no evidence in his speech or manner that he was intoxicated. "Anytime now," he said, "CNN is going to report breaking news regarding the shooting death in his garage of Congressman Elias Colston."

Lou stiffened and dug his fingers into the thick arms of his chair. Colston, the chairman of the House Committee on Armed Services, was one of the more popular congressmen in the House. Maryland District 1, Lou guessed, or maybe it was District 3.

"How do you know?" he asked.

"I was there," McHugh said flatly, wincing as he sat down in the other chair. "I saw the body. At least two shots—one to the chest and one dead center in the forehead."

"Are you absolutely sure? Did you check for a pulse?"

"Believe me, Lou, I checked, but I know dead."

"And the body temp?"

"Warm."

"When did this happen?"

"I got there at noon."

"And you had been drinking?"

There was an embarrassed silence, and then, "Yes. Fairly heavily."

Lou groaned. Gary McHugh seldom did anything in half measures. He could only imagine what *fairly heavily* meant.

"Why hasn't the story broken by now?"

McHugh shrugged. "I guess because I'm the only one who saw him—besides the person who killed him, that is."

"And why didn't you call the police?" Even as he was asking the question, Lou knew the answer.

"I . . . intended to find a phone booth and call them anonymously, rather than risk giving them my cell phone number. I knew if they caught up with me and I were found to be drinking, I could kiss my medical license good-bye."

"Oh, Jesus, Gary. But before you could call anyone, you smashed up your car and did this to your face, yes?"

"You got it. I must have skidded off the road and hit a tree."

"You don't remember?"

"The first thing I remember after seeing Elias's body, I was being transferred from an ambulance stretcher to a bed in the ER. Apparently, someone found me unconscious in my car. Somebody said something about having to use the Jaws of Life."

Blackout from alcohol or concussion, Lou thought. Most likely both. He probably should have been kept overnight.

"Which hospital?" he asked, checking the screen expectantly.

"Anne Arundel."

"Are you okay now? I have my medical bag in the car. Maybe I should check you over."

"They did everything—blood work, CAT scan. I had to beat the frigging residents and med students off with a stick."

"Did they want to keep you?"

"They wanted to, but I wouldn't consider it. All I wanted to do was get the hell out of the place as quickly as possible. Missy came and they let me go."

"Your alcohol level?"

"It was probably high. One of the nurses who knows me said a good lawyer could get me off any charges by saying I was head injured and couldn't authorize having my blood drawn. That may be the reason the police decided not to charge me on the spot."

"I'm not sure that's true if the ER people had good reason to draw your blood in the first place. Besides, you can always be charged later. But more important, the charges you're talking about may be significantly bigger than a DUI. Why do you think they would charge you with Colston's murder?"

McHugh rose and began to pace in front of the fire. "Colston is a patient of mine. I've been to his house many times before. There are security cameras."

"Then maybe one of them recorded the murder."

"Maybe, but it took place way in the back of the garage, by the stairs that go up to Colston's office. I don't remember any cameras being there—just outside on the driveway. I'll bet the only thing those cameras recorded is me, driving up and later driving away—maybe even with Elias's blood on me from when I checked him over. . . . What in the hell is going on? Why hasn't anyone found him and called the cops?"

"Gary, why would you be drinking in the morning and then go off to make a house call on one of your patients?"

"Because I wasn't making a house call, Lou. . . . Dammit, what is going on with this station? Why haven't they reported anything about this?"

McHugh grabbed a poker and stoked the fire as if he were spearing a wild boar.

Lou tightened his grip on the chair once more.

Again an inflated silence.

"Easy does it, Gary."

"Shit, I suppose everyone's going to find out anyway. I didn't go there to see Colston. I went there to see his wife, Jeannine."

"Not to treat her."

McHugh sighed. "No. We've been having an affair for more than two years."

"Oh, Gary," Lou groaned.

McHugh assaulted the fire again. "That's not all," he said.

CHAPTER 3

Lou stared across at McHugh and drew a nervous breath.

That's not all. . . .

What did he mean by that?

How much more could there be?

Before McHugh could explain, the news of Congressman Elias Colston's murder hit CNN like a wrecking ball. The report varied little from McHugh's account. Colston's body was discovered by his wife, Jeannine, after she returned from a meeting of a congressional spouses' group in Washington.

Jeannine Colston was not available for comment, but a spokeswoman for her said only that their son and daughter had been notified at college and were on their way home, and that Jeannine had no other comment at that time. The feed of the crime scene around the Colstons' tasteful country home was bedlam.

Lou waited for a commercial interruption to the first wave of reports, then turned to his host. "Okay, Gary," he said, "short and sweet. What else is there you haven't told me?"

McHugh threw an unnecessary log on the fire and began pacing again. "From what I can piece together, I skidded off the road and hit a tree just after I had crossed the bridge."

"Bridge?"

"I really don't remember a hell of a lot, Lou, but there's a stone bridge across a river about a mile down the road from the Colstons'."

Lou saw no significance to this latest revelation. "Explain," he said.

"Well, unless they find it at the scene, the police are going to suspect that I stopped and tossed the murder weapon off the bridge and into the river, then kept going and went off the road. There aren't many homes between Colstons' place and the bridge, so a logical conclusion would be that I was headed away from there."

Lou winced. "That's exactly what they're going to think," he said.

Then he remembered something else—something that McHugh had been required to discuss the first day his PWO monitoring contract began—his love affair with guns. McHugh owned several pistols and some hunting rifles. Years before, after a client's gunshot suicide, the monitoring contract was modified to demand that all guns be removed from a doctor's house, cataloged, and locked in a storage facility using a padlock provided by the PWO.

"The PWO has a record of the guns I turned in when I signed my contract," McHugh said as if reading Lou's thoughts. "They're all legally registered, so the police will learn about them, too, even though I know you people are protected from telling them anything."

Lou shrugged. *Not a big deal,* he was thinking. So why was McHugh being so dramatic about it, unless one of the guns registered to him was missing before he turned his collection over to the PWO?

No, there was something else.

"Gary, why were you drinking at that hour of the morning?" Lou asked. "What happened between you and Jeannine that led you to put your career on the line like that?"

McHugh's refusal to accept his alcoholism, and his failure to embrace a recovery program made him a setup for relapse. Still, he had managed to stay sober for several years. Often, in Lou's experience, the first drink after a long period of abstinence resulted from cutting down attendance at meetings followed by some sort of catalyst. Given the spontaneity of McHugh's early-hour intoxication, his rush to the Colstons', and the fact that he did not even know Jeannine wasn't home, Lou guessed that heartbreak might have been at the root of his relapse.

"She wanted to end it," McHugh replied, still staring at the screen.

"Did she say why?"

"Not really. She called me last night out of the blue and said I shouldn't try to contact her. I tried to get her to explain to me over the phone what was going on. All she kept saying was that Elias needed her, and she would call over the next few days."

"Elias needed her. What did she mean by that?"

"I don't know. I love her, Lou. I really do."

McHugh gestured toward the screen, where CNN was now reporting breaking news from an unnamed source that Maryland State Police had identified a person of interest in connection with the murder of Congressman Colston. They were not naming any names, but Lou and McHugh both knew who that person of interest most likely was.

Means, motive, and opportunity—in the absence of absolute proof or an eyewitness, these were the three critical circumstantial components of a crime, usually needed to convince a jury of guilt.

Lou felt his jaws clench.

Means—an affinity for guns and a place, the river, probably partially frozen, where the murder weapon might have been disposed of.

Motive—an affair with the victim's wife.

Opportunity—security camera footage placing McHugh at the scene close to the time of the killing.

But there was even more.

The suspect, himself, was probably operating in a blackout, and was incapable of providing anything useful toward his own defense.

Not good.

McHugh said he remembered checking Colston's body for pulses and finding none. Lou wondered now, as McHugh himself had suggested, if investigators would find blood, DNA, or other incriminating evidence in his Jaguar or on his clothes.

Not good at all.

"Did you call your attorney?" Lou asked. "We have you down as being represented by Grayson Devlin. It doesn't get any better than that."

"Actually, I called him from the hospital, but by then I knew I wasn't going to be arrested on the spot for DUI. He was busy with some sort of big case, but he promised he'd send one of his top associates over as soon as he could."

Before McHugh could expand on his answer, there was a soft knock on the office door, and Missy McHugh, petite and almost scarily thin, entered carrying a silver tray with a steaming teapot, sugar bowl, and spoon, and two blue china teacups.

"Here's the tea you asked for, darling."

Missy set the tray on their mahogany coffee table from enough of a height to rattle the dishes. She spoke the word *darling* as if it were a curse rather than any term of endearment. Her brown hair, streaked with silver, framed a pale, tired face that Lou knew had once been quite beautiful. He had been an usher at their wedding, but the closeness between him and Gary never carried over to her, and before he and Renee had split, she had never been able to warm up to the woman either.

"Nice to see you, Lou," Missy said without a glance at the television, "although I'm sorry it's under these unfortunate circumstances. Gary doesn't tell me very much, but I've been concerned about his not going to meetings, and I confess I wasn't all that surprised when he called me to get him away from the hospital and told me about the drinking and the accident. Now it appears he's going to lose his medical license."

Her baleful expression had Lou wondering how much she knew about other aspects of her husband's life. If the police and CNN reporters were doing their jobs, the answer to that question would soon be moot.

"I'm going to do what I can to help Gary put the pieces back together," Lou said.

"That's very nice of you. How are you feeling, Gary?" No *dear,* no *honey,* no contact between them. The woman's iciness put a chill in the room that even the crackling blaze could not offset.

"I'm feeling fine," Gary said. "Thanks for the tea."

She turned to Lou. The tension in her face seemed to have tripled. "I'm guessing you're here to revoke his license or something like that?"

"Like I said, I'm here to help him."

"But he is going to lose his license."

"I'm sorry, but I'm really not allowed to discuss anything pertaining to a physician's PWO contract, even with a spouse."

"Oh, you don't need to discuss anything. I know what's coming. It's a good thing the twins are in the last year of college, that's all I have to say. Otherwise, Gary might have to sell his precious plane. Look, I'm going out for a while. The Whitmans' Christmas party is tonight. Gary, I assume you won't be coming."

Grateful that Missy was about to break some of the excruciating tension in the room by leaving, Lou risked a peek at the screen. Still no mention of McHugh's name in the caption line.

McHugh ignored his wife's thrust and poured two cups of tea.

Without another word, Missy turned and, a moment later, was out the door.

"I'm sorry you had to be here for that, Lou," McHugh said.

"Nonsense. You had my back any number of times during the dark days."

"As I've told you before, it's been years since we had much of a marriage. I guess I don't have to explain my relationship with Jeannine."

"I don't require explanations. You called and asked me here. We've been close friends for years, so here I am."

McHugh rubbed at his stubble. "I didn't shoot Elias, Lou, but proving that isn't going to be easy. I called you because I'm afraid I'm going to need your help to check around about him—see if you can learn who might have wanted to kill him. Hire a detective if you think you need one."

"Gary, shouldn't that be a job for your lawyer or, better still, the police?"

"His *lawyer,* actually," said a woman. "But either would be correct."

CHAPTER 4

Lou turned, expecting to see Missy McHugh again. The woman in the doorway couldn't have been more dissimilar. She was tall and slender—an athlete, Lou guessed, dressed in a gray pants suit. Her straight ebony hair descended to just below her shoulders. She assessed him with intensely expressive eyes—an unsettling blue-green. There was something familiar about her, and Lou wondered if he was staring because of that—or simply because he couldn't pull away.

"Lou, I'm assuming this is Sarah Cooper, my attorney."

"You assume correctly, Dr. McHugh." She turned to Lou. "Grayson Devlin, Dr. McHugh's usual attorney, is in court with a case, so he sent me. Dr. McHugh, your wife let me in as she was leaving, so I just hung my coat in the foyer."

Sarah shook McHugh's hand, then, without waiting for a formal introduction, Lou's. Her fingers were long, and her grip confident. She wore a simple band on the fourth finger of her right hand, but none on her left. Her eye-to-eye contact was practiced and so firm that Lou felt he had been thoroughly analyzed by the time she turned away.

"Thanks for getting over here so quickly," McHugh said. "Grayson told me that he'd be at your disposal should you need him, but that you would take good care of me."

"Count on it," Sarah said.

"Lou, this woman was in charge of her firm's team in the Sandra Winkler trial. I assume you know about that case?"

Of course. That's where Lou had seen her before—in the papers and on TV. She wasn't easy to forget. The case made international news when an attractive young mother from Bethesda was accused of strangling her eight-year-old daughter behind the garage of their home. Cooper earned her client an acquittal, while she herself received a slew of death threats from outraged court vultures, who believed justice had not been served. Subsequently, a man accused of another, similar crime, admitted to guilt in the case.

"Nice job," Lou said. "Even after the verdict, I never knew what to make of that whole thing. I'm afraid to admit it, but until the killer confessed and the police found the proof in his room, I was on the side of those who thought she was guilty."

Sarah assessed him once again. "You were wrong," she said coolly. "And you would be?"

"Lou Welcome. I'm an ER doc at Eisenhower Memorial and a friend of Gary's."

He flashed on the first time he had met Renee. He

was a resident at the time, awkwardly trying to start up a conversation while the two were standing in the lunch line of the hospital cafeteria. Eighteen months later, they were married. Ten years and one Emily after that, they were facing a judge while Renee dissolved the union, citing the havoc wreaked by Lou's methamphetamine and alcohol addictions.

"Can I ask why Dr. McHugh called you here now?" Sarah asked.

"You can ask, but I'm professionally constrained from telling you."

"Well, that certainly gets us off to a strong start."

"Here," McHugh cut in, grabbing a sheet of paper from his desk. "If you really need to appease your boss at the Physician Wellness Office, I'll write you a release. Ms. Cooper, Lou is my monitor. I was required by the board to contract with Physician Wellness because of a DUI I once had. Lou is the only real human connected with the PWO, but he's still a company man."

"So if Dr. McHugh drinks, he loses his medical license," Sarah said. "Is that it?" Lou looked to McHugh, and Sarah groaned. "Great, so now we're playing charades."

"Yes," McHugh said. "If I drink, I lose my license."

"And what's Dr. Welcome supposed to do for us here, Dr. McHugh? From what I was told by Grayson, you may be facing some pretty serious charges. The fewer people you speak to about this, the better. I'd suggest you make that rule one."

"You can call me Gary. Lou is a friend of mine since

college. He's is going to help figure out who killed Elias Colston."

"No, he's not," Sarah said.

"Yes, he is," McHugh countered.

"Somehow, I think I must have a say in this," Lou cut in. "If Gary needs my help, and if I think his request is reasonable, I'm going to try to help him."

Lou had actually not decided if there was anything he could do, but Sarah Cooper was inadvertently discovering that the one sure way to get him to do something was to push in the opposite direction.

The attorney frowned. "His involvement could seriously compromise your case, Gary. Isn't there some sort of conflict of interest at work with his being your monitor at all?"

"He's going to help," McHugh said. "No matter what it looks like, I didn't kill Colston."

"Great," Sarah said. "That's just great. Listen, Gary, this isn't *The People's Court* or *Judge Judy*. If you are charged with this crime, there are people whose livelihood will depend on seeing that you spend the rest of your life in prison, and the laws that they will use to do it are built around rules and technicalities. So what happens when this man here does something dumb and amateurish that forces us to toss out evidence critical to your defense? Listen, we have plenty of investigators at our disposal—investigators highly trained in what they do."

"I don't care how good your investigators are," McHugh said. "I have a gut instinct about these things, and my gut is telling me I need him."

"In that case, Doctor," Sarah said, "I'm going to have to discuss things with my partners and see if we want to continue representing you."

At that moment, the doorbell rang. McHugh wandered over to the window, peeled back the drapes, and peered out into the dark. Blue and red strobe lights illuminated his face.

"The police," he said. "Guess they decided to keep CNN out of this until they paid me a visit. He looked first to Lou, next to Sarah. "Lou, as soon as possible, I need you to go and speak with Jeannine. She knows you've been helping me with my recovery, and is much more likely to speak with you than with any investigator. Now, please, I'm counting on you both. Please . . . please don't let me down."

The doorbell rang again.

Lou and Sarah Cooper exchanged unspoken questions.

"I'll go with you, Gary," Sarah said finally, "but our discussion about this issue is not done. Dr. Welcome, here is my card. Please use it before you try to be of any help."

CHAPTER 5

Staff Sergeants Bucky Townsend and Fenton Morales were the first pair in line to tackle the Big Hurt. To have gotten this far, Townsend, along with ninety-nine other members from Mantis Company, had to pass a series of rigorous tests—physical and mental.

The Big Hurt was their final exam.

Townsend wanted desperately to make the cut for Operation Talon, but all he knew about the most intense and intimidating obstacle course in the military was that its name was not undeserved.

A rolling fog, low enough to brush the frozen ground, spilled out from the woods surrounding the Mantis reservation, buried deep in West Virginia's Monongahela National Forest. The dense blue of the receding night was yielding to the flush of dawn. A thin coat of rime covered the frozen ground. It was a huge break that Townsend and Morales had drawn first team out. In another hour, the temperature would be well below freezing.

Townsend, determined to keep moving, bounced to

stay warm. He and the others had spent an hour sweating in the chill, when the door to the large, rough-hewn cabin swung open and, preceded by two aides, the legendary Major Charles Coon strode out onto the parade ground, his breath swirling out like a fighting bull's. Second in command to Colonel Wyatt Brody, he was solidly built, with eyes that glowed like the business end of an acetylene torch.

As one, a hundred eager marines snapped to attention—rows of wooden planks dressed in camo, eyes fixed forward, expressions blank as virgin slate. Had it been demanded of them, they could have remained in that position almost indefinitely. They were trained to endure discomfort. For them, this was the norm. They made even severe pain look manageable.

Coon slowly walked the line, probing the men's faces as if betting with himself which of them would make the cut.

"You are the elite of the elite," he said finally, his voice a mix of gravel and thunder. "Out of seven hundred Mantis warriors, you are the final one hundred to make it this far. Two thirds of you will not be chosen for Operation Talon. Many of you will consider that a failure." Coon paused here, but never turned his back on the men, and never lost eye contact. They might not be his equal, but they had earned his respect. "You will not have failed. None of you. Just getting to this point means you have succeeded. Delta Force can't tell you about the Big Hurt, and neither can the Rangers or the SEALs. That is because they have never run this course. Thanks to the vision of your leaders, this experience is reserved for Mantis only. It is the exclusive property of the best of the best, the bravest of the brave. You are Mantis!"

"Whatever it takes!" one hundred men shouted in perfect unison.

Whatever it takes, Townsend thought as he readied himself for the start.

Despite what Coon had proclaimed, failure was not an option. He would make the cut. He would be one of the men selected for Operation Talon. Of course, he still had almost no clue what the operation entailed. He knew only that it was high priority, high profile, and high prestige—his kind of work. He had come a hell of a long way from being a dairy farmer's kid in Muskogee, Oklahoma.

Mantis—the most decorated unit in the United States military.

I'm proud to be an Okie from Muskogee. . . . The Merle Haggard song ran like a tape through his mind, as it did whenever he was keyed up.

"Team One, are you ready to commit?" Coon shouted at Townsend and Morales. His stentorian voice roused a crow from its tree. It took off with an irritated caw.

"Sir, we are ready to commit. Sir!" Townsend and Morales shouted in unison.

Townsend saw a thin smile crease the man's chiseled face. "Gentlemen, this is what you've been working toward. This moment. We are alone out here on this course, but believe me, whether they can see you or not, the country is watching you."

Coon fired his starter pistol, and the duo sprinted

off, their heavy black combat boots crunching through the rime. A Mantis instructor indicated the first obstacle, labeled in crudely painted blue lettering on a board nailed to a tree.

BELLY FLOP.

The Big Hurt, the men had been told, was not designed to test a soldier's orienteering and navigation skills. It was about strength and grit—getting up, over, under, and through the toughest obstacles the military had to offer. Belly Flop was a fifty-yard crawl inches below barbed wire, through mud and frigid groundwater.

Twenty yards into the test, Townsend's muscles felt on fire, twitching as he clawed his way commando-style through thick, muddy clay. He rose up to negotiate a depression and tore his forearm through his sleeve on the teeth of an unforgiving strand of razor wire. The pain barely registered. There were medics along the course route, but to seek help meant automatic disqualification.

Whatever it takes, Townsend chanted to himself, grunting as he scrambled out of the mud. *I'm proud to be an Okie from Muskogee. . . .*

Slightly dazed, he drove ahead.

"You're not a tourist!" the Mantis guide waiting at the end of the obstacle shouted at them. "Move it. Move it!"

Townsend stumbled over a tree root, and then, following another guide's outstretched arm, sprinted toward the next challenge. Glancing over his shoulder, he saw Morales coming up alongside him.

"Let's go, Fenton! Let's go!" Townsend shouted.

UPSIE DAISY.

The two men easily ascended and descended a twenty-foot wall, and then sidestepped along G-STRING, a taut wire that crossed a dozen feet above a churning river with ice coating its banks.

"If you slip, you swim!" the guide yelled after them.

A hundred-yard sprint along a twisting, uneven forest path, and there was another guide.

"Get set for some climbing, ladies!"

As a boy, Townsend had been afraid of heights—too scared to ride the Ferris wheel at the county fair. But that was before Mantis. His acrophobia, once paralyzing, now was gone. He rapidly negotiated the largely trimmed branches of a massive, sixty-foot oak called SHISH-KA-BOB and then rappelled down.

"Not bad for an Okie," Morales said, panting to catch his breath after he landed.

"We're hot, baby," Townsend said, exuberant. "Hot as a two-fifty revolver."

ORGAN GRINDER . . . TWIST AND SHOUT . . . ALL IN . . . GUT BLASTER . . . TWOFER. Cheering each other on and, when possible, working as a team, the two marines completed the rest of the obstacles with relative ease.

"End of the Line!" a guide shouted, indicating the sign that announced the final obstacle.

Twenty feet up a thick, braided rope, a hand-over-hand dangling traverse for thirty yards, and a rope slide back to the ground, and it appeared the Big Hurt had been beaten.

Quickly, Townsend's adrenaline rush dissipated. His arms grew heavy, and he felt a cramp working its way into his right calf.

"Townsend . . . Morales." Charles Coon strolled over to them and motioned that standing at attention was unnecessary.

It was then Townsend noticed the portable gun rack standing just beyond the major. It held about twenty-five M4A1 assault rifles. The marine knew the gun well. The selective fire weapon used 5.56 mm rounds, and its four-position telescoping stock, slightly larger than the M4, had a distinctive curvature at the end.

"Gentlemen, this is your final test," Coon said. "There are twenty-five weapons for you to choose from. The target will be over there." He motioned through a corridor in the woods to a crudely constructed wooden wall, twenty-five yards away

Townsend had heard that the Rangers conducted a stress shoot as part of their training regimen, engaging targets after a grueling run. Maybe taking on the Big Hurt was designed to exhaust their bodies in a similar way.

"Sir, what will we be firing at, sir?" he asked.

"Did I give permission to address me, solider?" Coon barked.

Townsend felt his heart stop, then slowly resume beating again. "Sir, no, sir!" he managed.

The major smiled thinly, a crescent of white appearing between his lips. "Soldier, you are the target," he said.

"Sir, yes, sir!" Townsend bit back the urge once again to ask for clarification.

Coon continued. "We have loaded five of the guns in this rack with a live round. You do not know which gun has that live round. I do not know which guns have no cartridge. Do you understand?"

"Sir, yes, sir!" Townsend and Morales barked.

"You will each pick a gun, and I will fire that weapon at you. I will aim for the outside edge of your left chest wall. If you pick the gun carrying a live round, you will be shot through that spot. I assure you, I am a hell of a marksman, especially with that weapon and those ACO gun sights. My shot will inflict minimal damage so long as you do not move, but there will be medics here to check you over. Understood?"

"Sir, yes, sir!"

"Morales, what is the percent probability that within the next minute, you will be struck by a bullet?"

"Sir, twenty percent probability, sir!"

Coon nodded. "Gentlemen, pick a gun, set it in this holder beside me, and take up your position against the wall. Stand next to each other. I want both of you to be ready."

The men did as they were ordered. Townsend was bleeding and muddy. His bones ached. His skin was mottled and blue with cold. He fought to keep from shivering. Twenty-five yards away, Coon had gotten into a firing position.

The officer gave no warning, no countdown. Townsend kept his eyes fixed forward. He thought the rifle was the one he had chosen, but he could not be certain. He watched as in what seemed like slow motion, Coon pulled the trigger. The soft click was barely audible. Townsend glanced to his right and saw Morales still standing. Coon peered up from his scope and said, "Sergeant Morales, nicely done. You're dismissed."

Morales stepped away from the wall while the major switched guns.

Less than one percent, Townsend was thinking. That was the increased probability of his getting shot. *Less than one percent.* He kept his eyes fixed on the muzzle of the M4A1. Beyond it, he could see the commander press the gun barrel to his shoulder and peer into the scope. He saw the finger move and the trigger being pulled. Then he saw the flash and at virtually the same instant heard a crack that reverberated off the trees and sent more birds flying. The searing pain in his side dropped him to his knees. Still, he resisted clutching the wound.

Townsend struggled to his feet without assistance as Charles Coon studied the tablet computer held by his chief medical officer.

"How did Morales do?" Coon asked.

"His vitals were normal," the medical officer said. "No elevation in heart rate, muscle tension within normal range, oxygen levels reflected a non-stress state."

"And you're sure these patches are transmitting accurately."

"Absolutely, sir. Each man's patch broadcasts a unique radio-frequency identification that allows us to monitor their vitals at all stages of the test."

"What about Townsend?" Coon asked.

"He was no different from Morales," the medical officer said. "Cool as a cucumber. Even after he got shot, his tracings look pure Mantis."

"Colonel Brody will be pleased to have these two," Coon said. "Pleased as Punch." He was grinning as the next pair of candidates approached.

CHAPTER 6

Emily Welcome, wearing lime green headgear, bobbed about the ring like a buoy in rough seas. Shuffling and dancing across from her, Lou went through the rudiments of defense and the basic punches. The kid was a natural.

No surprise.

Lou had seen his daughter's athletic prowess evolve from her earliest days chasing butterflies, into a burgeoning passion for running long distances. But this was her first time in a boxing ring, and despite her natural ability, it shocked him to think how easy she was making it look.

Four days had passed since the arrest of Dr. Gary McHugh for the execution-style murder of Congressman Elias Colston. The murder weapon had not been recovered, but teams of divers continued to search the muddy bottom of the icy Pensatuck River. Still, the authorities sounded quite certain that they had their man. Apparently, the judge in his bail hearing felt the same way. Sarah Cooper's request for bail was denied.

Colston's funeral, certain to be a massive, celebrity-studded event, was scheduled for the day after tomorrow.

Without obtaining Sarah's blessing or, for that matter, Walter Filstrup's, Lou had decided he would try to arrange a meeting with Colston's widow, Jeannine, sometime after the burial. He knew four years ago that he might have crossed an ethical boundary or two by taking on a friend as a PWO client. But he was deeply connected to McHugh, and wanted desperately to help him get on top of his alcoholism. Once he agreed to be the associate director in charge of the case, he had set himself up for termination should Filstrup learn of their relationship. But now, there was no backing out.

"Hey, there, Papa, let's do some punching," Emily said, angling her mouthguard to make her words intelligible. "I'm liking this. I can't wait to see Kyle Smith's expression when I pop him in the nose. He's always bumping into me on purpose."

"You're not going to pop anyone in the nose. That's just Kyle's way of saying he likes you."

"I know. And a pop in the nose will be my way of saying that I like him back."

Lou stifled most of a grin. Emily had grown several inches in the past few months, and her shape was changing almost as rapidly. Growing up with her was going to be a hell of an adventure. Still hidden in his bureau drawer was the baggy gray T-shirt he had commissioned when he finally gave in to her repeated requests to train in the ring. HEY, GUYS, BEHAVE. I'M ONLY THIRTEEN! It read in front. The number *13* filled the back. Lou had

resolved to wait until he saw any serious flirting, and
then prepare for war and insist she wear it.

With his hands baking like two loaves of bread inside his gloves, Lou fixed his gaze on his daughter. Her
eyes were aflame with concentration as she circled him,
keeping her hands up, precisely as he had told her. She
had her auburn hair pulled back into a ponytail, giving
him a clear view of the sweat beading up upon her forehead. Beautiful. Just beautiful.

"Couldn't somebody call the cops on you for fighting me?" Emily asked.

"We're not supposed to hit each other," Lou reminded
her. "This is just to practice your footwork."

"Then why am I wearing headgear and a mouthguard?"

"Because you're my daughter, my only child, the light
of my life, and I'm pathologically overly protective.
Plus I'm not exactly a kung fu master when it comes
to stopping my punches an inch from your wonderful
face."

"Makes sense," Emily said after a protracted evalu-
ation. She slid her mouthguard back into place.

"Okay, let's do it again," Lou said. "Forward and
back, then side to side, then shuffle, and last do the pivot.
Ready?"

Emily ignored her father's instructions and instead
lunged forward and, moving as quickly as a firefly,
caught Lou off guard with a solid right to his gut. Only
countless hours of ab work in the gym and on his living room carpet saved him from something potentially
serious.

He stepped back and dropped his mouthpiece into the palm of his glove. "Do you know who Harry Houdini is . . . I mean *was*?" he asked.

"A famous magician?"

"Sort of. Before we step between these ropes again, I want you to be ready to tell me who he was and how he died."

Emily's eyes narrowed in her personalized teen-versus-parent way. As in their titanic *Monopoly* struggles, Lou already knew there was no way he was going to win this encounter.

"I have a feeling he got punched in the stomach," she said.

"The word is 'sucker-punched.' "

"That's two words. Besides, I gave you warning when I dropped my shoulder." Emily was a tribute to Charles Darwin—a perfect 50 percent genetic cross between Lou's obstinacy and Renee's cunning.

"Powerless," he said, as much to himself as out loud. The word was an AA mainstay. *We are absolutely powerless over people, places, and things.*

"It's your fault," Emily pressed on. "When you're in the ring, always be ready to be hit. That's what Cap told me."

"But he didn't tell you to sucker-punch anyone—especially your old man," Cap's rich bass echoed from ringside.

Emily turned and broke into a broad smile. "Cap!" she cried, kneeling by the ropes, wrapping her arms around the neck of the tall, muscular Bahamian and kissing him on the top of his shaved pate. Cap Duncan hugged her back and then climbed gracefully into the ring.

"Hey, Doc, your kid has fast hands. Girl, be careful when you hit that guy unless you're both ready. Around here, sucker-punching anyone anywhere can get you suspended for a week."

"Sorry."

The apology, Lou knew, a rarity for his daughter, was a clear mark of the respect she had for the onetime street pug and AAU light-heavyweight champion. Hank Duncan earned the nickname Cap'n Crunch because of the sound noses reputedly made when he hit them. His promising pro career lasted just six fights—until he stood up to the mob and refused to take a dive against a fighter they were backing. A short while later, he flunked a drug test and was suspended, even though he had never used anything.

He ended up working for the very men who had destroyed him, and turned to alcohol and narcotics to ease his humiliation. The path eventually took him to rehab, and then a halfway house. Cap had become a counselor in the house when Lou Welcome checked in, fresh from his own nine-month stint in a treatment center. Two years later, Lou had gotten his medical license restored, and Cap, his AA sponsor, was the owner of the Stick and Move Gym.

"I haven't trained a girl before," Cap said, "but from what I just watched, she might have pro stock in her blood."

Emily's face lit up. "Pro? Like I could be a professional boxer?"

Lou stepped in. "Pro as in you can be a professional anything so long as someone's willing to pay you for doing it. For now, I think you should keep your amateur status and keep getting A's in school. At least until you're eighteen."

"Sixteen," Emily said, dancing and throwing jabs at the air.

Cap's trademark laugh echoed through the gym. "Doctor, you have your hands full with that one."

Cap had poured his heart and everything he owned and could borrow into the Stick and Move—a converted warehouse just a short walk from Lou's apartment. The gym was well equipped with a row of heavy bags, a half dozen speed bags, stationary bikes, three regulation-sized rings, free weights, and plenty of room for jumping rope. Bit by bit, despite the fact that Cap let membership fees slide for anyone he knew couldn't pay, the place was inching its way into the black.

"Emily," Lou said, "why don't you practice your footwork in front of the mirror for a bit? I have to talk to the big guy, here."

"Sure thing, Pop."

Cap lifted the ropes and helped her from the ring. Lou waited until the two of them were alone at one corner.

"We gonna go a couple?" Cap asked, throwing a slow-motion left-right combo toward Lou's head.

At six-two, he was a couple of inches taller than Lou, and at fifty years old, he was still well down into the single digits in body fat percentage.

"Not today," was the reply. "I hope you remember

that Emily's going to stay here with you. At least for this afternoon, she is. I'm going to that funeral in Bethesda."

"Ah, yes, the congressman. Well, I have a bunch of chores mapped out for Ms. Emily, and maybe another lesson. You going to be back before dinner?"

"I expect so. The burial's in Arlington National, but I might not go. I should be back here way before five."

"In that case, we'll be here waiting. I promise you one thing, Doc: You're going to have one tired child on your hands."

"Ten bucks says she'll be running circles around you by the time I return."

"Make it twenty if she's asleep over there in the corner."

Lou remembered a story he had once heard about a man interviewing for membership in Mensa, the high-IQ society. He was asked only one question by the panel: What happens when an irresistible force meets an immovable object? The answer that got him immediate admission was "an inconceivable event." Cap's energy versus Emily's exuberance—an inconceivable event.

"My money's on the kid," he said. "Listen, pal, I need your help."

Lou checked to make sure Emily was out of earshot and following instructions. She was shadowboxing in front of the mirrors alongside four other fighters, all of whom were young black men in perfect shape. It was impossible not to smile at the scene. Lou's ex, Renee, was a social liberal and political moderate, but she was not a fan of Emily staying in Lou's hardscrabble neighborhood, and expressed more than a little displeasure at her daughter's sudden desire to take up boxing. Lou's position was that as good as the Carlisle School in Arlington was in terms of academics, it did little to expose its students to the richness of multiculturalism. The more time Emily spent in his world, the more aware she seemed of the sheltered homogeneity within her own.

"Feel like going a couple of rounds with your professor?" Cap asked.

"Ordinarily I would never refuse an offer like that—especially if you promise to take it easy on me when my kid's watching."

"And I will."

"But not today. Cap, have you read about the guy who got arrested for the murder of Congressman Colston?"

"A little. We've got a big AAU tournament coming up, so I've been spending my time with the kids and not with the news."

"Well, you've met the guy a couple of times, most recently at that fund-raiser for the gym last year, where you talked me into sparring two rounds with you. His name's Gary McHugh. He's a doc, and has been a good friend of mine since college. In fact, I was in his wedding."

"Did he do it?"

"He says no, but he was in a blackout and doesn't remember much."

"Lord. I would wager that ninety percent of those in jail don't really remember what they did to get there."

"So, I believe he's innocent until there's good reason

not to. At the moment, the police and the court have a strong enough case to arrest him and keep him without bail."

"He's in jail?"

"The Baltimore City Detention Center."

"That hellhole? How in the heck did he end up there?"

"No idea. He said something about overcrowding."

"Nasty, nasty place. Most jails are, even the newer ones, of which there ain't too many. Less space, less protection, fewer guards than a prison. I swear, neither one of them is a rose garden, but I would take a penitentiary over a jail anytime."

"Gary's having it tough there, Cap. Apparently word is out that he's a doctor, and the inmates want stuff from him. He's afraid. Is there anything we can do for him?"

"Let me check with the grapevine and see if anybody I know is doing time up there. The odds favor it. If there is, I can ride up there with you during visitors' hours and speak with them—see if we can get your pal a little protection."

"You're the best."

"Give me a couple of hours."

Cap headed up the flight of stairs to his office, perched on supports that suspended it out over the gym. In a minute, Lou could see him through the plate glass window, making calls.

Lou did a little foot and glove work himself and was about to motion Emily back into the ring, when he saw Cap stand up from his desk, wave, and start back down the stairs.

"That was way too easy, Doc. In the old days, it

would have taken a bunch of calls and a few hours or more to pin down someone doing time in any specific tank in the tristate area. Now, it's like two calls, and I've got a name. Seems like there's more brothers in the joint than out. That's sad, man, real sad. Rolando Booker's in Baltimore City right now for B and E. He's always been called Tiny. I suppose because he ain't. He and I used to run together after I was forced out of the ring. He's a good guy and a real artist with locks and safes of any sort. Great at plannin', not so good at gettin' away with it. Everything I know about B and E—and that used to be quite a bit—ol' Tiny taught me. We can find out when the visitors' hours are for their cell blocks and make a road trip."

"Thanks, pal. Gary's not exactly everybody's cup of tea, but he's always meant a lot to me, and right now, he's scared stiff."

"As soon as we have a time, we're there. It'll be good to reconnect with Tiny. He actually was a decent fighter at one time himself. Listen, I've got some pointers to give to Tommy, the kid with the red trunks shadowboxing to Emily's right. He has some serious potential if he can just stay in school and out of trouble."

"He's lucky to have you on his case."

Lou watched as his sponsor strode easily over to Emily, whispered something that made her grin, and sent her back to the ring. Then Cap turned to the boy and motioned for him to get his hands up. It was impossible to watch the man at work and not feel good. Lou knew that he had been orphaned at a young age, and made this way through some seriously hard times.

You never know, Lou found himself thinking as he watched his kid dancing across the gym toward him on her fawn's legs.

"Hey, Pop, I've got the best idea ever," Emily said, still holding her mouthguard.

"Let me guess," Lou said. "You want to be Cap's partner in the Stick and Move."

"Close," she said, her eyes sparkling. "I've decided to move in with you."

CHAPTER 7

Detective Christopher Bryzinski, of the Maryland State Police, hated funerals. With the exception of his wife, he had buried everybody who mattered to him, and this overwrought ceremony for a murdered congressman served only to bring those bitter memories to the surface. His father, Bart, a cop's cop, was run down ten years ago on a Maryland highway, killed by a drunk driver on a gray and rainy day like this one. His mother, who, much like himself, was a revolving member of Weight Watchers, died soon after, not surprisingly from a heart attack.

Bryzinski knew he needed to drop weight. He always needed to drop weight. His wife, Agnes, rode him about it mercilessly—that was when she wasn't riding him about his cigars. But then, what would be the point of it all? If he gave up food, booze, and an occasional smoke, Agnes might as well stuff him inside a wooden box as well.

Bryzinski shivered against the raw cold. He gazed absently at the guests who were shuffling across the depressing landscape of milk white gravestones, which reminded Bryzinski of soldiers on a perpetual death march. He had argued with the captain that sending him out here to take pictures with a lapel camera and record notes about the attendees was going to be as fruitless as trying to milk a bull, but the man must have been pissed off at him for something.

Dr. Gary McHugh was their killer, and that was that.

Only a fraction of the mob at the service in Bethesda had made the trip down to Arlington, but many of those who did were easily recognizable high-profilers. Jeannine Colston was trudging up the gentle slope, accompanied by her children and two or three others. She was a fine-looking woman, no doubt about that. Bryzinski tried to imagine how she was handling the damning stories about her affair with her husband's killer. With nothing much else to do, he moved closer and snapped off a few shots.

For a time, he wondered where Colston's son was buried. Mike? Mark? Something like that. He was killed in Afghanistan and had won an important medal for his troubles. Father and son. Both marines, both dead.

The final groups of mourners were headed from their cars toward the burial site. Bryzinski estimated two hundred or so would form the final gathering. Maybe a couple of unidentified or unexpected faces would show up. That's what the captain was thinking. Still, no matter what, nothing would change the conclusion that Bryzinski and his crew of seasoned homicide detectives had reached. Gary McHugh, the society doc, one of the beautiful people in D.C., was the man.

The wind kicked up in a sudden gust, spattering rain on beleaguered faces, and actually inverting some umbrellas. The priest, his white robes flapping like sodden sails, was settled beneath a canvas canopy, preparing to read from the Scriptures. Some people were openly weeping, but mostly what Bryzinski saw were people there to be seen. The military brass arrived in full peacock dress, while Secret Service agents stood at a conspicuous distance.

The chilly rain, mixed with windblown sleet, had peppered his face long enough for Bryzinski to declare his assignment a job well done. He took a few backward steps, turned, and eased away from the crowd and back down the hill. He had made it halfway to his Pontiac, parked parallel to the line of black town cars, when a deep voice startled him from behind. Bryzinski whirled, and his eyes widened with recognition. Secretary of Defense Spencer Hogarth stood alone and unaccompanied beneath a broad, black umbrella.

"Detective Bryzinski?"

Bryzinski's throat tightened. His exposure to politics never ventured past the Maryland governor's office, and he found himself speechless in the presence of the square-jawed, silver-haired, leathery-skinned admiral, whom many pundits thought to be a potential nominee for the presidency, or at least the vice presidency. A champion of traditional American values, and an all-American running back at the Naval Academy, Hogarth had become a fixture in all the news magazines.

"That's me," Bryzinski said, stunned more than flattered that Hogarth would know his name.

"Got a moment to talk?"

"Sure. How do you know me?" Bryzinski wiped his face with the back of his hand.

"Let's just say that when I have an interest in someone, I do my homework," Hogarth said.

"And you have an interest in me?"

"A sound conclusion. Detective Bryzinski—may I call you Chris?"

"Sure."

"Chris, I could use your help."

Bryzinski sensed the secretary wasn't a threat, and began to relax. "My help with what?" he asked.

"You are the lead investigator on the Elias Colston murder case, are you not?"

"I am," Bryzinski said, finding his mental footing now. Maybe this day wouldn't be a total loss after all. "Do you have information about the congressman's murder you want to share, Mr. Secretary?"

"No," Hogarth said, grinning. "Flip it around."

Bryzinski appraised the man curiously. Even in the gloom of the day, he felt riveted to Hogarth's eyes, almost an iridescent blue—the eyes of power. "You mean if I have information about Colston's murder, you want me to share it?"

Hogarth's smile was engaging. "No wonder your reputation as a fine detective precedes you," he said.

Over his career, Bryzinski had not been above accepting the occasional inducement for one favor or another. Every cop did it. He sensed an offer coming from the secretary of defense that he would not refuse. First, though, the obligatory feeling out on both sides.

"And exactly how will my sharing this information help in my investigation?"

"I have a strong interest in tracking the developments in this case," Hogarth replied. "You keep me informed, and I see to it you know how grateful I am." Again, that smile.

"I'm sorry, Secretary Hogarth," Bryzinski said. "With all due respect, sir, I realize you're a very important man, but if I understand you right, that's not how we go about our business at the Maryland State Police. I hope you understand."

"Let me walk you to your car," Hogarth said.

Bryzinski saw a pair of bodyguards lingering among the row of limos and executive sedans, watching the two of them but staying well out of earshot. "Maybe you should get to the point, sir."

"The point is, I'm not asking." Hogarth placed his arm around Bryzinski's broad shoulders, as though the two were duck-hunting buddies headed for a blind. Walking with slow, purposeful steps, he led the stunned detective toward the curbside row of parked cars. The rain played rhythmically on Hogarth's wide umbrella.

"Pardon?" Bryzinski finally managed.

"Here's the thing, Chris," Hogarth went on. "Let's make it short and sweet. Jamie Lambert. I assume that name means something to you."

"I don't—"

"Please, don't play games with me. Twelve years ago,

you shot and killed Lambert during a shakedown you and your partner were running. You planted a gun and some drugs on the kid—seventeen, I believe he was—and ended up getting off."

"I'm not going to admit to that. What, are you wearing a wire?"

"Not my style, Chris. Lambert's killing is not all I've learned about you. I know about your wife, Agnes. Thirty years next June, yes? I know you don't have any children. I know you don't have much money because you have the tendency to gamble too much—even tried Gamblers Anonymous, if my information is correct. I know your parents are both dead and that you're a reasonably well respected police officer. What I don't know is if you're a smart man, too—smart enough to know I wouldn't approach you like this if I didn't already have proof. Now, do we do business, or not?"

Bryzsinki's stomach lurched. At that instant, his foot sank above his shoe in a nearly frozen puddle. "And what would make me smart?"

"The people who do what I ask, Chris," Hogarth said, walking even slower now, "often find themselves with promotions or certain other—how should I say it—rewards."

"And what is it you want in this case?"

"What I want is to know anything and everything pertaining to the murder investigation of Elias Colston. I want you to personally feed me all the information you get—every tip, every lead, every name. I want everything you come across, not just what you think is important. I want you to let me be the judge of that."

Bryzinski's breath left him momentarily. He could barely feel the icy water that had filled his shoe and soaked his sock. The man was incredible. In just a couple of minutes, Hogarth had snatched his life away, and now was in the process of giving it back, with bonuses. Incredible.

"And if I don't do this," Bryzinski said, "then would that make me not smart?" Blood was thundering like river rapids in his ears.

"If you're not smart, Chris, then the Lambert murder will be just one of the things the world learns about you, starting with the detective's exam you didn't take yourself."

Bryzinski could only stare at the man. It had been years since the exam, and he was sure now that no one would ever find out. Shaughnessy had sworn that he had the switch to take the test for another man down to a science. *Goddamn mick bastard!* Now, his job, his pension—hell, maybe even the loss of Agnes. Everything was on the line for him.

Bryzinski scanned the slate gray sky, letting the chilling rain bathe his face. Spencer Hogarth was in a league unlike anyone he had ever encountered. It wasn't even worth asking how he had connected with so much information so fast.

After a minute, Bryzinski turned back to him. "I think you'll find that I'm a very smart man," he said.

Hogarth's smile this time was broader and more genuine. "I'm sure that I will, Chris," he said, releasing his arm from around Bryzinski's shoulder. "I'm sure that I will."

CHAPTER 8

Renee Welcome and Steve Gilbride shared a four-bedroom colonial in Arlington, Virginia. The upscale suburb, across the Potomac from Washington, owed its high real estate values to location and the child-oriented culture. Despite the highly regarded public schools, Renee chose to send Emily to the prestigious Carlisle School, where she, herself, had gone.

Steve's two kids, David and Alyssa, whom Emily tolerated with no great joy, stayed at the brick house on Fifth Street every other weekend and Wednesdays. In an attempt to get to know one another better, Renee had successfully pleaded with Emily to make the weekends with her father coincide with those when the Gilbrides, fourteen and twelve, were with their mother. The deal Renee caved in to was that in exchange, alternate Thursdays would be added to Emily's time in D.C.

Just the typical modern American nuclear family, Emily liked to tell her friends.

"Are there really such things as professional woman

boxers?" she asked now, as Lou swung onto the Roosevelt Bridge over the Potomac.

"Muhammad Ali's daughter fought professionally, and there was a great movie about women boxers starring and directed by Clint Eastwood."

"Who?"

"Clint . . . it doesn't matter. If you decide you want to box for a living, then go for it. But I'll tell you, unless you work your little bum off, you're going to get pounded into the canvas. Those women are tough and athletic."

"Well, I'm already athletic and I can learn to be tough. I think I should move into your place so I can train with you and Cap. I promise I'll do my homework every night."

Lou gulped. Why did he ever think he could stay even half a step ahead of his daughter?

"Now, don't get me wrong, kiddo, I love having you at my place, and I've been able to adjust my schedule at the hospital and the PWO to get you to school in the morning, but—"

"We should discuss it as a family. Isn't that what you and Mom are always saying?"

Oh, but the kid is good, Lou was thinking, feeling a fleeting pang for the significant other floating somewhere out there in the cosmos of her future.

By tradition, Lou always accompanied Emily into the house for the drop-off. Before her marriage to Steve, Renee, whose family counseling practice was full to overflowing, often used the time after Emily had raced up to her room to discuss her personal life and problems with Lou. Perhaps it was the strength of his recovery program, but it was as if the man she had loved and wed and slept with and divorced had become her confidant and best friend forever.

The problem was, as Emily not only suspected, but *knew,* Lou had loved his wife when she divorced him, and continued to have strong feelings for her.

This particular Sunday, Steve was at his office in the city, routine for those weekends when his kids weren't staying in Arlington. Renee, usually upbeat under any circumstance, seemed frazzled. Her wavy chestnut hair, which fell past her shoulders when it was unpinned, looked uncharacteristically unkempt.

Emily remained puttering downstairs rather than making her customary beeline for the solitude of her room.

"Hey, there . . . the place looks nice, Renee," Lou said, hoping to clear whatever was souring the air by acknowledging her holiday decorations. Renee, seated at the round kitchen table, which was littered with bills, clattered her reading glasses down, picked up a bill from the stack, and fixed Emily with a hard stare.

"Mom, I have the best idea ever!" the teen gushed as she squeezed past Lou to get inside the kitchen.

"What's the meaning of this?" Renee said, holding up an envelope Lou recognized as a Verizon bill.

"Meaning of what?" Emily asked, sidestepping her mother's disapproving gaze to retrieve a yogurt from the refrigerator.

Renee got to her feet. "There are three hundred dollars in text message charges here, young lady. Three hundred and twelve, to be exact."

Emily appeared confused. "What? That's crazy!"

"Crazy, huh? Well, then, tell me whose number is this?"

Renee crossed the room, bill in hand. Emily, who in the time it took her mother to reach her wolfed down several spoonfuls of yogurt, examined the bill, took another bite of yogurt, and said through a mouthful, "That's Katie. Isn't she in our Friends and Family network?"

Katie Willard was one of Emily's closest friends from school.

"No, Katie is not on our Friends and Family network," said Renee.

Emily looked offended. "Well, Steve was supposed to add her."

"Don't bring Steve into this!"

"Why?" Emily said. "I asked him to do it."

Lou moved to intervene, then pulled back. The core containment had not nearly been breached.

"And what on earth could you possibly be texting so much about?" Renee asked.

"Stuff. I dunno, Mom. It's just how we communicate."

"Well, you'll need to come up with another way of communicating that doesn't cost three hundred dollars a month."

"Then, duh, just add her to our Friends and Family network."

"Don't you dare talk to me like that," Renee said. "You are thirteen years old, and you will show me some respect."

The core was beginning to shed radiation.

Emily turned to Lou. "Do you see? Do you see why I've got to get out of here?"

"What's she talking about?" Renee said, now directing her ire at Lou.

"I'm moving in with Dad," Emily said.

Breach!

"Okay, time-out," he said, extending his arms. "Each of you, back off to a neutral corner and hold your breath for a minute. Renee, to preempt your question, no, this was not my idea. Em, to preempt what you were going to come back at Mom with, this is not a lily-white city where a redhead is the closest thing to a minority. If you think about it, you'll realize there is more cultural diversity here than there is in my neighborhood. Okay, breathe." Lou looked from mother to daughter. The tension between the two of them seemed to have lessened a tick.

"This so unfair!" Emily said, slumping down onto the kitchen's wide-plank cherrywood floor. "I can't even have a pet."

"A pet?" Lou asked.

"Steve's son, David, is allergic," Renee said.

Lou found himself considering Emily's request to move in with him, even though such a change would be a logistical nightmare. Now, it appeared he wouldn't have to take sides. Renee was a mother for the ages, always ready to cart Emily to track or play rehearsal, or even to adjust her work schedule to monitor a field trip. Emily's demands were a phase—a reaction to having things not go the way she wanted them to. But they still had to be handled carefully.

Gratefully, Emily had just given them an opening . . . a pet.

"Hey, why don't we compromise here?" Lou offered.

Emily rose up from the floor. "What kind of compromise?"

Renee appeared suspicious.

"I'll get a pet," Lou said, holding up his hands in a way that implied the scales of justice were now in balance.

"Mom?"

"If a pet would make you happy, and you can't have one here," Renee said, "then it seems fair for you to have one when you visit Dad's, provided there is no more talk about switching around your living arrangements."

"A pet is hardly a multicultural inner-city experience," Emily said, brushing aside the suggestion with her words, but not her eyes.

"It's called a compromise," Lou said.

"What kind of pet?" Emily asked.

"How about a flea."

"Very funny."

"Okay, a guinea pig."

"How about a dog?" Emily countered.

"How about I have a job and you're at my place only on the alternate weekends and one weekday."

"Then what about a cat?" asked Emily, homing in with the accuracy of a Sidewinder missile.

"A cat?" Lou's voice cracked.

"A cat," Emily said, grinning now at what amounted to absolute victory.

Lou's mind raced through alternatives from aardvark to zebra, but came up with nothing more practical. "Okay, okay," he said. "We'll get a cat."

"When?"

"Soon."

"Rescued from a shelter," Emily added. "And I've got to pick him out. And he's got to be neutered."

"But of course," Lou said, feeling his throat tightening at the ease with which he had been beaten.

Emily bounded over and kissed him on the cheek. "I'm sooooo super excited! Bye! I love you." She made a delighted little squeal on her way out.

"So what are we going to do about these text messages?" Renee called after her at the moment her bedroom door slammed.

"Gone," Lou said. He was gazing blankly at the staircase when he realized that he was wondering if Sarah Cooper was allergic to cats.

"You're really going to have to go through with this cat thing, you know," Renee said.

"We had a cat at the halfway house. As I recall, it tweren't much of a problem."

Renee smiled inscrutably and mumbled something that sounded like "You wish."

Before Lou could ask her to repeat the remark, his cell phone rang. The caller ID was just the number.

"Hello?"

"Dr. Lou Welcome?" a woman's voice asked.

"Yes."

"My name is Jeannine Colston. I believe you wanted to speak with me."

CHAPTER 9

Lou had seen the hollowed-eye look before—many times before. Jeannine Colston was beaten down, pummeled by exhaustion, loss, and the malicious snipings from her family and friends as well as the media. News of her affair with Gary McHugh, the man accused of brutally murdering her husband, had exploded in the press like a land mine. In some ways, Lou sensed, she was as dead as Elias.

"Thank you for seeing me, Mrs. Colston. I know it can't be an easy thing for you to do."

They faced each other across the front foyer of the Colstons' rambling colonial. Jeannine, whose striking patrician beauty was gray and tight-jawed, eyed him coolly. Despite the ravages of what she was enduring, it was still easy to see why McHugh could have lost his heart to her so absolutely. Out of reflex, it seemed, she dusted the light snow off Lou's coat, hung it in the closet, and motioned him to a sofa in the living room. There was an uncomfortable chill in the air, as if she had not bothered to turn on the heat.

"Given your friendship with Gary, I wasn't even going to return your call," she said.

"I understand. First let me extend my deepest condolences. I'm so very sorry for your loss and everything else that's been happening."

"Thank you. I appreciate that. Tea? Coffee?"

Lou shook his head and gestured to the dozens of luxurious floral arrangements engulfing the room. "Impressive," he said.

"I've thrown at least this many out. It's been almost a week, but they keep coming."

"The congressman was very popular."

"In case I didn't know that, so many reporters and former friends have gone out of their way to remind me."

Inwardly, Lou groaned. *What in the hell am I doing here?* According to McHugh's attorney, he was putting the man's defense at risk, and according to Colston's widow, he was sticking a salted knife into an open wound and turning the blade. Lou had seen the security cameras that filmed McHugh coming and going. He knew about the forensic evidence linking the man to Colston's murder. No other suspects had been approached or arrested, no new persons of interest identified. Open and shut. *What other explanation can there be? How can this not be the case of an alcoholic in a blackout bender, and a love affair gone horribly wrong?* Gary McHugh was sitting in a Baltimore jail, denied bail at his arraignment, and Lou was having a hard time convincing himself that his friend and client did not belong there.

"I'm sorry, Mrs. Colston. That was insensitive of

me. I like to think empathy is one of my strengths as a doctor. I didn't demonstrate much of it just now."

"I have been told by Gary that you are, in fact, quite empathetic. That's one of the reasons I agreed to see you."

"I'm afraid I don't understand. Did Gary speak about me very much?"

"Quite a bit, actually. But I saw you at the funeral. You were one of the very few there whom I didn't know, so I asked a close Washington friend who knows everyone, and she told me about you. After you left me those messages, I did some checking."

Lou gazed across the heavily furnished room at the large, empty fieldstone fireplace. If Jeannine Colston asked how he got into the funeral, he had decided not even to try for any answer other than the truth—that Gary had called in a favor from a judge in D.C. As it turned out, she never asked, possibly because the truth was the only logical explanation.

"Anyway," Jeannine went on, "you looked me in the eyes, and then you just turned and left me alone. I thought you had a very kind, interesting face."

"Thank you. I wasn't there to make any trouble. I just wanted to get a better sense of your husband and the people who were associated with him. I thought it might help me help Gary."

"I'm afraid Gary is beyond helping," she said.

The funeral for Elias Colston had been held at the National Cathedral. The media had gotten hold of the story of Jeannine's affair with the congressman's friend and physician, and turned the somber rite into a circus. Over a thousand were in attendance, including many of the military's top brass, who had come to pay their last respects to the man who oversaw their funding as chairman of the House Armed Services Committee.

"I'm assuming you want to know what I think happened," Jeannine said to Lou.

"If it's not too difficult for you."

"Difficult . . . not difficult. What difference does it make now?"

"I understand." Lou forced himself not to avert his eyes.

"Well, I think Gary did it," Jeannine said matter-of-factly.

"I know the police are certain that's the case, but why are you?"

"Because I ended our . . . relationship. Because he was drinking and getting more and more desperate to make things right between us. I can play you the messages he left on my mobile. I saved them after I shared them with the police because, as you probably know, Gary was a hunter and a gun nut. He's been on expeditions and hunting trips in the Rockies and Canada, and even a safari in Africa."

Lou nodded, thinking, *There it is again: motive, method, and opportunity.* It seemed that Gary was just a weapon away from spending the rest of his life in prison, or from becoming the first execution in the state in years.

"Do you feel like talking about why you ended things?" he asked.

"Is that why Gary sent you to see me? To find out why?"

"No," Lou said. "It's me who wants to know. Gary is steadfast that he didn't kill your husband. He knew I might be the only one on earth who would believe him and asked if I'd look into things. He's right that I tend to accept what I'm told by my friends until I have iron-clad reasons not to. So I'd like to understand as many of the events leading up to your husband's murder as possible."

Jeannine nodded. "Well spoken," she replied. "Put simply, I had a change of heart. Elias came to me the evening before he . . . was killed. He took me in his arms and kissed me in a way he hadn't in years. I felt it. I really and truly felt it like an electric charge shooting through my body. I'll remember that kiss for the rest of my life. It was like our first kiss, the kiss after he proposed to me, and the kiss on our wedding day all rolled into one. I had been having misgivings about Gary—thoughts about pulling out. Guilt. Having my husband kiss me that way and tell me how much he loved me and needed me made up my mind." She began to sob.

Lou waited. "It's okay," he said finally.

"No . . . no, it's hardly okay. My surviving children despise me now. They blame me for their father's murder. If I wasn't having . . . *having an affair*—" Another gut-wrenching sob cut her words short.

Surviving children . . .

Lou had researched Mark Colston's heroic death in

Afghanistan. The twenty-seven-year-old's platoon had come under attack by a group of Taliban fighters in the Ghazni Province, dubbed by many as being the most dangerous region in the country. Five members of the platoon were badly wounded in the ambush. Medical help could not reach them, because of heavy suppressing fire.

From the accounts Lou had read, Mark Colston strode into the line of fire with the calmness of Gary Cooper in *High Noon*. He shot and killed all but one of the Taliban militiamen. The one he did not kill, he mortally wounded. However, before he died, that Taliban fighter was able to toss a grenade at the fallen U.S. Marines. Mark immediately fell on the grenade, saving the lives of five men, while sacrificing his own. He was posthumously awarded the Medal of Honor for bravery above and beyond the call of duty.

"I'm sure things will work out with your children," Lou said. "Nine years ago, my wife divorced me while I was in rehab from an amphetamine and alcohol addiction. My daughter, Emily, was young then, but not so young that she didn't understand I had done something very bad. She blamed me completely. But things change. Now she's thirteen, and the two of us are as close as a parent and child can be. I have her nearly half the time, but just two days ago, she asked about moving in with me."

"What did you tell her?"

"She loves her mother as much as she loves me. It's just a teen thing. I said that if she left matters as is, I'd get us a cat."

For the first time since Lou's arrival, Jeannine Colston managed something of a smile. "Good luck," she said. She paused, her expression wistful, possibly recalling cats in her family's past. "Now, then," she asked finally, "are there any other questions you have? Anything else you want to know about?"

"Congressman Colston was shot in your garage."

"That's right."

"And his study is above the garage."

"Right again."

"Would you mind if I had a look around there?"

"As long as you don't need me to do it. I don't like being in either place. Besides, I feel a migraine coming on, and the only thing that ever really works at this stage is a nap."

"No problem."

"The code for both doors is five twenty-nine eighty-two, our wedding date."

Lou repeated the number, thanked her, and agreed not to stop back on his way out unless something came up that was important. "I assume the police are done here," he said.

"From what I could tell, they were done almost as soon as they started. They knew they had their man, and so did I."

CHAPTER 10

Sarah Joyce Cooper was on a partner track, or at least that is what she had been told by the firm's founder, Grayson Devlin. She was known for her intellect and composure in the courtroom, but when Devlin summoned her to a conference in his office, her nervousness was understandable.

The conference area, half the size of the one by the library off the main suite, was designed by one of Washington's most prestigious architectural firms to evoke feelings of regality and power. It was a legal sanctuary, featuring rich mahogany paneling and a floor adorned by one of the most beautiful Oriental carpets Sarah had ever seen. There were leather couches and chairs positioned with a designer's flair, bookcases filled with impressive legal tomes, and of course, a well-stocked bar. On one wall was a gas fireplace, and before it, an oval mahogany table with seating for eight.

When Sarah arrived, five of the firm's seven partners were at the conference table. She had no idea how long the partners had been there, and indeed, it was possible they did not know themselves. There were no windows in Devlin's private space, and no clocks. As Sarah found out during her first year on the job, the business of the senior partners of Devlin and Rodgers ended each day only when it had to.

She took her appointed seat and glanced at the papers set out for her, a stack considerably smaller than those in front of the others. She could see they had been reviewing the Gary McHugh case. It seemed a bit early for a strategy meeting of this magnitude, but she felt prepared. Still, she took a sip of lemon water against the raspiness in her throat. There were no prolonged greetings. The firm billed by the minute, and the senior partners' philosophy was to charge only for time spent serving their clients.

Grayson Devlin spoke first. A tall and lean silverback with a full head of hair and a love for designer suits, Devlin, even in his seventies, could intimidate as equally on the squash court as he could in the courtroom.

"Sarah, I see that Dr. McHugh is still in jail."

"The DA is certain he's the man. They don't want this to turn into a circus."

"He's been a good citizen. Any chance we could get him out?"

"He was having an affair with the victim's wife, and he was on the scene intoxicated at around the time the murder took place."

"Point taken. How is your defense shaping up?"

Sarah took another drink of lemon water. "Until we turn something else up, we're going directly after the evidence," she said.

Heather Goddard, the only female partner, made a disapproving sound. "I've read your brief, and that seems like a risky play to me," she said.

Sarah loved Heather's thinking, and did not feel at all on the defensive by having her question the strategy. The partners of Devlin and Rodgers were sharp and ethical, and they understood the critical nuances of the law. They also knew that in cases like McHugh's, their job was not to judge a client's guilt or innocence but, rather, to cast enough reasonable doubt to win an acquittal. When called upon, they functioned as a team to mount the best defense possible. If Heather had any concern, it was Sarah's job to address it.

"The evidence builds a circumstantial case at best. Without a murder weapon, I don't see any risk in attacking it," Sarah said. "But that's not to say I don't share your concern, Heather, which is why it's not my only strategy."

Sarah was pleased to see Heather smile. Next to Devlin, she was the partner Sarah most wanted to impress. Five years before, Heather's husband of twenty-six years had unexpectedly died in his sleep. Two years after that, following the death of Sarah's husband, David, Heather became one of her closest confidantes.

"What else do you have in mind?" Heather asked now.

"It goes without saying that politicians make enemies, especially ones with the longevity on Capitol Hill

that Elias Colston had. I've got an investigator checking around to see whose feathers he might have ruffled
over the years.

Gordon Rodgers, the most senior partner after Devlin,
appeared pleased by the plan. "Do you think a jury would
buy that?" he asked.

"Without the murder weapon, anything is possible.
The surveillance tape shows Dr. McHugh parking on
the drive and leaving his car. But the cameras aren't positioned to show him actually entering the garage or
even going around the house. The next time we see him,
he is more or less stumbling back to his car. Then he
drives away. The crime scene people are fixing the time
of death between eleven and two. That window would
include Dr. McHugh, but it leaves room for someone else
as well."

"Someone else?"

"It's a bit of a long shot, but I think we have an opportunity to focus some attention on Jeannine Colston."

"I thought she had an alibi—some sort of meeting."

"It was a meeting of congressional spouses. Quite a
large meeting, in fact. It featured a buffet brunch. People
milling around, then eventually sitting down. From what
we can tell, she hasn't produced any specific witness
saying she was there throughout the time window when
her husband was killed. It's likely the police were so
sure of themselves with Dr. McHugh that they never
even asked her for an alibi, let alone someone to support it. All we have to do is create doubt. The longer
we wait to ask her to produce an alibi witness, the less
chance someone will be willing to swear under oath

that Jeannine was at the meeting during the ME's window."

"Nice."

"So you're going to propose that Jeannine Colston shot and killed her husband before McHugh arrived at the property, and then left for the meeting in the Capitol?"

"Or after. Dr. McHugh was in a blackout. All bets are off. She could have been there and hid from him. Try this: Dr. McHugh shows up intoxicated. Jeannine and he have a fight. Colston overhears the squabble and confronts his wife about the affair. Tempers flare, and Jeannine Colston gets a gun and kills him."

"Does Colston even own a gun?" Devlin asked.

Sarah had her sixty-plus-page report memorized. "If you turn to page thirty-five in your brief," she said, "I have outlined our ballistics strategy."

The partners flipped to the page.

"The bullets recovered from Colston's body were fired from a .45 ACP," Sarah said, summarizing the lengthy report. "Forensics showed the slugs had a six-groove left-hand twist rifling mark. The Colt company is the only major U.S. handgun manufacturer that consistently uses a left-hand twist. However, several foreign handgun manufacturers also use a left-hand twist, including Taurus. The Colstons happen to have a registered Taurus PT1911. Reasonable doubt. That's our middle name, yes?"

It was no surprise how quickly the police had produced the ballistic forensic details. The Colston case was high-profile and demanded speedy processing of the evidence. Maryland also had one of the most comprehensive ballistics fingerprinting systems in the world. In fact, all new firearms sales were required to provide a fired slug to the state police, who then logged that information into their database.

Each year, Devlin and Rodgers sponsored a ballistics seminar for the firm. The comprehensive full-day session was one of the main reasons Sarah had signed on. Subsequently, several of her cases had hinged on ballistics evidence, and as a result, she had become something of an expert in the science. The inside of every gun barrel contained groove marks that helped a bullet spin and fly to where it was aimed. The "twist" referred to the inches of bore required for one complete rifling spiral.

The ballistics database contained measurements and photographs of the number and depth of each groove and right or left twist direction, in addition to a host of other identifiers. Those data were then used to determine a possible gun manufacturer and make of the weapon that did the firing. To get an exact match required the recovery of the murder weapon and a comprehensive firing test conducted by a ballistics expert.

"Did we test the Taurus?" Devlin asked.

"I plan to contract a three-fire test with one of our forensics experts," Sarah said. "I don't expect a match, but you never know."

Devlin smiled. "You never know" was a favorite adage of his.

The ballistics expert would fire Colston's Taurus

three times into a water tank. The technique would cradle the bullet and preserve the grooves.

"Of course," Heather said with a sly smile, "that doesn't mean the Colstons' couldn't own another Taurus."

"Always possible," Sarah replied, "and a seed of doubt I will be only too happy to plant. For now, all I'm going to show is that they owned a gun from the same manufacturer that is potentially the manufacturer of the weapon that killed Elias Colston. Maybe the Colstons didn't register all their firearms. Maybe the congressman received a Taurus as a gift from a lobbyist who knew he liked the make. Remember, he was a military man—a marine. Maybe Jeannine used that unregistered gun to kill her husband and then she hid the weapon somewhere. *Maybe*—one of our favorite words."

The partners murmured their approval.

Only Devlin looked concerned. "Well done, Sarah," he said. "Now, there's something else I want to discuss."

Uh-oh. Sarah tried not to read much into the change of topic, but that was like trying not to breathe. "Anything," she said.

"Succinctly put, I want to know if you think you should continue to head Gary McHugh's defense team. As his counsel for a number of years, I could rearrange my schedule and take over. That's an option we should discuss."

Sarah swallowed hard. "I'm sorry, sir," she said. "Is it something I've done wrong?"

Devlin cracked a thin smile. "No, Sarah. You've done

your usual stellar job and gotten things off to a great start. But there's a physician involved, and over the last few years, you have led us to believe you were not completely comfortable defending doctors."

Sarah tried to appear unaffected by the implication of Devlin's remark, but Heather's concerned expression suggested she had failed.

"I don't see that as a problem in the McHugh matter, Grayson."

Sarah struggled without success to push the image of David, immobile in his hospital bed, dying a prolonged, needless death, out of her mind. She reined in the terrible image. Shedding tears in Grayson's private conference room would not send a positive message to those who would be determining her future partnership.

Devlin glanced at the notes in front of him. "You've recused yourself from three cases dealing with physicians," Devlin said.

Sarah bit the inside of her cheek to keep from responding too quickly. "I'm fine to handle this one," she said. She kept her reply to a minimum. Weakness or bias of this sort was enough to delay her appointment or even to quash it altogether. She could be impartial. She could represent Gary McHugh—an arrogant doctor, for sure—without being clouded by thoughts of David.

"Well, I've read your brief, and it looks to me as if another doctor is involved now," Devlin said.

"That's true."

Devlin nodded. "So?"

"I can handle it," Sarah said.

Devlin fixed her with the practiced eye that had broken countless witnesses over the years. Then he silently polled the room. "You affirm in your brief that this second physician is Dr. Louis Welcome."

"That's correct. McHugh has enlisted his help. He's a doctor in the ER at Eisenhower Memorial, and a longtime friend. He also works part-time as an associate director of the Physician Wellness Office, helping alcoholic and chemically dependent physicians. My experience even before David tells me that involving physicians in our cases has a huge potential for blowing up in our faces. There is just too much ego involved—too much arrogance."

"And your position on this Welcome?"

"As you can see, I've already made it clear to Dr. Welcome that he is anything but welcome on our team. If he gets in our way or endangers our case, I will do everything in my power to get him to back off. For starters, I am going to have our investigators do a little background checking on him in case we need leverage. From what I can tell, there may actually be some conflict of interest at work if Welcome is professionally involved with McHugh through this Physician Wellness Office."

"So long as your investigation and your response to this Welcome is ethical."

The comment resurrected the image of David, tubes snaking out of him in all directions, backed by the thrum of the machines that were keeping him alive.

"I hope you know that I would never do anything that would adversely affect this firm," Sarah said.

But if Welcome gets in my way or jeopardizes my chance to make partner here, I will cut him off at the knees.

CHAPTER 11

Elias Colston had been shot to death in the center bay of a three-bay garage. The space was empty now, and if there had been a chalk outline of where his body lay, it had been scrubbed away. There was a black Mercedes C-Class sedan in the left bay, a silver Infiniti in the right, and some gardening equipment along the back wall. Nothing of any real interest.

Lou ascended a carpeted stairway and opened the door at the top using the punch-code Jeannine had given him—the day she and Elias had married, probably the biggest day of their lives.

Big wheel keeps on turning, he was thinking.

Elias's office occupied the entire second floor the garage. It was paneled in dark wood, and carpeted from the same roll as the stairs. Very male. An expansive bookshelf filled one wall, with double-hung windows centered on the others—blinds, no curtains. And carefully arranged in almost every available space were framed photos and testimonials, geometrically aligned, so that Lou wondered if the police who had investigated the office had even touched them. Colston, a former marine himself, had apparently never lost his ingrained desire for neatness and order. The books were arranged by height and type: hardbacks with hardbacks, paper with paper, larger tomes on the bottom shelves, more framed photos along the very top. The well-worn antique desk was absent of clutter, and the fine film of dust that had accumulated there, Lou guessed, arrived over the days following the murder.

The desk was augmented at right angles by a workstation that held a printer, two phones, a fax, file box, Rolodex, and a space for a computer, which he suspected had been disemboweled and dissected in some police lab.

The single row of photos on the top bookshelf was mirrored by one behind the desk chair, extending along the wall to the door that probably opened to the second floor of the house. Wedding . . . children . . . summer scenes . . . military units and buddy shots . . . a football team posed on risers . . . what almost certainly were honeymoon photos . . . Marine Corps ribbons separated from their rows and surrounding an obituary for Lance Corporal Mark Raymont Colston. The obituary and accompanying picture were ones Lou had seen before. Mark Colston was darkly handsome, with thick brows and gentle eyes more like a poet's than like a warrior's.

Lou checked the drawers of the desk. To his astonishment, they had not been emptied. It felt so clear that the police investigating the case were simply going through the motions. Dr. Gary McHugh had shot his lover's husband to death. Case closed.

He swept together the papers and envelopes in the top drawer and set them on the desk. A few bills; several letters of thanks from constituents, and several more making requests. *Replied* had been written on the top right corner of each of those, in what was almost certainly the congressman's hand. Lou scanned each one. Nothing that stood out. Beneath the letters was a Baltimore Ravens schedule for the present year, and a birthday card signed, *Love, Debbie*—one of Jeannine and Elias's surviving children.

Finally, there was an envelope addressed to Mr. James Styles at a post office box in Bowie, Maryland. The return address read "Pine Forest Clinic, Shockley, Minnesota." The logo featured three pines behind sedate lettering. The envelope was empty. Lou used a sheet of typing paper to record information from the notes and envelopes, folded the sheet, and slipped it into his pocket.

There was nothing of interest in the other two drawers. A trip to the Internet would help him see whether or not the Pine Forest Clinic or James Styles of Bowie, Maryland, fell in that category as well. For a time, Lou paced around the office. He wondered in passing what Elias Colston was doing in the garage when he was murdered. Just exiting his car? Getting set to leave? Waiting for someone? Perhaps searching for something?

The news for McHugh and Sarah Cooper was not going to be good.

At that instant, something caught Lou's attention. It was one of the ten or so framed photos of various sizes on the top shelf of the bookcase. But this one was different from the others. This one was facing the wall. Probably inspected and placed back carelessly, he was thinking as he reached up for it. The felt back may have caused investigators to miss that they had replaced it front side in. More likely, though, given their shoddy examination of the office, they simply hadn't noticed, in which case the photo might have been carefully placed that way by Colston.

Lou reached up, gently brought the frame down, and turned it over.

The medal on display against a black velvet field was a gold five-pointed star, each point tipped with tre-foils and encircled by a green laurel wreath. The star was suspended beneath a gold bar, which had the word VALOR inscribed in its center and an eagle perched atop.

The discreet gold plaque beneath it read:

MEDAL OF HONOR
MARK RAYMONT COLSTON

Lou caught his breath. He had no idea how many of the highest decoration the country could bestow for bravery had ever been awarded, but he knew it wasn't many. For more than a minute, he simply gazed at the medal, trying to imagine the horrible circumstances surrounding it, and wondering what had led the father of the recipient to turn it to the wall, if in fact that was what he had done.

It was then, he felt a distinct fullness beneath the felt backing.

Working on the desk, he released the eight catches holding the backing in place. It fell away, revealing a clear plastic sleeve.

And inside the sleeve was a CD.

CHAPTER 12

Three days earlier, Lou had driven to the Colston home, stopping just short of the driveway and then retreating to the bridge where police were theorizing that Gary McHugh had disposed of the gun he used to murder Elias. Their theory did not make sense to him then, and it wasn't making sense now, as he rolled slowly over the span, looking from side to side at the partially ice-covered river and wondering how McHugh, in a virtual blackout, after just shooting his friend to death point-blank, could have stopped, sized up the status of the water to be sure the gun would not simply end up on the ice, and then tossed it over the waist-high stone railing.

The tree McHugh had hit at enough speed to total his car and leave him battered and unconscious was down a slight embankment, fifty or so feet from the far end of the bridge. The deep gouge in the trunk suggested McHugh had quickly gotten up a head of steam before skidding or veering off the road. Possible, but not probable. At least, that was Lou's assessment.

Clearly the cops felt otherwise.

Immediately after the detectives arrived on the scene, before they began their investigation, Jeannine Colston had informed them of her relationship with McHugh. According to her, they next examined the recording from the security cameras covering the front drive. McHugh coming and parking. McHugh leaving his car and heading toward the house. McHugh returning and driving off. Word from the emergency room at Anne Arundel Hospital would have filled in some of the side pieces.

Motive, method, opportunity, alcohol.

Crank up the guillotine blade and light the torches. We've got our man. Tell the press to back off and wait for the DA's statement. Move along, now, folks. Move along. . . .

In their haste to finish the investigation of what they considered a slam dunk, the police had missed a strange and inexplicable finding—a matted and framed medal for valor, the ultimate valor, turned to the wall by . . . by—how could it not have been by Elias Colston?

Had the odd finding been an isolated one—an error by Colston after dusting the shelves, or a burst of anger at his son's death—that might have been that. But there was nothing isolated about it. The meticulous congressman and retired marine had carefully sequestered a recording of some sort, and left a sign indicating where it was that was as definitive, as unsubtle as Times Square on New Year's Eve.

If harm comes to me, if you are inspecting my of-fice, this is where you should look. This is where the money is.

Lou fingered the CD resting on the passenger seat of his aging Toyota, and began to scan the side roads for an isolated spot where he could listen in privacy. He had given thought to rousing Jeannine from her nap and listening with her, but it seemed wiser to get a pre-view. It was always possible that the disc had nothing at all to do with Elias's death—or his son's, for that matter. Perhaps, like his wife, he was having an affair. Perhaps he had made the recording and then changed his mind about sending it to someone, and had hidden it in the frame until he could decide.

A dirt road caught his eye, cutting off to the left. It was overhung with ghostly winter branches, many of them topped with snow. Tire tracks entered the woods along shallow frozen mud-packed ruts. Lou pulled in thirty yards, stopped by a NO TRESPASSING sign, and lowered his window three inches. The breeze was like a splash of aftershave. He cut the engine. Dense silence engulfed him. Finally, he turned the key to auxiliary and slipped in the CD.

There was a burst of static, and then a recording of two men, one younger, and one older. The older voice Lou knew immediately—Elias Colston. The represen-tative's funeral had featured the broadcast of an impas-sioned speech he delivered some months before to both houses of Congress, pleading in the memory of his hero son for a decisive decrease in military spending, and a shift in priorities from defense and satellite development to education. Wonderful, brilliantly constructed rhetoric from the head of the House Armed Services Committee.

The younger man was someone named Hector. He spoke with an accent Lou recognized from his years working at Eisenhower Memorial—Hispanic, etched by the streets. His vocabulary and the simplicity of his sentences suggested that he probably was not educated much beyond high school.

It took Lou just a short while to become convinced that the conversation was being recorded by Colston, and that Hector was unaware of it.

"Well, Hector, I confess I was quite surprised to hear from you. How long has it been?"

"A couple of years, sir. Since just after the . . . I mean since just after Mark was . . ."

"It's okay, Hector, you can say it."

"Since Mark's funeral. I really miss him, sir. I hope you know that. We all do. He was an all-American, a real-deal hero. The guys still talk about what he did."

"It's important for me to hear that, although I wish I didn't have to go to so many ceremonies in his honor. Those are making it tougher on me, not easier."

"I can dig it. You holding up okay?"

"Yes. Yes, I'm holding up as well as can be expected."

"And Mrs. Colston?"

"She has periods of great sadness, Hector, but then she bounces back."

"That's understandable. I enjoyed the couple of times she had me over with Mark for lunch, and that time for Thanksgiving. Give her my best."

"I will. Speaking of lunch, here's our sandwiches. Where would you like to talk?"

"Mind if we go out to those tables back there? As usual, the air-conditioning in this place ain't workin', and there's good shade and privacy."

Summer. Lou made a mental note. Whenever this conversation had taken place, it wasn't recent.

"That'll be fine," Colston said.

"Okay if I order a beer to bring along?"

"Go for it."

"Want one?"

"No thanks, Hector. I'm not that focused a driver under the best of circumstances."

There was a period of noise as the two men left wherever they were and settled in at one of the tables outside. Lou could not be at all certain, but it seemed as if Hector's speech was somewhat pressured and tense.

"So, sir," the marine said after a time, "let me explain why I asked to see you. It wasn't my idea, actually. It was our commanding officer, Colonel Brody. He asked me to speak with you."

"Wyatt Brody, yes?"

"Yes, sir."

"I met him briefly at Mark's funeral. He wasn't exactly the warm and fuzzy type."

"No, sir. That's not the colonel. Mark was one of his favorites, and believe me, the colonel doesn't have too many of those."

"Mark never spoke much about him, only about some of the other Mantis soldiers, like you."

"Well, the colonel is one tough dude, sir. And that's something of an understatement. He's very upset about some of the things you've been doing in your committee—cutting expenses to Mantis."

"It hasn't been just to Mantis, Hector. I feel our country is headed in the wrong direction, and it's time to adjust our priorities, specifically in the direction of more and better education. Drugs, street violence, welfare, crime, overcrowded prisons. There is no solution to the social ills that are dragging this country down other than more teachers and better schools, and the money has to come from someplace. Supporters call my proposals a blueprint for hope, and that's exactly what they are. Hope for our cities. Hope for children everywhere."

"Pardon me for saying it, sir, but education ain't worth much if towel-headed terrorists can just walk in here and blow up our schools. So long as they got the oil, they got the power. And the only thing they'll ever listen to is somebody else's power that's bigger than what they got."

"I believe we have enough intelligence and firepower to prevent that, provided they are used in the right way."

"Yes. Well, pardon me for siding with the colonel on this one, sir. He feels you should be showin' your son and his unit more respect, especially given that you're a marine yourself. We're the number-one best unit in the marines—hell, in the whole damn military. Please excuse the language. We are right up there with the SEALs, and rated even tougher than the Rangers or Delta Force. But our manpower and weaponry are being hacked away."

"Pushing for those cuts hasn't been easy for me, Hector. Several times it's come down to my son's memory or my conscience."

"Mr. Colston, sir, you got to reconsider," Hector pleaded, his voice half an octave higher than it had been. "The colonel is hard like no one I ever dealt with before. And he's got people around him."

"People?"

"Tough dudes, enlisted from the streets and put right in Mantis."

"What do you mean. Hector?"

There was a prolonged emptiness before Hector responded, this time in a strained whisper. Stunned, Lou listened to the exchange.

"We call them the Palace Guards, and wherever the colonel is, they're not far away."

"Are they like a gang?"

"In a way, maybe. I really don't know."

"So, Hector, is this meeting some kind of warning from Colonel Brody?"

Extended silence. Another harsh, whispered reply.

"Mr. Colston, for Mark's sake, for your sake, you gotta pull back and take some of the pressure off of Mantis. Mark gave his life for the company and this country."

"You seem nervous, Hector. Has Colonel Brody threatened you if you don't succeed with me?"

"It's Dr. Brody, sir. Did you know that?"

"Doctor? Like a medical doctor?"

"Not like any medical doctor you ever had, and nobody talks about it much, but yeah, he's a doctor of some kind. I tell you 'cause that's how smart he is. Smart and tough and backed up by some of the hardest men this side of hell."

"Hector, you know I'm a pretty powerful man in Washington. Just say the word, and I can bring some serious clout down on your Colonel Dr. Brody."

Lou heard some shuffling and imagined Hector pushing to his feet.

"Those guys smoking back there against the restaurant. At least two of them are Palace Guards. All I want is your word, Mr. Colston—your word that you will lighten up on Mantis and replace some of the money you got taken away."

"The best I can do is to promise I'll think about my position."

"Please, do that, sir. Please."

"All right, Hector. I promise. One last thing."

"Yes?"

"Do you know anything about Mantis soldiers being killed at a place called the Reddy Creek Armory?"

"Never heard about nothing like that. What is it?"

"I don't know. There was a blog I came across written by a reporter in North Carolina that mentioned it. When I tried learning more, the blog was gone, wiped off the Internet. I couldn't find any other mention of any killings anyplace. It's as if they never happened."

"No idea, sir. Never heard of no Mantis marines bein' involved with any killings."

"Okay. Thanks, Hector. Let me know if you hear anything like that."

"I will. Now, please, do what I asked and help keep Mark's unit strong. He died for Mantis and our country."

"You have my word."

The disc went silent.

Eyes closed, Lou sat alone in the late afternoon chill. Suddenly, he realized he was soaked with sweat.

CHAPTER 13

The American flag outside the state police barracks in College Park, Maryland, still flying at half-mast to honor Congressman Elias Colston, fluttered in a light breeze. Lou parked his Toyota and remained in his seat for a time, thinking about the violent deaths of Elias Colston and before that, his son. He wanted to feel exhilarated about his discovery of the CD—a discovery that might ultimately connect the two, but the only emotion he could connect with at the moment was sadness.

For a time, his thoughts drifted to work. Walter Filstrup, irritated that a client Lou was monitoring had been arrested for murder, had assigned him two more difficult cases—a pediatrician with bipolar disease who had decided to stop her meds and had become frighteningly argumentative at work before going on a shoplifting rampage, and an anesthesia resident who had started sampling the narcotics on his tray, and was in immediate need of hospitalization and detoxification. The result, in addition to shifts in the ER and the strain of trying to get to the bottom of the Colston murder, was a mounting exhaustion that tempered any feeling of accomplishment at finding the disc.

Lou had listened to the recording twice, and had made a copy for Sarah, which he buried beneath the socks in his bureau drawer next to some personal papers. It was all there on that disc—everything the police would need to divert their attention away from Gary McHugh and onto Colonel Wyatt Brody, commander of the elite fighting force Mantis, under whom Mark Colston served until his death.

Just before entering the police barracks, Lou tried, once again, to call Sarah. She was taking a deposition and would probably be out of touch for at least the rest of the day. Her assistant, a pleasant-sounding woman named Andrea, turned him over to her voice mail. At least there was proof Lou had tried to get in touch with her.

The investigating and arresting officer, a detective Chris Bryzinski, sounded amiable on the phone, and anxious to do the right thing, although he also sounded convinced of the guilt of Gary McHugh. Lou had significant experience with the Maryland State Police. At what he hoped was the beginning of the end of his active addiction, he had been arrested in Baltimore buying amphetamines from an undercover cop. The police treated him fairly then, and he had every reason to believe this detective would appreciate the significance of the remarkable conversation between Elias Colston and Colston's son's best friend.

If things went the way Lou anticipated, Wyatt Brody

would immediately become a person of intense interest in the murder of the congressman. Brody's motive for the killing was at least as strong as the one being attributed to McHugh. Elias Colston had been spearheading the reduction of funds to all aspects of Mantis, the crème de la crème of marine fighting units, as well as to virtually every other aspect of the military.

In addition to wanting to keep his unit afloat, Brody appeared to have surrounded himself with some hand-picked toughs known to the rest of Mantis as the Palace Guards. It was not clear from the recording exactly how far the guards were willing to go to protect Brody's interests, but there was no doubt that Hector feared them.

The compact, one-story, gray brick station was situated just off the Capital Beltway in a section of town that had a number of one-story businesses and not much that Lou could see to attract people to them. Lou spoke to a uniformed officer through a Plexiglas shield and took a seat on a well-worn chair in the waiting area. He was right on time, if not a little early. Five minutes passed, then ten. When they spoke on the phone, Bryzinski had seemed eager enough to meet.

Now? . . .

Another five minutes. Lou fingered the disc, sleeved and wrapped, in the pocket of his jacket, and thought about leaving. He was about to do just that when the door to the inner sanctum of the station opened and a bowling ball of a man motioned him in. He was five-six or -seven and seemed close to that wide across, huge-headed and balding. His brown suit coat, buttoned at the middle, failed to hide the bulge of his shoulder holster.

"Detective Bryzinski," he mumbled, not bothering with a handshake.

So much for impressions over the phone.

"Lou Welcome," Lou said, matching mumble for mumble.

He followed the detective past a NO SMOKING IN THIS BUILDING sign into his office, a featureless, wildly cluttered space that reeked of stale coffee and possibly Bryzinski himself. Stacks of folders and loose papers covered virtually every square inch of desk, as well as a portion of a laptop and an ashtray shaped like Florida, filled with loose change.

Without being asked, Lou took the steel-armed institutional seat on the guest side of the desk. Bryzinski settled into his high-backed Staples standard, looking immediately like an overindulged pooh-bah. A diamond ring cut into the flesh of his right pinkie, and a narrow gold band did the same to the wedding finger on his left. Lou tried briefly and without success to form an image of the wife who awoke each day next to the man.

"Sorry to keep you waiting," Bryzinski said after a time. "We're short two men—one home sick and the other shot."

"Shot?"

"Don't ask."

Lou didn't. "Well, thanks for seeing me," he said.

"I don't have a lot of time."

Why am I not surprised? This was a man who was chronically inconvenienced.

Bryzinski pursed his lips in a gesture that said, *Okay, let's get this over with.* "So now," he said, "you told me who you were over the phone, and I checked you out. Let's skip the 'friend of Gary McHugh' part and cut to the chase. What's going on, and how does it affect my case?"

And remember, I don't have a lot of time.

Lou hesitated, seriously considering simply bolting from the toxic office. After a few empty seconds, he put the CD on Bryzinski's desk, beside a tower of files and other papers that looked on the verge of collapse. He reviewed his visit with Jeannine Colston, and his inspection of Elias's office, carefully choosing his words to avoid any implication that Bryzinski and his cohorts had underdone their jobs.

The detective seemed to be listening with one ear, occasionally looking out the window and not bothering to take any notes or to record Lou's statement. It was not the least bit difficult for Lou to imagine the cop forming a conclusion before the investigation had actually begun, and tailoring his inspection to support what facts he had.

"Did you bring the frame?" Bryzinski asked when he had finished.

"The frame?"

"Yes, the frame." Irritation replaced the ennui in the detective's voice. "The thing that might have fingerprints all over it."

Lou began to feel dumb. He wanted to snap back something like, *How about you try to spend an hour running a busy inner-city emergency room?*

"I'm sure it's still in Colston's study," he said instead.

"Look," Brezinski countered as if he were lecturing a third-grader, "I bet you think that you've cracked this case wide open. Well, take it from me and twenty years as a cop: You haven't." He patted the stack of papers closest to him. "You see these? These are from other people—lots and lots of other people. People who also think *they've* cracked the case wide open. Get what I'm saying?"

"I think this is more than just a random tip," Lou said.

"Do you know what I've got to do?" Bryzinski continued on as though Lou had not even spoken. "I've got to go through each and every one of these. And guess what they are? They're all shit. Total and complete crazy shit. You know why? Because everybody wants in on the action when it's somebody big who gets killed. Everybody, even the marginally sane ones, has a fact or a theory. And you know what else? See these other piles? I got about thirty-eight active cases, and I can't get a frickin' tip on any of 'em. Know why?"

"Well, I'd guess—"

"Because they're nobodies. They're just people. Regular joes. All ages. All races. Bad guys, good guys. But none of them are a congressman, and none of them had a wife who was shtupping a big-shot society doctor."

"Well, Gary and Jeannine's relationship isn't really—"

"So, I'll take this CD, since you're so insistent on dropping it off in person, and we'll put it through the sniff test. And even though I have better things to do, I'll drive back to the Colstons' place and get that frame."

"I can go back and get the—"

"You can go to your hospital or your crazy junkie doctor office, and let us do what we get paid to do."

"You're not going to listen to that disc right now?"

Bryzinski sighed. "Look, Doctor."

"Yeah?"

"I'm going to tell you how this really works. You see, like I said, I've been doing this job for a long time. Trust me when I tell you that I know guilty when I see guilty. Your buddy, McHugh, may be a great guy ninety-nine percent of the time, but he wasn't so great when he blew away Congressman Colston. It happens—the way of the world. Someone loses it, someone else dies. So, you can add your CD to the pile of conspiracy theories for me to investigate, and I'll listen to it. But I'm not going to rush and do it this minute, and I'm not going to do it with a big, happy smile on my face. Does that make sense?"

"No, it doesn't make sense," Lou said, "but it's obviously how it's going to be. I'll tell you one more time before I leave you to all your overwhelming piles of work. Listen to this disc, and you'll realize there's a motive for another man to have killed Elias Colston."

"I'll hear it, all right," Bryzinski said. "But on my time." He stood with some effort, and lumbered to the door.

Lou followed, giving one last forlorn look back at the CD. "Should I call you?" Lou asked.

Bryzinski grinned. He was Abbott having just been served up a slow softball pitch from Costello. "Don't call us," he said. "We'll call you."

CHAPTER 14

The Baltimore City Detention Center loomed like a medieval castle, plunked down in a neighborhood advisable to keep away from after dark. The gray stone edifice featured four tall towers framing a steep-pitched roof, each tower topped by a metal turret. Stone-arched frames held rows of grimy windows, each several stories high and nearly obscured by rusty bars. *Impenetrable, imposing,* and *inescapable* were words that popped into Lou's head as he and Cap passed underneath an entrance awning built against an expanse of chain-link fencing and razor wire.

Lou swallowed hard as he entered the brightly lit whitewashed lobby. It was one thing to be reminded of his arrest a decade ago, but something far more terrible to be back inside a detention center. This was the purgatory of the corrections system—a hellhole, lumping together guilty and innocent, each awaiting trial or transfer to a more long-term incarceration in prison. These were men who could not make bail or, worse, whose alleged crimes were deemed so severe that a judge had denied them bail of any size. Gary McHugh fell into the latter category—alleged murderers, who almost never got bail. In fact, Lou needed special permission from the Maryland Department of Public Safety and Correctional Services just to arrange this face-to-face meeting.

Lou and Cap approached the lobby window together. They turned over their IDs, and after explaining to the woman working the counter whom they were here to see, a metal door to Lou's right buzzed and they were ushered inside by a stone-faced armed guard. Lou startled when the heavy door slammed behind them and the cannonlike sound echoed eerily down a long stretch of empty corridor. Their footfalls snapped against the linoleum tile, creating a mournful tattoo.

Their next stop was the locker room area, where they were instructed to remove and lock up all personal effects—wallets, jewelry, pens, keys. A second guard, equally as somber as the first, escorted them through another heavy door that clanged shut with the finality of a thunderclap. They passed through the metal detector without incident and followed the guard along a warren of corridors that eventually brought them to the visitor center.

"That was fun," Lou said to Cap, realizing his palms had gone clammy and his pulse had ticked up several notches.

"I never get used to this," Cap said, "but it's a good reminder of where I could have ended up."

"Amen," Lou said.

Lou took his assigned seat on a long bench with partitions on either side of him. Cap got placed somewhere to Lou's right, perhaps five or six partitioned spaces away. There were eight or nine other visitors here, their conversations subdued. Handprints marring the thick Plexiglas were the echoes of the devastated and desperate loved ones who had cried into the black phone Lou would soon use to speak with McHugh.

The one good thing about this jaunt to jail was that it made Lou forget about the hugely disappointing encounter with Detective Chris Bryzinski. The man's lack of enthusiasm was very high on Lou's list of irritants. Maybe after he finally brought himself to listen to the striking conversation between the high-ranking congressman and the young marine, Bryzinski would call Lou with a little more energy. And with luck, once that happened, the icy atmosphere between Lou and Sarah Cooper would begin to thaw.

A loud buzzer pulled Lou's attention toward the door and Gary McHugh's somber entrance. The flamboyant physician looked absolutely miserable in his orange prison jumpsuit. He had clearly lost weight, and his usually buoyant complexion had gone sallow. McHugh slumped into his chair as he and Lou picked up the wall-mounted phones.

"Thanks for coming, Lou," Gary said, his voice rife with torment. "It's great to see a friendly face. Any face, for that matter."

"How are you holding up?"

"Not so good. I keep telling people I didn't do it, Lou, and nobody will believe me."

"You'll get your day in court," Lou said. "But you've got to stay strong."

"Yeah, stay strong. Not so easy here. Lou, this place is a nightmare. We get the same thing to eat every day. Every blasted day. It's dirty and overcrowded. There's no decent exercise yard. You don't get a single second of privacy. Not a second. You can't even take a dump here without somebody whistling at you. And the gangs—the gangs run the place, and they are really bad. If I have any positive news to report, it's that after listening to one guy after another blame alcohol or drugs for the mess he's in, I've begun to realize that if I ever get the chance, I need to put more effort into my recovery."

"That's great to hear you say. See if you can get your hands on any AA literature."

"I'll try, but I'm really terrified speaking up about anything."

"We're working on that," Lou said.

Lou knew that McHugh's being a doctor did not help matters at all. In fact, the inmates were certain he could get drugs, which only heightened the enmity toward him in a number of quarters when he couldn't deliver. There was little or no sympathy for him in jail, just as there was little compassion in the press or hospitals for most of the other PWO clients. They had been given the Great American Dream, elusive to so many, and through their appetites, their lust, their passion for excess, or their psychiatric illness, they had destroyed it. Never mind the good they had done over the years, or the patients they had cared for so meticulously and selflessly. From the beginning of his recovery, Lou had argued on any number of platforms that, like anyone, doctors had the right to be sick, although they also had the obligation to seek treatment.

McHugh was constantly being threatened; his wife and children refused to visit him; and even his attorney had been acting somewhat distant and clinical.

Lou debated trying to boost his friend's mood with an account of the recording he had found, but until Sarah finished her deposition and listened to the CD herself, it did not seem like a wise idea at all. He also worried about raising McHugh's hopes without first seeing a change in Bryzinski's attitude. Instead, Lou tried to cheer him up by talking medicine and, without naming names, the new cases he had been assigned by Walter Filstrup. Nothing had much effect.

"So, what do you think?" McHugh asked, obviously tired of the small talk.

"About?"

"Come on, Lou. What have you learned? What did Jeannine say? Does she think I did it?"

"She's hurt, Gary, rejected by her kids just like you have been, and angry as hell. At the moment, there isn't much doubt in her mind that you're guilty."

"Damn. Lou, I swear, I didn't kill him. You've got to keep searching for proof of that. I don't care if I never get to practice medicine again, but if I get sent to prison, I swear I'll—"

"Easy, pal. Remember that 'day at a time' stuff? It's not just words. It saved my life."

McHugh wiped the sleeve of his orange jumpsuit

across the sweat beading up on his brow. "Okay," he managed.

Cap came up behind Lou, bent down, and whispered in his ear, "We're all set."

The guard eyed Cap with suspicion.

"Gary," Lou said into the receiver, "look down the row, to your right. You see the large black guy with the Mohawk? His name's Booker—Tiny Booker."

"I've seen him around. He's hard to miss."

"Well, Tiny has got your back now. He and his pals are your protection in here until you get out. Don't lose faith Gary. We're going to find proof that you're innocent."

"Yeah? Tell that to my kids, will you?"

"When it's right. I'll do that—promise."

The guard approached and motioned to his watch that the visit needed to end.

"Stay strong, pal. I'll be back soon."

"Thanks. It's good to know someone's got my back."

"And Gary?"

"Yeah?"

"What you said about not caring if you ever practice medicine again? Believe it or not, that's pretty healthy thinking."

The guard led Lou and Cap back to the locker area, where they retrieved their things. Cap opened his wallet, checking to see that his money was still there.

"What?" he said, responding to Lou's *come on, now* look. "There are a lot of criminals in here."

"I shudder to think of how close I came to getting

myself locked up. So, Cap, do you think your friend Tiny will have any luck protecting Gary?"

Cap worked his jacket back on. "I dunno. Like you said, these are bad places, Lou. Tiny told me it'll be tough to keep watch all the time, but he's got enough juice with the gangs that it'll probably turn out all right."

"And what if he can't?" Lou asked.

"Well, I know that looking at those sausage-sized fingers of his would hardly make anyone a believer, but Tiny Booker is the best B and E man, the best lock-picker in Baltimore, and maybe one of the best anywhere. I've seen him get past alarms that would make Willie Sutton go dizzy in the head."

"And how's that going to help, Gary?"

"Because if Tiny says he can do something, my bet is on him doing it. But if it turns out he can't help McHugh, there's a better-than-even chance he could break him out of here."

CHAPTER 15

Lou used the hours before his graveyard shift to nap, read fifty or so pages of Dickens's *Pickwick Papers,* and hit an AA meeting. The sparsely attended discussion group dealt that day with Step One of the twelve steps—admitting one is powerless over his or her addiction and that their life had become unmanageable. Gary sounded as if he were inching toward that vital first step on the road to true recovery.

"You can't be too stupid to get this stuff," Cap had said when he and Lou first met, "but you can sure as heck be too smart."

Hopefully, Gary was in the process of being given the gift of desperation. From his own experience, Lou had learned that the harder that gift was to obtain, the better.

When he finally left the ER, it was, as usual, an hour after his shift should have ended. The thirteen hours were hectic enough to make them pass quickly. Lou, pleasantly bone-weary, headed down to the hospital caf for what he now realized was his first real meal in most of a day. Grapefruit juice, poached eggs on an English muffin, home fries, milk. Because of his reluctance to use any disposable dishes or utensils, he as usual annoyed the server by insisting on metal, glass, and ceramic. Renee, who considered herself a die-hard green, had continuously lectured him on how much less environmentally friendly it was to wash dishes than to go paper, but he defended his reluctance to change anything by demanding statistics.

He had just reached an empty table and set his tray down when his cell phone began vibrating.

It was Sarah Cooper, and she did not sound at all pleased. "Are you somewhere where you can pick me up?" she asked.

Lou looked longingly at his breakfast, none of which was transportable. "When?"

"Five minutes ago."

"I suppose so. I'm at Eisenhower Memorial. I just got off—"

"We need to go and speak to that detective you left me a message about. I just got off the phone with him. He's waiting at his office for us, but he says he's got to leave soon. I need to hear from both of you exactly what you said to him."

"Do you want to listen to the disc first?"

"Dr. Welcome, what part of 'he says he's got to leave soon' are you having trouble with?"

"Attorney Cooper, does the approach of being snide and nasty usually get you what you want?" Lou picked at the edge of an English muffin, which was already becoming soggy.

"I'll be just inside the street door to my office," Sarah said.

The line went dead.

Over the ten-minute drive to Sarah's office, Lou mustered the ten years of serenity that defined his recovery. From their initial meeting at McHugh's place, something hadn't been right between the two of them. But what?

Lou pulled to the curb, and as promised, she hurried out. There was no question that he found her attractive. It was hard not to. But if she wanted to push him away, she was doing a near perfect job.

"Drive!" Sarah ordered, slamming the door behind her and snapping her seat belt in place.

"Wait, I think we should talk," Lou said.

"About what? What could you say that you haven't already?"

Lou flashed on the time in grade school when he had tried to impress some older boys by shoplifting a wind-up robot from a toy store. He had been desperate for their approval then, just as he realized he was for Sarah Cooper's approval now. That, in all likelihood, was what lay behind his rush to turn the disc over to the police. And if her reaction was any measure, he was screwing up just as badly as he had by pilfering the robot. The difference was that unless he was way off base, he had done nothing wrong this time.

His punishment for the shoplifting gaffe was the payment of a month's allowance to the proprietor of the store, and a two-page essay about why it was wrong to steal. He glanced over at the attorney he had wanted so much to impress, and wondered if he was going to get away that easy.

He slipped the car into the flow of traffic and headed west.

"Do you mind telling me what's going on?" he asked finally. "Why the rush to go back to see Bryzinski?"

Sarah's look held all the warmth of concrete. "Do you think you went into medicine because you were arrogant, or did you become arrogant because you became a doctor?"

"I don't know what you mean."

"All right, let me try this another way: Do you think it would be right for me to stroll into the emergency ward and start sewing up patients?"

Lou was about to go for a flip answer, but bit it back at the last instant. "No," he said solemnly. "That wouldn't be appropriate."

"So, do you think the rules we have for handling evidence in legal cases is any less crucial and binding than the rules you have for treating patients?"

"I suppose not, but—"

"There is no 'but.' You may have messed up. You physicians screw up all the time because you just don't listen. The rules to follow are there, starting with, Listen to the patient. But you decide when you're going to pay attention to them and when you just don't feel like it. Even if this Bryzinski has taken perfect care of that CD, the potential is there for disaster. Trouble at home, an alcohol problem, some sort of scary medical report from his doctor. He loses his concentration or isn't paying attention to you in the first place, and all of a sudden, all your good intentions fly out the window. When your patients tell you something, do you listen?"

"Of course I listen."

"And what about when I told you something back at Gary McHugh's house. Did you listen?"

Lou could not understand why she was so upset. It wasn't as if he were a naïve idiot. He had made a thorough, even brilliant, search and had turned up a CD that was going to help his friend and her client. Then he had made two copies of the CD, and took the original to the police. What was wrong about any of that?

She should have been ecstatic about the discovery. Perhaps her vitriol was nothing more than a stab of jealously at Lou having proved his worth to McHugh's case in just a matter of days. He decided to push the envelope.

"Sarah, I found evidence that should at least infuse doubt into the case against Gary. I don't see why you're so upset."

She sighed deeply while Lou weaved through the increasing volume of early afternoon traffic. "You just don't understand how things work," she said.

Lou wanted her to look at him. The angrier she got, the more he wanted to appease her. They should be forging an alliance—for Gary's sake, they needed to be on the same team.

"Why don't you explain to me how things work instead of getting so upset with me? I did try calling you."

"But then you decided you could just handle things yourself. The old M. Deity."

"What's your deal?" Lou asked. "All that matters is the police have the evidence you'll need to help Gary."

Finally, Sarah turned to him. He immediately wished she hadn't. "Do they?" she asked. "Just in case, did you make sure the copies you had made were flawless reproductions?"

"No, but—"

"And did Jeannine Colston see you find the CD?"

"She was sleeping off a migraine and asked me not to wake her unless I had to. I didn't even know what was on the disc yet, and I felt she had done enough, spending so much time with me. She was really a mess."

The Toyota picked up even more speed.

"So nobody knows that you found this evidence that will possibly help cast doubt on the guilt of Gary McHugh?"

"Well, Bryzinski does."

"You told me he didn't listen to the recording in front of you. Did Bryzinski know that nobody else had heard that recording?"

The speedometer's needle inched ahead.

Lou nodded. "I understand what you're getting at."

"At last, light dawns. Doctor, this isn't a child's game. A man's life is at stake here."

Lou began to boil. "I think I appreciate what's at risk."

"Do you? You think this is just about evidence? A congressman has been murdered, Lou. Don't you get it?"

Lou realized it was the first time she had called him by his given name.

"This is about sound bites and CNN and twenty-four-hour-a-day news coverage. It's about getting somebody fingered for the crime, winning in the court of public opinion, and lastly putting the so-called scumbag who the DA says did it away for life. It's about elections and promotions, and that has nothing—*and I do mean nothing*—to do with evidence.

"Who looks bad if Gary McHugh isn't the killer? Who looks bad if your tip capsizes somebody's boat— someone with a lot more power and influence than you and I have, someone who doesn't want the public to think that an investigation into a congressman's murder was shoddily handled? Whose ass is in a sling when the media starts reporting that the Keystone Kops bungled yet another high-profile investigation? I'm not talking evidence. I'm talking the facts of life in the law—real and often very ugly facts."

Lou glanced down at the speedometer and saw that he was now traveling eighty in a fifty. "We'll be there soon," he said.

CHAPTER 16

The remainder of the ride to the state police barracks in College Park was made in absolute silence.

Breathe in . . . breathe out . . .

Lou used the mantra to keep focused on the speed limit and on the likelihood that in a short while, there would be no further tension between him and Sarah Cooper. The detective in charge of the Colston murder would produce the CD, and Gary McHugh would no longer be the only suspect. Case closed—or, more to the point, just beginning.

Sarah Cooper had an edge like honed steel. It was humbling and not a little embarrassing to be spoken to the way she had spoken to him, but he could see her point. His enthusiasm and, yes, maybe his arrogance had overwhelmed his objectivity. And for whatever reason, Sarah was disinclined to cut him any slack at all.

The flag outside the low brick building was still at half-mast. With all the violence in the world, Lou wondered if its condition might be permanent. The two of them were kept waiting only a short time before Chris

Bryzinski lumbered into the waiting room and motioned them to follow him into the inner sanctum. Lou watched as the man's girth nearly brushed against each side of the doorframe, and he mused about what would happen if the detective were ever forced to chase a criminal. They stopped in the hallway just beyond the door.

"Dr. Welcome, welcome back," Bryzinski said, his expression suggesting he took some pleasure in the double use of Lou's last name. "What can I do for you now?"

Sarah introduced herself and shook hands with the man. "Thanks for making time for us," she said.

"Hey, no problem. No problem." Bryzinski replied, giving Sarah the once-over. "It just can't be long, though. We're swamped today. Four accidents and one homicide."

"Detective, could we speak in your office?" Sarah asked. "These matters are sensitive, and I'd prefer a more private area in which to discuss them."

Bryzinski grunted a reluctant concession and asked the desk officer to buzz them through the next door. Then he led them down the corridor to his office. The policeman's desk was, if anything, even messier than when Lou had been there. He suppressed a grin, watching Sarah's distaste as she breathed in the fetid air and surveyed the cluttered landscape. They remained standing while Bryzinski took a call and quickly dealt with whatever it was.

"So?" he asked, not inviting them to sit down or bothering to do so himself.

"We won't take up much of your time," Lou said.

"Attorney Cooper just wanted to talk with you about the CD I dropped off yesterday."

"In the interest of discovery," Sarah added, "I'd like to make sure to give a copy to the district attorney's office as well. Have you listened to it yet?"

"Actually, no. It's been really crazy here since the congressman's murder. Tips keep coming in. Despite the fact that we are confident we have our man, we still have to—"

"Could I see it, please?" Sarah asked.

"Detective Cartwright's in charge of managing everything that comes in on this case. By the time we've had the chance to follow every one of them up, there'll be buds on the trees and flowers in the garden."

"I certainly hope not," Sarah said. "My client, Dr. McHugh, is in jail, and we're counting on you and those tips to help us get him out."

Bryzinski mumbled something that sounded like *fat chance,* and unclipped the radio from his belt.

"Hey, Mike," he said, "it's me. What'd you do with that disc?"

Crackle and static spit back, making it hard to hear all the words, but Lou picked out the two most important ones: *what* and *disc.*

Bryzinski pushed the Talk button on his radio. "The one in the brown cardboard jacket," he said.

More static.

Lou heard Cartwright clearly say, "Hang on."

"Hang on," Bryzinski interpreted for Lou and Sarah.

The static and crackle returned. Lou wondered if

there was a special button on the detective's radio to make it that way.

"It's not there," Cartwright said.

"What do you mean, it's not there?"

"Not . . . in . . . pile," were the three audible words this time.

"All right. Keep looking," Bryzinski said. "When you find it, bring it back here and leave it on my desk." After some difficulty managing the truck tire above his belt, he replaced the radio. "Cartwright's having trouble locating it," he said. "That happens sometimes. But it's there. I promise you. Nothing to worry about."

Lou turned to Sarah, who looked as unfazed as she had while staring out the windshield from the passenger seat of his car.

"I don't understand," Lou said, his voice up half an octave. "I dropped it off just yesterday morning."

Lou felt Sarah squeeze his wrist. *Cool it,* was the message.

Bryzinski did not back down. "Sorry, Doctor. If I wasn't so damn busy, and I had more time, I would go down to Cartwright's office and find it myself. I did sign for it, didn't I?"

"I don't think so," Lou said, feeling his cheeks flush.

"No big deal. Listen, tomorrow, if things slow down, I'll have it for you." He turned to Sarah. "I told the doc, here, my department had too many tips to follow up on for him to be rushing us. We process these things as they come in. Now, if you'll excuse me, I am falling farther behind by the second."

Lou was about to say something when Sarah's grip around his wrist tightened even more.

"Thanks for your time, Detective," she said. "Here's my card. I'll be waiting for your call."

"My pleasure," Bryzinski replied, sliding the card into his pocket without even glancing at it. He then escorted them back to the waiting area for a perfunctory good-bye.

In the parking lot, Lou waited for Sarah to erupt.

Silence.

"Look, I'm sorry," he said finally, quickening his steps to catch up to her. "But I still believe it's going to turn up, and I do have the copy. These are cops, not criminals."

Sarah stopped, spun around on one foot like a ballet dancer, and stared Lou down. "Do you have time to get that CD for me?"

Lou flashed longingly on his bed and considered asking if she had ever worked an all-night shift in a busy ER.

Instead, he nodded. "I'll drop you off and then take the disc to your office."

"If it's not too much trouble, could you drive me by your place? I want to get it right now."

The subtext of her request was obvious: *I don't trust you.*

"No problem," Lou said.

Sarah pulled her coat around her and took her place on the passenger seat of the Toyota. "And no more grandstanding," she felt the need to add. "We get this done, and you back off and let us handle things from here."

Lou began his breathing mantra, and finally climbed behind the wheel. "I've only been doing what I felt was right to help an old friend," he said.

"You are too much. Never budge an inch. Is that something from the Hippocratic oath?"

"I won't cause you any trouble."

"Hope that you don't," Sarah said, her eyes flashing. For a time, they drove on in silence.

"So, tell me," Lou asked finally, "do you think Wyatt Brody's the one?"

"Let me hear what's on that CD before I decide anything. What I really want to know at this point, is what Spencer Hogarth has to do with Detective Chris Bryzinski?"

"Hogarth, the secretary of defense?"

"Bryzinski had what looked like a to-do list on top of that pigsty of a desk of his. Tops on that list was to update 'S. Hogarth.' There was a number there, but I couldn't make it out."

"Curiouser and curiouser," Lou said.

Spencer Hogarth, the controversial, polarizing secretary of defense, had a love–hate relationship with the media, Congress, and the public. Many viewed the former secretary of the Navy's politics as a throwback to the days when America answered the world's most pressing challenges with firepower rather than diplomacy. To some, he was an incendiary with a frighteningly short fuse. To others, he was a crusader standing firm against terrorism in any and every form. For years, his prime adversary on Capitol Hill had been one Elias Colston.

"Could it be another Hogarth?" Lou wondered out loud.

"Correction, another *S*. Hogarth. I suppose anything's possible. But Hogarth and Colston were rivals over some pretty important stuff, and now a note to update him shows up on the desk of the cop who's investigating Colston's murder. Coincidence?"

"I think not," Lou said in perfect unison with her.

They laughed, and for the first time, Sarah's expression softened. "You know," she said, "it's hard for me to believe, but it appears you might actually have a sweet side to you. Sweet and idealistic. I'll bet you're even a half-decent doctor."

Lou glanced over at her, but aside from her words, there were no giveaways. "Thanks," he said. "I've been thinking the same about you. You know, I always thought of Hogarth as being tough, but never dirty. Maybe he's just anxious to keep on top of the case because of the history he and Colston had."

"I wish *I* could believe that everyone wanted to play by the same rules you want to play by, Lou. Your naïvete, at least until it wears thin, is sort of endearing."

"Bryzinski will turn up that disc," Lou averred.

Sarah's expression was strained. "Dr. Welcome," she said, "I don't know if I believe in global warming, UFOs, or Bigfoot, but I am a thousand percent sure of one thing."

"Yes?"

"Detective Christopher Bryzinski is up to something."

CHAPTER 17

Lou could tell much about a person from their reaction to his neighborhood. The less they shrank at the sight of graffiti, boarded-up windows, and loitering bands of kids, the more likely it was that Lou would get along with them. Surprisingly, Sarah seemed completely at ease, if not indifferent, to Lou's street. Perhaps they were destined to overcome their differences after all. Either that, or she was too absorbed in getting her hands on the copy of the Colston CD to notice the surroundings.

Lou parallel parked his car directly in front of Dimitri's Pizza, which occupied the entire lower level of his building and featured, he would tell anyone who would listen, the tastiest, most lovingly prepared pies and calzones in the city. The aroma wafting out from the shop said the ovens were already in action. As usual when he arrived home to that distinctive bouquet, Lou began fantasizing about a large vegetarian—his and Emily's favorite.

"I'll wait here," Sarah said.

"It's fine for you to come up. You can meet Diversity, our cat."

"Our?"

"Mine and my daughter Emily's. She lives in Arlington, but spends a lot of time here. She and I train at the Stick and Move boxing gym across the street."

"Sounds like my kind of gal. Please don't take this the wrong way, but most of the doctors I deal with live in places, well, more like Dr. McHugh's."

"No offense taken. Living here helps keep me right-sized. Emily, too. The place and what's left over after every month's rent payment helps fill in a hole I once dug for myself."

"I think I know something about that. And you both feel safe here?"

"This is a great neighborhood with terrific people. We're careful enough not to leave our doors unlocked, but that's about it. My ex wishes I would move out to the burbs, but I feel perfectly safe. Time for coffee?"

Sarah climbed out of the car, checked her watch, and frowned. "Thanks, but I've got to hurry, actually. I have back-to-back meetings that will take the rest of the day."

Lou picked up his mail in the dimly lit foyer and led Sarah up one flight. The first few steps, he found himself hoping that Tiny Booker and his cronies could provide the promised protective services for Gary. The last few, he was focused on Sarah, trying to get a read on why she was still so distant, and hoping that once she had the copy of the CD he had made for her, things between them would lighten up.

Then he saw that his apartment door was slightly ajar.

We're careful not to leave our doors unlocked, but that's about it.

Instantly, he was on red alert, every fiber tense. He turned, held a finger to his lips, and motioned toward the door. Then he slipped his parka off and dropped it silently to the floor. His senses were crackling like a defective jumper cable as he mentally retraced his steps when he left for the hospital last evening.

We're careful not to leave our doors unlocked. . . .

This was not carelessness on his part. He was sure of it. Something was wrong—very wrong.

"Go back outside and call 911, Sarah," he whispered. "Four fifty Clinton Street."

"Is there a rear entrance?"

"Yes, but I keep it double bolted."

They listened.

"I don't think anyone's in there."

"Please go down and make the call."

"What are you going to do?"

Damn lawyer! he wanted to scream. *This is no time to be standing here taking a deposition.*

"I'm going in," he said.

"Wait until I get back up here."

Damn it, just go!

"All right, but hurry."

As Sarah headed softly down the stairs, cell phone in hand, Lou debated crashing into the apartment. If he did, what little ground he had gained with the woman would certainly be lost. In fact, if this open door had anything to do with the disc he had hidden in his bureau drawer, the ground was lost already.

He knelt and made a careful study of the locking mechanism and the door itself. There were scuff marks along the base of the door that he had a hard time believing were there before. Again, he held his breath and listened.

Again, only silence.

Where is she?

His pulse hammering, Lou was about to ease into his apartment when Sarah opened the foyer door and started back up the stairs. Without waiting, he pushed against the door. The hinges creaked, as if reluctant to reveal what secret lay inside. Lou could feel Sarah behind him, her breathing rapid and uneven. Light spilled through the door and onto the landing. Lou was certain he had left the apartment dark except for a small lamp in the bedroom.

This was going to be bad.

The first sign of destruction, an overturned end table by the couch, was just the beginning. Lou pushed the door open more fully, swallowing back the bile that was percolating into his throat. He took one footstep inside and then another, now not only assessing the carnage, but also scanning the place for Diversity.

In the kitchen, he slid a huge carving knife from his butcher block holder.

"Don't you want to wait for the police?" Sarah asked.

Now who's being naïve?

"They don't rush to these neighborhoods," he replied. "Besides, I don't think anyone's here."

"Just the same, I would wait," Sarah said. "Whoever did this might be in the back room, in a closet or something."

I hope they are, Lou thought, tightening his grip on the knife handle.

He turned on the overhead light.

The search, at least from what he could see in the kitchen and living room, was professionally thorough. The cushions of his couch had been slashed open, spilling out clumps of stuffing like the fatty tissue of a wound. Chairs were upended. End table drawers were pulled out, the contents tossed onto the floor. His laptop was gone. The kitchen was a total shambles. Cabinet drawers were pulled open and solid cat food, mixed in with shards of his dishes, littered the floor.

The back door at the end of the hallway was closed, and he could see it was bolted. It looked as if the intruder had entered and exited through the front.

Still tense and brandishing the knife, Lou approached his bedroom. As he stepped through the doorway, Diversity dashed out and across Sarah's shoes.

"Jesus!" she cried out, lurching back against the wall.

"That's Diversity."

"I know," she said acidly, recovering her breath. "You told me in the car. Doctor, not that I don't care about your cat, but where did you put the CD?"

One look into his bedroom, and Lou knew they were in trouble. The room had been taken apart as meticulously as the others. His attention went immediately to his bureau, where the drawers had been pulled out and their contents dumped onto the floor. Sarah, arms folded, watched as he searched through the pile of his clothes.

"It's gone, isn't it," she said. "That's what they were after."

Lou continued throwing aside clothing, but he knew the effort was fruitless.

"It was hidden in that drawer under some papers. I . . . didn't think anyone would do this. They took my computer, too."

Sarah didn't bother to retort.

"You tried," she said finally. "Whoever did this knew exactly what they were after and how to find it. It would have been easier on you if you had just left it on the kitchen table."

"Feel free to say you told me so."

"Okay, I told you so."

"Now what?"

Still holding the knife, he led Sarah to Emily's room. There was not a thing out of place. Not a pillow, not a game, not a stuffed animal. The closet was similarly intact.

"I guess that clinches what they were after," Sarah said.

Diversity had returned and now was doing a figure eight around their legs, purring loudly. Ignoring him, Lou left the room and buried the blade in the wall.

"I feel so damn stupid," he said.

"I would say this wasn't your best day. I'm sorry about your place."

"That's just stuff. I can't believe I did this to Gary."

"Well, we'll do our best to fill in the pieces. Now we have two questions we need to answer: Who? And why?"

"I'm really sorry," Lou said.

"I know you are." In the distance, they heard the siren of an approaching police car. "No sense crying over spilt milk. You stay and take care of this business. I'll take a cab back to the office."

CHAPTER 18

It took most of two days for Lou to put his apartment back together—two days during which he had not heard a word from Sarah. No surprise. His next step would be to re-create as best he could the clandestinely recorded conversation between Elias Colston and the young marine named Hector. Not exactly evidence Gary's attorney could use in court, but the closest he could come to another apology.

First, though, it was Emily's weekend. Lou watched from the kitchen as the teen made a curious check of the apartment. He had done a decent job putting things back together, and she never turned the sofa cushions over, so his hasty suturing job remained undiscovered. Crate & Barrel still carried white china, and a new Mac was no problem, especially since she had brought over her own laptop.

Still, even though Emily's room remained intact, she was stunningly intuitive, and Lou wondered if sooner or later he would have to go from omission to outright lying, a skill at which he was totally inept. For a time, he debated if he should even allow her to spend the weekend, but finally decided that whoever ransacked their home had left with what they came for and weren't likely to return.

Gradually, it began to feel as if his gambit had succeeded, and it was back to business as usual. Emily was alternating string games with Diversity with setting up a game of Monopoly on the alcove table. She and Lou had a movie lined up for the evening. But now their day would feature lunch with Lou's father at the Wave Rider, virtually the only restaurant the three of them ever ate at together.

Dennis Welcome had four great loves in his life: his family, his red Chevy pickup with 200,000 miles on it, his union, and the Wave Rider's double bacon burger. Though Dennis lived in Virginia, Lou shared a meal with him frequently, including Emily whenever possible. With the senior Welcome between carpentry jobs once again, and his inability to distinguish solitude from solitary confinement, Lou felt glad this was an Emily day. His father's lunch invitation, ill timed as it might seem, offered a much-needed break from what had been an extremely stress-filled couple of days.

The Wave Rider, a surfer-themed sports bar that had rarely served an actual surfer, was pleasantly busy. All twelve flat screens were playing some variant of an ESPN sports show. Dennis, distinguishable by his salt-and-pepper crew cut, stood up from his customary booth and waved to Lou and Emily as soon as they set foot inside the place. He wore faded blue jeans, dusty work boots, and one of his collection of flannel shirts, this day red.

"Grandpa!" Emily squealed, dodging waitresses and patrons as she sprinted into Dennis's burly arms.

"How are you, Dad?" Lou asked.

"Oh, great and great," Dennis said, tapping his knuckles on the top of Emily's head. "Okay, then, enough chit-chat. I've got me a man-sized craving."

"You know they do serve a nice variety here," Lou said. "Rumor has it that the double bacon burger may be slightly less than healthy."

"Blasphemy!" Dennis cried, looking to Emily for corroboration.

"Put Dad on trial for food treason," Emily said.

"Instead, I'd suggest you spend a little time researching arteriosclerosis," Lou said.

"And I'd suggest you spend a little time mending your shirt." She pointed to a one-inch tear just above his belt.

"Diversity," Lou groaned.

"What?" Dennis asked.

"Diversity is my new cat," Emily said without looking up from the menu. "He and Dad aren't exactly getting along."

"You got a cat? Who named him?"

Emily pointed a thumb at her chest. "It's in honor of my mission to bring multiculturalism to the Carlisle School. I was going to move in with Dad, but Mom wouldn't let me, so we got a cat."

"So when you're in Arlington, that makes your dad the guardian of Diversity. I like it."

Lou poked a finger through the hole in his shirt. "The cat and I are getting along just great."

"That's sarcasm," Emily said. "Diversity hates Dad because Dad blames him for things he could never have done."

" 'Hate' is a very strong word," Lou said. "I would prefer you didn't use it."

"Would you prefer 'despise'? Detest? Dislike? Abhor? Resent?"

"Any of those," Lou said. "How about 'is adjusting to'?"

Emily executed a textbook-perfect eye roll. "Okay. Diversity is adjusting to how much he resents my dad."

Dennis's laugh was always good to hear. The year-long assault on his spirit since his wife's cancer death had been hard on all of them.

"Grandpa," Emily said, "can you order me a veggie burger, side salad, and a sparkling water?"

"What about the bacon burger? I thought you loved those?"

"She's thinking about going vegan," Lou explained.

"I'm almost vegan already," Emily said. "Another year, and I'll be a hundred percent."

"You always set goals and you always achieve them," Dennis said. "Just one of the many things I love about you."

"Oh, look," Lou chimed in, "they've added catburger to the menu."

"That's not funny," Emily said.

The folks at the ASPCA shelter, where the two of them had adopted Diversity, could not have been happier to make the match. For Emily, it was love at first purr. On the ride home, Diversity, a two-year-old orange and white tabby with amber eyes, nestled in her lap. Later he chased thread, batted a piece of paper, and clawed the carpet-fragment-on-a-pole Lou bought at the pet superstore for forty-nine dollars.

However, when Lou returned home after dropping Emily back at the house in Arlington, Diversity had become an altogether different cat. He hissed, hid under the bed, and made a flying tackle to dig his claws into Lou's legs every time the guardian of Diversity crossed the living room. At some point, he turned the top of the refrigerator into his own personal fortress. But of course, whenever Emily was around—or anybody else, for that matter—the cat was an angel.

Lou perused the menu long enough for his father to complain and call the waitress over, rushing Lou into a Cobb salad.

"So . . . you involved with the doc who killed Colston?" Dennis asked once their server had moved on.

"Shhhh!" Lou said. "Keep it down. Dad, this isn't appropriate lunch conversation."

Emily broke away from her texting. "I know that Congressman Colston was murdered by his wife's jealous lover," she said, holding up her smartphone. "We get all the news on these things. So, *are* you involved?"

"The two of you!" Lou said. "Enough."

"I spoke with your brother yesterday, and he thinks you are," Dennis said. "Told me one of his clients is connected with someone important who told him that before he shot Colston, McHugh was under monitoring with the PWO for a drinking problem."

"Graham should not be spreading rumors," Lou

said. "A PWO contract is very confidential. It's not something that he or his over-the-top-rich clients should even be discussing."

"I'm just curious is all," Dennis said. "No need to get all snippy."

"I'm not being snippy," Lou said.

"You were being a little snippy, Dad," Emily said.

"Will you guys just drop it, okay?"

"Dropped," Emily said, holding up her empty hands.

"Dropped," Dennis followed.

"Good," Lou said.

Dennis broke the ensuing silence less than a minute later. "So, do you think he did it?"

Lou threw up his hands. "Oh for goodness' sake, okay. Okay. I admit that I do know Gary McHugh. He's asked me to help him out—see if I could come up with reasons why somebody other than him might have wanted Elias Colston dead."

"And did you?" Emily asked.

"I'm working on it, but McHugh's high-powered lawyer, Sarah Cooper, wants me to stop interfering with the case. She thinks the only thing I'm capable of is getting in her way."

"Sarah Cooper," Dennis exclaimed, "the one from the Sandra Winkler trial?"

"That's right."

Lou explained to Emily what the Winkler case was about. Not surprisingly, she already knew a few of the details.

"So this Sarah Cooper sounds pretty peeved at you," Dennis said after Lou had finished.

"If by peeved you mean uncooperative and hostile, then yes, she's peeved, all right."

"Do you know why she's so angry?" asked Emily.

"Not really. I came across something that I thought would help McHugh's case, and I gave it to the police rather than to her. Now it looks like they may have misplaced it."

"No wonder she's upset," Dennis said.

"Actually, she was irritated with me from the moment we met."

"First the cat and now this lawyer," Dennis said. "Maybe you should change your deodorant."

Thankfully, their food arrived, sparing Lou from having to respond. Throughout most of their meal, Emily seemed preoccupied. She would eat, do something on her phone, and then eat some more.

"I've got a new investment chance," Dennis said between bites of his burger.

"Not the replacement window company?"

"No. With the economy tanking, people aren't fixing up their places as much these days."

"So, what is it this time?"

"Online gaming," Dennis said.

"Online gaming?"

"It's a Polish company. They've got three games in development. Virtual fish farming and virtual gold mining look like their biggest winners."

"Virtual fish farming?"

Lou was hardly incredulous. For as long as he could remember, Dennis was always looking for the big score, and never finding it. At one point, he went through the funds he had set aside for Graham's college tuition, and turned to Lou to bail him out. Hopefully, the younger Welcome brother would never know, but the amphetamines Lou ended up taking to help him through several moonlighting jobs, and the alcohol he used to come down from the speed, were what led to the suspension of his medical license. On the other hand, they also led to his subsequent recovery.

"Graham is already looking at the brochures," Dennis said. "Problem is, they're in Polish."

"I'll wait for his assessment," Lou said, knowing that Graham was as conservative with money as their father was cavalier.

"Your loss, sonny boy. Can you pass me a napkin?"

Suddenly, Emily cried out, "Oh, so that's her beef."

"Whose beef?" Lou asked.

"Sarah Cooper."

"What are you talking about?"

"Did you ever Google her?"

"Never occurred to me."

"It's all here. Her husband died and she sued his doctor. She won, too. One of the articles says six million dollars."

"I thought you were texting your friends, not doing research."

"Believe it or not, I can do both at the same time. All us kids can. I was just trying to help you out. Look, read it for yourself."

Emily handed him her smartphone, which had a Safari browser open to a five-year-old article from the magazine section of *The Washington Post*. According to the detailed feature, David Cooper, an attorney and tireless crusader for Washington's homeless, had been complaining of headaches for some months. The world-renowned neurologist he went to diagnosed migraines, even though Sarah argued that her husband never had a headache or illness in his life. David, a rock climber and kayaker, expressed to the doctor that the pain seemed more in his neck than his head. Sarah was quoted as saying that every time she massaged his neck David would complain about pain in his head.

Despite their concerns, the neurologist, whom Sarah referred to as "unbearably arrogant," refused to order an MRI of the cervical area, or nerve conduction studies in his arms. He also refused to involve an orthopedist or neurosurgeon in the case, but rather continued to prescribe anti-inflammatories and physical therapy. Then, beset by increasing pain, David awoke one morning, turned his head quickly, and partially severed his spinal cord, paralyzing himself from the upper neck down. After two miserable years on a ventilator, with little quality of life, David Cooper died. The jury in the malpractice case concluded that more careful attention to his complaints would have enabled the neurologist to seek a life-saving spinal fusion.

Stunned by the tragic account, Lou handed Emily back her phone.

"She doesn't have a thing just against you, Dad," Emily said. "She's got a thing against doctors."

CHAPTER 19

Bucky Townsend and Fenton Morales clanked Bud bottles and toasted their good fortunes. Enjoying a night out at the Willows was nothing new for the two marines, but tonight they had special cause for celebration. A yelping, chest-thumping, fists-in-the-air reason to imbibe. Major Charles Coon had given each the word that they were no longer finalists for Operation Talon. They were in.

Even though the two of them knew little of the objective of the mission, what mattered was its importance to national interests and to the security of America. For some time, OT had been priority number one at Mantis—the specifics of what the operation entailed were secondary.

"This is why we became marines," Morales said, taking another swig.

"Forget that—this is why we chose Mantis," Townsend countered.

"Yeah, though I still can't believe you made it. Heck, you're just an Okie from Muskogee."

"And a badass one, at that."

"To OT, and whatever our crazy-ass future holds."

"To OT," Townsend repeated.

"To Mantis and the chance to make a real difference."

They clanked their bottle necks again and raced to chug their beers. Townsend banged his empty bottle on the table just a second or two before Morales.

"This Okie knows how to handle his suds, compadre. Never forget that."

Morales's laugh was warm and heartfelt. They ordered another round, then another. An hour later, Morales checked his watch. "We should get going," he said.

The jukebox spit out a Stones tune, while Townsend watched more men from the base trickle in, followed by a couple of townie girls wearing dresses far too short for the outside cold.

"Why go, man?" he asked. "Isn't the night still young?" He exchanged smiles with a leggy young brunette in a blue sequined party dress.

Morales's look was admonishing. "You want Coon thinking you're more into booze and babes than you are into this mission?" he asked. "That guy is like a ninja— everywhere at once. We gotta get real about this, buddy. Set an example. We're not only Mantis now, we're Talon."

Townsend shared one last, longing look with the hot brunette. Then, sighing loudly, he pushed back his stool and stood. Morales did the same. "Whatever it takes," Townsend said mournfully.

Morales put an arm around his friend and led him to the door. "Whatever it takes," Morales repeated, chuckling softly.

Outside, the winter air slapped Townsend across the face. The gunshot wound to his side was healing rapidly, just as Coon had promised it would, but it still acted up in the cold. Even so, Townsend never once considered mentioning the unusual training practices of Colonel Brody and Major Coon to his family, not even to his younger brother Terry, his best friend. The Palace Guard would not take kindly to anybody challenging the integrity of Mantis. *Whatever it takes* were not just words; they were a way of life. The way of Mantis.

"Glad you shut me off," Townsend said, exhaling a swirling tendril of mist into the dark night. "I was starting to feel it. I can't even remember where we parked."

"We're right down here," Morales said, pointing to a side street not more than a block from the bar. As they turned the corner, powerful high-beams flashed on, momentarily blinding them. An engine revved up, followed by the angry whine of tires searching for traction against the nearly frozen pavement. Alcohol slowed their reaction time. The side door of an all-white cargo van slid open as the vehicle screeched to a stop beside them.

Four men dressed in black leapt out from the van, their faces obscured beneath head coverings that Townsend associated mostly with al-Qaeda. The men, each heavily armed, tossed Townsend and Morales into the van like sacks of laundry. Two other men waiting inside the van shoved the muzzles of assault rifles up under the marines' chins. The van peeled away from the curb and turned the corner, momentum slamming the side door closed.

Townsend's world went black as duct tape was tightened across his mouth and a coarse, moldy hood was pulled over his head. He tried unsuccessfully to shake it off, but it was tied quickly around his neck. All he could think of was a video his platoon had been shown where hoods like this one were pulled over captives' heads just before they were decapitated. Next came plastic cuffs, which dug painfully into his wrists. He sensed Morales was lying close by, but their captors would not allow them to touch.

For an indeterminable amount of time, perhaps half an hour, the van sped down a fairly smooth highway. Then it slowed and bounced along an uneven road, violently jostling Townsend about. He heard the men shouting at one another in Arabic.

Do they want to kill me? . . . Torture me? . . . Film me making some sort of confession, broadcasting me on a Web site espousing some jihadist cause?

Townsend breathed in and out slowly through his nose. He had no idea what was in store for him and Morales. What he did know, unquestionably, was that regardless of whatever awaited them, he was not afraid.

With the bag still covering his head, Townsend allowed himself to be guided into a room cold enough to store meat. There would be time, he told himself, probably soon, to struggle and to make it difficult for them. But before he could react, they snipped his manacles off, cut his shirt away, and shoved him down onto a sturdy wooden chair. In seconds, they had lashed his ankles to the legs and his wrists to the armrests. Finally, the hood was removed.

Townsend needed a minute for his vision to clear. He and Morales were tied on identical chairs in a barren, ten-foot-square windowless room, beneath a bare bulb. They were stripped to their undershirts but still had on their camo pants and black boots.

Three men crowded into the room with the two guards. Their heads were covered except for the opening in their bandannas displaying reptilian eyes. Their complexions, what Townsend could see of them, were dark bronze, further confirming his suspicion that his captors were Arab terrorists. The fifth man, wearing a turban but no bandanna, had a hatchet face buried behind a thicket of dark beard. He appraised Townsend and Morales as if they were lambs destined for slaughter.

"What is Operation Talon?" he said in near perfect English.

Are they part of a sleeper cell? Townsend wondered. *How long have they been hiding in plain sight? How much do they already know?*

"My name is Sergeant Bucky Townsend. I am a citizen of the United States of America."

Townsend had scored near perfect marks at SERE school—Survival, Evasion, Resistance and Escape training. He knew how to respond during an interrogation. As long as it seemed there was a possibility they would talk, nothing would happen to them—nothing, that was, except some torture.

"What is Operation Talon?" the man asked again, this time addressing Morales specifically.

"My name is Sergeant Fenton Morales. I am a citizen of the United States of America."

The man nodded dully, assessing both marines with complete disinterest. He turned his back to the hostages, and when he faced them again, he was wielding a pistol, which Townsend recognized as a Glock 19. With his arm extended, rigid as a steel girder, the terrorist pointed the barrel of the gun at Morales's head.

"Last chance, Sergeant Morales," he said with absolutely no inflection in his voice. "What is Operation Talon? When will it be taking place?"

"My name is Sergeant Fenton Morales, I am a—"

Morales's words were cut short by a loud pop, followed by a bright flash of light mixed with the acrid stench of gunpowder. In the same instant, Morales's head recoiled back violently as the bullet splintered through his skull. Blood, bone, and brain splattered across the wall behind him, leaving a grotesque spin art pattern of red and white. Morales slumped forward in his chair, lifeless, blood still dripping from the gaping hole in the center of his forehead. Townsend stared wide-eyed at his friend.

Whatever it takes, he recited to himself. *Whatever it takes. . . . Whatever it takes. . . .*

Townsend felt sick, but he did not feel panicked. He would kill these men or they would kill him, but there was no way they would learn even one word about Operation Talon. Morales was a lesson for him—a warning to cooperate or die. That just wasn't going to happen . . . ever.

"Now, what is Operation Talon?"

"Fuck you."

Townsend stared straight ahead with unblinking eyes.

The terrorist leader slapped him viciously across the face, then motioned for Morales's corpse to be removed. Two guards cut him free. As they dragged him away by his undershirt, the heels of his boots left long rubber streaks across the gray linoleum floor. Bucky Townsend clenched his jaws. All he could think of was getting a crack at even one of them. Just one.

The leader ushered the remaining guards out of the room and followed them, closing the door softly. When he returned minutes later, he was wheeling a steel push-cart containing an array of instruments, most of which Townsend could identify. Some, though, he could not.

"What is Operation Talon?" the man said.

"My name is—"

The terrorist held up his hand, cutting Townsend's words short.

"Bucky," the man said, crouching down to get eye level with Townsend. "My name is Abdullah, and I do not wish to cause you harm, but I need information from you, information that I will hurt you to get. Do you understand?"

"Yes," Townsend said. "I understand. Hey, Abdullah, take these ropes off my wrists and give me your Glock. Just for a minute."

"I'm now going to blindfold you, Bucky. You will hear my footsteps walking around your chair. In my hand I'm going to be holding this." Abdullah picked up a ball-peen hammer and showed it to Townsend. "I am going to strike your body with this hammer," he said.

"Maybe your knees, an elbow, your neck. You won't know when I'm going to hit you, or where, and you won't know the blow is coming. You can avoid all this unpleasantness if you answer my question. Exactly what is Operation Talon, and when will it be taking place?"

Townsend's nostrils flared as he fixed his gaze on the hammer gently tapping away against Abdullah's meaty palm.

"My name is Bucky Townsend—"

Townsend's world went dark again as Abdullah pulled a cloth blindfold across his eyes and tied it tightly in the back. Then, as promised, there were footsteps circling around him.

Breathe in . . . breathe out . . . in and out . . . whatever it takes . . .

The footsteps stopped and Townsend waited for the pain, sucking down air in preparation. He waited . . . and waited. Nothing. Then the footsteps began again; round and round they walked.

"You don't need to die like your friend Morales. You don't need the excruciating pain you are about to suffer. Tell me about Talon, and you can go."

"Fuck you."

The footfalls continued, then came to another stop, this time to Townsend's left. He felt the ball-peen hammer bouncing on his left knee, though not with any great force. He braced himself for the strike. The pain he knew would be unimaginably intense.

I'm proud to be an Okie from Muskogee. . . .

"One last time. What is Operation Talon? When is it going to happen?"

Townsend stiffened and muttered another stream of curses. All he could think of was dying with the class and bravery of Morales. He would make every marine in Mantis proud.

At that instant, instead of the pain he was anticipating, Townsend felt the blindfold being loosened. His eyes adjusted to the light, and he cried out. On the chair next to him, with an artfully done gunshot wound at the center of his forehead, sat Fenton Morales, beaming.

"What the—?"

"Nice going, pal," Morales said. "I knew you could do it."

The door to Townsend's left opened, and Major Charles Coon entered the small room, followed by a gangly man in his thirties wearing paint-stained fatigues.

Coon was grinning even more broadly than Morales. "Sergeant Townsend, meet Sergeant Brett Coughlin, the best illusionist and makeup artist in the military. We use him and his special skills for jobs like this. That directed spray of blood and bone is a miracle—a friggin' miracle."

Coughlin nodded toward Coon, then to Townsend. Then he set about peeling off the gunshot from Morales's forehead.

"Sonofabitch," was all Townsend could say. "Sonofa rat-nosed bitch."

The tall man who had identified himself as Abdullah used a ten-inch razor-sharp Bowie knife to slice through Townsend's restraints. Then he helped him to his feet.

"Orders are orders," the man said without emotion, peeling off his fake beard and revealing himself to be one of the Palace Guards.

Townsend understood fully. This was his final test for Operation Talon. There would be others who would be exposed to Brett Coughlin's magic, or else they already had been. But he was done.

Coon set a strong hand on Townsend's shoulder. "You did well," he said. "Damn well."

He motioned a graying man into the room, whom Townsend recognized as Coon's chief medical officer. The CMO held an open laptop. "His vitals were well below expected this time," he said. "He was basically at rest, almost in a sleep state. Heart rate, muscle tension, oxygen levels, everything. It's rather remarkable. I think we're there."

Coon nodded. "Sergeant Bucky Townsend, I'm pleased to inform you that you are now an official team member of Operation Talon."

"Sir, thank you, sir," Townsend said, snapping to attention. "You won't be disappointed."

Coon smoothed out his uniform. "I'm sure that I won't be," he said. "In fact, I'd bet my career on it."

CHAPTER 20

Lou picked up a pen and flipped to a blank page in his yellow legal pad. He was seated at his kitchen table with a steaming mug of cocoa, looking, he hoped, like a suave, unrumpled novelist in a coffee commercial. He started with the first few words he recollected from the conversation between Elias Colston and Hector.

Hi, Hector.

Or did Hector say hello first?

Lou tore off the sheet and started again.

He made another attempt, feeling more foolish by the minute for not waiting to give the disc to Sarah rather than rushing to take it to the police. *Arrogant.* According to the article Emily had dug up, the word was one that, for some years, Sarah had associated with physicians. Now it appeared she had good reason to be using it again—Lou was arrogant to believe he could recall anything verbatim. Another try, another crumpled ball of yellow lined paper. He simply had not listened to the recording closely enough or for enough times for the conversation to take precise root anywhere in his memory. God, but he hated being wrong.

"That's why lawyers never say anything that will matter without having a stenographer typing it down."

Hadn't Sarah been smiling when she said that?

For his fourth attempt, Lou tried an entirely different approach, jotting down words, phrases, and recollections in free association.

Long time since they last met. . . .
They ordered sandwiches. . . .
Colonel Brody requested the meeting. . . .
Colston wanted to cut funds for Mantis. . . .
The palace guards . . . toughs that are never far
    from the colonel . . .
Ever heard of the Reddy Creek Armory? . . .
Don't know nothing about no armory.

Something about a blog.

Lou set down his pen. This was hardly the detail Sarah had in mind. He hated giving her another reason to be disappointed in doctors, but this effort was fruitless. The best he could do was to bank on Detective Bryzinski coming up with the disc. He went to get some carrots and celery sticks, and spied Diversity manning his fort atop the refrigerator. The cat mewed, then hissed. For a moment, Lou thought he was going to spring.

"Come on big fella, let's be friends."

He opened a can of gourmet cat food he had bought at Whole Foods for what seemed like the price of a restaurant meal for himself. Diversity eyed Lou until he had returned to the legal pad, then leapt to the floor via the counter and began chowing down.

Nice kitty.

Another page or two, and Lou finally admitted defeat. There had to be another way.

"What do you think, pal?" he said to the tabby. "Should I try to find this Hector?"

Diversity turned his head toward Lou's voice, licked his lips, and mewed.

"I'll take that as a yes."

Lou crossed to the phone by the couch. Jeannine Colston answered on the second ring. She sounded as if she had been sleeping or crying, or possibly, Lou guessed, both. Many things were going to have to go right before life made sense to her again.

"I found something when I was looking through Elias's office," Lou said. "It was a CD, secretly made, I think, recording a conversation between Elias and a marine named Hector."

"Hector Rodriguez? Mark's friend?"

"I believe that's who Elias was speaking with, yes."

"That's strange," Jeannine said. "Why would Elias do such a thing?"

"Colonel Wyatt Brody, who heads up Mantis, asked Hector to arrange the meeting. I think that Elias wanted to have a record of the conversation because he knew what they were going to talk about."

"And what was that?" Jeannine asked.

"Your husband's controversial position about cutting

support to the military and, in particular, to Mantis Company. He wanted to keep slashing funding, and Brody was using Mark's best friend to get Elias to change his position."

"I really think you should have told me about this, Dr. Welcome." For the first time, there was a spark of energy in her voice.

Lou knew that she was right. "I'm sorry I didn't," he said. "You were sleeping when I found it behind the backing of Mark's Medal of Honor. I didn't know what it was until I listened to it after I had left. It seemed like something the police should have, so I took it to them."

There was a prolonged silence during which Lou feared Colston's widow might erupt. Dealing with Sarah had certainly prepared him well should that happen.

Ultimately, though, Jeannine sighed. "I'm going to give you the benefit of the doubt, Doctor," she said finally. "I know your mission was to exonerate Gary. But I'd prefer it if you kept me in the loop from now on."

"I understand. Believe me, Jeannine, all I want is to ensure that the person who is ultimately tried and convicted of Elias's murder is the one who did it. If that's Gary, then it's Gary."

"In that case, I will tell you that if Wyatt Brody thought he could change Elias in any way, he did not know my husband very well. He may have had his faults, but Elias was a rarity among politicians. He was elected as a Republican, but was truly an Independent— never one to be influenced by lobbyists, his party, or at times even his own constituents. He thrived at the polls and on Capitol Hill by adhering to three very simple principles—honesty, transparency, and doing the right thing."

"He was a good man," Lou said.

Jeannine again went silent, clearly regaining her composure. During that time, Diversity finished his meal, left the room, then padded out from the bedroom with one of Lou's socks and sequestered it someplace behind the cereal boxes on top of the refrigerator.

Gone, forever, Lou thought, wondering about using a chair to check what else might be stashed up there.

"Yes, he was a very good man," Jeannine was saying. "It was wrong what I did."

"Perhaps. But I don't think it's anyone's place to judge. I'm sure you had your reasons. The human heart is very complex, and as Gary's longtime friend, I know how exciting and charismatic he can be."

"That's kind of you to say."

"So, did Elias ever talk to you about Wyatt Brody?"

"No, never, although we didn't talk politics as much as you might think. So, what do you need now?"

"I need a way to contact Hector."

"I'll get it for you. Tell me, how did the police miss all of this?"

"To tell you the truth, I don't think they were looking very hard. They had a theory of what happened, and they just looked for the evidence that fit that theory."

"And you believe the recording might somehow be connected to Elias's murder?"

"Anything's possible. I'll be able to tell better after I speak with Hector, hopefully in person."

Jeannine retrieved her address book and read off two numbers. "I don't know how easy he'll be to reach. Elias never said so, but I assume Hector's still on active duty with the marines. If you'd like, I can try to reach him to say you're going to be calling."

"If it's not too much trouble, that would be great."

"I want the same thing you do, Dr. Welcome—justice for my husband. Now that I think about it, there's another number you should have. His name is Steve Papavassiliou—Papa Steve, we call him. He's an ordnance specialist working with Mantis now, but he may have transferred there from another unit."

"Papa Steve?"

"He is . . . was Elias's closest friend, and Mark's godfather. He and Elias served together in the marines. Elias would brag that Papa Steve could blow the antennae of a fly without killing it. They were like brothers. If Elias spoke about Wyatt Brody with anybody, it would have been with Papa Steve."

Jeannine gave Lou Papa Steve's number and promised to call Hector right away.

"One last thing," Lou said. "Did the congressman ever mention a place called the Pine Forest Clinic?"

"Not that I recall. What's that?"

"I guess from the logo that it's a clinic of some sort located in Shockley, Minnesota. I found an empty envelope in the top drawer of Elias's desk addressed to a James Styles at a P.O. box in Bowie."

"Bowie, Maryland?"

"Exactly. And the return address was that clinic in Minnesota."

"No idea. If I make any connections with that one, I'll let you know."

After repeating her promise to try to contact Hector Rodriguez, Jeannine ended the call.

Lou left a message for Papa Steve. The man's gravelly voice mail greeting made Lou think of what Santa Claus might have sounded like if he carried a bazooka and a bag of C-4 explosives in his sleigh. He was on his way back to the kitchen table when Diversity attacked his leg from the side of the couch as if he were being chased by a coyote and Lou was an oak. The encounter lasted only a few seconds before Lou could shake free from his new nemesis, but the pain would endure considerably longer.

Cursing, he rolled up his pants leg, blotted away the blood from three neat rows of gouges, and swathed the area with soapy water and Neosporin. Then he added buying Band-Aids to the to-do list taped on the door of the fridge.

Twenty minutes later, the phone rang.

"Dr. Welcome," he said, thinking it might be Papa Steve returning his call.

A youthful, somewhat anxious voice, said, "My name is Hector Rodriguez. Mark Colston's mother called me a little while ago. She said you wanted to speak with me about Congressman Colston's murder."

Lou explained his involvement with the case.

"What's that got to do with me?" Rodriguez asked.

"Elias Colston wrote down some notes regarding a conversation you had with him. Do you recall speaking with him at a bar a few years back? You talked about a bunch of things—Mark Colston, Wyatt Brody, and a group you guys call the Palace Guards."

Lou thought about telling him the conversation had been recorded, but did not want to risk spooking him even more. He could usually tell when a patient was holding back on him, and Hector was giving off the same vibes.

"Yeah, well, I don't know what you're talking about," the marine said after an edgy pause.

"Hector, a good friend of mine is facing life in jail for a crime he might not have committed. I think your conversation with Colston could be the key to sorting things out. Listen, I'll come all the way out there to speak with you. I won't need more than an hour of your time."

Lou held his breath while Hector went quiet again. "One hour," Hector said. "And not a minute more."

CHAPTER 21

Lou finished an all-nighter in the ER plus an extra three hours covering for a doc with some sort of GI nastiness. Occupational hazard. Finally, he trudged to the on-call room and dived facedown on the narrow, industrial bed. His nightmare this day, what he remembered of it, anyway, featured cats.

By the time the alarm clock sounded at one in the afternoon, Lou was totally disoriented and probably as distressed in his gut as the doctor he had replaced. The trapezius muscles across his shoulders had developed knots the size of golf balls, and the grit in his eyes refused to wash away. It was the way of the typical late-night ER shift—feelings no less familiar to him than breathing.

Lou stopped at the hospital's Starbucks for what he called road juice—espresso macchiato. Then he headed for the doctors' parking lot, which was tucked at the center of the hospital complex, among a dozen or so buildings, half of them outdated and antiquated, and half under new construction.

Before leaving the lot for the four-hour drive to Hayes, West Virginia, Lou called home, wishfully expecting some sort of message on his answering machine from Detective Chris Bryzinski, telling him to stop by the station to pick up a copy of the disc. Nothing doing. Between Sarah's scorn and Jeannine Colston's rebuke, he wasn't exactly feeling at the top of his game. He had learned many invaluable lessons from his years of sobriety, but he still balked at accepting anything less than perfection in himself.

Nothing doing there, either.

Traffic was reasonably light as he headed out of the city and toward the Monongahela Mountains, a segment of the Appalachian range straddling West Virginia and Virginia. A Talking Heads CD helped battle back the blearies, and the notion of meeting face-to-face with Hector Rodriguez more or less completed the job.

Would Hector be able to remember enough details of a conversation from years ago to satisfy Sarah? Lou had his doubts. He wondered how Gary was doing in jail. Being locked up was certainly the ultimate lesson in humiliation.

It was just after sunset on a day that was hovering around freezing, when Lou rolled into Hayes. The EN-TERING HAYES sign was legible, but pocked with bullet holes. His plan was to spend some time before his rendezvous with Hector getting a feel for the place. Hector had provided detailed directions to their meeting spot, but Lou needed only to exit the highway to find the Wildwood Motel. Pulling into the driveway, he took in the folksy look of the weather-beaten sign suspended on a pair of rusty hooks. Judging by the dearth of cars in the motel parking lot, he suspected it was not frequent that someone tacked up a NO before the word VACANCY.

The Wildwood might not get a five-diamond rating from AAA, but the clean, single-story motel was head and shoulders above the residents' quarters at Eisenhower. Having phoned ahead, Lou already had a room waiting in his name. If things did not go well with Hector, and there were no notes to compile, he would probably just put on another Talking Heads CD, leave a tip on the unmade bed for housekeeping, and drive home.

Hayes was a military town—pretty much as expected, but on a smaller scale. Lou drove around some of the back roads, but quickly concluded that Main Street was where most of what passed for action took place. It had two bars, one Chinese restaurant, a burger joint, and a dilapidated lumber mill that still appeared to be active. Wanting to get more familiar with the home of Mantis Company, Lou made a pit stop at a bar called Ralphie's, which possessed the grungy charm of the dives he once loved to frequent but, at this day and hour at least, none of the patrons.

He ordered a Diet Coke from the bartender—mid-forties, apron, tattoos, nicotine stains, five o'clock shadow—and rated the fountain Coke a surprising seven and a half for taste, temperature, and carbonation. On the Welcome scale, developed after Diet Coke replaced Wild Turkey as his drink of choice, three was undrinkable unless he was touring Death Valley, and two was undrinkable under any circumstances. He had yet to meet a perfect ten.

"You ain't from around here," the bartender said with an Appalachian twang.

"You did that without even pulling out your Ouija board."

"My what?"

"How'd you know I was an outsider?"

"Hayes is a small place. Everybody knows everybody. Even the visitors to the base."

"Name's Lou Welcome."

"Bell," the bartender said, extending his hand. "Ralphie Bell. You said Welcome?"

"Just like the mat."

"Like the wh—? Oh, I get it." He chuckled until he laughed. And then he laughed until he doubled over in a spasm of cigarette-driven coughing.

"So, where is everybody?" Lou asked

"Hayes stays pretty quiet until after eight o'clock or so. That's when the boys from the base are allowed to come into town. That is, if they have the night off."

"Is the base far from here?"

"The entrance is 'bout a half mile away. But careful that you don't stumble onto their property without you knowin' it."

"Why's that?"

"The base is 'bout fifteen square miles that includes some of the wildest country in these mountains, and not much of it is fenced in. There are lots of 'No Trespassing' signs posted about, but the number-one crime in Hayes are hunters who trespass without realizing what they've done. Trespassin' and carryin' a weapon around here is really frowned on." Bell loaded and shot an imaginary pump-action rifle.

"Ouch!" Lou said, clutching his chest. "Tell me something, Ralphie, does Wyatt Brody ever come in here?"

Bell scoffed. "Once in a great while he pops in for a drink an' stays a few minutes. But the truth is, Colonel Brody don't really socialize with nobody that I know of. Soldiers say he's on some sort of mission from God, and sometimes he sure acts that way."

Lou tried, but could get no further insights on the man who might have murdered Elias Colston. On the chance he was going to need to try again with Ralphie Bell, he left two dollars for the drink, plus a ten. It was going to be up to Hector Rodriguez to fill in some huge gaps.

Lou had no trouble finding his way back to the Wildwood, but he had a harder time locating the way to the bonfire pit, where Hector insisted they meet. The path, leading off from a pair of worn picnic tables at the rear of the motel, was partially overgrown with brush, and the ground was crunchy with thin ice. A stiff breeze had cropped up, and Lou was grateful that he had steered clear of the bargain aisle when choosing his parka at Eastern Mountain Sports.

Using his cell phone as a flashlight, he emerged after a hundred feet or so into a wide clearing. At the center of the clearing, a broad, stone-rimmed pit still emitted the potent scent of recently burnt wood. Beyond the pit, a sliver of moonlight escaping from clouds scudding overhead revealed the silhouette of a stocky man standing more or less at attention. The vapor from his breathing swirled eerily in the thin light.

"Dr. Welcome?" Hector's voice and accent were unmistakable.

"That's me. Thanks for doing this, Hector." Lou approached him, prepared to shake hands, but Hector remained as he was. Even in his bulky, military-issue parka, he was powerfully built, and through the evening gloom, he looked swarthy and handsome.

A warrior.

Lou spoke again. "I appreciate that you allowed me to meet with you, Hector. I think it might be important."

"Tell me what you want to know." His coolness matched the evening.

Lou shifted his weight from side to side to get the blood flowing to his feet. He reached in his pocket for his gloves and realized he had left them on the front seat of the Toyota.

"If it's okay with you," he said, "I'd rather talk indoors. I rented a room at the Wildwood, so we could speak there if you want."

Hector shook his head dismissively. "Can't do that. People might see me with you. Coming or going. That's why I got here early and took the back way, through the woods. Talking to a stranger in this town will lead to questions, and questions aren't good for my career."

"Understood," Lou said, blowing on his hands now.

From the clouds of frozen vapor, Lou could tell that Hector was breathing at about half the rate he was. He suspected that the marine's pulse was a fraction of his as well.

"So let's do this," Hector said. "What do you want to know?"

"First, I want you to know something," Lou said. "I didn't tell you the complete truth when we spoke by phone. Elias Colston didn't take down any notes about your conversation. He recorded it and transferred the recording to a CD. I gave that CD to the police, and now it's gone missing along with a copy I had in my apartment."

He left out about his place having been ransacked, and that was probably just as well. Even from six feet away, Lou could see the younger man tense and go pale.

Hector inhaled deeply and tilted his head skyward. "Congressman Colston was my best friend's father," he said. "I said things that night I wouldn't want certain people to know about. Why didn't you tell me this when we talked on the phone?"

"I was worried you'd panic if you knew and refuse to meet with me. Look, I'm sorry, Hector, for misleading you in any way, but we've got to come as close as possible to re-creating that conversation. Every detail. Every point you made. Everything you said. I have a tape recorder here." Lou extracted a miniature state-of-the-art instrument from his parka. "We won't know what's going to be important or not until we get it all down."

Hector eyes flashed. "You don't get it, man," he said. "I told the congressman stuff that I shouldn't have told him. I loved that man. He was like a father to me. That's why I was trying to warn him to back off from Colonel Brody and Mantis. But if word gets out that I talked about the Palace Guards, then I'm a dead man walking. What in the hell could have happened to that disc? Who has it now?"

"I . . . I don't know. The police have it. I'm sure of that."

"Damn."

"As I recall, you didn't say much about the Palace Guards at all. Can you tell me about them now?"

"I shouldn't tell you nothin'. It's not safe for you to know. These guys—the Guards—they're badass, man."

"Please, Hector. You've got to help me help the man who's in jail for Elias's murder. I don't believe he did it."

"The news said he was havin' an affair with the congressman's wife. Why should I care what happens to him?"

"Because Mark's father would have cared. He would have wanted justice to be done no matter what, even if it meant freeing his wife's lover."

Hector looked about furtively. "Okay, listen, I'll help you because I love that family. But you got to find that disc."

"I'm doing my best."

"The Palace Guards are sort of picked by Colonel Brody before they even join the Corps. They mark themselves with a tattoo of barbed wire wrapped around their wrist. That's how you can tell who's Guard. We all have one of a praying mantis right here on the bottom of our forearm. That's how you can tell who's Mantis."

"So what's the connection between Brody and the Palace Guards?"

"Just what I said. If someone starts actin' up and gets on Brody's bad side, the Guard might pay them a visit, rough them up a little, remind them that they don't want to be on Colonel Brody's bad side, and that the next step is they're out of Mantis."

"Do you think Brody's desperate for money to fund Mantis?" Lou asked. "I mean, your outfit has been hit pretty hard by budget cuts that were initiated out of Colston's office."

Hector just shrugged. "Probably," he said. "Everyone's desperate for money. The colonel's always complaining that D.C. is squeezing Mantis harder than any other branch of the marines or even the rest of the service."

"Do you think Brody could have murdered the congressman because he knew about the Palace Guards?"

"I doubt it," Hector said. "Either way, I sure as hell hope that recording doesn't get back to the colonel. If it does, I may find myself with a visit from—"

The night exploded with a series of bright flashes and loud pops that came from somewhere down the path to the clearing. The top of the picnic table in front of Lou splintered, spraying fragments of wood into his face. More gunshots . . . more flashes.

"Run!" Hector screamed. "Split up and run!"

The two men broke for the woods at the same time. They were separated by about a hundred feet, when another shot rang out. Lou saw Hector stumble, then fall, clutching his leg. Lou stopped running and headed toward the marine, but a hail of bullets sprayed snow in front of him.

Hector lurched to his feet, still holding his leg. "I'm all right!" he cried out. "Get out of here! Run!"

Lou watched the marine vanish into the woods.

Then he spotted an opening in the dense underbrush and plunged through it.

CHAPTER 22

Lou stumbled as he reached the woods, but he managed to grab a tree trunk and keep from falling. The icy ground provided all the traction of a hockey rink. Branches lashed out like claws, gashing his face and hands. His foot caught a root hidden beneath the snow and sent him sprawling. He landed heavily onto the hard, packed ground and skidded across the rocks. From somewhere in the distance, he heard more gunfire. Then he heard something else—something that sent him scrambling on all fours, across the frozen snow and hard, packed dirt until he regained his footing.

Voices.

It seemed like there were two men, and they definitely were after him. The woods diffused the sound, making it difficult for Lou to make out where they were.

"I can see his tracks," a raspy voice called out from somewhere behind him. "Keep the flashlight steady."

Lou's only recourse was to keep on running, but his ankle-high hiking boots made every step feel leaden and uncertain. In the icy, blowing night, breathing quickly became a problem. Again and again he had to pause to draw in enough air to push ahead. His lungs burned, and a fearsome stitch had developed in his left side.

"This way!" a man with a Hispanic accent yelled out. "Over here."

Moonlight would occasionally illuminate a pathway through the woods; then clouds would obscure it, plunging the forest into near total darkness. Lou thought he had put some distance between himself and his pursuers, when the ground beneath him turned steeper. Before he could slow his stride, he was skidding downhill. His right foot caught the edge of a rock and he went down, tumbling at an awkward angle and landing heavily at the bottom of a small ravine. He touched his left temple and felt blood. His shoulder on that side throbbed, and he wondered if his contused knee would hold weight.

The moonlight was gone now, and the darkness seemed impenetrable. Dazed, he hauled himself to his feet. The knee held. Then, from far up the steep slope, he saw two shafts of light dancing erratically off the trees and underbrush.

"Sonofabitch," he murmured, wondering whether he should use what time he had to hide or to run.

For most of a minute, he remained motionless and listened. From among the rustling winter branches, he heard the distinct sound of rushing water coming from his right—a stream or waterfall. Not the direction he wanted to go. Hobbling, he headed away from the sound, angling along the shallow swale at the base of the hill. Every twenty feet he stopped and listened again. There were no voices from above, but he sensed the men were there. Trying to deal with his tracks, he walked backwards for a time, until he reached some rocky ground. Then he cut uphill and to his right.

Probably fruitless, he thought. *No, not fruitless . . . dumb, and a waste of time.*

At that instant, above and ahead of him, he saw the shafts of light once more, cutting through the blackness. He whirled and, ignoring the stabbing pain on the side of his knee made worse by the unevenness of the terrain, he headed back toward the running water. The stream was wider than he had expected—more a river lined with ice and snow, moving rapidly from his right to his left, rippling across nearly submerged rocks and boulders the size of refrigerators. He peered ahead, getting what help he could from his cell phone's display light. The wind was to his back, and several times the voices were carried down to him.

Clearly, the two men were more adept at moving through the winter forest than he was. The debate of what to do next lasted only a few seconds. Prying a stout branch from the snow, he broke off the dead twigs and braced himself as he stepped into the frigid water. In an instant, his boots had filled and his socks became sodden. The numbness was sudden and utterly unpleasant. Rather than go directly across, he followed the flow, using his branch for balance and praying he could stay upright.

One step . . . then another . . . and another.

Oddly, he found himself flashing on nights in his college library, memorizing an endless list of organic chemistry formulas, knowing that if he studied for twenty-three hours, somebody at another table was studying twenty-four.

Discipline. One step. Another. One formula. Another. Discipline.

Carbocation with three valence electrons is carbenium . . . with six is . . . is what? . . .

His distracted thinking seemed to keep the burning numbness in his feet at bay. Gradually, he angled for the far side of the river. The longer he could stay in, the better chance he had. The water reached his knees. If he fell over now, he was dead. Simple as that. And if the water became much deeper, he was going over.

Concentrate.

Oxidation plus carbocation is . . . is what? How in the hell did I ever pass?

The water level held just above his knees. His jeans were soaked to the groin. At a bend, he risked a glance backwards. The lights were there, still some distance away. How much of a trail had he left? How much more could he take? Standing in the middle of the river, Lou crouched behind a boulder and watched as the beams cut irregular paths through the darkness.

"I got tracks here," he heard one man say.

"He might have followed the river," said the other.

"Or he might be in it."

"Let's separate. You head up the hill. I'll go this way. Fire if you've got him spotted."

Lou risked a relieved breath. Two against one were not odds he embraced, but one on one? At least he had surprise going for him. Surprise and the water. . . . And Emily.

He stood and kept working across the river. His knee and shoulder ached and the water burned but, one step at a time, he was moving. He checked back again. Judging by the single flashlight beam, maybe fifty yards separated him and his pursuer. The water level had dropped back to his knees, but the slippery rocks were a constant challenge. Still, he was feeling increasingly comfortable moving ahead.

Mistake.

Without warning, his boot skidded off a mossy rock and he pitched forward into the water, arms extended. His knees slammed down into the rocks lining the bottom. His ankle took the torque from the fall and twisted unnaturally. For a moment, Lou feared it might have broken, but he got back to his feet, now totally soaked and beginning to shiver. After a few hesitant attempts, he managed to put decent weight on the foot. A sprain.

Once again, he was on the move, but traveling at a much slower rate this time. His lungs were again on fire, and the agonizing stitch had returned to his side. From behind, he heard splashing.

Keep moving . . . keep moving. . . .

The shivering had become ferocious now. Hypothermia was taking over. It probably wasn't going to help much, but he had to get out of the river. At that instant, there was a gunshot.

"You out there?" The raspy voice called out, taunting him through the dark. "I'm gonna find you, an' I'm gonna kill you."

Two more pops. Though the gunman may have been shooting blindly, a branch to Lou's right splintered. He was ten feet or so from the bank. Ignoring the numbing cold, he forged ahead. Now, without his support stick, he was slipping with each unsteady step. Ahead, he could make out what seemed to be a broad clearing of some sort—a field. Then he realized that the blackness wasn't a field at all.

It was a lake.

CHAPTER 23

Lou hauled himself onto the bank of the frigid river and stumbled across to the shore to what seemed like a nearly circular lake, frozen as far out as he could see. It was impossible to be certain of the circumference, but Lou would not have been surprised if it were a mile or more. He tried to will himself to stop shaking. Was he better off with or without his freezing, water-soaked clothes?

To his right, twenty feet away, there was a dilapidated boathouse. Its roof had partially caved in and the windows were smashed out. Dense cobwebs filled what eaves there were, and tall weeds had taken over the surrounding ground. There was a rotting rowboat, long past any ability to float, propped up against the side of the shack closest to him. A basketball-sized boulder set on the upper gunwale held it in place.

The wind had picked up intensity, swaying the tall trees until they groaned like stiffly moving joints. The odds on there being something in the house to wrap himself in were small, but it was worth checking. He had to move quickly, though. The boathouse was the first place the man heading downriver to kill him would check. Incredibly, the door to the place was firmly closed and secured with a rusty bolt. Lou rejected the notion of forcing it open and instead peered into the darkness through what had been a window. After its prolonged submersion, his cell phone and its light were useless.

From what he could see, the place was empty.

Time was running out. Lou was shivering mercilessly. The only plan he could conceive of was to drag himself along the lakeshore and get shot.

At that moment, still some distance away, he heard branches cracking. It was almost over for him. Trying to run had as much chance now as having his cell phone light up. Then he glanced over at the rotting boat, and the glimmer of an idea began to take shape. A feint— one of the moves Cap loved to use in the ring.

Silently, using all his strength, Lou set the huge rock aside and flipped the rowboat upright, cushioning the landing with his shoulder. Some wood splintered off, but for the most part, the sorrowful craft remained intact. He shoved it to the lakeshore and slid it out onto the ice, which creaked but held firm.

Now for the feint.

Moving on his knees and pushing the boat ahead to keep his weight distributed, he eased across the ice. There was a restless cracking, and a strained creak, but again, no give.

"Hey, brother," the voice called. "You're running out of room. How about you don't make it hard on yourself? I promise I won't."

Five more yards onto the ice. Then another five. He was twenty yards from shore now. The ice seemed set to give way, but his chips were on the table. Lou turned the boat ninety degrees, then gingerly removed his parka and threw it on the ice not far away. In the ring, the move would have been equivalent to dropping his right hand and dipping his right shoulder, announcing that the next blow was going to be an uppercut from that side, when the real punch was going to come from the left.

Then, crawling on his belly military marine-style, he eased back to shore. He hauled the boulder to the far side of the shack and tested that he could lift it. Knees . . . belly . . . chest. The rock was lighter than the 225 pounds he pressed in sets of ten at Stick and Move, but it was absolute dead weight, and it seemed like chest high was the limit here. When the final moment came, he would have to do better than that . . . or die.

Kneeling by the boathouse, Lou felt his adrenaline rush begin to fade, and once again his teeth were chattering. He peered around the corner toward the woods. At that instant, a dark shadow moved cautiously from the forest, a flashlight in one hand, and a handgun in the other. Lou pulled back and flattened against the wall.

"You here, brother?" the man called out.

The ground crunched as the killer approached the wall where the boat had been. Through the window above him, Lou saw the flashlight beam scanning the inside. He clenched his jaws and willed his teeth to remain quiet.

More crunching. The beam swung toward the lake, then out onto the ice and onto the dark silhouette of the rowboat. Finally, the light stopped on Lou's parka.

"You ain't fooling me, bro. I know you're behind that boat."

He stepped out onto the ice and fired two shots. Lou could sense him checking around his feet, following the tracks he had left.

"I hit you yet? Don't worry, I will. I'll come right out there and shoot you between your eyes."

It seemed like the gunman was firing a semiautomatic pistol, but Lou had no idea the number of rounds the weapon held. What he did know was that the diversion of the boat and the parka was occupying the man's focus and confusing him. One cautious step at a time, the gunman moved onto the lake. A quarter of the way, Lou guessed. . . . Now maybe half.

Lou hoisted the boulder to his chest and moved forward. He could feel the adrenaline of fear pounding in the muscles of his chest and arms.

The gunman fired three more times.

Go ahead, big guy. Keep shooting . . . keep shooting.

Lou neared the lake's edge. The huge rock was on his shoulder now. In order to make an effective throw, he had to venture onto the ice again.

But not too far.

Lou needed to close the twenty-foot gap between them by at least half.

"I hit you yet?" the man yelled, oblivious of the figure closing in behind. "I've got a lot of ammo, bitch."

He inserted a fresh magazine and snapped off several more shots. Five feet.

The killer, whom Lou could now see was about his height and build, finally sensed something was wrong and began to turn. Lou brought the rock over his head and heaved it with all the strength he had. The momentum sent him sprawling backwards and landing heavily on the ice. He felt it crack beneath his weight, sending frigid water seeping up around him.

The gunman was spinning toward the commotion behind him when the rock landed precisely at his feet. The ice beneath him gave way instantly and before he could raise his weapon to fire, he vanished. Lou heard the splash, but scrambling for the shore, he could do nothing to help the man. The killer cried out once. Then there was silence. Desperately cold, Lou reached the bank and staggered along the wooded shoreline, tripping over roots and stumbling through skeleton-like, densely packed, leafless bushes.

He was alive, but only long enough, he knew, to freeze to death. He pulled himself to his feet and pushed ahead, unable to pull in a useful breath. Leaning against a tree trunk, he risked a glance behind him. He had put some distance between himself and the rotting boathouse, but what difference did it make? In the childhood debate with friends about the worst way to die—burning, drowning, or freezing—he had always argued for burning. Now, he wasn't at all sure.

Gasping for air and shaking violently, Lou sank

down on a fallen tree. He bent forward to check his injured ankle, and was rolling down his sock when he felt the muzzle of a gun press firmly against the back of his neck.

"Don't turn around," a youngish man's voice said. "Put your hands up and get facedown on the ground. Do it now, or I shoot!"

Teeth snapping like castanets, Lou did as instructed.

Strong hands wrenched his arms behind his back.

The last thing he felt before he lost consciousness were handcuffs being secured around his wrists.

CHAPTER 24

Lou came to slowly, carried into awareness by a pounding headache. He was handcuffed to a stretcher in a van equipped as an ambulance. His sodden clothes had been replaced by military fatigues, and he was covered by a pile of blankets. He guessed his core temperature to be somewhere in the eighties.

The van jounced over a rutted road, each dip firing off a howitzer shell in his head. The young man sitting next to him wore a red cross armband. The driver, considerably more grizzled, had one that read MP. Neither man seemed in the mood to speak with him. There was no reaction when Lou told them who he was and how he came to be in this situation.

"I'm telling you one of your own guys was shot," Lou said. "Hector Rodriguez. He could still be back there someplace. Don't you care?"

"What we care about is our orders," the driver said finally, "and our orders are to bring you to the base. Whatever story you have to tell, you can tell it there."

That's not going to help anybody, Lou thought.

Lou had little doubt that Brody sent men to kill him and Hector—perhaps members of the Palace Guard Hector had spoken about. Somehow the contents of the missing CD had to have gotten back to him. No other explanation he could think of made sense. The ambulance slowed and came to a stop at a security checkpoint manned by a team of heavily armed marines.

The MP and medic flashed their security clearance, and a razor-wire gate slid open on a narrow track. A minute later, the van was on the move once again. When Lou craned his neck and looked back, he saw the fence closing. He wondered if he would ever be getting out.

They traveled along some dirt streets, past two long buildings Lou assumed to be barracks. Off to the right there was a target range lit by a series of powerful floodlights, and to the left was the start of what appeared to be an obstacle course. They came to a hard stop at a dirt courtyard that housed three single-story buildings—clapboard siding, tiled roofs. The largest of them was up on short stilts with a porch running across the length. A sign at the center of the group read:

MANTIS COMPANY
WHATEVER IT TAKES

"Just remember, I'm a civilian," Lou said as the men released him and guided him out of the van. "I've got rights."

"Not when you trespass on military land, you don't," the MP replied.

The men took hold of Lou's elbows and escorted him into the center and largest of the three buildings. They stopped in front of a shuttered wood door, upon which, painted in perfectly rendered black lettering, were the words:

MANTIS COMPANY
COL. WYATT BRODY, COMMANDER

The fierce praying mantis painted beneath the lettering looked as if it could eat a cow. The MP knocked and waited until being invited to enter. Then he set Lou's soggy wallet on the austere wooden desk. Only a few neatly arranged files were set atop the unvarnished surface. Wyatt Brody glanced at the wallet disdainfully. The dimly lit office was rustic, with exposed beams and wooden bookcases filled with memorabilia and military tomes. No photos, no artwork, no awards, no certificates of merit.

The most impressive aspect of the office was two huge, beautifully crafted glass display cases covering the wall behind Brody's desk, and the one opposite it. Inside the well-lit cases was a museum of polished handguns—more than Lou had ever seen in one setting. The guns were mounted on green felt, and labeled with brass placards detailing the make, model, and year of the weapon, as well as some text. Through a partially opened door behind the commander, Lou could see more cases and more handguns.

"Impressive, isn't it, Dr. Welcome," Brody said from

his seat behind his desk. "Several of them are one of a kind."

Lou wasn't startled to hear his name. The MPs obviously searched his wallet and called ahead.

Brody nodded toward the door, and the two men left.

"One of your men has been shot," Lou said as soon as the door clicked shut. "He may be badly injured."

"I've already got a search party looking for him," Brody said. "Just as I had several looking for you."

Lou scanned the man's expressionless face, but could not fathom a guess at his level of truthfulness. Brody, dressed in a beige shirt and tie underneath an olive green jacket, was in his late fifties, distinguished in every way, with closely cropped salt-and-pepper hair that rested high on a creaseless forehead. There was a Slavic quality to his appearance—narrow face, aquiline nose, pronounced cheekbones, glacial blue eyes. Yet of all Brody's features, it was his mouth that troubled Lou the most. His thin lips seemed to frown and grin simultaneously, as if to suggest he derived the same satisfaction from administering pleasure as he did from inflicting pain.

"Take a seat," Brody said, motioning to the plain wood chair set in front of his desk.

"I prefer to stand," Lou said.

"It wasn't a request. I haven't arrested you for trespassing yet," Brody continued, "but all that could change with the push of a button. The cells in our brig become unbearably small after just a few hours. Now, take a seat."

Lou hesitated, then acquiesced.

Brody interlocked his fingers and assessed Lou with his ice blue eyes. When he finally spoke, Lou sensed how Brody's dominating voice, stern yet without much inflection, could have a hypnotic effect on the men under his command.

"Why don't you tell me what you were doing trespassing on the property of the United States Marines," the commander began.

"I'm a taxpayer. Doesn't that make me a part owner? How can I trespass on my own property?"

"Look, Dr. Welcome, and yes, the MPs radioed ahead, and I had my people run you. Where you work. What you do. Even where you box. Let me be clear about something: Cute and evasive is the fast track to getting yourself locked in one of those cells. So let's try this again. Why were you on Mantis property?"

"Is running for my life a good enough reason?" Lou said. "There were at least four guys trying to kill Hector Rodriguez and me. And I think I know who they were, too."

"And exactly who where they?" Brody asked.

"Have you ever heard of the Palace Guard?" Lou asked. "Rumor has it they work for you."

He studied Brody's cryptic face, looking for an extra blink, a slight tic that might tell him something. A corpse would have given him more information.

"Never heard of them," Brody said, his smile conveying many meanings. "Are they a gang of some sort? Members of nearly every major gang have been identified on military installations throughout the world. It's pervasive in all branches and across most ranks, especially the junior enlisted men."

"So, do you want to explain why your men tried to kill me and Hector?"

"My men? We don't hunt civilians. We go after the other side—the bad guys. If you were attacked, it wasn't anybody directly connected to Mantis."

Brody's eyes never wavered from Lou's face, and Lou wasn't at all sure he would enjoy facing those eyes in the ring.

"Well, why don't you tell me," he said, "since you seem to be an expert on gangs in the military, why the Palace Guard, or whoever those men were, would want me dead?"

"I told you, Doctor, I don't know who this Palace Guard is. I can tell you that gangs have their own agendas. Maybe it wasn't you they were after. Maybe you were just in the wrong place at the wrong time."

"Maybe I could accept that if you could explain why they would want to kill Hector."

Brody continued to size Lou up. "If you have to know," Brody said finally, "Hector Rodriguez was not the most well regarded soldier on this base. You've heard of the Thin Blue Line?"

"In association with the police, sure," Lou said.

"Well, we have a line of our own here in the military, and Hector Rodriguez had crossed it many times over. He was about to get kicked out of Mantis, in fact, for performance reasons, and as retaliation, he started spreading lies about the company, about me, and about guys in his own platoon. So it wouldn't surprise me at all if Staff Sergeant Rodriguez stepped on the toes of the wrong person with the right connections. So, Doctor, that's your answer. Now it's time for you to do the answering. What were you doing talking with Hector Rodriguez in the first place?"

Lou tried for an inscrutable look of his own, but felt certain he missed. He thought of bobbing and weaving with the man à la Muhammad Ali, but finally decided to hit him with a couple of straight-on body blows, just to see what he might jar loose.

"I came here to speak with Mark Colston's best friend," he said. There, he'd put it on the table—the first hint that his visit to Hayes had something to do with Elias Colston's murder. But there was no reaction from Brody at all, not one tell, as poker players called it.

"And why would you be doing that?" Brody asked.

"Well, some things have come to light, and I'm following them up as a favor for the guy accused of killing Congressman Colston."

"Tragic what's happened to that family," Brody said.

"Funny thing is," Lou continued, "the more digging I do to help out my friend, the more your name keeps coming up as a possible reason the congressman is dead."

"Me?" Brody's laugh was unrevealing. "I can only tell you what everyone knew—that Elias Colston and I were never the best of friends."

"Funny how his son's death didn't bring you two closer together."

"Mark Colston was one of the bravest men I've ever had the privilege to lead," Brody said. "But it's no secret that I stood in strong opposition to the congress-man's agenda. He wanted to cut our funding, and naturally I wanted to expand it. That sort of conflict is commonplace in our government. It's a form of checks and balances. And while we may have had our political differences, I don't go around killing people, if that's what you're insinuating."

The body blows had been like punching a stone wall. It was time to try a Cap'n Crunch—a straight-out jab to the face.

"I confess the thought has been crossing my mind," Lou said.

Lou felt the room charging up, like the moment just before a thunderstorm.

"You listen to me, Welcome," Brody said, his face now crimson. "I wasn't the one sleeping with Colston's wife. And I wasn't the one who was at their house drunk when he was killed."

Crunch!

"The timetable for that isn't at all clear," Lou said. "It only takes a second to walk up to someone and pull a trigger. Any person could have avoided the security cameras by coming through the woods out back, and shot the congressman before or after Gary McHugh was there."

As quickly as it had arrived, the thunderstorm passed, and Wyatt Brody was ice once again. "Well, that person could not have been me. Not that I have to make any excuses to you, but I was at the Marine Day parade on the day Colston was killed. So there are a thousand or so witnesses who can attest to that."

"Arranging for someone to be murdered is no different from pulling the trigger yourself."

"Keep that in mind, Doctor."

Are you threatening me?

Lou swallowed the melodramatic retort at the last moment. Of course he was being threatened. "I keep everything in mind," he said, "including what it felt like to see that boy get shot."

"And I think we're done here," Brody said with a dismissive wave. "You're free to go."

"Great. So, are Tweedledum and Tweedledee going to give me a ride back to Hayes?"

The corners of Brody's mouth tightened. "My men are busy searching for Sergeant Rodriguez," he said. "I'm afraid you're going to have to make it back to Hayes on your own."

"What? On foot?"

"You seem pretty adept at traveling through the woods. And that's a good thing, too, because there are plenty of woods to go through before you reach the main road. You just have to watch your step. As you have learned, a lot of bad things can happen out there." Using the tip of one finger, he pushed Lou's wallet across at him.

"Thanks for the heads-up," Lou said.

"I want you to have time . . . to think."

Lou looked past Brody at the gun cases and wondered if the weapons were loaded, and how quickly he could smash through the glass and get at one of them. Fat chance.

Brody reached under his desk drawer and, without

subtlety, pressed a button. In half a minute, two men knocked and entered. They were dressed in parkas, fatigues, and heavy-duty boots, almost identical to the two who had chased him through the woods. The Palace Guards. One of them carried an extra parka.

"Men, escort this gentleman to the river trail and point him toward the town. Have a good morning, Dr. Welcome. I'll be sure to let you know if our search teams find your friend Hector. I know you're concerned."

The guards had moved to where Lou was seated when a man dressed in camouflage appeared behind them and knocked on Brody's partially open door. He was tall, ruggedly handsome, and fit for any age, let alone the sixty or so years Lou guessed him to be. He wore a down vest, but had the sleeves of his shirt rolled up, giving a glimpse of a faded tattoo of an explosion on one meaty forearm, and the letters TNT splayed across what looked to be a stick of sparking dynamite on the other. His light hair was cut short, military standard, and level on the top.

Brody flashed an aggrieved look.

"Sir, I'm sorry to interrupt, sir," the older man said. His leathery voice matched the weathered condition of his skin.

"What is it?" Brody demanded. "If it was anybody but you, I'd have your ass for busting in on me like this."

"Colonel, can I speak to you for a moment?"

"Go ahead."

"In the hall?"

Brody sighed and followed the chiseled marine into the anteroom. The door was pushed nearly closed, but remained ajar enough so Lou was able to catch most of what was said.

"Sir, the police are here," the man said. "I was checking inventory in Building Two when they rolled into the courtyard and asked me where they could find you. Apparently, there's a new man at the gate, and he let them in."

"Get me the name of that guard," Brody said. "What do the cops want this time?"

"Apparently, there were gunshots fired behind the Wildwood Motel in Hayes. The proprietor thought the men might be wearing military camo. The police are checking out if it involved anybody on the base because of the camo. I thought you should know, in case you wanted to talk with them."

"I don't," Brody said.

"Hey," Lou called out, "there were gunshots there. Some men were trying to—"

The Palace Guards were quick. One of them forced his hand across Lou's mouth. The other pulled an eight-inch knife from his boot and held it to Lou's throat.

From the anteroom, there was the sound of new arrivals.

"Colonel Brody, I'm Sergeant Kendall. This is Corporal Walsh. Sorry to barge in on you, but we're investigating reports of gunshots being fired behind the Wildwood Motel."

"Yes," Brody said. "We have a man in there who was caught wandering on base property. If you fellas want to take him in for questioning, that's fine with me. Just make sure he knows that the next time he trespasses on Mantis property, we may not be so charitable."

He reentered the office and motioned for the guards to back off.

Lou reflexively rubbed at his throat. "You know," he said, "I think I'm going to accept a ride from those gentlemen out there." He stepped away from the two guards. "I'm fine to see myself out, boys. Thanks for the chat, Colonel."

Brody stared at Lou, unblinking. Then the trace of a smile turned the sides of his mouth. "Lucky day for you," he said.

CHAPTER 25

Lou understood his obsessive nature could be a great asset one minute and an even greater shortcoming the next. Friends from college still talked about the day he studied twenty-four hours straight for an organic chemistry test. He ended up getting sick halfway through the exam and, were it not for being allowed a redo by an understanding professor, would have flunked.

Once he secretly agreed to bail out his father and assume much of the burden of Graham's tuition, nothing would deter him from that goal—not even the need to take stimulants to go from one moonlighting job to another. His addiction lasted for years. Eventually, to survive, he was forced to approach his recovery with as much determination as he had his drug use. Over the years, the intensity of his obsession had settled down, and staying straight and sober had become a way of life. Now, with his passion for recovery on automatic pilot, that intensity had been manifest in the need to learn everything he could about one man, Colonel Wyatt Brody. Hours rolled past as Lou, hunched over his lap-

top, picking through the endless Wyatt Brody items sent
by his browser.

Seven hours . . . eight . . .

Lou's eyes were burning from the connection with
his monitor screen. He looked up only to scratch a note
on his yellow legal pad, and got up only for bathroom
breaks and more coffee. The wrist of his mousing hand
throbbed, a warning sign the muscles and tendons were
being dangerously overworked. His legs were stiff as
chilled motor oil, and his stomach felt knotted and raw.

Brody!

Diversity lingered on the carpet nearby, keeping a
low profile, surprisingly reluctant to resume his role as
Lou's tormentor.

Nine hours . . .

Brody's name came up many times in Lou's multiple
searches, but never with startling information. There
was nothing about the man's personal life or career in
the military that helped connect the dots. Married once.
Long ago divorced. Born and raised in the East. One
child—a daughter. U.S. Marine Corps since his graduation from the Naval Academy.

*What was it that Hector knew that Brody wants si-
lenced?* It seemed the more Lou looked for answers, the
fewer he found.

Mantis proved to be equally enigmatic. The outfit—
formed in 2002 under the direction of then Major Wyatt
Brody—had, according to a Web site that tracked military statistics, the highest percentage of marines killed
in action and the most number of medals bestowed for
valor. It was a model unit in what many believed was

the toughest, most demanding branch of the military. Unlike the SEALs, Rangers, and other Special Forces outfits, there was no recruiting Web site for Mantis. Members, it appeared, were all hand-selected by Wyatt Brody himself.

So why would a man so dedicated to his unit want to kill one of his own? Lou had been sick with worry for Hector. None of his projections were pleasant. Captured or dead. There were no other realistic options for the young marine. If he had been captured by Brody's Palace Guards, it seemed reasonable he would be tortured for whatever information they believed he possessed relative to Elias Colston.

Lou had stayed in Hayes long enough to file an official report with the tiny police department, but from the onset, it was obvious that jurisdiction presented a major obstacle to any investigation. The police could search the national forest and the woods behind the motel, but the base itself remained off-limits.

A military matter. Lou had heard the phrase enough to put it to music if he wanted to.

He checked the *Hayes Examiner,* a small biweekly, and followed the paper's Web site and online sources covering the surrounding towns for news of Hector. He had even called the bartender at Ralphie's, thinking that if anybody had heard something, it would be the man whose clientele purposely loosened their lips with booze when they came in his joint. What he got from Ralphie Bell instead was zip, zero, and nada—so much of nothing, in fact, it was clear word was out, making the subject of the gunfire behind the Wildwood Motel off-limits.

Lou's only lead, if it could be called such, came from Hector's mother, a widow living in San Antonio who spoke only minimal English. All Lou learned from their brief phone conversation was that Hector had been officially reported as AWOL. He did not upset her by sharing his true suspicions. Captured or dead.

Ten hours . . . keep searching . . . This man may have killed Colston. . . . He well might hold the key to Gary's freedom.

Lou was clicking through pages of Google search results, when his eyes drifted to the horizontal menu, specifically the "image" option.

He hadn't looked there earlier, simply because he already knew what Brody looked like. What else could there be?

As expected, the images—what there were of them—were not at all helpful. A few PR headshots of Brody, some random book covers authored by people with his last name, family photos (but of a different Brody family), a flower, a dog, a superhero, a baby, and on and on—randomness at its most frustrating.

Lou went forty search pages deep, scanning through image after image, when something caught his eye. It was a photograph that appeared moderately old, scanned and uploaded to someplace on the Internet. Lou positioned the cursor on top of the image and saw that it had been, in fact, uploaded to a Facebook page. He clicked the link to open the Web site for the image, and up came the Facebook page for a retired professor named Dr. Derek Vaughan.

Dr. Vaughan either did not bother to make his images private or, given his age, maybe did not know how. Emily was always teaching Lou how to do things on the Internet. Even though he and Vaughan were not Facebook friends, he could still see Vaughan's images, and read the captions.

The picture showed a much younger Wyatt Brody, dressed in a cap, gown, and hood, receiving a plaque from a well-dressed, bespectacled man who was smiling broadly. The caption read:

I present my favorite student, Wyatt Brody, graduating from the USU's MD/PhD program, the Dean's Medal for Research Excellence, 1985. His thesis: Studies on the Neurochemistry of Fear.

The Neurochemistry of Fear.

Lou sat motionless, staring at the screen, unaware of the aching in his neck and shoulders, or the gritty exhaustion burning his eyes.

He knew the USU stood for Uniformed Services University of the Health Sciences, a university run by the federal government, with the mission of preparing graduates for service in the U.S. Medical Corps. He strained to put the pieces together. An MD/PhD does award-winning research into the neurochemistry of fear. Some years later, he helps found a company of marines with a remarkable record of bravery, including at least one winner of the Medal of Honor. His company, Mantis, holds the distinction of having the highest percentage of soldiers killed in action, coupled with the most medals of valor awarded.

Who are these marines? Lou wondered. *Why are they such outliers from the others in the Corps?*

There was something unusual about Mantis Company and their commander, and Lou could not shake the suspicion that the explanation had something to do with Wyatt Brody's thesis. He sent the Facebook image to his printer and listened as it materialized on his desk.

This was it, he was thinking. This was the first step on the path toward unraveling the mystery of Colonel Wyatt Brody.

He smiled grimly. Not only had he taken the initial step, but he knew precisely where to take the next one. He set his fingers on the keyboard. In seconds, he was connected to the Web site of the library of the Uniformed Services University.

CHAPTER 26

The Nimitz Library, named after Fleet Admiral Chester W. Nimitz, was a centerpiece of the plush campus of the U.S. Naval Academy in Annapolis. Lou had familiarized himself with the protocol for visitors, and now approached the reference desk with his photo ID in hand.

The pert librarian, Adele Green, according to her nameplate, was at least ten years his junior. She glanced up from her terminal and appraised him. "May I help you?" she asked.

"Yes, I called ahead," Lou said. "I'm the D.C. doc from—"

"Dr. Welcome," she said without breaking eye contact.

"That's right I—"

"Wanted to read Wyatt Brody's thesis paper from 1985," Green said, smiling.

Of all the professions Lou had ever dealt with, librarians—and reference librarians, in particular—were high on his list of favorites.

He returned her smile. "I suppose you've heard this before," he said, "but have you ever seen—?"

"*M*A*S*H*? If you're referring to Gary Burghoff, who played Corporal 'Radar' O'Reilly in the 1970 film and TV show, the only actor beside George Wood to reprise his role from the Altman film on the television show, the answer is, yes, other people have told me I reminded them of a female version of him. I've decided to accept that as a compliment—at least as a comment on our work habits."

Lou laughed. If there were a reference librarian's hall of fame, Adele Green was ticketed for it.

She reached below her desk and removed a modestly thick, eight-and-a-half-by-eleven, leather-bound book. "I'll hand this to you once I check you in and you go through our screener. You don't want to set off the alarm."

"You seem like someone who really enjoys her job," Lou said.

"I enjoy connecting people with information, if that's what you mean."

She jotted down his pertinent identifying details, while he eyed the bound thesis eagerly.

"Funny," she went on, "we have theses that get filed here and then don't get requested at all for decades. You're the second person in five years who asked to see this one."

The statement instantly grabbed Lou's attention. "Oh?" he said, trying for a modestly casual tone. "That's interesting. I wonder who else was researching into Wyatt Brody's genius?"

"I have it right here," Green said, checking her screen. "Oh, my. The last borrower was our congressman, Elias Colston."

"Colston?"

"It's awful what happened to him. Just terrible. I only hope they have the man who did it."

Adele Green's revelation hit Lou like a spear. Elias Colston was not only interested in Wyatt Brody, but he had also uncovered the unusual subject of the man's Ph.D. thesis. *But why?*

"Justice will be served," Lou said, picturing Gary McHugh in his hideous orange jumpsuit.

He took the volume and settled inside an out-of-the-way carrel, then flipped open the bound thesis and read the title page:

Studies on the Neurochemistry of Fear
Clinical Experiments and a Review of the Literature.

Divided into the standard scientific form the thesis was extensive and impressive.

Introduction
Materials and Methods
Observations
Discussion and Literature Review
Conclusions
Bibliography

The bulk of Brody's research, Lou quickly learned, focused on the centers in the midbrain known as the amygdalae and the hypothalamus—hardly lightweight stuff. Even with the advent of real-time MRI, which over recent years had opened the doors to so many neurologic mysteries, the mechanisms of function of the amygdalae and the related limbic system remained the source of contention. But in the mid-'80s, Wyatt Brody had formed solid, fascinating hypotheses, and his laboratory work seemed to bear his theses out.

Brody's experiments, many of them simple to the point of absolute elegance, involved rats that were programmed with electrical shocks to the feet to fear specific benign stimuli, such as a pet toy or specific food. "Learning to fear," he called the process. By measuring the response activity in the rat's brain chemistry, Brody homed in on a number of structures that created the state of fear. Then he set out to identify the neurotransmitter chemicals produced and released by those structures.

Simple . . . not!

Hours passed. Lou was in med school mode—processing, dissecting, memorizing, scratching notes on his ubiquitous yellow legal pad. None of med school had ever been particularly easy for him, but the sense of achievement when a concept was mastered was one he loved.

Lou could not help but smile at Brody's absolute brilliance. He wondered how much Elias Colston, with a background in the law, had gleaned from the sometimes quite dense explanations of the experimental findings—especially the theories on how to block the fear reactions once they had been learned.

At the center of Brody's work on the neurochemical

blockade of emotional arousal was a set of receptors located throughout the midbrain. This portion of Brody's thesis seemed to Lou to be more ragged and less authoritatively expressed than the others. It appeared that Brody had identified three or four transmitters. But his ability to block these transmitters with other chemicals had not been clearly worked out at the time he wrote the conclusions to his research.

Strange, Lou thought. It was as if in a heartbeat, Brody had lost confidence or possibly even interest in his work. But even so, from what neurochemistry Lou knew, this was still cutting-edge work, deserving of the Ph.D. Brody had been given.

He read through the final portion of the thesis, looking specifically for any hint as to why Brody did not push harder into the discussion and conclusions of the paper. There were no shimmering revelations or revolutionary, Nobel Prize–worthy contributions to the field, but there was one surprise, and a huge one, at that. Brody believed that the most promising antagonist versus the chemicals released by the fear centers of the amygdalae and rest of the midbrain was an old friend of Lou's— methamphetamine.

In its back alley form, methamphetamine looked like rock candy and carried the name crystal meth. Besides booze, Lou's drug of choice had been Adderall, a prescription dextroamphetamine. But from time to time, he drifted down the dark road to crystal. He had managed to steer clear of it most of the time by reminding himself that the substance was one of the most dangerous and addictive drugs ever cooked up—a stimulant that, taken long-term in high-enough doses, could actually produce distinctive, irreversible lesions in the brain.

He had been intervened upon before he could become addicted at a high level, but he had seen his fair share of meth heads over the years—fidgety, loquacious, and quick-tempered, with horrible tooth decay, dilated pupils, wasted muscles, and sores.

Though mentioned, Brody's observations on methamphetamine lacked a powerful discussion and a dynamic conclusion. If there were a practical application for the drug or the drug in combination with others, the future creator of Mantis did not spell it out.

Strange.

Bleary, Lou took some final notes, and then prepared to return the thesis to Adele Green. Nearly four hours had passed since their initial meeting. During those hours, some doors had been opened, but a myriad of questions remained.

If Wyatt Brody was responsible for the break-in at his apartment, how had he learned about the CD? Given the attack by the Palace Guards, it was unlikely that Hector had talked. Even though it seemed Brody had given up on the final stages of his research, had he subsequently developed a neurochemical agent capable of blocking the fear response? If so, was he actually using it? To what end? What, if anything, did all this have to do with the Reddy Creek Armory and Elias Colston's murder?

His thoughts swirling, Lou closed the cover, gathered

his things, and returned to the reference desk, his legs trying to recall exactly how they were supposed to move.

Adele Green looked as though she had just arrived at work. "I walked past your carrel a couple of times to see if I could be of any help," she said, flipping absently through the pages of Brody's thesis. "I suspected you might be asleep, but that was hardly the case. You never even looked up to see me."

"Whatever the opposite of ADD is, I think I have it," Lou said.

"I'll bet you're a very good doctor."

"I try."

"Did you find whatever it was you were looking for?"

"Not as much as I was looking for, but I did find some useful information."

"I'm glad. From what I just noticed, in addition to Congressman Colston, Dr. Brody had some other pretty important connections."

"What do you mean?"

"Here, look at this." Adele slid the volume around to face Lou. It was open to the last page—the dedication.

Instantly, Lou experienced a midwinter chill.

Dedicated with deepest respect to my mentor, friend, and advisor, Admiral Spencer Hogarth

"I think that's pretty interesting," Adele said. "Don't you?"

CHAPTER 27

Lou sat in Devlin and Rodgers's opulent waiting room, nervously tapping out bongo riffs on his briefcase and trying to arrive at a truce with the stiff leather armchair he had chosen. He had not been in contact with Sarah since the break-in, and felt certain when he finally did call to set up this meeting, she would refuse to see him. But here he was.

He had feared that what relationship existed between the two of them had vanished along with Elias Colston's CD. After trying his best to ignore the subject, he finally admitted to himself that Sarah had made a strong impression on him both as an attorney and as a woman. He had pinned his hopes for a reconciliation on her professionalism and concern for her client, and was prepared to take any port in this storm.

For the moment, at least, it seemed as if he had read her correctly. Sarah Cooper was a lawyer first and foremost and would want to be made aware of all the evidence pertaining to Gary McHugh, including what Lou had uncovered regarding Mantis and Wyatt Brody. He had been in the waiting room for ten minutes when she emerged from behind a paneled door, dressed sharply in a gray business suit and crisp white linen shirt. Her expression, as usual—at least in his presence—was stony.

"We'll go to my office," she said, not even bothering with a greeting or handshake. *Any port in a storm,* Lou reminded himself. At least he had made it through the door. But if Sarah's lack of warmth were any indication, his hope for rapprochement was teetering on the brink. Undeterred, Lou gratefully left his chair behind and followed her down a lengthy corridor, his feet sinking into the plush carpeting as if he were crossing a putting green.

Not surprisingly, Sarah's office was decorated with tasteful, understated elegance. Light from a gray, overcast day filtered in through floor-to-ceiling windows. For someone who had yet to make partner, she had a space featuring an impressive collection of artwork, a leather sofa with two matching chairs, and built-in mahogany bookshelves filled with legal tomes. The few photographs on display spoke of a woman into fitness, friendship, and the wild outdoors. There was one nearest her desk of a tall, tanned, exceedingly well conditioned man standing proudly beside an ocean kayak. Lou sensed strongly that it was her late husband, David.

"Your office is really beautiful," Lou said.

"Thank you."

"I always wondered if people with offices like this one worry that their clients will think the fees they are handing over are going for lavish furnishings."

"Actually, we believe our clients want to think that we make enough money so that we can afford it," Sarah said, settling in behind a desk roughly the size of a polo pitch.

"Touché."

"So, did you come here to tell me that you found the CD?"

"Touché again," Lou said. "Nice thrust. When's the last time someone bled to death on your carpet? Look, Sarah, I've decided to issue one blanket apology that will cover all my wrongdoings from talking back to my folks through sneaking a kiss from Arlene Silver in the back row of the Bing Cinema to not being more careful with the CD."

"That's not much of a list," Sarah said. "I hope it's the abbreviated version."

"Actually, I had to make up the part about Arlene. She wouldn't even let me hold hands. All I'm trying to say is you're going to have to forgive me if you want my help."

"Is that what you've been doing?" she scoffed. "Helping me?"

"It might not come across that way at first," Lou said. "But I'm more helpful than you know . . . so far."

Sarah set her elbows on the desk, rested her chin atop her interlocked hands, and leaned forward, her eyes mischievous. "Please, enlighten me," she said.

Lou began with his prolonged, ill-fated attempts at creating a verbatim transcript of the CD recording.

"I told you it would be impossible," she commented.

"Like I said, no more apologies—just a plea to give

me a chance to make amends. I've been at this nonstop since the break-in, and I've got some stuff for you."

Sarah leaned back in her chair, her body language suggesting a bit more openness.

"*The Persistent Little Puppy,*" she said.

"What?"

"It was my favorite book when I was a little kid. The puppy kept trying and trying until she got whatever it was in the end. I could never get enough of that story. Drove my mom crazy. Please go ahead, I'm sorry to have interrupted." She gestured for him to continue.

"After I gave up on the transcript, I made a call to Jeannine Colston."

Lou detailed the conversation and his subsequent meeting with Hector. Color drained from Sarah's cheeks as he recounted the events in Hayes, and the chase through the woods, which had probably ended with the frigid death of the Palace Guard marine who was chasing him.

"Look me in the eyes and tell me you're not making any of this up," she said.

Best offer I've had today, Lou was thinking as he did what she asked.

"There's more," he said. "Much more. What did you say that book was called?"

"*The Persistent Little Puppy.*"

"You never struck me as the kind of person who would fall in love with a book with redundancy in the title."

Sarah got it immediately. Lou loved her smile.

"Funny," she said. "I read that little picture book well into high school, and never noticed that."

"I told you I'd be of use somewhere along the line. I'm not sure what the moral is here, but I'm sure there must be one."

"You said there was more."

"Chapter two of this tale deals with Wyatt Brody. You may want to strap yourself in for this one."

Sarah listened, spellbound as Lou took her through the Mantis fortress, Brody, and his arcane handgun gallery.

"He actually threatened you?"

"Not in so many words, but he was preparing to send me back to town alone along a mile or so of freezing, pitch-black trail. It's hard to believe there wouldn't have been some of the boys from the woods waiting out there for me."

"My God."

"If the cops hadn't shown up when they did and been brought to the office by one of the soldiers, I guarantee you I'd have been frozen toast."

Sarah rose from her chair, turned away from Lou, and gazed out the window. When she turned back, her arms were folded tightly across her chest and her jaw was set. "Who is he?" she asked, as much to herself as to Lou. "Who is Wyatt Brody?"

"Funny you should ask," Lou said, unclasping his briefcase.

He extracted a folder of notes and photocopies, set them on the desk by her hand. Then he went over his hours in the library.

"The persistent not-so-little puppy," she said, not bothering to cull the awe from her voice.

"Just call me Big Dog. Anything that's not clear," he said, "just ask."

For several minutes, she examined the copies, diagrams, and notes.

"You mention here that Brody seemed to stop writing analytically as he got nearer and nearer to the end of the thesis. What do you make of that?"

Lou shook his head. "It stuck out, is all I can say."

"Do you think it means that his experiments were a failure?"

Lou met her gaze and could tell she knew exactly what he was thinking. "Or a success," he said.

"I'll read through this later. What next?"

Lou had been waiting for this moment. "That depends," he said. "Have you had a cardiogram lately?"

"Heart like a horse," she said, patting her chest. "Devlin requires every one of us to have a yearly physical. He doesn't want any of us conking off in the middle of a big case."

"Okay. If you're sure, take a look at this." With as much drama as he dared, Lou slid the dedication page across to her.

Her reaction lit the room. "Hogarth! Dammit, it's dedicated to Spencer Hogarth!"

"I couldn't believe it when I saw it."

"So, what do we do now?"

This time it was Lou who grinned.

"What?" she said. "What's so funny?"

"You just said 'we.' That's all. You said, 'Well, what do *we* do now?' "

"Okay, you got me. We're a 'we' on this thing starting right now. That said, I think I should start with an apology of my own—an apology for treating you the way I have."

"You can say what you want, but I believe I already know."

Sarah's eyebrows rose. "Have you been doing research on me, too?"

"No," Lou said, "but my thirteen-year-old has."

"Smart kid."

"You don't know the half of it. Thirteen going on thirty, she is. I told her you and I weren't getting along too well, and I didn't know why. She went online and learned about your unfortunate experience with . . . with your husband's doctor."

"Fair enough. I'm dealing with it the best I can, but sometimes the whole thing just pops out. That's about the most I can say."

"That's more than enough. If you ever want to talk about it, I'm here."

"Thanks. So, what now? We can't use this thesis to go and get subpoenas. A decent judge would laugh me out of her chambers."

"No," Lou said, "but we can try to figure out if something on that missing CD cost Elias Colston his life."

"Like what?" Sarah asked, flipping through Lou's notes on Wyatt Brody.

"Like Reddy Creek," Lou said.

Sarah looked up at him. "Explain."

"I don't have much. Colston asked Hector if he knew anything about someplace called Reddy Creek, but he didn't—or at least he said he didn't. Colston said he read in some reporter's blog that two Mantis soldiers were killed there, but I don't think he gave any more details. I looked it up. No blog that I could find, and I looked pretty hard. It's a military armory in Raleigh, North Carolina. That's all I've learned so far. I can't find any mention of soldiers being killed there at any time."

"How did Colston know they were Mantis?"

"No idea, except Hector told me that each member of the company has an identifying tattoo of a praying mantis on the inside of his forearm."

"You said the blog that's vanished was written by a reporter. Any idea what paper?"

"Not really. One in Raleigh, I suppose."

"Do you think it's important?"

"I'm not sure. Maybe Colston was fishing. I don't think *he* could find any official report of two dead Mantis marines, either."

"Two dead marines at a U.S. armory . . . a blog written by a reporter . . . and no trace of either now. I smell cover-up."

"Then I'll keep looking."

"No, let me take this one. We're a 'we,' remember."

"You going to start online?"

"Actually, I thought I might start with my boss, Grayson."

"Why him?"

"Over the years, Grayson has made just about every connection that's worth making. A newspaper in Raleigh and two dead marines sounds like it would be duck soup for him. Grayson Devlin knows everybody, and if anybody can find this missing reporter from North Carolina, then my money is on my boss."

"Terrific. I'll wait to hear and keep digging on Brody and Hogarth. Meanwhile, if there's anything you want me to convey to Gary, just let me know."

Sarah's eyes sparkled. "You did it, Doctor!" she exclaimed. "You did it."

"What did I do? What?"

Her smile was a thing of dreams. "Rather than charging off to meet with Gary, you asked."

CHAPTER 28

Another graveyard shift came and ended, this one fairly serene. Buoyed by thoughts of his new connection with Sarah, Lou packed his stuff and headed out of the hospital to the doctors' parking lot. Despite the early hour, he felt charged. At the head of his to-do list was purchasing a ticket from Dulles International to Minneapolis, and arranging for the rental car he would drive to the Pine Forest Clinic in Shockley, eighty minutes north of the city. The medical director of the clinic, Dr. Gerald Sherwood, had agreed to give him a one-hour consultation, but to get even that, Lou had been forced to bend the purpose of his visit.

The clinic, according to a modest Web site, was an exclusive facility for the diagnosis and treatment of medical and neurological disorders. Even after researching the place, Lou was uncertain of its scope. It appeared that privacy and discretion were at the center of its services. Sherwood was board certified in internal medicine and neurology, and educated at the Mayo Clinic and other top-notch training hospitals. Pine Forest was in its twentieth year. Insurance did not cover the initial one-hour consultation, he was told before being scheduled with Sherwood.

Payment of $1,000 had to be in cash or cashier's check at the time of the visit. Lou discarded the notion of mentioning James Styles of Bowie, Maryland, the name on the envelope he had found in Elias Colston's drawer, and went instead with his brother Graham's address and vitals. If necessary, he might hit up Graham for the thousand as well. Including airfare, the cost of the trip and the appointment would put a dent in Lou's discretionary bank account, but he sensed it was a move he had to make. Like the framed Medal of Honor turned to the wall, the envelope bearing Styles's name seemed significant.

As he wended his way between buildings to the doctors' lot, he became immersed in memories of the morning of his first night as an intern at Eisenhower Memorial. He had dragged himself out of the hospital to the doctors' lot after a tense, grueling shift marked by more uncertainty, anxiety, and insecurity than any one person should ever have to bear. His ancient Chevy was up on blocks, and three men were expertly spinning off the wheels.

"Hey, what are you guys doing?" Lou had managed.

"You keep out of this, Doc," one of them said. "This doesn't concern you."

"Of course it concerns me. That's my car."

"Oops. Hey, guys, it's the doc's car. Sorry, there, Doc."

The three nonchalantly replaced the wheels, tightened the lugs, lowered the car, and wheeled their jack away.

Welcome to Eisenhower Memorial.

This winter morning, with dawn having just made an appearance, there were no men stealing his tires. What there was instead, was a uniformed cop, slipping a ticket beneath the driver's-side windshield wiper. His cruiser was parked a few feet away.

"Hey!" Lou shouted as the cop turned to leave. "What's going on?"

The officer, strong-jawed with eyes deeply set beneath the shadow of his hat brim, tilted his head back to give Lou a curious look. "You're a doctor here?" he asked.

"Of course I am. We have our own security people. They don't give tickets."

"The hospital asked us to handle this. You haven't got a sticker. That means you get a ticket."

Lou's hopeful mood evaporated. "Nobody has a sticker, just look around."

"Well, they will."

"This is ridiculous."

"Look, pal, I don't make the laws, I just enforce them. This is just a notice, but now we have your license plate number. If you don't see the parking office and get a sticker, next time will be a twenty-five-dollar fine."

"This is totally ridiculous," Lou said.

The cop sheathed his ticket book like he was holstering a gun, climbed into the cruiser, and opened the window nearest Lou. "Have a great rest of your day," he said. "And make sure you look your ticket over carefully. It summarizes all the new regulations on the back."

The patrol car turned into an open row and then drove away.

Bryzinski, Lou was thinking. *This harassment must have something to do with that crooked cop.*

He slid the ticket out from beneath the wiper, brought it into the car, and turned on the interior light. One side looked like a standard orange ticket. On the other side was a note, printed in a heavy, masculine hand.

Dr. Lou Welcome,
You have to be very careful, but you also have
to trust somebody. You can trust me. The police
officer who gave you this ticket is a marine and
a good friend of Elias Colston and me. We want
to get to the truth about Elias's killer. If it is
Wyatt Brody, we will nail him and he will pay.
Meet me Tuesday at the following coordinates:
38.84783,-76.73744. Nine P.M. sharp. Stay
hidden beyond the wood line. You'll know
when I arrive.

Your friend,
Steve Papavassiliou
(Mark Colston's Papa Steve)

CHAPTER 29

You'll know when I arrive.

Creepy.

What in the hell had Papa Steve Papavassiliou meant by that? Judging from the way he had chosen to deliver his message, and the use of map coordinates to specify their meeting point, the man was either an inveterate game player or paranoid, possibly both. Even though Lou's life with Emily had turned him into a pretty good game player himself, he did not feel particularly trusting of Papavassiliou. Nevertheless, he had decided to play.

Not that surprisingly, a Web site allowing him to input the GPS coordinates pinpointed the ninth hole of a public golf course in Midwood, Virginia, twenty-five miles outside the district.

Creepy.

It was half past eight when Lou arrived at 38.84783,-76.73744. Sharpton Hills Golf Club was dark and completely deserted. He negotiated a steel pole security gate, concealed the Toyota behind a cart shack, and walked out onto the ninth fairway carrying a printout of the course layout. The night was cloudless and below freezing, and the ground blanketed with a thin layer of crunchy snow. Lou took up a position inside the nearby wood line and shivered away the cold.

The cloudless night and bright moonlight afforded him an unobstructed view of the par four ninth hole, and he wondered just how Papa Steve would make his dramatic arrival known. Too little snow for a dogsled. Just enough for cross-country skis. Too much for a golf cart. A snowmobile or ATV seemed the best bets. From his jacket pocket, Lou removed the folded-up parking violation and reread the first lines of Papa Steve's note.

You have to be very careful, but you also have to trust somebody. You can trust me.

Lou thought back to what Detective Chris Bryzinski had probably done, possibly in collusion with Spencer Hogarth.

You have to be very careful. . . .

Reassuring or not, Lou was intent on keeping Papavassiliou at arm's length until the man's agenda became clearer. He and Sarah had discussed the note by phone and agreed it would make sense for Lou to go through with the meeting, but cautiously. Later, they would decide how far Papavassiliou could be trusted.

Lou had spent an anxious day catching up on Physician Wellness work, including progress reports and an especially unpleasant hour with his boss, director Walter Filstrup, whose rant against alcoholism being an illness was especially annoying.

"I have your last dictation regarding Gary McHugh," Filstrup said. "Get this—your words: 'Physician 307 seems to be on automatic pilot. It has now been more than four years since his last drink or drug. Random weekly urines have been negative. I continue to be concerned about his lack of reliance on recovery meetings and other forms of support, but no one can question his resolve to keep his illness under control.' You really blew this one, Welcome. At least the man who had his illness under such good control is where he's supposed to be. Behind bars."

"Even alcoholics are human," Lou had replied, "just like most of the rest of you."

"Okay, Mr. Recovery, whatever you say. Meanwhile, McHugh's given this program a hell of a black eye, and by association, so have you."

"He didn't kill Colston."

"And I didn't have scrambled eggs for breakfast this morning. Why don't you go on back to work while you still have a job. If you run out of things to do, practice spelling *guilty.*"

"I'll do that, but McHugh is innocent. And, Walter?"

"Yes?"

"You've got some of those scrambled eggs on your tie."

Nine o'clock arrived accompanied by what felt like a ten-degree drop in temperature. No Papavassiliou. Lou pressed against a tree and said silent thanks for the replacement parka, watch cap, and gloves he had picked up at L.L. Bean. As each minute passed, he became more and more suspicious of a setup. What was Papavassiliou's connection with Brody? Did he have evidence that would exonerate McHugh? Were the Palace Guards approaching from the trees behind him?

Ten minutes passed. Time to leave. Cautiously, Lou stepped clear of the wood line. The landscape was as cold and desolate as the moon. Maybe something had happened. Maybe Brody had found out about the note and sent the Palace Guards to stop Papavassiliou. Questions. More questions. Lou turned and panned the woods. Nothing. Not a sound. He cursed himself for not bringing a flashlight.

At that moment, from the distance, he heard a faint machinery thrum. Half a minute later, he saw the powerful lights of a chopper—like an alien spacecraft cruising low across the rolling landscape. The small, single main rotor helicopter stopped twenty feet from the ground and dropped down right in front of him, just below the ninth green.

You'll know when I arrive.

Nicely put.

Lou shielded his eyes from the transient blizzard created by the rotor-generated winds. Quickly, the engine and light were cut off and the door to the small cabin opened. A tall, broad-shouldered figure jumped down, pulling up the fur-lined hood of his parka. Ten feet separated the two men when Papavassiliou pushed his hood back. Lou recognized him instantly. If he took off his jacket and rolled up his sleeves, Lou would

have seen faded tattoos on his powerful forearms—
one of a mushroom cloud explosion and the other of a
calligraphic rendering of the letters *TNT*. All at once,
the timely arrival of the police that night at the Mantis
headquarters no longer seemed like a fortunate coincidence. Steve Papavassiliou worked on the base, and it
was he who had saved Lou from Wyatt Brody.

Does that mean I can trust him? Lou wondered. *Or
was that an elaborate setup to earn my trust?*

"Told ya you'd know when I got here, Dr. Welcome."

"It's Lou," he said.

"Papa Steve will do for me. That's what comes from
being the age of most of the guys' daddies." He shook
hands with a grip that would have pressed garlic.

"Why the helicopter?" Lou asked.

"Guess the answer is the same as to why a dog licks
his genitals."

"Because he can," Lou responded.

"I've been flying whirlybirds for about as long as I
been blowin' things up. Got friends in the business, so I
borrowed one of their toys. Wyatt Brody is a head case.
A damn smart head case, but a head case nonetheless.
The men close to Brody are known around the base as
his Palace Guards. They are tough and skilled and willing to do most anything for him. We got to be really
careful. No matter how cautious I was, the guards could
follow me. At least on the ground or the water they
could. But no way could they could keep up with me in
the air."

"Why is Brody following you at all? What's going
on with him?"

"What's going on is I think Brody is the one who murdered Elias."

"You have proof?"

"Call it strong suspicion."

"Not one of the Palace Guards?"

"Possible, but I doubt Brody would give any of them control over him like that. He's all about keeping control to himself."

Lou peered through the darkness at the man. To this point at least, he liked what he saw. Still, trusting Chris Bryzinski with Colston's CD had cut him badly. "What can I do?" he asked.

"Brody's taken a liking to me since I moved over to Mantis, but he doesn't let anyone get too close. If he did kill Elias, I want to nail him, Lou. I want to nail him real bad. Elias and me have been through a lot together. I miss him. You can help me because that would mean helping your friend McHugh. It would also be payback for Hector."

"Payback?" Lou took a step back. He could feel his jaw tighten.

"Sorry. I should have reasoned out that you might not know yet. Searchers found his body late yesterday."

"Where?" Lou asked, swallowing against the lump that had materialized in his throat. Hector's death was as much on him as on the men who had killed him.

"They found him on a wild part of the base," Papa Steve said. "Word is he'd fallen off a cliff and broke his neck. Died instantly. Apparently, he'd been drinking, but the full toxicology report will take a few weeks. I heard they recovered an empty bottle of vodka near to where he landed. People think the guy was despondent about the rumor that he was going to get the boot from Mantis. Some people think he might have jumped."

"That's a lie," Lou snapped. "I was in the woods when guys he said were the Palace Guard tried to kill him and me. Hector was nowhere near the base. He wasn't drunk either. It's all a setup orchestrated by Wyatt Brody."

Papa Steve's eyes flashed. "You think I don't already know that?" he said. "Let's have a seat in the cockpit and talk where it's warm. We've got some things to discuss."

The interior of the helicopter was an aviator's dream, compact and loaded with high-tech gadgetry.

"When you defuse bombs for a living, you make a lot of friends in high places. I'm the guy you call when you don't know which wire to cut. I'm also the guy who rigs up the wires in the first place."

"I saw your tattoos that night at Mantis," Lou said. "I think you saved my life."

"So do I. I saw the ambulance bring you in. Hector and I are—were—pretty tight because he was my god-son's closest friend in Mantis. He asked if I thought he should meet with you. I told him I didn't see why not. The cops showed up because of the gunshots. I just led them to Brody."

Lou started wondering again about Papa Steve. Someone had to have told Brody about the meeting be-tween him and Hector. There was also the matter of the policeman delivering Papavassiliou's note to the doctors' parking lot. Clearly, Papa Steve had the man checking on him, maybe even following him.

"So what are we doing here?" Lou asked. "Now it seems we've got two killers to catch, Colston's and Hector's."

"We're after Wyatt Brody. He's all that matters. But we need to go at this very carefully, and I need to know that you're all-in. Brody has been up to something for years. I made a promise to Elias when I agreed to transfer to Mantis that I wouldn't bring anyone into the fold who isn't a thousand percent committed to finding out what that something is. And I haven't . . . until now."

"So you've been helping Colston investigate Brody?"

"That's the reason I transferred," Papa Steve said. "Colston wanted to shut down Mantis, not because his son died serving the unit, but because he felt, as did others in Congress, that the unit was redundant. The functions of Mantis could be integrated with the SEALs and other Special Forces outfits for better efficiency. I think you can guess that was not a popular idea with Wyatt Brody."

"What happened?"

"Brody had a vendetta against Colston because of the funding issues. He's promised to ruin him anyway he could. I think he just lost patience."

"He doesn't know about your connection with Colston?"

"Can't tell. You know the old adage, keep your friends close and your enemies closer. That may be what he's doing."

"Jesus," Lou murmured. "And you think what Elias was doing in Congress gave Brody enough motive to commit murder?"

"I think anybody who threatens Mantis is putting themselves in harm's way."

"Including you."

"And you," Papavassilious said.

Lou had theories of his own—connections between Brody's thesis on fear and Colston's interest in Reddy Creek—that he was not yet ready to share with Papa Steve.

"So, what have you found out?" Lou asked.

"Just that no matter how much funding Colston hacked from Mantis, Brody always has found a way around it."

"Maybe he ran out of tricks."

"That's what I think. Elias was squeezing too hard, and Brody finally decided to take him out."

"Where does that leave us, then?" Lou asked.

"I need something from you."

"What's that?"

"I've been following Dr. McHugh's case. I know of his lawyer's firm. They are famous for their in-house approach to explosives and ballistics. A friend of mine—one of the best in the connect-the-wires-and-watch-things-go-boom field—once got paid big bucks to give some lectures to the lawyers there. He said they were all brainiacs. You being friends with McHugh, I wondered if you knew his attorney, a woman named Cooper, Sarah Cooper."

"I know her," Lou said.

"Well, I need to see the ballistics report on the slugs that killed Elias."

"Why?"

"You saw Brody's gun collection, right?"

"It's an image I'm having a hard time forgetting."

"Well, I'm willing to bet that one of those weapons was used to kill my friend. I need that ballistics report to narrow down the choices, and I need it done quietly in case whatever weapon was used is still around."

The bullets. Lou wondered if this was the whole point of Papa Steve arranging this meeting. Maybe Papavassiliou was completely on the level, but maybe Brody wanted to know if he had anything to fear from the ballistics report, and he had asked Papa Steve to find out. It worried Lou to involve Sarah with anyone from Mantis.

"I'll see what I can do," he said, "but you're not going to be able to prove that Brody had the opportunity to kill Colston."

"Why is that?" Papa Steve asked.

"He told me he was at a Marine Day parade on the day Colston was murdered. People saw him leading Mantis into the stadium. They can prove he couldn't have been the shooter."

Papa Steve appeared unfazed. "I've been keeping an eye on Brody for several years," he said, "and I've seen things that contradict what Brody told you—a pattern."

"Pattern? What do you mean?"

"Brody leaves the base at the same time every single Wednesday. *Every single Wednesday.*"

"Where does he go?" Lou asked.

Papa Steve shook his head. "That I don't know. Wish I did," he said. "He's not easy to follow. The Palace Guards keep a close watch on him. But I do know he leaves to go someplace every Wednesday. He usually comes back after three or four hours."

"You were at the parade, weren't you?" Lou said.

Papa Steve smiled. "I wanted to see if Brody would disappear from the parade, too—you know, keep up with his pattern. He did. Walked out like he was headed to the bathroom. I followed him for a while, but the Palace Guards picked up my tail, so I had to back off. They've gotten in the way every time I've tried to follow him. What I do know is that Brody was headed west, toward Elias Colston's house. And that is irrefutable evidence, because I've got it all on videotape."

Lou quietly pondered the implications.

"What does that tell you?" Papa Steve asked.

"That he's a liar, but I already knew that. What now?"

"What now is that you get me the ballistics report and we take it from there."

CHAPTER 30

After two sets of woefully misleading directions from two locals, Sarah eased her rental car to a stop in front of the office of the *Belmore Current,* the newspaper Edith Harmon had taken over four years ago after fleeing North Carolina.

EASTERN MAINE AT YOUR FINGERTIPS, the sign over the front door proclaimed.

Sarah pulled on the door handle before realizing that the interior lights were shut off and the place was locked. *Damn.* She felt momentarily deflated. Then she noticed a small handwritten note secured to the door by a suction cup.

Gone to Laundromat. Be back soon.

In her experience, nearly every town, no matter what size, had at least one Laundromat. Belmore had the Caribou, located across the street from the office of the *Current.*

I might not be an investigative reporter, she thought,

but I have a pretty good idea where I'm going to find Cassie Wilkins, née Edith Harmon. Before heading there, she surveyed Edith's office through the glass front door. She had seen the inner workings of a newspaper before, but never one so small. Edith, it appeared, had a talent for economical use of space. Shelving units lining the walls were stacked with legal-sized boxes, all of them clearly labeled.

The printer sat atop a three-drawer filing cabinet, and a foldout table in the center of the room provided a work area for two of the smallest laptop computers Sarah had ever seen. The *Current* was at most a two-person operation, which truly surprised her. She had picked up a copy of the newspaper on her drive into town and been impressed by the depth and breadth of coverage. Edith Harmon, it would seem, was as good at writing and running a newspaper as she was at disappearing.

This is it, Edith, Sarah thought as she traded the chilly morning air for the humid heat of the Laundromat. *I've found you. Now, let's see what you have for me.*

The powerful odor of detergent hit her head-on, and reminded her of the piles of unwashed clothes she left back at her condo—a common occurrence anytime a major trial took over her life. There were two rows of stainless-steel washing machines, and double-stacked dryers of the same brand lined the walls. Sarah had not used a coin-op since her days at Princeton, back when there were gladiatorial battles for every available machine.

Looking around, she saw four people in the Laundromat, two of them under the age of five. The mother of the rambunctious boys playing peekaboo through the round glass door of a front loader was a heavyset woman decorated by a mural of tattoos on her thick, sleeveless arms. The other woman was folding clothes fresh from the dryer at the far end of the room. From behind, she was petite, with shoulder-length curly dark hair. She was dressed in jeans, worn Western boots, and a wool-blend bomber jacket that fit snugly to her slender body.

You've got to be Edith. I just hope you don't bolt when you learn why I'm here.

Finding this woman had proved to be no simple feat. As resourceful and connected as Grayson Devlin was, Sarah had given him precious little to go on—a no-longer-extant blog from years ago, and something about two Mantis soldiers killed during an apparent robbery attempt at the Reddy Creek Armory in Raleigh, North Carolina. She had found no news stories about any armory robbery, Reddy Creek or otherwise, and no other blogs that mentioned anything about the place.

As it turned out, what little Sarah had to go on was more than enough information for her boss. Sarah did some advance legwork before approaching him with her request for help. The mystery blogger, she concluded, had to have been an investigative reporter. There were three newspapers in the Raleigh area that would employ a reporter interested in a robbery at Reddy Creek—*News & Observer, Raleigh Downtowner,* and the *Metro.* Not surprisingly, Devlin had contacts at each. After less than two days, he called Sarah into his office.

Pay dirt.

"Her name is Edith Harmon," Devlin said. "She used to work for the *News and Observer.*"

Sarah's eyes brightened. "That's great news," she said. "Where is she at now?"

"She's dropped the Edith Harmon name and goes by Cassie Wilkins," Devlin said, glancing down at his notes. "She runs a small newspaper in Belmore, Maine."

"Why did she change her name and leave the paper in Raleigh?"

"Don't know. It wasn't easy getting the information I got from her editor."

Sarah shrank at the revelation. For Devlin to admit something did not come easily was significant. Years ago, he told her, Devlin and Rodgers had won a major libel suit that could have bankrupted the North Carolina newspaper. Edith's new identity and whereabouts were a closely guarded secret, and Devlin had given his promise that her confidentiality would be protected by Sarah.

"Meaning I'm expecting you to come back from Maine with something that's going to help us win the Gary McHugh case," he said.

Winning the McHugh case would more than make up in media coverage for whatever price Devlin had had to pay or whatever marker he'd had to call in to get information on Edith Harmon. Losing the case, however, would have just as powerful an effect in reverse.

Devlin had never threatened Sarah's future as a partner in the firm, but she had heard stories of others in the past who had been ignored to the point where they had wilted professionally and eventually resigned, and she knew that possibility was constantly looming.

"I'll do my best," she said.

It took every ounce of willpower to keep from telling Devlin what she really thought about the McHugh case—how his acquittal might be the tip of an iceberg that extended to the highest levels of government and a massive conspiracy that Edith Harmon might very well hold the key to unlocking. Until Sarah and Lou learned more, they agreed it would be best to keep the reveals to a minimum, even if that meant the potentially risky move of keeping Devlin in the dark.

Sarah's excitement at the prospect of finding Edith Harmon was tempered by one painful, nagging question.

Can I go back to coastal Maine? Can I really do it?

The question was an anvil over her head. As soon as her plane touched down at Bangor's airport, the heavy reality of the trip set in. Sarah knew returning to Maine would be emotional, but she was caught off guard by the intensity of her reaction. Twice, on her drive to Belmore, she found herself hyperventilating, and had to pull off to the side of the road and park until there were no more tears to cry.

Unexpectedly, Sarah's resolve to persevere came in part from Lou. Back in her office, she had referred to them as "we," and if her tenacity in the courtroom demonstrated anything about her, it was her unwillingness to disappoint a teammate. Lou was genuine and down to earth—a great mix of toughness and spirit. She felt determined not to let him down, even if it meant painfully reliving the magic days with David.

As she drove past the sign welcoming her to Belmore, thoughts of her last time in the state filled her mind. It was summertime then, and she and David were on one of their no-particular-place-to-go drives—David's name for their annual road trip.

Each July, they would pick a new state to visit, rent a car and sometimes bikes, and spend a week or two just driving around, meeting the locals, searching for the equivalent of Earth's Largest Ball of Twine, all while savoring every second of their stress-free time alone. These were designated nonworking vacations. Cell phones and laptops were verboten. The same went for any GPS. Map use required a unanimous vote.

Sarah had loved her road trips with David, but the drive through Maine proved especially poignant because it was the last one they ever took. Six months after the trip ended, David turned his head quickly to say good morning to her, and paralyzed himself from the upper neck down.

"Hey, sweetie—"

Snap.

Did she actually hear the spinal cord snapping as the ligaments cut through it, or was that just in her mind?

Snap. Snap.

Real or imagined, Sarah awoke to the sound in her head each and every morning since.

"David! David!"

She cried out his name over and over again. Her husband's only response had been to stare blankly up at the ceiling, wide-eyed and absolutely still.

David . . .

Though covered by a light dusting of snow, downtown Belmore was similar to several of the towns she and David had passed through. Beautifully restored redbrick buildings, none higher than three stories, mixed in with elegant old New England homes, funky antique stores, and an excellent selection of restaurants. Sarah took in a deep breath of cold sea air and felt every bit of its restorative powers. Of all their journeys, David had loved Maine the most.

Standing just inside the Laundromat, Sarah inhaled the detergent-laden air, then walked down the row of machines to the petite woman folding clothes. The husky, tattooed mother, a full basket in her hands, led her two kids out into the street.

"Cassie Wilkins?" Sarah asked.

Would you run if I called you Edith Harmon? she wondered.

The woman turned, catching Sarah a bit off guard because she did not expect her to be wearing dark, oversized sunglasses indoors on a December afternoon. She was in her late thirties or perhaps early forties, strikingly pale but pretty and feminine.

"Yes?" the woman said, not smiling. "Can I help you?"

Her lack of wariness was not surprising. She was, after all, the town's newspaper editor.

"My name is Sarah Cooper. I'm an attorney from Washington defending a man in a murder trial. I was hoping I might speak with you."

"About what?"

Sarah held her breath, then decided simply to go for it. "About Reddy Creek," she said.

Edith Harmon's jaw tightened. Even through her dark glasses, her eyes seemed to flash. Still, she made no attempt to check around to see if anyone could be overhearing them. In fact, they were now the only two in the place.

"I'm sorry, but I don't know what you're talking about," the woman said, under control.

"You're Edith Harmon," Sarah said. "It's important that I speak with you about Reddy Creek."

"I'm sorry, but—"

"Please," Sarah said in an urgent whisper. "I promise I'll keep your secret safe, whatever it is. An innocent man's life is at stake. I just need to know what you can contribute that will help me with my case."

"You want to know what I can contribute?" the woman said.

"Yes," Sarah replied, "that's all."

Angrily, the woman ripped off her sunglasses. Sarah reached her hand to her mouth and took a backward step. Edith Harmon's eyes were ringed by gruesome dark scars and grotesque indentations. Her milky gray eyes showed no trace of an iris or pupil.

"I think I've contributed enough," Edith said, unfolding the white cane Sarah had not seen resting beside her laundry basket. "I've contributed plenty."

CHAPTER 31

Edith slipped on her sunglasses and went back to folding her laundry as if nothing were happening. Perhaps she believed that tuning Sarah out would be enough for her to make the phantoms from her past simply disappear. Sarah stood several feet away, trying to figure out her next move, when she noticed safety pins attached to various articles of Edith's clothing. One pin seemed to designate blue, two for green, and three for white. Some of the clothes, Sarah now could see, had metal tags sewn into the fabric with what had to be Braille abbreviations for the other colors. Edith kept her socks together and organized using sock savers, a contraption Sarah had seen advertised on late-night infomercials.

"I'm no threat," Sarah said. "I'm not here to hurt you. I'm not going to tell anybody your secret."

No response.

"Please, talk to me, Edith."

Still nothing. Edith continued meticulously about her business.

Sarah continued searching for an opening—any opening.

"Do you use those pins to help you match your clothes?" she asked, suppressing an exasperated sigh.

Edith turned around and faced Sarah. "Well, now, Attorney Cooper," she said, "you just earned yourself a point."

"I did? For what?"

"In all the time you've been standing here, you never once said I'm sorry, despite that it was clear when you came in, you didn't know I was blind. I really detest pity."

Sarah laughed uncomfortably. "But . . . but how could you tell I didn't know?"

"For one thing, I heard your feet scrape against the floor when I took off my glasses. Shocked, you took a step backwards. Then the contents of your purse jangled about like you had made a sudden movement—another step backwards. It was quick. You were surprised by something unexpected."

"You're right, of course, but like it or not, I am sorry. And I want to know if your blindness is related to Reddy Creek. I want to know why you ran from North Carolina."

Edith folded a white blouse into four perfect creases. Her gaze never veered from Sarah's face. "I've been dreading someone would track me down," Edith said. "Were you followed?"

"No, I wasn't. I'm sure of it."

Even without vision to guide her, Edith looked unconvinced.

Sarah flashed on a psychology professor in college

who told her class that 75 percent of memory and thought came from sight. Where did the substitute come from when that 75 percent was lost or had never existed at all?

"If you found me," she said, "they can find me. Who was it? Who gave me up?"

A woman and little girl entered the Caribou Laundromat. Edith's head whirled toward the door before Sarah had even reacted to the sound.

"It's okay," Sarah said.

"I know. Thin mom, three-year-old daughter, both bundled up, wearing boots."

"Can we go somewhere and talk?" Sarah asked. "Please, I won't take up much of your time."

Edith scoffed. "No, you won't take up much of my time. You'll just come here and blow my world apart instead." With her finely shaped mouth tight, Edith tucked her laundry basket under one arm and used her free hand to flip her cane open.

"Please, talk to me. I need your help. A man's life is at stake."

"What about my life?" Edith breathed in deeply and exhaled slowly. Her body language softened. "Okay, you can come to my office. I'll give you ten minutes. I'm not promising to answer all or even any of your questions. But you're going to answer mine. Got it?"

"Ten minutes," Sarah repeated. "Thank you. Thank you so much."

She marveled at Edith's balancing act—how she maneuvered herself to the front door of the coin-op carrying a full laundry basket while working the cane.

Could I live without sight? She wondered. *Could I make it seem so natural?*

"You're wondering if you could go on if you lost your sight, and if you can help me with my basket," Edith said. "What did I tell you about pity?"

Sarah smiled at Edith's insight. "Can I at least hold the door open for you?"

"Well, now," Edith said, "that's not pity. That's just plain being polite."

Once outside, Edith found the curb with several practiced taps of her cane, and waited a few moments while listening for traffic sounds. Then she walked unhurriedly across the street, with Sarah several steps behind. Edith had a number of keys on her key ring, but she found the right one to unlock the *Current*'s front door without any fumbling, something Sarah rarely accomplished with any of the keys on her own set.

Inside the cramped office, Edith moved about like a woman with sight. She hung her jacket on the coat tree by the door and motioned Sarah to do the same. Then she stoked the low fire in a small woodstove, crossed to the microwave at the back of the room, took a box of tea from the shelf above, and filled two mugs with water from a small sink nearby.

"I have the steps memorized," Edith explained as if reading Sarah's thoughts.

"I was wondering about that," Sarah said. "And also that you seem quite fluent in Braille."

"Metsa metz. It's like moving to Italy with no chance of ever moving back. You learn Italian as quickly as possible, or you can forget about getting the toppings you want on your pizza. I was always pretty good at languages. Braille is just another one of them. I hope you don't mind decaffeinated tea. Caffeine makes me anxious."

"I'd love tea," Sarah said, "Any kind. No milk, no sweetener. But to be honest, I'm a little surprised you're not more anxious. I know my showing up here was quite a shock."

Edith pushed some buttons, and soon the microwave was heating up the two mugs of tea. "When you've lost your sight after thirty-six years of seeing," she said with her back to Sarah, "you tend to get kind of philosophical about things."

"How so?"

"There's absolutely nothing I can do about you having found me. Nothing that my getting angry or upset is going to change, anyway. But I can keep calm and level-headed, so at least I can listen carefully when you tell me how you managed to locate me and, more importantly, why."

Soon, the two women were seated at the foldout table in the center of the coffin-sized office, sipping at their tea. Sarah glanced over at Edith's computer and saw the attached keyboard was Braille compatible. She also noticed that all the tags attached to Edith's neatly stored legal boxes were labeled with Braille as well.

"What happened to your sight?" Sarah asked.

Edith held up a finger. "No, you first," she said. "How did you find me?"

Sarah told her about Grayson Devlin and his contact at Edith's former paper.

"Wow," Edith said. "Your boss must have some pretty serious dirt on Bruce."

"Bruce?"

"Bruce Patterson. He's the editor-in-chief at the *News and Observer,* my former boss, and the only person who knows my secret. Well, the only person besides you and your boss, I suppose."

"We haven't told anybody else," Sarah said.

Edith took a lengthy sip of tea, breathing in the steam and contemplating. "I have no place to go now," she said. "And I'm not leaving Belmore. Even if they do come after me, they'll never find my son."

"Son?"

"Yes, my son, Ian. He's the reason I ran," Edith said. "After they blinded me, I knew they were capable of anything, including using my son to get at me."

"So he's safe?" Sarah asked.

"Nobody knows his real name or where he lives. Not even Bruce. Ian's a college student now, but he was just fourteen when all this happened. I had him when I was twenty-two. His father was what you could generously call narcissistic and possessive. He didn't want anything to do with us as a family, he wanted me all to himself, so he panicked and took off before I gave birth. Ian and I did better as a duo anyway. He became everything his father wasn't. Although he wasn't living here, he encouraged me to learn how to see without eyes. Even helped me to stop feeling sorry for myself and learn Braille. Without him, I never would have had the confidence to take over this rag."

"Who did this?" Sarah asked. "What happened to you?"

"I don't know exactly. What I do know is that I was working on an investigative piece on the handling of weapons at the Reddy Creek Armory when a young soldier named Mike Fitz arranged a secret meeting with me, claiming no one would believe his story."

"What story?"

"According to him, two marines from Mantis Company—each had the tattoo of a mantis on his forearm above a ring of barbed wire—tried to rob the armory. Mike was on guard duty. There was a gunfight, and he shot and killed them both. His commanding officer took an extensive report, medical corps hauled away the bodies, and then everything disappeared. Somebody covered up the whole damn thing. The marines were reported as AWOL. The families put up a fight, but no one paid any attention."

Sarah's eyes widened and her hand went to her chest as she bit down on her bottom lip. She wondered if Edith could sense the tension in her face—the shock and surprise in her body language.

"Did this Mike know what they trying to steal?" Sara asked.

"Weapons, naturally. Only the weapons they were after made little sense to him. There were better weapons to take—larger, more sophisticated ones. But they left those alone. Why? They took assault rifles and some rocket-propelled grenades and ignored a clearly marked crate of Bushmaster ACR assault rifles—one of the absolute best weapons in the world. That was a big red flag for Mike."

"How so?"

"Because it meant they weren't looking, unless, of course, they were killed before they could get at the Bushmasters. It seemed they knew what they were after from the get-go. They knew exactly what weapons to take. They were doing what marines are trained to do."

"And what's that?" Sarah asked.

"They were following orders. These weren't a couple of lone wolves after a thrill. They were on a mission."

"How did they get inside the armory in the first place?"

"Good question," Edith said. "According to Mike, they couldn't have gotten in there without having access. There were no alarm wires cut. No automatic locks disengaged. Somebody arranged it. At least that's what he believed."

"An inside job," Sarah said.

"Exactly."

"Who is this Mike?"

"Was," Edith corrected.

"I'm sorry." Sarah looked confused.

Edith held up a finger, wagging it from side to side. "The word *sorry* is not in my lexicon, remember?"

"Got it," Sarah said, thinking how much she was growing to like this woman.

"I used the word *was*," Edith went on, "because my informant, Mike Fitz, is dead. He died when the car I was driving was forced off the road and over a cliff. He was in the passenger seat. His neck was broken and my face was so horribly smashed in that I lost my sight."

"You were forced off the road?" Incredulity strained the pitch of Sarah's voice.

"In retrospect, it was clear we were being followed," Edith said. "Whoever it was waited until we were on a particularly winding stretch of road before making their move. Three good sideswipes were all it took to force my car off the cliff. Of course, it was night and there were no witnesses, but I swear it was a military truck that hit us. From what I heard, as far as the police were concerned, I lost control of my car. I had no way of proving otherwise."

"But they took you to a hospital," Sarah said. "Wouldn't whoever was trying to kill you be able to find you there?"

"I was secretly transferred to another hospital."

"Secretly?"

"My boss Bruce is a man of great influence and boundless resources."

"Why would he put himself at risk for you?"

"Guilt," Edith said, wistfulness in her voice. "Bruce wouldn't run the story about Reddy Creek when I brought it to him. He insisted on more proof, but we didn't have a credible source. Still don't."

Sarah shook her head in disbelief. "I don't get it," she said. "You had Mike."

"Not exactly. After the cover-up at Reddy Creek— surprise, surprise—Mike was dishonorably discharged on a trumped-up charge. In a random urine screen, he tested positive for a large amount of cocaine. One hastily conducted court-martial later, and my informant had lost all credibility with my boss. Bruce wouldn't run the story. Not for anything. He thought Mike was just out for revenge and didn't believe there was any cover-up."

"Your blog," Sarah said. "You wrote the blog because you couldn't get your article published."

Edith removed her dark glasses again, displaying the scarring that marred what Sarah sensed might have once been very beautiful eyes.

"Guess I found a way of convincing Bruce that Mike was legit."

"So while you were being stonewalled by your boss, you and Mike went out on your own, didn't you?" Sarah asked. "That's why you were together. You were still investigating Reddy Creek."

Edith nodded. "How'd you know?" she asked.

"Because that's what I would have done."

"We were together because somebody wanted us to be," Edith said.

"Who?"

"We had a new informant, or so we thought. A marine contacted Mike anonymously. Said he had proof that Reddy Creek was an inside job. He wanted to meet in person."

"But it wasn't a real tip?"

"No, it was a setup, luring us onto the road where Mike was killed and—" For the first time, Edith was unable to continue.

"We can't let this go," Sarah said. "We've got to find out who did this to you and why."

"Let me ask you something," Edith was finally able to say, "why do you care so much?"

"Because Elias Colston, the congressman whom my client is in jail for allegedly murdering, was asking questions about Reddy Creek before he was killed. I suspect if we connect the dots, we'll find a link to whoever killed Mike and came close to killing you."

Edith stood quickly and turned her back to Sarah. "I'm afraid our ten minutes ended a while ago," she said softly.

Sarah stood as well. She came around front and took hold of Edith's slender wrists. The newspaper woman did not pull away.

"Please," Sarah said. "What happened to you is beyond horrible. I can't possibly imagine what you've gone through. But an innocent man is going to be sentenced to death for a crime he didn't commit. Nothing can be done to take back what happened to you, but you can still fight. You can still hurt these people. You can still help me get to the truth."

"Why me? I'm just a blind reporter from a small-town paper. You have the power of a major Washington law firm at your fingertips."

Sarah took hold of Edith's hands now. "No, I'd be blind if I thought I could do this without you. You know it, too. But if you feel you'd be putting Ian at risk in any way, just tell me, and I'm out of here. I mean it."

"No, he's with cousins. He has tremendous spirit. I risk Skyping him every couple of weeks. He's the one who's kept me going when I started coming apart. If he hadn't pushed it, I never would have learned Braille."

"He sounds wonderful."

"A little fresh at times, but I sort of like that. He also encouraged me to find a way to protect myself." She reached in the pocket of her cardigan and extracted a small pistol—a derringer, Sarah knew from her courses at the firm—with piggy-backed barrels and a jewel-inlaid handle. "A man in town taught me how to shoot this derringer Snake Slayer. Give me a noise, and I'll give you a hole. Wanna see?"

"No thanks, Edith. I believe you."

Edith broke into an intense smile.

"What?" Sarah asked.

"Ever since I was blinded, I've been waiting for two things to happen."

"Tell me."

"First, for my boy to grow up to the point where he can go out in the world and live his life."

"Sounds like that's happening," Sarah said. "So what's your second thing?"

"For my eyes to show up here in Maine so I can get some revenge on the bastards who did this to me. Sarah Cooper, will you be my eyes?"

"You know I will," Sarah said.

Edith dropped the derringer back into her pocket. "In that case, I have more to share with you."

CHAPTER 32

It was a Wednesday morning.

From the moment Steve Papavassiliou lifted off the frozen fairway of the Sharpton Hills Golf Club, Lou had been obsessed with finding out where Wyatt Brody was going nearly every Wednesday. Papa Steve claimed he had done what he could to follow the Mantis commander, but the Palace Guard, covering Brody's back, made it dangerous to the point of impossible. If Papavassiliou's suspicions were right, four Wednesdays ago, during a military parade, Brody had veered off his usual destination and shot Elias Colston to death.

Today, Lou's problem would be to keep Brody in sight without ending up in Palace Guard handcuffs again. From what Papa Steve reported, the guard returned to camp after an hour or so, leaving Brody to tend to his business alone.

Weather was no problem. Freezing or just above. Bright sky, scattered clouds. Patches of frozen snow. Lou's front-wheel-drive Toyota, though dependable, was not the best in the winter mountains. With memories of his deadly trip to Hayes never far from the surface, he had spent the night at a motel an hour east of the town. After a better-than-average mushroom and Swiss omelet, he had positioned himself down a cross street with his third cup of coffee, not far from the entrance to the road leading to camp.

Papa Steve had not been easy to read. It certainly seemed as if the two of them were on the same page, but Lou could not shake the notion that Mark Colston's godfather was holding some things back. His story, including the role of the Palace Guards in protecting Brody's Wednesday forays, had been persuasive. The man was confident and tough. He had stepped in when Lou needed it, and probably saved his life that night in Brody's office.

Lou wanted to believe the story of how Papa Steve lost Brody on the day of the Marine Day parade. Why not? He struck Lou as supremely competent. He was a guy who flew helicopters for fun while disarming bombs for a paycheck. It seemed that tailing Brody would be a piece of cake for a guy with his abilities. Was there any reason for him to lie? Lou struggled with the question. Was there something about Brody's Wednesday jaunts Papa Steve didn't want Lou to know?

Having made the decision to tail Brody, Lou turned to the source he knew he could trust for the best and most up-to-date information on how to do it. He turned to Google.

How to follow someone in a car.

Lou felt foolish at first, typing in the request, but that was before more than twenty-five million results were returned in about three tenths of a second. Lou clicked on the first link—a wikiHow article that listed eight tips for following somebody without getting caught. The tips were basic but helpful, starting with knowing precisely who you are going to follow. Seven more tips to go:

Stay alert and avoid distractions.

Use a crowd whenever possible.

Avoid sudden turns or quick moves.

Stay four to six car-lengths back.

Where more than one lane is available, stay in the one to the target's right—the less-used mirror side.

Keep a clear view of your target at all times. Don't give in to any distractions.

If you lose contact, don't give up. Become even more vigilant and keep going, checking convenience stores and gas stations in case your target has turned off.

The road from the Mantis base was two lanes wide, and it emptied into State Route 10, soft-shouldered and well paved. Lou's first problem might well be his worst: He had no idea what Brody might be driving. If he had stronger trust in Papa Steve, he would have asked. Probably he should have.

Too late now.

Nine forty-five . . . ten . . .

No Brody.

Traffic out of the base was light. Even without

knowing what Brody was driving, it was hard to believe he could miss the man and the Palace Guards backing him up.

Gradually, Lou's thoughts drifted to Sarah. Late yesterday, she had phoned from Belmore, Maine, having made contact with Edith Harmon. The reporter—who had tried to blow the whistle on the Reddy Creek shootings and ended up sacrificing her sight—sounded like an amazing woman, with every reason not to get involved in this case. But Lou was not at all surprised to learn that Sarah had convinced her to join their efforts to replace Gary McHugh with Wyatt Brody in a jail cell.

Sarah was continuing to pile up points in Lou's head like a pro basketball team. More and more, he found himself wondering what it would be like to spend time together—and more and more, he warned himself to keep his notorious impatience in check. Sarah hadn't kept her feelings toward him a secret when they first met, and he felt confident that when she had something more to say, he would hear it.

Again, Lou checked his watch. Five minutes past. He drummed his fingers on the steering wheel and kept his eyes locked on the access road.

Come on!

Ten fifteen came and went. Lou slumped down in his seat, defeated.

Why did you lie to me, Papa Steve? You were Elias Colston's best friend, Mark's godfather. What don't you want me to know?

At that moment, through the half-opened window,

Lou heard an approaching car. Seconds later, a glistening, silver BMW sedan came barreling out from the access road, and rocketed past, down Route 10. Behind the wheel, wearing aviator sunglasses, was Wyatt Brody. Lou put his Toyota in gear, and suddenly realized he was about to violate the main tip for successful tailing. He was about to lose his target. The BMW was already accelerating south, and in seconds would be out of sight. To Lou's left, there was no sign of the Palace Guards.

He kept his foot jammed tightly on the brake pedal. Five seconds more, he decided, glancing at the now-empty highway to his right. Four . . . three . . .

The roar of a truck engine filled the air, and a military Range Rover with two men in the front rumbled out of the access road. Both men wore sunglasses similar to Brody's, and one of them was speaking into a two-way.

Clearly these guys knew what they were doing. Lou was outmatched, and was lucky to have gotten this far. He grinned at the notion that the Palace Guards might have read the same Web sites as he had, then waited until the Rover had disappeared after Brody, and pulled out onto Route 10, checking to his left to be sure he wasn't about to be sandwiched between the Rover and yet a second car. The chase was on. He adjusted his target from Wyatt Brody to the Palace Guards and stayed six car-lengths back.

Piece of cake.

Gradually, traffic increased, and Lou risked a calming breath. The military SUV was easy to spot.

He could do this.

Stay alert and avoid distractions.

Half an hour passed. They were going fifty-five now. Route 10 had expanded into four lanes. Following tip three, Lou shifted to the right one. The Range Rover was a reasonable distance ahead, but Brody's silver BMW was nowhere. That was when Lou saw the blue strobes flashing in his rearview mirror. A Statie!

Fuck!

Thirty minutes on the road, and the game was already over.

Lou slowed, signaled right, and began searching for a place to pull over. There was still the chance that the trooper would flick on his siren and zoom past, but Lou knew in a second that wasn't going to happen. For years, he had meant to change to MD plates—not because he wanted protection against getting a ticket while making a house call, but because he wanted people to see that not all docs drove a Mercedes or Lexus. Now it was too late.

The entry to a small strip mall provided a safe landing area. As always when he was stopped, Lou debated whether he'd be better leaping out to meet the trooper halfway or whether he should slouch meekly, license and registration in hand, and wait.

Well, Officer, I was following the man I believe murdered Congressman Colston. No, not the philandering doctor, but the highly decorated marine colonel. I was going exactly as fast as he was, but I guess I'm the one who got caught.

Lou tried out the truth, rejected it, and was searching for a substitute when he was asked for the usual documents.

None of your witty repartee, he warned himself. In his less mature days, he often managed to convert a minor traffic encounter into a trip to the station. The trooper, an impressively buxom white woman with a pretty enough face, probably would have looked sexy-tough in any garb, but she looked especially so in the black-tie, broad-brimmed hat, and stately olive of the West Virginia State Police. She spent a few minutes in her cruiser checking him out, then returned bearing papers. Four words, "License and registration, please," were all she had spoken. Now she added a few more. Quite a few.

"You're not in line to make the drivers' hall of fame, Doc."

"I thought I was doing pretty well."

"What kind of doctor are you?"

Easy . . .

"Trade. I'll tell you if you tell me what I was doing wrong."

"You changed lanes without signaling. We frown on that in West Virginia."

Damn. So much for wikiHow tips.

"I'm an emergency doc in D.C. Eisenhower Memorial. I promise you, I always signal when I change surgical instruments."

"That's funny. Lucky for you I like funny. Well, Doc, this is your lucky day twice over. Believe it or not, but you might have saved my mother's life last year. Somebody in your ER did. She had a coronary while she was on a Silver Belles bus tour of D.C. Needed to get a shock in the ER for fibrillation. I don't remember if I ever knew the name of the doctor who gave it to her, but the people at the hospital told me it saved her life."

"Were they able to get a stent in her?"

"Two."

"And she's doing okay now?"

"She's doing terrific. That was very nice of you to ask."

"I would have asked even if you weren't about to add a bunch of points to my insurance record."

"Well, because you're a nice guy and you asked about my mom, and you might have saved her life, I'm just giving you a warning. Also because you're not one of those pompous doctors with MD plates."

"Thank you, Officer."

"Lemon. Judy Lemon. Here's my card, in case you find yourself in these parts again." She fished one out from what seemed like a stack of fifty. "Also, you might want to slow down. You were five mph away from getting nailed for that."

"You got it, Officer Judy. Slow."

Now, just leave me alone.

"No sense in speeding, either. There's a mile backup ahead. Construction."

Lou felt his pulse jump. A mile backup. His brain began working through the possibilities. At that moment, he glanced across the road in time to see the Mantis Range Rover approaching from the other direction, headed back toward Hayes. No silver BMW in sight.

Had the king separated from his Palace Guards?

Cautious not to go too far overboard, Lou put himself into modest flirt mode. "Listen, Officer Judy, it's not the best of circumstances, but I really do appreciate just getting a warning."

"You're welcome."

"You were just doing your job."

"Sounds like there's something more you'd like to say." Her smile oozed pheromones.

"With that construction you told me about, getting stopped has made me hopelessly late for an appointment."

"So?"

"How about another trade: If you could guide me past the holdup, I promise you dinner at the restaurant of your choice. Believe me, I'm good for it and I'm good, period—especially if I get the position I'm interviewing for."

The trooper gave Lou's offer some thought—perhaps a nanosecond's worth. "You know what they say about scorning a woman with a gun," she said, playfully patting her hip.

"I don't know, actually, but I think I can guess. No scorning. Promise."

"I like steak."

"You got it. The biggest, juiciest one in the county."

"Deal. Follow me, cowboy."

Lou thought he saw a skip in her step as Officer Lemon hurried back to her cruiser. He wondered how many business cards would be left in her stack by the end of her shift. No matter. It seemed fairly certain that this scenario was not among any of the twenty-five million hits in Google.

Judy Lemon's blue strobes flashed on, and in ten minutes they were an odd, two-car caravan, cruising in the breakdown lane past a long, frustrated line of slowly moving motorists. After half a mile, Lou spotted the silver Bimmer, pulled on his faded Redskins cap, and slouched down in his seat until he was peering between the bottom of his steering wheel and the top of the dash. Clearly, Brody felt the backup tail from the Palace Guards was no longer necessary.

A quarter of a mile past the construction, Lou slowed, pulled off the road, and gave Officer Judy Lemon a thumbs-up and a good-bye wave. Fifteen minutes later, Wyatt Brody sped past. His jaw set with anger, he was paying no attention to anything other than the road ahead.

Traditionally, Lou's Camry could handle seventy before it began to shimmy. Brody was hitting seventy-five. Lou did what he could to maintain both distance and contact, but it was a struggle. He thought about the irony of having Brody get pulled over by Judy Lemon, but it wasn't to be. Instead, he caught a glimpse of brake lights and a flash of sun on silver as the Mantis commander turned hard left, following a sign toward Billingham.

With one car between them, they headed west, parallel to a swell of foothills. Eventually, the wooded landscape gave way to a more industrialized section of Billingham. Auto repair shops lined both sides of the road, tucked between a few fast-food joints and a number of warehouses, many of them corrugated steel. Brody's Bimmer signaled to make a left turn, and Lou slowed to watch the car glide into the parking lot of a large self-storage facility.

Lou got a fix on the unit Brody was interested in, and kept his distance. The outdoor facility was divided into rows, with garage-sized storage structures on either side. Lou guessed there were fifty or so on the premises, each of them featuring a green roll-up door.

He cruised down the access road parallel to the one Brody had taken, then shifted to Park and moved ahead on foot. He was in adrenaline-fueled, high-level, ER mode now, and he loved the tension. Ambulances were on their way in with multiple victims from a major crunch. Keyed up and ready for anything, he worked his way along the side of the last storage unit in the row, inching closer and closer to the corner.

The silver BMW, without a driver, stood idling beside an open storage door. Moments later, a white, windowless panel truck—maybe seventeen feet, no markings—backed out. Brody, looking calmer and more energized than he had when leaving the construction site, pulled the truck over and replaced it in the garage with his Bimmer. Then he used a pull-cord to lower the door and replaced the heavy padlock.

Lou raced back to the Toyota and waited until he heard Brody accelerate. Then he shifted into Drive, inched into the open, waited for a battered pickup to insert itself between him and the van, and followed.

CHAPTER 33

The ride south would have been quite beautiful had Lou taken more than a few seconds at a time to appreciate it. The Monongahela Mountains seemed to be constantly shifting against the pale early-afternoon sun. The road was winding, and he was forced to stay closer to Brody's van than he would have liked. On one narrow stretch, the side of Lou's Camry barely avoided a huge, jagged rock. Lou had been following the man for almost two hours. It seemed more as if the Mantis commander was on a schedule than in any particular rush.

A gas station would have been an oasis here. There were no cars to provide any sort of camouflage, and Lou had to back way off his tail. His initial adrenaline rush was gone, replaced by the tension of losing the white van at any turn or, even worse, of being spotted.

He was considering simply taking his chances by speeding up, when he eased around a sharp bend and spotted Brody's truck several hundred yards ahead. The brake lights were on, and seconds later, the van turned right. As soon as it was out of sight, Lou accelerated. The road, if it could be called such, was an unmarked path cut into the woods—twin ruts that ran upward along the side of a foothill. The frozen snow, an inch or so of it, was much more of a problem for the Camry than it probably was for the truck.

Violent jolts from rocks and holes snapped Lou's teeth together more than once. The Toyota skidded sideways in places and completely lost traction in others. A quarter of a mile . . . half. Lou was forced to slow. Then, just as he seemed to have regained control, he veered off the rutted road entirely and slid down an embankment to a parallel pathway on the right—this one actually more navigable than the one Brody was on. It occurred to him that the best he might be able to hope for was leaving the Camry and walking out of the forest. Then he got a break.

Looking upward and to his left, he saw the van brake and then stop in something of a clearing, perhaps a hundred yards ahead.

Cautiously, Lou backed up until the road he was on flattened and widened for a brief stretch. Backing all the way out to the highway or even turning around were now possibilities. In fact, there was enough room behind a huge boulder to pull his car over to the side of the road and conceal it. He opened his door, cringing at the creaks, and eased out into the chilly mountain air. From above and to the left, he could hear that Brody was keeping the truck idling. It appeared he was still behind the wheel.

Lou decided to chance the slope to his right. If he

could get high enough, he would be looking down on the van. Pulling himself up by icy tree trunks and rocks, it did not take long for his hands to go numb. Twice he slipped, sliding several feet down on his stomach. It seemed certain that only the reverberating engine noise kept him from being discovered. Twenty-five feet above the van, Lou was able to crawl out onto a rocky bluff that featured enough brush for some concealment. He breathed into the sleeve of his parka and waited.

Five minutes and he heard the rumble of an approaching vehicle. He briefly lamented not having brought binoculars, but gave himself a pass. A second van, identical to Brody's, jounced down the hill and skidded to a stop almost nose to nose with the van. From his vantage spot, Lou could just make out his Toyota on the road below and fifty yards behind the two trucks.

The doors to the new arrival flew open, and two men stepped out. Moments later, the back of the truck creaked open and three more men emerged, dressed for the cold. All were olive-skinned, with either shaved heads or thick waves of ebony hair. Latinos. Maybe Mexicans. Brody climbed out of his truck. One of the men saluted him.

"Manolo," Brody said, his voice carrying clearly to Lou.

The other four arrivals circled to the back of Brody's panel truck and pulled the doors open. Lou noted the lack of small talk. The moves were practiced, choreographed, business. Made perfect sense, he thought. If

Brody made this drive nearly every Wednesday, they'd done this dance many times before. Two of the men jumped up into the back of the truck, while two others positioned themselves to receive the cargo within. Brody stood silently beside the man named Manolo: heavyset with a carefully waxed handlebar mustache and a thick neck featuring 360 degrees of tattoos. Lou sensed what the crew were offloading even before he saw one of the wooden cases pried open.

Guns. Sophisticated military weapons, and lots of them.

Brody stood a few paces away as Manolo inspected the cargo.

"These are good," he said to Brody, hefting one of the rifles. "Very good. Our people in Juárez will be pleased, amigo. All M4s?"

"Easier to get now that we've scaled back in Afghanistan."

Brody spoke mostly English, but used fluent Spanish when he had a mind to. Lou was never a Spanish scholar in school, but he could still handle the simple stuff. He held his breath and stayed low.

Hello, Reddy Creek, he was thinking, mentally dropping one piece of the Brody puzzle into place. Brody ponies up sophisticated weapons to a Juárez cartel in exchange for . . . for what?

Soon after the weapons inspection concluded, Lou got an answer—at least a partial one. Manolo signaled to one of his men, who opened the rear of the second panel truck and lugged out a huge cooler. Then another.

As Lou watched from above, transfixed, Manolo set

one of the coolers on the ground at Brody's feet and opened the top. White vapor from dry ice billowed upward.

"This is the best batch we've cooked yet," Manolo said, extracting one of what looked like a number of large plastic freezer bags. "Seven hundred capsules per bag, Señor Colonel. Counted and recounted. Filling the capsules and counting them took my men many hours."

"I've told your boss over and over again," Brody growled in English, "don't screw with the formula."

Formula . . . Lou tensed.

"We make it better," Manolo said.

He whistled loudly using two fingers, and a man, thin as the leafless branches overhead, approached.

"Sí?"

This time, Lou could only ferret out a few words—one of them, *Pedro.*

Brody brought a thermos from the passenger seat of his van and poured a clear red liquid into a small plastic cup.

"Why don't you want to tell me what that drink is?" Manolo asked.

"Do you tell your wife the name of your mistress?" Brody responded. "It is enough for you to know that what you make for me does not work properly without what my other source makes for me. It is better that way, *sí*?"

"I suppose so. My wife and my mistress. I like that one, Señor Colonel."

The man, Pedro, took the cup of crimson liquid, studied it for a few seconds, and then swallowed it in one gulp along with the capsule.

Manolo checked his watch. "Give five minutes to have an effect," he said to Brody.

"How long has this man been taking the formula?" Brody asked.

"A month, more or less. Every day."

"Give it fifteen minutes at least. I can wait."

"I told you, this stuff is good."

Manolo went to the front seat of his truck and brought back what Lou thought might be a portable electrocardiogram machine. Pedro unzipped his jacket and unbuttoned his work shirt, exposing his bare chest to the elements without the slightest trace of discomfort. As Manolo pasted on several electrodes to Pedro's chest, the rest of the crew formed a tight perimeter to watch. Pedro's stoniness did not come as a surprise to Lou. Even without a drug in his system, the man seemed the sort who could wolf down a breakfast of nails and glass without so much as an orange juice chaser.

Manolo gave Brody the cardiogram machine to hold. "You'll see how good, amigo," he said. "You'll see."

Pressed onto the leaf- and snow-coated ground, Lou watched from above as Manolo pulled a huge revolver from the waistband of his pants. He chambered a round and made it a point of showing Brody the weapon now was loaded with a single bullet. Then he flicked his wrist and locked the cylinder back in place. Finally, dramatically, he spun the cylinder fast enough to make the sound of a whirling roulette wheel.

Then he handed the gun to Pedro.

Lou did not need his Spanish to interpret Manolo's instructions.

The younger man stared off into the distance as calm as if he were bird-watching, and slid the muzzle of the weapon deeply into his mouth. The crew around him were shouting words of encouragement. Brody seemed to care only about the readout on the cardiograph. Lou sucked in a breath and held it, stunned by the barbarity of what he was witnessing. Every fiber demanded he try to stop the madness. But he knew better. Pedro shouted something from his throat and, with no more preparation than that, pulled the trigger.

Click.

Empty chamber.

Lou silently released his breath.

Smiling, Pedro handed the gun to Brody who, making no eye contact, fired at a tree twice before a shot rang out and splintered wood. Then he handed Pedro an envelope, passed the revolver to Manolo, and continued studying the machine.

"Unbelievable," he said. "This reaction time is spectacular. What did you guys do?"

"Like I said, Señor Colonel, we made it better," Manolo said. "Better, purer ingredients."

"The meth?"

"New cook. New recipe."

Brody simply nodded.

The transfer continued in silence. The man, Pedro, who had cheated death, went right back to offloading weapons. Brody returned the plastic bag to the dry ice and checked to be certain the coolers were secure in his van. Then, without another word, he climbed into the cab of his truck, reversed direction, and headed down toward the highway. Lou had no chance to follow, but he had learned most of what he needed to—except who these men were, and where they were headquartered. Manolo, the mustachioed leader of the group, turned his truck around without difficulty and headed back up the mountain.

Lou remained crouched on the bluff until the engine noise had been replaced by a heavy silence. Then he clambered down to where the exchange had taken place and cautiously began following the van tracks uphill. The sun was beginning its descent, but the midafternoon chill was tolerable.

Guns for drugs.

Mantis and some sort of Mexican cartel.

Was this the knowledge that had gotten Elias Colston killed? Was there more?

Lou had his suspicions about how Brody was using his portion of the deal, but at this point nothing was certain, including the role of the secretary of defense.

About thirty minutes up the hill, the woods thickened and the snowpack became deeper. Achy and chilled, Lou trudged ahead, sticking to the edge of the road and keeping a sharp eye out for guards. A clearing up ahead drew his attention. Sunlight, peeking out from behind a cloud, cast a spotlight on a dilapidated-looking structure.

The ramshackle building, a drug cartel version of a still, Lou guessed, was made of corrugated steel and framed with rough wooden beams. It seemed to have more chimneys and smokestacks than it did windows. White smoke, thick and heavy with the pungent odor of ammonia, wafted out from the stacks and stung Lou's lungs. The white truck was parked to the right of the building, alongside a gray SUV—possibly a Honda. Pedro and three others from the weapons exchange were taking guns from the back of the truck and carrying them around to the other side of the still. Lou watched from behind the trunk of a large pine.

Drugs for guns.

Some sort of super amphetamine for M4s.

A classic barter, no more elegant than a quart of moonshine for a Colt .45 in the Old West. Manolo emerged from inside the still and peeled off a paper surgical mask. This time, however, he was not alone. Leashed to his wrist was the largest German shepherd Lou had ever seen. The dog's keen ears were bent back. Its eyes seemed to be focused on the air itself. Lou watched the animal's nostrils flare and its head dart about.

Oh shit! he thought.

Was the dog's arrival on the scene coincidence, or did they suspect something?

Manolo rattled off some Spanish. Then he started to walk down the road toward Lou—a leisurely stroll, just exercising his dog, or so it seemed. But the shepherd resisted. Manolo took four steps, and the dog dug in its heels. Its lips peeled back in an angry snarl. A growl, low and threatening as thunder, echoed off the trees. Then its eyes locked on a target and the growl turned into angry barking. Its jaws began snapping in a way that begged for flesh to tear. Its open mouth, dripping with saliva, showcased a finely sharpened set of white daggers. Lou traced the dog's line of sight and felt a wave of heat roll up his back.

The animal was looking right at the tree where he was hiding.

CHAPTER 34

The huge German shepherd continued snarling and straining at his leash.

"What's happening?" one of the gang asked.

"I don't know. He's in a very bad mood."

"Matador's always in a bad mood. Maybe he smells something—a rabbit or a rat. Pedro probably left the lid off the trash again."

Matador. The name meant "bullfighter," but it also meant "killer."

Lou's mouth went dry.

Thirty yards away, he flattened himself against the pine. He was never much more than a B student in Spanish, and he was doing about C-plus work translating now. But for whatever reason, he knew Matador.

Manolo battled to keep the shepherd in line, and began scanning the woods for the source of the animal's angst.

It would not be long before he discovered the answer.

Despite the chill surrounding him, Lou was sweating. Matador had downshifted to a low, rumbling growl, as if he had decided to conserve energy for what lay ahead. Lou remained concealed, desperately playing through scenarios of escape, and finding none that had any promise. He thought he heard Manolo say the word *ardilla*, and hoped he remembered it as "squirrel" or "chipmunk," and not "dinner." The dog's constant growling sparked in Lou a deep-seated fear, possibly from a scare in his childhood.

Lou silently added "mauled by an animal" to his list of horrible ways to die. The shepherd's teeth were designed to latch on to flesh and tear it away one agonizing bite at a time. Lou imagined the terror of pushing haplessly against the powerful animal's salivating snout, while its jaws bore into his gut, drilling him hollow. The image came to him so visceral, so real, that he swallowed at an imaginary copper taste of blood percolating in the back of his throat.

Matador.

Lou kept his body rigid, trying to will some control over his ragged breaths and scattered thoughts. *Breathe in through the nose . . . out through the mouth, just like I'm in the ring, just like sparring . . . in through the nose, out through the mouth.* The gospel according to Cap Duncan.

Lou thought about Emily. All his focus should have been on escaping, but that was the thing about having a kid. He thought about how his death would impact her. Would anybody even find his body? Probably not. Manolo and the crew would bury him in pieces somewhere in the woods, torch his car, and then *voilà*, gone. Missing person, whereabouts unknown. Posters would be circulated. Search teams would be organized, maybe even a modest reward offered. Officer Judy Lemon would tell the Staties all that she remembered of the man who, just yesterday, it seemed, changed lanes improperly. Manolo and the Juárez cartel would dismantle the lab and rebuild it many miles away. The end.

The growling intensified again.

You cannot die up here in the woods. You cannot let it happen.

Lou's controlled breathing began having a positive effect. His thoughts became more logical and focused, although none of them carried hope. He could try to crawl backwards and take a new position farther down the road, but he'd be exposed between trees. He had no idea how sharp Matador was—how little movement and shift of smell it would take for him to go into attack mode. At the moment, he was a decent distance away, but if Lou simply bolted, the dog would close the gap in seconds. Game over.

Then, as if reacting to Lou's unspoken prayer, Manolo tied the snarling animal to a post and went around to the back of the still, possibly to check on the guns. Lou backed up carefully and, amidst a renewed crescendo of barking, added ten more yards to the distance between him and death. A couple of more moves like that, and he would make a break for the Camry.

Again, the barking dipped to a simmer. The dog's back stayed arched, its keen eyes constantly probing, like a marine on patrol. Lou hunched over and took another precious ten yards. Then another. Manolo had returned and again took Matador's leash. He tugged hard, but the mammoth dog strained in the opposite direction. Lou seized the distraction and raced to another tree. Killer, possibly hearing the rustling of fallen leaves or smelling the fear thickening the air, snapped his head around. Manolo, consumed by winning his power struggle with the beast, yanked on Matador's leash, trying to force the dog to heel.

Lou could see the smoke but not the lab. He dropped to his butt and eased down the mountain. In retrospect, it had been stupid to try to check out the still, but he had done stupid before, though perhaps not with these consequences. The rocks tore through his jeans and left painful scrapes on his legs. He could still hear excited barking, but could not tell if the sounds were getting any closer. Finally, he risked pulling himself to his feet.

Almost there.

He made it another fifteen minutes and thought by now he'd gone far enough so the dog would be out of earshot. A volley of barking said he wasn't. The slope had steepened, and the temperature was dropping. Ice was now a problem. An all-out sprint to the car might work, but it also might well result in a sprained ankle or, worse, a broken one.

Lou eased around the clearing where the guns-for-drugs exchange had taken place. Maybe seventy-five yards to go. The time for caution was over. He began to trot down the steep embankment toward the boulder where he had concealed the Toyota. Then, from up the hill, he heard the sound of crunching ice and leaves, followed by an intense growl. Spinning around, Lou saw Matador streaking across the ridge above him, dragging his leash.

His heart threatening to explode, Lou broke into a chaotic sprint. His feet skidded on the ice-slickened slope, slowing his steps.

Careful . . . careful.

Ahead he saw a glimmer of red—the front of his car—poking out from behind the boulder. Behind him, no more than fifty feet away, the streaking brown missile intent on tearing him to pieces was locked in and headed down the embankment. His teeth were bared. Saliva hung down from his snout like streamers.

Lou glanced ahead at his car and did some quick math. Twenty or thirty feet to the driver's-side door, plus two seconds to get inside, equaled dead. No question about it. He imagined the beast launching itself at him from behind, knocking him face-first to the ground, then going at his neck.

It wasn't going to happen—not without some sort of response. Could he make it onto the roof of the car? What would happen then? How about over the roof and in the passenger-side door? The images flashed through his mind like a passing bullet train.

From behind, the snarling grew louder—closer.

Then Lou tripped.

The villain was a partially buried root, thick as a fist. Lou fell heavily, air exploding from his lungs. His face slammed against the frozen ground, dazing him. Still, he managed to roll to his back. It was a complete surprise at that moment to realize his hand was wrapped around a dead branch—four feet long, heavy, leafless, and gnarled as an arthritic limb.

He was scrambling to his feet when the blurred outline of Matador came into sharp focus—ten feet away and about to go airborne. Instinctively, operating on rubbery knees, Lou turned sideways and gripped the end of the branch with both hands. Between blinks, he flashed on a memory, processing it as fast any computer.

He was twelve years old, playing Little League baseball. Always a decent fielder, he was doomed in the sport by his inability to hit. The bases were loaded with two outs in a tie game. His team, the Dodgers, needed just one run to win the league championship. The resulting scene would stay with him forever—teammates charging the mound, all laughing, high-fiving, piling on one another. Just one hit. God, but he wanted it so badly. Three pitches, three swings, three strikes. Nobody from the Dodgers did any celebrating that day.

The shepherd was crazed. Its jaws were wide open; its fangs, dripping with saliva. In moments, its mouth would be red with blood, his blood. Lou tightened his grip on the branch and forced himself to focus on the animal's maw. Then, with a step forward, he swung from his heels. One hit . . . just one. The impact was ferocious. The dog's momentum knocked Lou backwards onto the ground. But Matador was stunned as well, and went down heavily at Lou's feet, yelping plaintively while trying to right himself.

Without a glance at matador, Lou sprinted the remaining five yards to the car, climbed into the driver's seat, slammed the door, and fumbled his key into the ignition. At that instant he felt the weight of the car shift forward. Through the front windshield, Matador stood on the hood, snarling. The corners of his mouth were torn and bleeding, but his teeth were still bared. He forced his muzzle against the windshield, leaving bubbly trails of saliva and blood. Lou turned the key and slammed the gearshift into Reverse.

The shepherd stayed on the hood for as long as he could—a surfer determined to ride his wave all the way to shore. Finally, he jumped off, landing on his feet. Lou backed down the road. Manolo and his mammoth six-shooter had to be close by.

As he backed onto the highway, his thoughts were consumed by Wyatt Brody's doctoral thesis, and the odd lack of a strong discussion and conclusion. The exchange Lou had just witnessed was proof that his research had not only succeeded, but was also being used on Mantis servicemen. But to what end? Lou wondered as he accelerated north. To what end?

CHAPTER 35

Wyatt Brody strode into the packed dining hall. Seven hundred marines—many of them decorated for valor, some of them more than once—remained seated along Spartan wooden benches. Set out on the long folding table in front of each of them was a seven-ounce plastic tumbler filled halfway with a clear, crimson liquid. Next to each tumbler was a capsule, also crimson. Pale light from the early dawn filtered into the dining hall. The daily ritual had begun.

Major Charles Coon followed close behind Brody. "Attention!" he called out as soon as they reached the center of their table.

The sound of benches scraping back echoed through the hall as the soldiers of Mantis rose to their feet, a forest of the bravest, most skillful fighters the military had to offer. Brody scanned the room, taking in the scene as though he were appreciating fine art.

The men, most of them preparing in small groups for clandestine missions around the globe, were waiting for Brody's selection for the morning presentation.

The honor was not doled out lightly. Typically, Brody or Coon or one of the other officers led the men, but at times an enlisted man who strongly embodied the principles of Mantis would be selected for the privilege. In truth, almost all of them were eligible. The seven hundred remained at attention and waited.

"Staff Sergeant Bucky Townsend!" Brody called out.

Townsend, already stiff as a corpse, forced himself to stand even straighter. "Sir! Staff Sergeant Bucky Townsend, present and at attention, sir!" he shouted.

Nobody looked at Bucky. All eyes stayed forward, locked on Brody as though he were the only living presence among them.

"Staff Sergeant Townsend."

"Sir, yes, sir!" Townsend remained outwardly emotionless and still as stone, even though it was the first time he had been chosen.

"Come forward to present."

Townsend stood beside Brody and saluted, his arm at perfect angles. *I am Mantis.*

"My brothers," Townsend said, "glasses up."

Moving as a single entity, each man held a capsule in one hand and his drink in the other.

"Crimson is the color of courage," they said in perfect unison, "the color of blood spilled in battle, the color of valor. To justice. To country. To God. To Mantis. Whatever it takes!"

Then, as one with their commanding officers, each set the capsule on his tongue and drained the symbol of their collective strength and bravery. They were Mantis, a brotherhood bound by the power of the crimson liquid.

When breakfast ended, Brody once again stood at his place to address the men. Glancing down at a clipboard, he read a list of twenty names—the tactical team of Operation Talon.

"If your name was read, we will convene in the briefing room immediately," Coon said.

"Sir, yes, sir," the twenty responded.

The briefing room was situated inside a crude wooden building about the size of a one-room schoolhouse, only a short walk from the dining hall. There were maps, projection machines, and several computers. The room was kept warm by portable heaters. Coon stood at the front, with Brody seated at a desk to his right.

"Gentlemen," Coon began, "you have each had a preliminary briefing on Operation Talon. You are the tactical team, the men who will be feet on the ground. Behind you in support will be dozens of your Mantis brothers. The success of this ambitious mission rests in your hands. From now on, this building and the equipment within it will continue to be at your disposal, but the door will be locked to all except you. The keys are in the envelopes at your desks. I would suggest you spend all your waking hours studying. The time for fun and games is over."

"We will be studying, sir," Townsend said, "but as this is the first time we're all together, could you review the overall strategy of the mission?"

"Of course, Sergeant. Operation Talon is a 'shock

and awe' style attack whereby we will take out ten high-value terrorist targets in a simultaneous, synchronized strike."

"Sir, are these targets centrally located?" Fenton Morales asked.

"Negative," Coon said. "These targets are in ten different geographic locations, five different countries."

"Will we be using drones in the attack?"

"Negative as well," Coon said. "We cannot one hundred percent confirm the validity of the location intelligence we have received. Therefore, we cannot confidently strike using our drones without risking high civilian causalities and significant global blowback. We need visual confirmation of our targets before making any kill. We don't want a mess of dead women and children to give a bunch of jihadist wannabes a reason to join the cause. We ran an operation back in '03 in Khewa that resulted in a successful target kill, but with lots of local dead. We don't need a repeat of that."

"Are we still going to be deployed in ten teams of two?"

"Ten teams of two is correct," Coon said.

"What's the timing of this?"

"Deployment in five days or less. What else?"

"And after we locate our target?"

"Each team will infiltrate a suspect location, verify the validity of the target, and in a synchronized manner use a bomb to kill that target. Any team who does not make precise visual confirmation will have to wait for their target to show before detonation. We want ten dead in a twenty-four-hour period. 'Ten in Twenty' will be your war cry. This is going to cut the head off of the hydra."

"Where will we procure the explosives?" Morales asked.

Coon turned to Brody, who stood and faced the men.

"You will be wearing them," he said.

CHAPTER 36

Lou drove some distance before he found a stretch of highway that offered reliable cell phone reception. He was three hours from D.C. provided the Camry kept chugging, maybe more because it was already getting dark. His hands were still trembling from lingering adrenaline as he keyed in Sarah's number. It was hard to wrap his head around the ways he could have died in just the past few hours. Mexican drug cartel. Palace Guards. Wyatt Brody. Angry dog. And that did not count Officer Judy Lemon of the West Virginia State Police.

With each piece of the Brody puzzle that fell into place, other gaps seem to have appeared. The power of the man and the pervasiveness of his program left Lou feeling bewildered and frightened for Gary. If Lou's suspicions were correct, then the murder of Elias Colston was part of a major conspiracy involving supremely powerful players who would stop at nothing to protect their secrets.

Sarah answered on the third ring, and Lou felt his beleaguered spirits lift at sound of her voice. They were a team—maybe not a well-oiled machine yet, but a bond between them had formed—a deepening friendship accelerated by extraordinary circumstances.

"Hey, I've been worried sick about you," she said. "Are you all right?"

"Well, considering I almost became a can of Alpo, I'm doing just fine."

"Explain," Sarah said.

Lou recounted for her Wyatt Brody's guns-for-drugs exchange and his own close encounter with Matador.

"Why do you think Brody is involved with a Mexican drug cartel?" Sarah asked when Lou had finished.

"The cartel's chemist is concocting large quantities of the drug Brody created for his thesis—a drug that eliminates fear. Sarah, you should have seen how calmly this guy Pedro stuck a revolver in his mouth and played Russian roulette. He was absolute ice."

"That's terrible."

"I came really close to screaming at him to stop before he pulled the trigger, but I don't think that would have been such a great idea. One of the ingredients of Brody's juice is methamphetamine, which isn't something easily obtained via a military purchase order. I'm fairly certain he's using this concoction on Mantis soldiers."

"For what reason?"

"That I don't know," Lou said. "Wish I did. I could come up with some theories, but they would be speculation. The cartel is cooking up the meth, but they're not involved in the entire production of the Mantis cocktail."

"So how does this connect to Reddy Creek?" Sarah asked.

"I've been thinking about that," Lou said. "There's a logic chain here we can follow—a chain that I think leads us to a conclusion that's irrefutable and surprising."

"Go on."

"We agree that Reddy Creek is Mantis, right?"

"Well, according to Edith, the two marines who were shot and killed raiding the armory had Mantis tattoos—so, yes, Reddy Creek is Mantis."

"And we agree that Brody is Mantis."

"Without question."

"And Brody's thesis is dedicated to whom?"

"Spencer Hogarth," she said. "I got it."

"So if Hogarth is Brody and Brody is Mantis and Mantis is Reddy Creek, then . . ."

"Then Hogarth is Reddy Creek," Sarah said. "Goodness, Lou, what is this?"

"I'm not sure. But I think my pal Gary inadvertently got himself stuck on the flypaper. I also think the whole business goes far beyond Reddy Creek."

"Meaning?"

"Meaning the guns-for-drugs exchange is an ongoing thing. I can't imagine Brody and his Palace Guards keep hitting the same supply depot each time they need to feed the cartel."

"Multiple armories?"

"A nasty conclusion, but an unavoidable one, I think. And I suspect Brody would need somebody high up on the food chain to help him pull it off. Somebody with enough political capital to buy the information and co-operation needed to make this scheme work."

"Hogarth," Sarah said in a half whisper.

"That's right."

"Do you think he would know if Wyatt Brody killed Elias Colton to keep him quiet?"

"It's possible," Lou said. "Even if he doesn't know, we can help him find out. He's not going to want to be embroiled in any major scandal. Not with his political ambitions on the line. Either way, we get Gary off, which is our goal here."

"That's not our only goal," Sarah said. "I promised Edith I'd help her find the people responsible for blinding her and killing Mike. Now I know where to start."

"All roads lead to Hogarth," Lou said.

"It may take a while for me to get a meeting with him, but I'll make it happen."

"You've got to be careful. Your friend Edith may be proof of how dangerous Hogarth can be if he's threatened."

"We'll keep our backs to the wall, don't worry."

"Teammates worry about teammates."

"And there's no *I* in *team*," Sarah said. "Got it. Thanks for caring about me, Lou."

"Thanks for letting me."

"Okay, so I'm going to go after Hogarth and be extremely careful doing it. What are you going to do in the meanwhile?"

"I think I'm going to hug my daughter and play a marathon session of Monopoly."

"You're lucky to be alive," Sarah said.

"Don't I know it."

"You need to lay low," Sarah said. "Don't go poking hornets' nests with any sticks. Let Edith and me work on Hogarth. And remember, Brody may not know it was you there in the forest, but he's been alerted someone may be on to him, and you're on a very short list of people that might be."

"Consider me hung low," he said.

"I mean it, Lou. You could have at least told me you were going to do this."

There was an edge to her voice. Clearly their newly established alliance was a branch that would hold only so much weight.

Lou cringed at the notion that he was in the process of holding back the truth from Sarah, but given her reaction, he felt convinced that his decision was the right one. In fact, his scheduled weekend overnight with Emily was just a couple of days away. Much as he would have loved to hang with her today, there was no marathon *Monopoly* game in his immediate future. Instead, resting in his bureau drawer was a round-trip plane ticket for a late evening flight tomorrow—a flight to Minneapolis.

CHAPTER 37

The Pine Forest Clinic, as Lou had suspected, was not for patients faint of wallet. The directions took him well off any beaten track to a walled and gated entry-way surrounded by snow-covered gardens, with a uniformed guard, who checked a guest list and passed him through to a sprawling mansion. The atmosphere was sedate, but the air inside was still tinged with aromas Lou knew well—scents of disinfectant, human illness, and treatment.

Lou accepted tea from a doe-eyed receptionist who spoke with a British accent and looked as if she might have stepped from the pages of *Vogue*. A clipboard of demographic forms and a brief medical record followed, but nothing extensive. Dr. Sherwood would take care of that, he was informed. He felt fairly certain he would not be kept waiting long, and in that regard was not disappointed. The real question was how long he would last when the doctor learned the purpose of his visit.

The heavy mahogany door opened to Gerald Sherwood's office, and the doctor stepped out for formal greetings. He wore a starched white coat with his name and degree embroidered in blue over the left breast pocket. His stethoscope, a top-of-the-line Littmann, dangled from his neck. He was, as expected, distinguished—sixty or so, with razor-cut graying hair and bright, aquamarine eyes. From the instant of their meeting, Lou sensed for no particular reason that the man suspected the motive for this visit was something other than advertised.

As he walked to the chair across the desk from the director, he took in the dozen artfully matted and framed diplomas and certifications on the walls. One of them caught his eye immediately—a diploma from the University of Virginia, Elias Colston's alma mater. He strained unsuccessfully to remember Colston's graduation year, but it would not have mattered. Colston spent time in the marines before going to college. No matter what, it seemed quite possible that the two men were classmates. It was hard to believe the connection was a coincidence.

He decided this was a time for directness.

"So, Mr. Welcome," Sherwood said in a rich, melodic voice that could have fit behind a radio microphone, "it says here that you have been having trouble with migraine headaches."

"Actually, Dr. Sherwood, I have never had a disabling headache in my life, and my name is Welcome, but my first name is Lou, not Graham."

"*Disabling.* What an interesting choice of words. Are you a physician, Lou Welcome?"

Lou tried to grin, but his face felt frozen. The man was sharp. "Emergency medicine. I work at Eisenhower Memorial in D.C."

"I see. Are you looking for employment here?"

"No. Why do you ask that?"

"Since we are not looking for colleagues, I can't imagine another reason why you would use a false pretext and pay so much to get in to see me."

The man's expressive eyes were truly a window to his thoughts. Lou remained focused on them.

"I need information," he said.

"About?"

"About a patient of yours. A man named James Styles of Bowie, Maryland." Lou passed across the envelope with Styles's name.

The spark in Sherwood's eyes was transient, but revealing nonetheless. "It appears you have made the long journey here for nothing. As a physician yourself, surely you know that even if this name meant something to me, I would never tell you. Confidentially is more than a word here. It is the way we attract patients and do business."

Lou slipped a photo of Elias Colston from his briefcase and set it next to the envelope. "Congressman Elias Colston was murdered two weeks ago in Maryland. I found this envelope in his desk while I was searching for clues as to who might have shot him in cold blood." Lou waited for a reply, but there was none other than a shrug. "I am here because the man who is currently in jail for the murder, also a physician, is a friend of mine. He's an outdoorsman and pilot, a bit wild and at times unpredictable, but utterly devoted to his patients. . . ."

Nothing.

". . . I see you graduated from Virginia at about the same time as Colston. It seems possible you two were classmates. I wonder if he could have come here for some sort of medical problem because of that connection."

Nothing again.

"Dr. Welcome," Sherwood said finally, "I am going to do you a favor and not charge you for this consultation. But I will not answer any questions about any person, real or imagined, living or dead. That's the way it is. Now, if you'll gather your things and excuse me."

Lou stood and slipped the envelope into his briefcase, but he left the eight-by-ten head shot on the desk, facing his host.

"I'm a very principled man and physician," Lou said before he turned to go, "but I am also pragmatic and proud that I am capable of reasoning out ethical problems for myself. HIPAA laws are what they are. So is the ancient oath we took at med school graduation. But when push comes to shove, the most important voice I must listen to and answer to is the one inside my head that tells me what is right and what is wrong in any given situation. I believe my friend is innocent of murdering Elias Colston. At the moment, he is petrified and living in a filthy cell in a Baltimore jail. The DA is determined to see that he spends the rest of his life there. You hold one of the clues that might help set him free—the clue as to whether the murder victim had any preexisting medical conditions, and whether he came here under the assumed name of James Styles. If it is too difficult for you, you don't have to say anything. Just slide that picture back to me and I will know."

Sherwood did not move.

"Dr. Welcome," he said without emotion, "please don't force me to call security to remove you."

Leaving the photo, Lou turned and retreated to where his rental car was parked. It was going to be a hell of a long trip home.

Lou had never felt that comfortable in crowds. Not surprisingly, the Minneapolis–St. Paul Airport was mobbed. He was wedged in line, shuffling toward the TSA screening equipment when his cell phone began ringing.

"Dr. Welcome," he said.

The voice on the other end was a woman's with a British accent. "Dr. Welcome," she said, "you left a photo here today. The doctor says the answer to your question is yes."

CHAPTER 38

A sprinkle of dirt rained down on Lou's face. He blinked rapidly, although each blink seemed to push more grains against his eyeballs. He tried to brush them clear, but his wrists and ankles were bound with thick rope. More dirt fell, this time landing in his open mouth, gagging him. Lou heard the scrape of the spade slicing into the mound of damp earth. Another shovelful fell, peppering his face, neck, and arms. Already his legs were completely buried, along with much of his torso. Manolo was saving the head for last.

"You enjoying your little bath, amigo?" he asked.

More soil. The last chunk included a meaty earthworm that landed on Lou's cheek and wriggled about, searching out an opening in which to hide. It found one just inside his mouth. More dirt. His throat filled up.

I'm sorry, Em. I'm sorry I let you down. I love you more than anything. I'm so sorry. . . .

Lou forced his eyes open, but the world was black. He drew in a nervous, wet breath, but inhaled only fur. He was crammed on the living room sofa, a vicious kink in his neck. Diversity was nestled on his face. Consciousness returned grudgingly. It was one of the most unpleasant, relentless nightmares he could remember. He dug his fingers into the cat's thick mane, and was about to hurl him across the room, when he became fully awake.

"Hey, big fella," he said instead, gently setting him aside, "thanks for helping me to keep from suffocating."

Through the open blinds, he could see that dawn was just making an appearance. In the hospital, he was known for being able to battle stress and sleep depravation to a standstill. Clearly he had lost this encounter. He felt like a raptor, circling around the mystery of Elias Colston's death. But soon he would be ready to home in. He shook his head to dislodge the nightmare. With no small effort, he stood and stretched.

Diversity meowed. The gang downstairs at Dimitri's Pizza had taken charge of his feedings during Lou's trip to Minneapolis, and he seemed to have gained five pounds.

"How long has Wyatt Brody been hooked up with a Mexican drug cartel?" he asked the cat. "Is there any more information I can try to get from Dr. Sherwood?"

Diversity cocked his head.

"You don't care how long, because all you care about is tuna. Tuna, and now, pizza."

Lou was making an attempt at bonding with Diversity when he noticed a brightly colored flyer lying beneath his front door. Another restaurant menu. Clearly the building's lack of any decent security had become known throughout the neighborhood. Still, he realized, it was strange that someone was out distributing flyers at this hour. Probably it was there when he got home last night, and he had simply stepped over it.

Lou retrieved the flyer, intending to move it to the trash. He had eaten at most every restaurant in the area, but he'd never heard of a place called Al's All-American Grill. When Lou noted the address, his curiosity grew. The diner was located in Alexandria, Virginia, across the Potomac and eight or so miles south of the city, making this the worst flyer distribution strategy imaginable.

Lou flipped open the menu and was not all that surprised to see a note from Papa Steve written in black marker. The man was a will-o'-the-wisp—resourceful and elusive.

Dear Doc,
Come to the restaurant today between eight and
noon. Let's talk.

Your pal,
Papa

Two hours later, Lou had showered and was parked out front of Al's All-American Grill. A small brass bell above the door announced his entrance. The diner looked like many Lou had visited before, but the distinct aroma told him the place served some fine greasy spoon food. About half the eight red leather booths were occupied. A well-worn counter with wooden swivel stools separated the patrons from the two cooks serving up eggs and hash browns almost as fast as they were ordered. Lou strolled up and down the narrow passage between the stools and the booths, searching for Papa Steve. No sign. He checked the flyer and the time. It was just quarter to eleven. Finally, he took a seat at a booth to wait.

A stocky, olive-skinned waitress with tousled dark hair took Lou's coffee order. Despite feeling famished, he figured he'd wait for Papa Steve before ordering something to eat. The waitress returned a moment later with not only Lou's coffee, but also a plate of steaming scrambled eggs and corn beef hash cooked to perfection— crusty around the edges.

"I'm sorry," Lou said with an apologetic smile, "I'd love to eat this, but it isn't my order."

"Oh, yes, it is, sir. Our chef made it special for you."

Lou looked beyond the narrow passage between the counter and the kitchen and saw Papa Steve dressed in a cook's apron and hat, standing behind the grill, waving at him with a spatula.

"So, Doc, how do you like the hash?" he called out.

Lou had grown accustomed to the man's eccentricities, but this latest move still was a surprise. "You're a cook?" Lou said.

"Only once or twice a month when I can get away. I love cooking any meal, but especially short-order breakfasts, and especially working for my buddy Alex." He gestured to the waitress. "Most important meal of the day. She's been a friend for years."

"Let me guess. She's ex-military."

"When you defuse bombs for a living—"

"You make a lot of friends," Lou said, finishing Papa Steve's sentence.

Mark Colston's godfather removed his apron and announced to his cooking partner that he was going on break. A moment later, he emerged through a set of swinging double doors and took a seat in the booth across from Lou. "You seem like a wheat-toast kind of guy, so I went with that," Papa Steve said.

"Spot on. Guess you got my message."

After calling Sarah from the highway in West Virginia, Lou had left a brief message for Papa Steve.

"It's not safe to talk by phone," Papa Steve said, scanning the diner, suddenly deadly serious. "I told you that. That's why I had Paul, our dishwasher, deliver you my message. Fortunately, you didn't say anything we have to worry about."

"Yeah, well, from now on, no more phones. I've seen firsthand how unsafe dealing with your commanding officer can be."

"Talk to me," Papa Steve said.

Lou repeated the same story he had told Sarah.

Papa Steve listened intently, but his expression was grim. "So it's not just vitamins Brody's feeding us, eh?" he said.

"Is that what he told you it was? Vitamins?"

"Yup, a special blend, courtesy of Uncle Sam and Brody's personal research. He's a doctor, you know."

"Oh, I know. Not a doc who's going to win any Nobel Prizes for medicine, either."

"We were told the juice and the capsules were engineered to boost our strength and our immune systems. I can see now why we all believed the stuff actually improved our outlook, and why the Palace Guards had a little talk with anyone who refused to take them. To tell you the truth, I didn't really mind doing it, and I couldn't say it did anything bad to me."

"I wouldn't be surprised if there was some sort of withdrawal syndrome associated with stopping it."

"You know, following Brody like that was pretty dumb, Lou. You could have gotten yourself killed, or worse."

"Worse than killed?" Lou asked.

"I've seen people who have survived a dog attack before. Yeah, there's worse than killed."

"It was worth the risk," Lou said. "Now we know that somehow Brody is behind Elias's murder, and we know why. We've just got to prove it."

"If your pal Sarah is as resourceful as you say, then maybe Hogarth will crack and sell out his protégé."

"That's what we're counting on," Lou said. "This is a great breakfast, by the way."

"Throw on a little of that hot sauce I mixed up," Papa Steve suggested, pointing to a small red bottle with a skull and crossbones on the otherwise plain label.

"Maybe I should chug a cup of that ruby juice before I do."

"For our mission. For valor. For justice. For our country. For God. For Mantis. That's the oath we swear every day before we down the shit. Well, my friend, you were dumb, but you done good. Real good. Now it's time we nail the bastard."

"What do you mean?"

Papa Steve moved closer. "We're going to get the murder weapon," he said.

Lou aspirated hot sauce and began gagging.

"Ice water. Drink the ice water."

It took two minutes before Lou could speak. "Now I understand the label on that stuff," he said. "So, where do you think we're going to find the murder weapon?"

"Wyatt Brody's gun case."

"Clearly you know something I don't. What makes you think the murder weapon is there?"

"Because of that ballistics report you faxed me," Papa Steve said.

"Explain."

"According to that report, the gun that killed Elias is a .45 ACP that fires slugs which have a six left rifling mark."

"So?"

"So Brody has a few .45-caliber pistols in his gun collection, but only one that fires a slug with that rifling mark. I took an inventory of all of Brody's .45-calibers and ran it by a friend of mine who knows a lot about guns."

"You've got a lot of helpful friends," Lou said.

"I've saved a lot of people's lives by not letting them get blown up," Papa Steve replied, "and some others by blowing up people who had it in for them. Anyway, according to my source, the only match in Brody's collection is a Colt/U.S. Army 1911 .45 ACP five-inch-barrel military pistol. Nice antique weapon. Retails for about two grand on the open market. You and I think Brody is our shooter, but now I know which weapon he used to do the killing. We get that gun, we run the ballistics test again, and we've basically got ourselves a murder weapon tied to the owner."

Good as Papa Steve's cooking was, Lou lost his appetite. The notion of returning to the Mantis base held all the appeal of taking Matador for a walk.

"I've been inside Brody's office, remember?" Lou said. "Assuming we can even sneak onto the base, his gun case probably has some seriously sophisticated locks. Let me guess—you have a friend who knows how to pick locks?"

"As a matter of fact, I do," Papa Steve said. "But first she's got to break herself out of jail. If push comes to shove, I can run a diversion and whip up a little something that will blow the office lock and then the display case. But it will reduce the operation to a snatch, grab, and run, and in addition to seven hundred soldiers, there are bound to be alarms."

"Well, I do know someone," Lou said, "but I'm worried it's going to be too dangerous."

"You stumbled into this quagmire, Lou," Papa Steve said. "If you want to get out of it and help your doctor pal, as I believe you do, then we've got to go on the offensive and take some risks. How good is your contact at B and E?"

"Cap is good at almost everything he does."

"Then bring him on board. It's great that Sarah is going after Hogarth. Power to her. But we can't trust that she'll get him to flip on Brody. We've got to have more evidence."

"The gun case," Lou said.

"I'm working on an idea and some diversions that will help get us inside."

"Terrific."

"So what do you say? Are you with me?"

Don't go poking sticks at any hornets' nests.

Sarah's warning resonated. Stealing a major piece of evidence was bound to sit poorly with her, and might well trigger some sort of arcane courtroom battle. *Not* stealing it, or delaying, risked a completely different set of problems, including Wyatt Brody's becoming wary of being a suspect in Elias Colston's murder, and simply deep-sixing the gun in one of the Mantis base's many lakes and bogs.

"Well?" Papa Steve asked.

Lou resumed poking at his meal. Cap would say yes in a heartbeat to doing his part with the locks, despite the risk. Everything would depend on him and on Steve Papavassiliou's plan. Lou's embryonic relationship with Sarah might not survive, but then again, if it did, it would be so much the stronger.

And finally, of course, following orders had never been one of his strong suits.

"I'm in," Lou said.

"You're a good man, Charlie Brown. We go on Tuesday. That gives us four days. Details to follow."

The marine set his hands flat on the table, and Lou covered them with his own.

"Tell me something," Lou asked as he stood to go, "does the name James Styles mean anything to you?"

Papa Steve thought for a moment, then shook his head. "Nope," he replied. "Why do you ask?"

"Oh, nothing," Lou said. "Just a name I came across while I was searching through Elias's desk."

CHAPTER 39

La Cucina Dolce smelled of tomato sauce and aromatic Italian spices. Sarah took in the ambiance of the casually elegant restaurant, feeling as though she had just been teleported to Tuscany. The distinctive voice of Andrea Bocelli, played at the perfect volume, provided an authentic dining soundtrack. The walls were adorned with landscapes in gilded frames, and the ebony tables were set with crystal, silver, and bone china.

The restaurant's maître d', jet pomaded hair with sophisticated touches of gray, escorted Sarah to a private dining room, unoccupied except for one corner table. Secretary of Defense Spencer Hogarth, his back to the wall, nodded vaguely in her direction and returned to his meal as one of his three-man security detail helped her off with her coat. Another slid a wand from a black leather case and waved it around her body like a philharmonic maestro.

Recording devices.

None found.

In anticipation of being frisked, Sarah wore tan slacks

and a tight-fitting black sweater accented only with a single strand of pearls. No pockets. The men took a position just outside the door while the maître d' escorted her to Hogarth's table.

The secretary motioned with a nod to seat her catty-cornered from him. "My dinner just arrived. Would you care for anything to eat or drink?"

He gestured toward a plate of seafood linguine, alongside tomato bruschetta, an antipasto appetizer, and a porcelain dish piled with olives of varying sizes and colors. Sarah, who never felt intimated by any judge or high-profile client, found her throat had gone dry in Hogarth's presence. She had seen the man on television so many times that to see him in person crossed the threshold of surreal.

"We should keep this to business," she said.

"At least enjoy a glass of wine with me."

Hogarth filled the glass in front of Sarah from a half-empty bottle. She inspected the wine and took a sip. There was no worry about Hogarth trying to poison her—at least not until he knew what she had come here to tell him.

"I'm no more than an amateur," she said, "but this is very nice."

"It should be," Hogarth replied. "It's a Monfortino, 1997."

"Sounds expensive," Sarah said. "I sure hope that's not our tax dollars at work."

Hogarth responded with a tight, humorless smile. "If you know anything about me, then you know I've made my own money. Plenty of it."

"Well, if you know anything about me," Sarah said, "then you know I'm the lawyer for Gary McHugh, who's currently in jail for murdering Elias Colston. You may also know that Dr. McHugh is innocent. I'm about to get the charges against him dropped, and one of those who will be moved up the list to chief suspect is you."

Hogarth's expression darkened, then quickly responded to a sip of wine. He took a forkful of his linguine, and dabbed at the corners of his mouth with a linen napkin, taking no obvious pleasure from the food.

"I agreed to meet with you, Ms. Cooper, because Elias Colston was a dear personal friend of mine. I want to be of any service I can to help bring his murderer to justice. But I must confess I had no idea you were here to levy threats and allegations against me. If I had known that, I would have poured you a glass of less expensive wine."

"I'm not certain I would have known the difference. Secretary Hogarth, you can be of service and help to honor the memory of your friend if you tell me the truth. Did you kill Elias Colston?"

Hogarth huffed. "What are you talking about? What possible motive could I have for killing an old friend? Over recent years we've had our disagreements over his views on military allocations, but we debate those differences, we don't start shooting over them."

"Does the name Reddy Creek mean anything to you?" Sarah gave Hogarth an enigmatic smile and took a healthy swallow of his expensive wine.

"Reddy Creek is a place," Hogarth said, "a town in North Carolina, I believe."

"It's also the name of one of your armories."

A spark of anger flared in Hogarth's eyes. He snapped his fingers, and a waiter standing just outside the doorway came rushing over. "The linguine tastes terrible tonight," Hogarth said, pushing the plate aside. "Tell Joseph to prepare it properly or tell him he can find another place to work."

"Yes, Mr. Secretary. Right away, sir."

Sarah observed the exchange with keen interest. "You enjoy controlling people, don't you?"

"I'm lifetime military. I enjoy when things are done properly, like my meals. What I don't enjoy is having some snot-nosed pretty-girl lawyer show up at my restaurant, where I like to conduct my personal business affairs, and fling unsubstantiated allegations at me."

Sarah was unruffled. "I can assure you, my allegations are anything but unsubstantiated."

"Enlighten me, then. Tell me what motive I would have for murdering my friend. And don't tell me it's because of his stand on military spending."

"The motive is that you've been feeding information to Wyatt Brody on gun shipments to various armories along the East Coast. His men then go ahead and steal the weapons while someone on the inside, someone with allegiance to you, covers up the thefts."

"To what end?"

"The weapons are being used to fund an illegal drug trade that somehow benefits your Mantis Corps. How does that motive sound to you?"

"It sounds like something you could never prove," Hogarth said.

"Does proof really matter?" Sarah asked. "I mean, your political ambitions are not exactly a closely guarded secret. I hear vice president. I hear secretary of state. I think one whiff of this scandal will be enough to derail your political career forever."

"What do you want, Ms. Cooper?"

"I want your help in bringing down Wyatt Brody. That's what Elias Colston tried to do, and it cost him his life. I think Brody is the triggerman, and you're close enough to Brody to help us get him."

"Elias proved that going after Mantis is not a popular action. It nearly cost him his reelection."

"Maybe it's political suicide for you to help me, Mr. Secretary, but I think your other option is far less desirable."

"This is all bullshit!" Hogarth exclaimed, his cheeks reddening.

His security detail started into the room, but he calmed them with a raised hand. Control. Everything about Spencer Hogarth revolved around control, and Sarah was prepared to turn that penchant into weakness.

"In the courtroom, we call it evidence," she said.

"You have nothing," Hogarth said, jabbing an accusatory finger across the table at Sarah. "You think you can come in here and threaten me? Nobody threatens me, young lady, especially lawyers without any proof."

At that moment, the maître d' appeared in the doorway, escorting Edith Harmon on his arm. She was wearing dark glasses. The security team started after them, but Hogarth again stopped them with a gesture.

"Over here," Sarah said.

Edith crossed to the table using her folding cane. "Do you mind if I sit down?" she said to Hogarth as if she were looking directly into his eyes.

"Who are you?" he demanded.

"This is my friend Edith Harmon," Sarah said, studying Hogarth's expression for any glimmer of recognition. There was not a flicker.

Edith took the seat next to Sarah. The two women had become fast friends, and Sarah felt emboldened by Edith's presence. It was remarkably brave for her to confront the man who both women believed held some responsibility for Edith's blindness.

"I have the invoices," Edith said flatly.

Hogarth shook his head derisively.

"She can't see your body language," Sarah said. "She has no idea that you're pretending not to know what she's talking about."

"I don't know how you induced battalion supply sergeants to cooperate," Edith went on, "extortion or maybe just a little bribe. But I do know that we have the identity of at least one man behind the forged invoices."

"What on earth is this woman talking about?" Hogarth said to Sarah.

She had defended enough criminals to know when one of her clients was lying, and Hogarth had just tipped his hand.

"She's talking about the invoices you had doctored," Sarah said. "The inventory at the armory needs to match the number of weapons shipped there from the manufacturer. If there are fewer weapons than the invoices say should be on hand, questions will get asked by the agency assigned to audit the account. But if the invoices are doctored, then Brody or whoever can divert a not suspiciously large number of weapons, and nobody would even know to ask."

"This is ridiculous," Hogarth said. "Get out, both of you."

"So, on a prearranged night and time," Edith said, "at a specific armory where a guard is paid off, there's a theft. Only at one armory—the one at Reddy Creek, there's a screwup. Maybe a guard gets sick and the rotation gets changed. Maybe he forgets that this was to be the night some guys were coming by to pick up a truckload of weapons. So, a poor fellow named Mike Fitz gets caught in the middle and does his job, and two men with Mantis tattoos on their forearms get killed, and he ends up getting murdered."

"Ridiculous! I don't need to take this sort of abuse from the likes of you."

"By 'likes of you,'" Edith replied in a calm voice, "are you referring to me? A blind woman? A woman whose life you helped to destroy because I was seeking the truth? A woman who just so happens to be an investigative reporter with a lot of useful connections, including Mike Fitz. A woman who obtained the original invoices from the gun manufacturer who supplies Reddy Creek? For all your power and privilege, Mr. Secretary, you don't know the half of what a woman like me can do to you."

A contemplative look washed across Hogarth's face. *Resigned,* Sarah thought. *He's going to cave.*

"What do you want me to do?" he asked finally.

"Mr. Secretary, if you want any hope of salvaging your political career, we need you to wear a wire and get Wyatt Brody to confess to Congressman Colston's murder." Sarah stood up from the table and dropped her business card in front of Hogarth. "I'll give you twenty-four hours to make up your mind. If I don't hear from you by then, we go public with our information."

The waiter returned to the table with a freshly prepared plate of linguine nettuno. "The chef assures me this will meet with your very discerning tastes, Mr. Secretary," he said. "Is there anything else I can get for you?"

"Yes," Sarah said, pointing to the open bottle of expensive wine. "We'll take two of those, please. To go."

CHAPTER 40

From the moment Papa Steve first shared the elements of his plan to break into Mantis headquarters, Lou had felt uneasy, but at this moment, he was more concerned than ever. The plan's timetable had been changed, and everything had been pushed up by two days. To Cap's dismay, the alteration meant less time to dust off his lock-picking skills.

Deviating from his own rules, Papa Steve had called Lou to break the news. "We're going on Sunday," he had said, "not Tuesday."

"Sunday? Why so soon?"

"Can't tell you over the phone. You still in?"

"I'm in. I'm in."

"And your pal?"

"In. I'm sure of it. I just have an aversion to change."

"Just meet me at the place, and I'll explain everything."

The place, transmitted to Lou in another under-the-door menu, was twenty miles southeast of the Mantis base, near the town of Dudley. Lou and Cap waited in the woods on the side of a rutted dirt road by a sequential Barbasol shaving cream sign. They were in a part of town devoid of houses, businesses, or much traffic. The bright sun, cast against a cloudless sky, did little to warm the morning.

Even though Cap was wearing gloves, a jacket, and fleece, he needed to dance his trademark boxing moves to keep warm. "Bahamian blood has a high freezing point," he said. "Why couldn't this buddy of yours have just met us at the motel?"

"He's quirky—cautious drifting toward paranoid."

"Great. So long as he hasn't crossed over the invisible line."

Following the plan, Lou left his car at a motel he rented for two days in Dudley, and he and Cap walked half a mile out of town to the rendezvous point.

"I guess this is why he wanted us to dress warm," Lou said.

He pushed back the sleeve of his parka to check his Mickey Mouse watch. Papa Steve was due now, but in what mode of transportation Lou could only guess. Plane? Helicopter? ATV? There were fields around that made any of them possible.

Cap exhaled a weighty breath, sending up a cloud of vapor. "Man, Welcome, I haven't had nerves like this since my last prizefight."

"We can still back out," Lou said. "I'll tell Papa Steve we didn't have enough time to plan. Look, Cap, I don't want you getting hurt or worse because of me."

Cap just laughed. "You think after what you told me about your last visit to that base, I'm going to let your sorry white ass go back inside there without me? I thought about trying to talk you out of this little escapade, but I know better. You've got your mind made up, and *I've* got your back."

"You're the best. If it makes you feel any better, I'm nervous, too."

Cap ruminated a moment. "Nah," he said. "That doesn't make me feel better at all." Then he smacked Lou playfully on the arm.

"Well," Lou said. "I've added a little contingency plan of my own just in case things come unglued."

Cap hugged himself and shivered off a chill.

Lou was about to explain when they heard the rumble of an approaching engine. The headlights of an olive-green military truck appeared from beyond a hilly rise a quarter mile away. The canvas tarp covering the back of the lumbering vehicle shook and ruffled in the steady breeze. A minute later, it groaned to a stop.

Papa Steve, wearing a fur-lined parka, hopped down from the cab. He had the grin of a charter boat skipper ready to depart for a tuna-fishing expedition. "Hiya, Cap," he said, taking Cap's hand in both of his. "It's a real pleasure and an honor. I was a big fan of yours back in the day."

"Thanks for the props. Any friend of the doc's is a friend of mine."

"Before we get started, I know I cut you short of time. You need any tools?"

"Brought my own. I practiced breaking into our motel room last night."

"I've been up close and personal with Brody's system, Cap. I can promise you, whatever his locks are, they ain't no motel."

"I can only do what I can do, brother."

"I think he's a keeper, Doc."

"What happened?" Lou asked. "This wasn't supposed to go down so fast."

"That's life in the military, son," Papa Steve said. "When we talk about tomorrow, God laughs. Brody's presented us with a situation too good to ignore."

"Tell us."

"Can't we talk while we're driving?" Cap asked. "You must have some heat in the cab of that khaki junker."

"Actually, you boys won't be riding in the cab. You'll be under the chassis like a couple of Mexican border sneaks." Papa Steve knelt and pointed to a steel platform he had rigged to the undercarriage. "I've got a way to conceal the sides, but you've got to climb on board the platform before I can secure it in place."

"You want us to ride underneath this truck for twenty miles?" Lou said.

"Um, the truth is, you're going to be under the truck for a wee bit longer than that."

"How long?" Cap asked. "I have trouble with tight spaces. I can do them, but I don't like them much."

"Until evening."

"That's hours from now!" Lou exclaimed.

"When I said a wee bit, I really meant a lot. Hope you both took my advice and dressed real warm. I brought helmets and the oxygen masks our parachute jumpers wear. Those will help you breathe on the drive over."

"Can't we just ride in the back?" Cap asked.

Papa Steve shook his head. "The cargo in back is going to get inspected before I can drive onto the base. It's too risky to hide back there. And I don't want anyone seeing you guys going from the back of the truck onto my platform anywhere close to Hayes. There are eyes all over the place right now."

"What are you hauling?" Cap asked.

"Fireworks. Lots and lots of fireworks. Brody's asked me to rig up a big-time Fourth of July–type show. That's part of the reason I changed the plan. Only he's gonna get more than he's bargaining for."

"Talk to us," Lou said.

"Something is going on at Mantis. The start of a mission. Whatever it is, it must be important because Brody is going with them at least part of the way."

"You don't know any more details than that?"

"I've heard the words 'Operation Talon' bandied about for some weeks now. Brody's been putting the guys from Mantis through a grueling series of tests. A couple of 'em even got shot. No life-threatening injuries, but they were wounded running an obstacle course we call the Big Hurt."

"That is a big hurt," Cap said.

"Brody's been winnowing down the mission pool candidates for weeks now, looking for the best-of-the-best of Mantis. He's got his crew selected, and he's ready to roll. Brody asked me to run a big fireworks send-off for the men tonight. He's done that before for various missions, but on a smaller scale than the one he wants here. There's a trio of Chinook helicopters parked on the heliport that's going to take them to an airfield someplace, probably for staging. Brody wants the Chinooks to fly out surrounded by the rockets' red glare. If you ask me, the guy has seen *Apocalypse Now* a few too many times—but, hey, who am I to deny the man his spectacle? He's even recorded the music and wants me to do my best to match it up with the fireworks."

"When do we know to break for Brody's office?" Lou asked.

"Wait until you hear the '1812 Overture.' You know that piece?"

"I know it," Cap said.

"Great. When you hear it, you'll rush for the office, break in without setting off any alarms, and do your thing. Believe me, no one will be watching. They're going to be having their own problems, courtesy of *moi*. Are you guys sure you're up for this?"

Lou stared at him. "The '1812 Overture'? Are you kidding me?" he asked.

"What? What?"

"This is either the best of signs or the worst of signs," Lou said. "Get this. In college, I roomed my freshman year with a guy named Bob, who was known on campus as Dr. Strange. He was a mile or so south of eccentric in just about everything he did. He had money, plenty of it, and he owned the most incredible, expensive stereo system I had ever seen. A Bang and Olufsen."

"So?" Cap said.

"So, believe it or not, he only had two albums—just two. One was *Scheherazade* by Rimsky-Korsakov, and the other was the '1812 Overture.' Depending on his mood, he played one or the other of them all day every day. I tried to switch rooms. I tried reasoning with him. I even moved my bed from our bedroom to our living room. Nothing worked, nothing. Until one day, he paid me off."

"He what?"

"I was on scholarship, and he gave me like fifteen hundred bucks to leave him alone and let him listen to his albums whenever he wanted."

"You took it?"

"Of course I took it. It was only for a year. Gradually, I actually embraced the music. I not only came to not mind either piece, but sometimes when he wasn't there, I actually played one of them myself. I know just about every note of the '1812,' and exactly when various portions take place."

"Too much," Papa Steve said. "Well, may the spirit of Dr. Strange be with you tonight."

"Amen to that," Cap said. "Believe it or not, for years, when I'm working out, I usually do it to the theme from *Rocky*. But sometimes—"

"Don't tell me, the '1812 Overture.' "

"You got it, Pops."

"Okay, then. Doc, you ready to lock and load?"

"Not just yet," Lou said.

"What's the delay? I'm due back on the base in an hour."

"My contingency plan isn't here yet."

Papa Steve glared at him. "Contingency plan? What the—?"

At that instant, a state police car, headlights on, appeared in the distance and sped toward them. It stopped just behind the truck.

"Let me do the talking," Papa Steve said.

"Not to worry," Lou said. "I've got this one."

Judy Lemon, looking fit and fine in her state trooper uniform, approached with a swaggering sway of her hips that caught the attention of both Cap and Papa Steve. She came right up to Lou and took off her mirrored sunglasses. "I should arrest you for obstructing my steak dinner," she said, scolding him with a wag of her finger.

"Doctor's honor I'm going to take you out for that," Lou said, holding up his hand as a sworn promise.

"Honor isn't something I'm looking for from you, Doc," Lemon said.

Lou swallowed hard at her come-hither smile. "Guys, this is Officer Judy Lemon, a-k-a our backup."

Papa Steve flashed Lou an angry look. "I didn't say anything about needing a contingency plan! Lou, what have you told her?"

"Not much," Lou said. "Just, well—"

"Don't worry," Lemon said. "I've looked the other way for worse things than sneaking onto a military base and stealing a gun."

"Good to know," Papa Steve said insincerely.

"Besides, Brody's been sticking it to the Staties so long now that I'd love to stick it right back at him.

We've pulled over more DUIs from Mantis than could fit in the state barracks, but have any ever gone to trial or even lost their license? I don't know who Brody has bribed or blackmailed, but I'm more than happy to bend the rules to get the bad guys."

Papa Steve did not appear at all satisfied. "Lou, this isn't some little snatch-and-grab job. There are a lot of big boys on that base with a lot of big guns. I don't see how the police are going to help out here. No offense."

"None taken, sweetheart," Lemon said. "And if Lou here doesn't want to take me out for dinner, you might do just fine as his replacement. In the meantime, Lou has a way of getting in touch with me and I have a way of getting you some help if those big boys with big guns develop itchy trigger fingers."

"Not that I don't trust this plan of yours, Papa Steve," Lou said, "but I've got a kid who needs a father."

Papa Steve set his hands on his hips. He had the look of a man ready to call the whole thing off. Instead, he fixed Lou with a pointed stare. "Okay, so that's it," Papa Steve said. "We've got backup. Lou makes the call when we need it, which we won't."

"Glad you see it my way," Lou said.

"I didn't say I saw it your way. Now, gear up. It's going to be cold riding under that truck."

"I'll be as close to the base as I can get without attracting too much attention," Lemon said.

Lou and Cap donned the helmets, masks, and portable oxygen supply, climbed under the truck, and shimmied their way to the center of the cold steel platform. Lying on their stomachs, heads on wafer-thin pillows, the pair had room to squirm, but precious little beyond that.

Papa Steve secured the metal sides of the platform to hooks he had welded to the truck's chassis, and the steel cocoon was closed. Moments later, the cruiser drove off. Then the engine rumbled, and the cantankerous truck lurched forward.

Next stop, Mantis.

CHAPTER 41

Lou could not say how long he and Cap rode inside the box. While they were locked in total darkness, time slowly lost all meaning. Fifteen minutes? Fifty? All he knew was the vehicle had come to an abrupt stop and did not move for some time. They had to be at the Mantis base guardhouse.

The ride to Hayes from Dudley was a violent voyage that had jostled Lou and Cap against each other like passengers on a wooden roller coaster. Lou's limbs were stiff, and every pressure point was screaming. Twice, his foot cramped up, but without room to maneuver, he had to grit his teeth through the pain. As long as they were moving, he could cry out, but now that they were still, he could only bite at his lip and wait. His fingers and toes felt brittle and numb from the cold. Vibrations from the idling engine were like electric shocks.

Most of Lou's thoughts, though, were with his boxing coach and AA sponsor, the gentle battering ram of a man huddled next to him. It was a lot to say Cap had saved his life, but it was by no means exaggeration. Now Lou found himself wishing that he had never thought to bring him along. He shifted his body closer to Cap's and could feel him shivering.

"You okay?" Lou whispered, nudging his own gas mask aside.

"Been better, been worse," Cap said.

"Sorry for roping you into this, pal."

"Don't be. I make my own choices."

They heard footsteps crunching on the hard, packed ground outside. Lou worked his body over to the side of the platform, hoping to catch any snippets of conversation.

Sure enough, he heard Papa Steve's commanding voice engage with some of the Mantis guards. "Howdy and a fine afternoon to you, good gentlemen."

"We're checking IDs today, Papa Steve. CO's orders."

"The Brody asks, the Brody gets. Here you go, Chuckie."

"What's in the truck?"

"Fireworks for the big show tonight."

"We gotta search the back."

"Oooh, Paranoid City. Just make it quick. I got the Mantis version of the Big Bang to set up."

"Can't wait."

Lou held his breath. From what he could hear, at least two men had climbed inches above where he and Cap lay, and were conducting a thorough search of the cargo. It sounded as if some cases were even opened.

Paranoid City was right.

"You're all set, Papa Steve," one of guards called out.

The truck bucked as it was slipped into gear. Lou groaned and worked his legs, pleading with his muscles to stay forgiving for just a little while longer. Minutes later, they stopped once again. The driver's-side door opened, then slammed closed. The back panel was lowered.

"This may be it," Lou whispered.

"Next time I complain that a workout is too hard, remind me of this trip."

"Same here, big guy."

From just outside where they were lying, they heard Papa Steve whisper harshly. "Lou, Cap, you boys all right down there? Knock on the side. Once for yes, twice for no. It's safe."

Lou banged once against the side, and battled back the urge to add a few extras.

"Good. Now, you just hang tight. A couple more hours is all. The show will feature some short speeches blasting from some pretty intense speakers, followed by a couple of marches accompanied by fireworks. The '1812 Overture' will be last, Howitzers and all, with more fireworks than you can shake a stick at, mixed in with enough of the real deal to get some serious attention. Soon as you hear the 1812 music, head for Brody's office. By the time things begin to blow up, you better be back at the truck. I unhooked the back, so you can push yourselves out. But listen close. Timing here is critical. If things go right, we'll be able to drive right off the base without too much trouble. Knock once if you've got all that."

Lou knocked.

"Hang tough, boys."

Lou felt a gentle tap on his leg.

"How else are we supposed to hang?" Cap whispered.

Lou guessed ten minutes had passed when they heard footsteps approaching. Then a voice.

"Hey, there, Papa Steve, how's it going?"

Brody!

"Getting ready to be offloaded," Papa Steve said. "I think you'll be happy with my selection, Colonel."

"Will this be enough to make it a spectacle?"

"I've got boxes of aerial repeaters, shells, rockets, Thor missiles, display tubes. It'll be a spectacle, all right."

"Good," Brody said. "These men are going on a very dangerous mission. They deserve a fitting send-off."

More footsteps.

"Papa Steve."

"Major Coon."

Lou did not recognize the new voice.

"Ready for the big send-off?"

"I have my crew ready to empty this truck and place everything on the firing platform. Then I'll hook it all up and ka-boom. Fourth of July in December. How about the howitzer gunners, Major. Are they all set?"

"Champing at the bit," Coon said. "Excuse me, Commander, but I wonder if I could have a word with you."

"Papa Steve," Brody said, "why don't you give us

five minutes, then bring your men to help you unload these boxes."

"Yes, sir."

Footsteps, probably Papa Steve leaving, followed by a minute of silence.

"Okay," Brody said finally, "what is it, Charlie?"

"I wanted to let you know that I've decided to handle the notification to the families myself."

"All of them?"

"I think it's better that way, sir."

"I'll probably go with you to some of them. What's the final story?"

"Just as we discussed. Helicopter crash after the assassinations were completed and the men had reassembled for the trip home. It's the most believable way for twenty soldiers to be killed at once."

"Makes sense," Lou heard Brody say. "This is a major milestone in the evolution of the new war, Charlie. It's been too long that we haven't been fighting on a level playing field. Our technology has proved only that we have more money, not more resolve. But all that is going change with Operation Talon. Terrorists everywhere will soon be aware that Americans are willing and ready to replicate every tactic used against us, including those that involve a life for a life."

"You've done a good thing here, sir. In time, this will put an end to terrorism and change the course of the war. And most important, it will alter how our resolve is perceived. These parasites will learn not only to respect us, but more important, to fear us. I just left the men. They're ready, sir. I also wanted to let you know that we've moved the takeoff from the Langley airstrip to Dover, as you advised."

"Better Dover," Brody said. "Their security is reasonable and I want as few people as possible to know anything about this."

"Understood and agreed."

"Let's get ready, my friend."

"Yes, sir."

Footsteps . . . Brody and Coon walking away.

Lou's stomach had knotted up. Combined with what he saw in the woods while following Brody, what he learned from Papa Steve, and what they heard just now, he had learned enough to put together a truly frightening scenario. Operation Talon was a mass suicide mission. Twenty soldiers, primed by Brody's ruby drink, ready to die for their country violently and without fear. He might not know the targets or other specifics, but the intent of the mission was as evident as it was ungodly. Lying in the darkness beside his friend, Lou recalled how easily the cartel man named Pedro had slipped a partially loaded revolver into his mouth and pulled the trigger.

Click!

Now, Mark Colston's wonderful heroism, surprising even to his father, made sense. Clearly it was only a matter of time before Elias Colston put all the pieces together. In megalomaniac Wyatt Brody's warped mind, the man had to die.

But now a new problem had arisen.

Instead of trying to prove Brody killed Elias Colston, Lou had the responsibility of at least twenty brave, essentially innocent lives in his hands. The lives soon to be sacrificed on the altar of Operation Talon.

He waited until he felt it was safe to talk. "Cap, do you know what that conversation meant?"

"I know that I'm dying in here, Welcome. My limbs have gone completely numb and I'm so damn cold."

Lou could feel Cap shivering beside him. Only then did he realize he was shivering himself. "We can't quit now, Cap."

"I was just talking, pretty boy. Anything to keep from thinking about my own misery. It sounds like your buddy Brody doesn't care too much who he steps on."

"The man's crazy. Absolutely drunk with power and his misguided theories of patriotism. Unless he's stopped, a lot of people are going to die."

Silence settled in again, and the seconds dragged on. It was nighttime, Lou thought, more because he wanted it to be than because he was sure. The hours of waiting on the steel platform had taken a huge physical and emotional toll. Papa Steve had long ago returned with a crew from Mantis and unloaded the boxes of fireworks. The moment of action had to be close.

"I can't do it, Cap. I can't make it another—"

"Gentlemen, this your commander speaking," Brody's voice boomed from giant speakers, cutting Lou short. "Tonight we honor the men who will represent Mantis on the most important mission since the founding of our young outfit. From the beginning, Mantis has embodied the virtues of the true solider. Please join with me in affirming those virtues."

"The color of our drink is the color of courage,"

seven hundred voices barked out in perfect unison. "It is the color of blood spilled in battle, the color of fire that burns for freedom. For our mission. For valor. For justice. For our country. For God. For Mantis . . . Whatever it takes!"

Lou felt a tremendous surge of adrenaline and sensed that beside him, Cap was experiencing the same thing. At all costs, the sacrifice of these men had to be averted.

"Alone we are powerful," Brody was saying. "Together we are unstoppable. Let us honor the men who will endure the most dangerous and important mission Mantis has ever had the privilege to undertake, the men of Operation Talon. As I call your name, would you each please climb onto either of the trucks that will transport you to the heliport.

"Staff Sergeant Bucky Townsend, Muskogee, Oklahoma. . . . Corporal Luis Sanchez, Vicksburg, Mississippi. . . ."

The cheers became more rapturous after each name. When the list was completed, Souza's "Stars and Stripes Forever" blared through the loudspeakers, accompanied by a barrage of fireworks and the rumbling of truck engines.

One more march, some more fireworks. Then, from the massive speakers, the "1812 Overture" began.

It would be just what the colonel ordered—three huge Chinook choppers lifting up at once, fireworks exploding around them, with Tchaikovsky's iconic cannonade providing the soundtrack. Protected by the fireworks, Lou stretched, then rolled to his side, imagining what Wyatt Brody would be experiencing while the pistol was being removed from his fabulous gun collection—the pistol that would help prosecutors put him on death row.

Majestic strings, slow and sonorous at first, filled the air.

Music to die for, Lou thought.

"Get ready, my friend," he said, no longer confined to whispering. "We're on."

CHAPTER 42

Lou and Cap jammed their heels against the rear panel of what had been their prison, and felt it fall away. It landed with a muted but satisfying thud. Sliding backwards, they dropped to the ground in a crouch behind the truck. A rush of cool air bathed their lungs. From no more than fifty feet away, the nearest huge speaker, mounted on a tall pole, had begun broadcasting the gentle opening string passage of the "1812 Overture." Cap stood and straightened up, groaning obscenities at his joints.

Lou looked to his right and took in a familiar sight. They were parked on the dirt courtyard housing Brody's headquarters and two smaller structures. Overhead, a variety of fireworks were turning the moonless sky into a fantasy garden. The explosions accompanying the display shook the earth.

Aside from the music, the core of the base was ghostly quiet and appeared completely deserted. Windows in the three buildings and nearby barracks were dark. There were no guards on duty, at least that Lou could see. Papa Steve had mentioned that the ceremony was set for the assembly area, some distance away. He was smart to have sped up the timetable. If ever there was a perfect time to penetrate Wyatt Brody's world, this was it.

When he pushed himself off the platform, Cap pulled out a compact knapsack he had wedged by his head. Small length of clothesline, powerful flashlight, leather pouch of tools, headlamp, stethoscope, hunting knife, and a pistol.

"Sorry, not my style," Lou had said when offered a similar weapon.

"I love our soldiers," Cap replied. "Love 'em, respect 'em, am grateful to 'em, too. But if these Palace Guards are what you say they are, I ain't going down without making a noise."

Mantis Company
Whatever It Takes

The sign was as Lou remembered from his previous harrowing trip to the base. In a perverse way, Brody was right in his speech to the troops. It *was* more than just a motto. . . . For the twenty soldiers of Operation Talon, it was a death sentence.

Lou tapped Cap on the shoulder and pointed to the target building. The fighter glanced around, nodded back at Lou, and made a surprisingly limber dash across the hard ground to Brody's office. He reached the perimeter without incident and waved for Lou to join him. Keeping as low as he could manage, Lou shambled across the open area, giving back all the style points Cap had just won. His legs were still weak and stiff, and he stumbled once. Working for each breath, he reached the short flight of stairs to the porch and flattened against a support next to Cap.

The first bridge of the "1812 Overture," a series of chromatic runs that depicted anxious Russians anticipating battle, reverberated from the enormous speakers, accompanied by the rumbling of some low-level fireworks. The music precisely reflected Lou's growing sense of urgency. For a moment, his ultra-odd college roommate's elegant stereo flashed in his thoughts.

Lou set his watch and started it.

"We've got eleven minutes before the cannonade," he said.

Cap looked over at him. "You really know the '1812 Overture' *that well*?"

"Some day after this is all in our rearview mirror, I'll play it for you on kazoo. Come on, buddy, it's time to do this thing."

They ascended the wooden staircase to the outer door. From the PA system, the strings were now beginning battle with the horns. Distress . . . worry . . . mounting panic . . . determination. War.

Cap turned on his headlight and took the lock-pick kit from his backpack. "It's a dead bolt," he said, examining the front lock. "Harder than it looks, but a diamond pick ought to get this puppy open." He removed a long silver wand with a little bend at the end.

"Where'd you get those?" Lou whispered.

"Online. Where does anyone get anything these days?

A year or so ago, I couldn't find my old kit, so I went to Lockpickingtools.com."

The fireworks intensified as the horns began the powerful "Marseillaise." The French counterattack was under way.

"An artiste needs quiet," Cap said, stepping back and gesturing up at the explosions and light. "Seriously, boss. Don't panic. We're in."

Lou turned the knob, and the door opened easily. "You hot shit," he murmured.

"La Marseillaise" peaked. The tide of battle had turned. The two friends moved quickly to the shuttered wood door of Wyatt Brody's office. Outside, the decrescendo of violins played a soft romantic melody.

"Maybe seven minutes," Lou said.

The rustic office triggered unpleasant memories. If not for Papa Steve, this place would have housed his last minutes on earth. They went directly to the case in the small room behind Brody's desk. Papa Steve's intelligence was on the button—the polished antique Colt military pistol was at the center of the display, right where he said it probably would be. It would leave a six left twist rifling mark on any bullet it fired.

In the distance, the soft sounds of impending triumph. The tide of the conflict had turned. The mop-up was beginning.

"Okay, time to get cracking," Lou said, checking his watch. "We're at about the five-minute mark now."

Cap spent a few moments studying the situation—a sculptor eyeing a block of marble before putting mallet to chisel. "The case is alarmed with glass-break sensors, anticipating a smash-and-grab, but the actual lock wasn't a priority. It's a Yale. Tough but not killer tough."

Cap deftly slid another long hooked tool into the lock. His muscular frame, the body that had battered dozens of fighters in the ring, seemed calm and totally at ease. From his years of suturing facial and tendon lacerations, Lou had no trouble relating to the all-consuming concentration.

"The plug hole has beveled edges," Cap said, speaking much more to himself than to Lou, "and the ends of the key pins are rounded off. I've got to do a bit more scrubbing because the driver pins are set on the bevel. Can't turn the plug if the driver's caught on the bevel. Shouldn't be too hard."

The music outside was intensifying—frenetic string runs, crashing cymbals, horns blaring the French national anthem, a timpani foreshadowing the cannonade to come. Then, the penultimate passages—pastoral melodies, the utter exhaustion of the troops. Lou guessed they had four minutes to get the case open, unhinge the gun, and make it back to the truck.

"Damn. I've got the pins set, but the lock isn't opening," Cap murmured. "Reduce the torque and keep scrubbing over these pins. That's all I can do."

"Two more minutes, and we've got to smash the case and take our chances with the alarm," Lou said.

He shifted on his heels, watching his friend work. Outside, the music was again building. The fireworks explosions were rattling the display cases. The finale was near. At the instant bells began chiming in the soundtrack, the lock popped with a satisfying click, and the case opened. The Colt, not fixed to the velvet-lined back, rested on a pair of hooks. Cap lifted it free and placed it in his knapsack along with his tools.

"We've got to move, Cap! Now!"

Lou shifted a pistol from the bottom row to fill in the space the Colt had occupied. Then he carefully closed the case and followed Cap through the office to the porch. They reached the courtyard just at the start of the overture's dramatic climax. The speakers blared out the brass section's recapitulation of earlier themes. Branches shook as runs by the strings and woodwinds blended in versions of "God Save the Tsar."

The fireworks had slowed. Off in the distance, to his left, Lou saw the lights of three helicopters rise slowly and majestically into the smoke-filled sky. The moment the choppers lifted off, the cannonade began. The finale. Howitzer booms reverberated through Lou's chest and seemed to rattle the fillings in his teeth as massive rosettes—red, purple, and blue starbursts—filled the sky. For a moment, Lou was in his college dorm room, getting psyched for finals with Dr. Strange.

Up ahead, Papa Steve was standing by the truck, urgently motioning for them to hurry. He was holding something up in his left hand.

Lou had no doubt it was a detonator.

CHAPTER 43

Shoulder to shoulder, Lou and Cap had taken three steps toward Papa Steve when a Mantis guard stepped out from a building to their left.

"Freeze right there or I'll shoot!"

Lou whirled in the direction of the voice and dropped facedown on the hardened dirt. The overture climax continued, with cannon fire booming from the PA system as though the base were under siege.

And then, in an instant, it was.

Military vehicles parked along the road began to explode, one after the other. Bright orange flames shot into the night. Glass shattered, sending jagged shards in all directions. Trucks and jeeps thrown into the air landed with a bone-rattling crunch of metal. A pair of smaller explosions sprayed a potpourri of dirt and rocks high into the air.

Papa Steve was either going to have a hell of a lot of explaining to do, or he was planning on going AWOL before the commander returned.

"I said stop!" the guard shouted.

A burst of machine gun fire followed. Bullets slapped at the ground by Lou's feet. Frantically, he searched for cover, but Cap had other ideas. He rolled over once and then again. The second time, he had the pistol in his hand. One shot, and the soldier cried out, dropped his gun, and fell, clutching his shoulder.

"Nice shot!" Lou exclaimed.

"Nice shot, hell! I was aiming at his leg."

"Get to the truck!" Papa Steve was hollering.

Pistol drawn, he was providing them with what seemed like random cover fire. Small explosions continued to erupt throughout the woods. Assuming chaos and fear were Papa Steve's goals, he was the Picasso of demolition. Lou and Cap were moving again, hunched over, weaving across the courtyard. More guards had materialized near the wounded soldier. Bullets whizzed past Lou's head as he angled for the truck. If he tripped now, he'd be dead. Just like that, dead.

The situation was surreal. He was on a military base in rural West Virginia, weaponless, locked in a goddamn firefight with highly trained soldiers who were pathologically prepared to die to protect their world. Back in Arlington, Emily was probably in her room, listening to music, getting ready for bed, totally unaware of the horror that was evolving three hours or so to the west. Another bullet struck the ground close by. Lou fought the urge to drop and roll. There was no cover, and he would be shot before he could take another breath. Cap was firing over his shoulder as he ran, the knapsack and its precious contents at times bouncing off the ground. Papa Steve continued to fire, but each series was quickly answered by a return volley.

As Lou reached the truck, he heard the distinct snap of bullets against metal. Next there was the thud of bullets against rubber, followed by a loud hiss of air. The left rear tire instantly deflated. Moments later, the right was flat as well.

A final burst of speed and Lou reached the passenger door with Cap on his heels. They scrambled inside while Papa Steve fired one last burst and dived behind the wheel. As torturous as their situation was, he seemed exhilarated—a cowboy mounting a two-thousand-pound bucking bull.

"You got the gun?" he asked as they lurched ahead.

Breathing heavily, Lou nodded. "How're we gonna get out of here with two flat tires?"

Papa Steve, his tan knuckles white from gripping the wheel, glanced over at him. "I thought you were the one with the blond bombshell contingency plan."

"Let's get to the guardhouse. I'll make the call on the way. Can you get any speed from this thing?"

"As long as it doesn't realize it has two flat tires."

Lou had Judy Lemon's phone number on speed dial. The "1812" was over now, and the smoke from the fireworks was drifting away. Papa Steve's explosions, too, were on the wane. Bewildered soldiers were emerging from the woods, weapons ready, trying to determine what had happened and whom to shoot.

The truck roared ahead, sending up rooster tails of dirt and dust, seeming as if it were stripping a gear every few feet.

"Dr. Lou? Is that you?" The voice of Judy Lemon, barely audible, crackled in Lou's ear. Sporadic gunfire had resumed, and several bullets hit the truck.

"Judy, can you hear me?" Lou had no idea if she answered. "Judy!" Lou shouted. "Meet us at the gate! At the gate!"

The truck was slowing down, its engine screeching.

"Not far now!" Papa Steve yelled. "We may have to run."

Up ahead, Lou caught sight of the end of the road and the guardhouse. The truck was about to breathe its last. Steve pushed a button on his detonator, and to their right, twenty feet or so from Cap, an explosion disintegrated a jeep, sending up smoke, flame and noise.

"Jesus!" Cap cried out, ducking from the blast.

"I had forgotten about that one until I saw the jeep," Papa Steve said, laughing as dirt and stones rained down on the roof. "Truck's dead. Guns out! We've got to run for the gate. Lou, where's that backup?"

As if on cue, up ahead, blue and red strobes appeared. With Papa Steve's handiwork disrupting the night, the front gate to the Mantis base was unguarded.

After a brief sprint, during which Papa Steve easily kept pace, Cap opened the gate to let Lemon's cruiser inside.

The driver's-side window opened, and Lemon leaned out. Her hair had been tucked under her trooper's hat, but Lou noticed that she had probably painted on another layer of makeup. "Hey, boys. Need a lift?"

The three clambered inside the cruiser just as a small nearby shed exploded.

"I know, I know," Lou said. "You forgot about that one."

"Which of you guys got the fireworks permit?" Lemon asked.

"That would be me," Papa Steve said.

"Operation Talon," Lou said, breathing hard. "We've got to stop it."

"Why?" Papa Steve asked. "We've got the murder weapon. Let's use it to get Brody."

"Talon is a suicide mission. Twenty guys are coming back in body bags unless we do something to prevent it."

"Did you hear where they're going?" Papa Steve asked.

"Dover Air Force Base. They were going to take off from Langley, but they changed their plans. I don't know where their ultimate destination is, but I got the sense from what I heard that it's more than one place."

Papa Steve hesitated. The muscles in his face went taut, and he seemed to be having difficulty assimilating the new information.

"What's the deal, boss?" Cap asked impatiently. "We've been lucky so far. I don't think we should be hanging here too much longer."

Finally, Papa Steve shrugged and pointed to a narrow dirt road in front of them. "That's the road to the heliport. Officer Judy, would you mind taking us there?"

"Brody's gone," Lou said. "What good's that going to do?"

"Trust me," Papa Steve said.

"Okay, then. Judy, go for it!"

The cruiser rocketed forward, fishtailing twice before being expertly brought in line. A minute later, they were at the heliport. A guard, possibly alerted by radio, stepped out from behind a utility shed and trained his rifle on the cruiser car.

"Down!" Lemon shouted.

The four of them ducked as a bullet struck the front windshield dead center and exited out the back, leaving perfect spiderwebs in the glass. Driving like a NAS-CAR champion, Lemon hit the brake and skidded into a smoke-and-rubber-filled 360. Then, before the cruiser had fully stopped, she rolled out the door, rising to her feet with lightning quickness, her pistol trained on the center of the Mantis guard's chest.

"Drop that weapon, soldier," she said. "That's an order."

Papa Steve climbed out of the car. "Do as she says, son. We got no beef with you."

The standoff was short lived. The baby-faced soldier lowered his weapon, and within moments Lemon had his wrists handcuffed behind his back, and he had shown the three men lockers containing radio helmets for each of them.

"I don't get it," Lou said. "What are we doing here? We've got to stop Brody."

Papa Steve gestured toward a weathered army helicopter, one of two remaining on the helipad. "Gentlemen," he said. "If we want to stop Wyatt Brody, then we're going to need to go for a little ride. Follow me, and I'll teach you boys how to hot-wire a chopper."

CHAPTER 44

Sarah could never bring herself to sell the town house she and David bought ten years before. Beckman Place was one of only a handful of gated communities within the D.C. city limits. Situated on a hill with majestic views over Sixteenth Street and Florida Avenue, Beckman Place sat on a piece of land that once housed a castle built for Senator John Henderson, coauthor of the Thirteenth Amendment, abolishing slavery. David fell in love with the location's history enough to ignore the strain the 1,500-square-foot property put on their limited budget. Now, the stone entrance gateposts were all that remained of Henderson Castle, and memories were all that Sarah had of David.

After spending the day with Edith, Sarah had grown even fonder of the remarkable woman she had come to regard as a friend. Edith had not visited Washington since before the so-called accident that blinded her, but she navigated the streets almost like a woman with sight. Once, on their way to Devlin and Rodgers to make copies of the Reddy Creek invoices for safekeeping,

Edith used her cane to keep Sarah from crossing a street in front of oncoming traffic.

"Open your ears," she had said with a smile.

When they arrived at Sarah's office, there was a surprise waiting for them. Bruce Patterson, Edith's former boss at the *Raleigh News & Observer*, had sent a FedEx box containing all the files, notes, and, research Edith had compiled during her Reddy Creek investigation. She and Sarah spent the remainder of the afternoon locked away in Sarah's office, going through the material with the meticulousness of archeologists at a dig site.

It was late afternoon, and Hogarth still had not called to accept Sarah's offer.

"Are you going to go public?" Edith asked.

"We can't back off," Sarah said. "He made his choice. Besides, thanks to you, we have a wealth of evidence here, even without Hogarth's cooperation, to establish a very strong motive for Brody to commit murder. I'm confident a jury will have more than enough reasonable doubt to acquit McHugh, if the prosecutors go to trial at all."

The two women returned to Beckman Place by Metro with only hours to go before Hogarth's deadline expired. Sarah waved her electronic key in front of the card reader. Automatic gates rolled open on well-oiled wheels. The guard seated inside a tollbooth-sized stone guardhouse did not break away from his TV set as Sarah and Edith strolled past. Sarah even waved and said hello, but the distracted man ignored her. Even with the windows in the guardhouse closed, Sarah could tell he was watching some sort of sporting event.

"I guess he's more into basketball than he is into security," Edith said, using her cane to feel the ground in front of her. "Third quarter, Wizards are losing by ten to the Celtics."

No longer surprised by anything Edith did, Sarah merely glanced over at her and smiled. "Maybe that's why crime here goes up during football season," she said.

She locked arms with Edith, feeling warmed by the bond they had formed, and guided her the last hundred yards to the town house.

"What's that?" Edith asked.

Sarah looked perplexed. "What's what?"

"I thought I heard something moving. A rustling."

Sarah went still as the dead, listening. Nothing. Not a sound. "The wind?" she asked

"Maybe."

Sarah checked the branches on several nearby trees, wishing they were rustling. She took out her key and tentatively inserted it. At the instant the bolt turned, an exceedingly hefty man looped around the shrubbery and came up behind them. It only took Sarah a second.

Detective Chris Bryzinski.

The College Park cop trained his gun on Sarah, barely giving Edith a glance.

"Inside. Quickly. Not a word from either of you."

Sarah's heart stopped. Barely able to move, she inched the door open and led Edith inside the small, lighted foyer. Bryzinski grabbed Edith by the arm and swung her rudely onto her knees on the living room rug. Sarah moved to help her, but the massive policeman called her off. She saw determination in his cold eyes, buried deep in fat—a man with a mission.

Not good.

"Hogarth sent you, didn't he?" Sarah said.

"Shut up and sit in that chair."

"I'll scream."

Shoving Edith aside with his boot, Bryzinski rammed the barrel of his gun into Sarah's belly. She gasped and stumbled backwards into an Eames chair—one of a pair she and David had picked out together. Only then did she notice that the gun had a silencer.

"I'll shoot you both dead, right here, right now," Bryzinski said. "You've still got a chance to live, but only if you do everything exactly as I say."

Sarah's blood was ice. She could read people, and this man was there for only one purpose. She had no doubt that within minutes she and Edith would both be executed. A weapon of some sort? An escape path? A scream? A frontal attack? Nothing made sense except to stay calm and reason with the man. Ten feet away, her dark glasses lying on the rug beside her, Edith had worked her way to her knees.

"Please," Sarah said, fixing on the detective's eyes. "You don't have to do this. I don't know what Hogarth is paying you, or what he has on you, but this is murder, plain and simple."

"Shut up!"

"You don't want our blood on your hands. We're not just things to be removed. We're people. Please, Chris, you swore an oath to protect and serve. Hogarth is a monster. An ambitious monster. He'd step on you like a bug if you were in his way. Don't give in."

"Shut up, dammit!"

Sarah could see some confusion in his eyes. She needed to push. She had to convince him he wasn't a demon.

As if in answer to her thoughts, Bryzinski glanced down at Edith and, without warning, kicked her over onto her side.

Sarah knew what was coming now, and there was not a damn thing she could think of to stop it from happening. A china figurine stood on the end table to her right, a wedding present from her parents. She could throw it at his face and attack, relying on her quickness and perhaps Edith's help to overcome his massive bulk.

"Is it money, Chris? Is that what this is all about? Is that why you're going to murder two women who never did anything to hurt you?"

Sarah inched her hand closer to the figurine and at the same time sized up Bryzinski—his stance, the position of his gun, the commitment in his eyes.

"I wish it was money," he was saying. "I'm afraid you've made a powerful enemy. There's nothing I can do."

"What about your wife? What would she think of you if she knew what you were about to do?"

"You keep her out of this."

To Bryzinski's right, Edith was back on one knee. Sarah forced herself not to look at her. The figurine was only a couple of inches away. Sarah could think of nothing else to do but continue to talk . . . to try to reason . . . to plead.

"You don't look ready to do this, Chris. Have you ever killed someone in cold blood?"

"I'll put the shot where you won't feel a thing. Her, too."

"At least tell me how much Hogarth's paying you. I have millions from the settlement of my husband's death. Millions. I'll give all of it to you—every cent. I mean it. Just let me get up and I'll show you my bank statement. Whatever Hogarth is paying, I can beat it."

Edith was up in a crouch, with one knee still on the rug.

"I wish it was money," Bryzinski said again, ruefully. "Unless you've got a magic wand to erase the past, I got no choice here. Look, I'm sorry. I really am. But this is how it has to go down."

"I thought you said we were going to talk," Sarah said.

"I lied." Bryzinski raised his gun and aimed it dead center at Sarah's forehead. "God forgive me," he muttered.

His gun came up, the muzzle of the silencer an ebony hole in the universe. Sarah grabbed the figurine and hurled it at his head at the instant she heard the gunshot. In the same motion, she threw herself and her chair over backwards. Her head slammed against the oak floor beside the rug. A brief burst of white light, and all went black.

A second? A minute? Ten? The first thing Sarah experienced when she came to was the ecstatic realization that she wasn't dead or, for that matter, in any pain. The first thing she saw was Chris Bryzinski, lying facedown, trying desperately to pull himself across the rug. The first thing she heard was Edith's voice.

". . . I mean it! Move one more inch, and you're going to see how accurate I am with this thing. And with you panting like a water buffalo, I promise you I won't miss."

"Fuck you, you bitch. You shot me."

"Keep talking, my friend," Edith said. "Keep talking. Your voice and your buffalo breathing are the only ways I can keep a bead on you, and this derringer Snake Slayer still has one shot." She waved the jewel-handled, double-barreled weapon in his direction.

Shaking, Sarah scrambled to her feet and raced to Edith, pausing only long enough to kick Bryzinski in the side of the head, and then to pick up his pistol and throw aside the silencer.

"You okay?" Sarah asked, her arm around Edith.

"Did he bleed on your rug?"

"Sort of."

"An oriental?"

"Only sort of. Pottery Barn."

"I'm glad he said that little prayer before he pulled the trigger," Edith said. "I wouldn't have been able to get a precise bead on him otherwise."

"I completely forgot about your offer to have target practice in your office just to show me you could do it."

"My instructor taught me never to carry a gun unless I was prepared to use it. I was so ready."

"Will someone help me?" Bryzinski moaned. "She shot me."

"Packs a wallop, doesn't it," Edith said. "Beware the blind guy."

Sarah left Bryzinski writhing on the floor, clutching his tree-trunk thigh, and returned moments later with a white bedsheet and a kitchen knife. She ripped the sheet with the knife, using one strip to gag the detective, and several more to bandage his leg. Blood was continuing to flow, but not at a rate she deemed life threatening. Next, she found a pair of handcuffs in a fabric pouch latched to his belt, and manacled his hands behind his back.

"What now?" Edith asked.

"Now I'm going to get a dolly from the maintenance shed."

"What for?"

"We've got to go drop off this dirty laundry."

Sarah hugged Edith hard, unwilling to let go. It felt as if she were embracing a sister and not just a friend.

CHAPTER 45

"A helicopter's main job is to kill you," Papa Steve said into the helmet's microphone, "and the pilot's job is to not let that happen. So far, so good."

The aging twin-engine UH-1N Huey bucked against a strong headwind as it flew a northeastwardly course toward Delaware. From the copilot's seat, Lou watched, fascinated, as the man who self-admittedly could blow the antennae off a fly without blinding it demonstrated a completely unrelated skill set.

In the backseat, Cap was looking far worse than Emily had during their one ill-fated whale watch together in choppy seas. The Huey dipped again and yawed severely before Papa Steve settled it down.

"I told you I didn't want to get in this thing!" Cap yelled from the backseat.

"Haven't you been in a helicopter before?" Papa Steve asked.

"I've only been in a plane, like, twice. I don't like the idea that there's nothing between me and the ground but air."

"You can handle it," Lou said. "Heck, you've stood up to the mob."

"And it cost me my boxing career."

Papa Steve banked the chopper hard right, flying at a thousand feet over a stretch of Virginia woodland.

"Do you want an air sickness bag?" Lou asked.

"No," Cap said, shaking his head and looking precisely like a guy in need of an air sickness bag. "I want a pizza."

Lou gave Cap a big thumbs-up sign, and Cap responded by giving Lou the finger.

"I need to call Sarah," Lou said. "She's been working on Spencer Hogarth, trying to use him to get Brody to admit to Colston's murder. But now we've also got to find a way to get him to stop Operation Talon."

"You can make a call using the Huey's sat phone," Papa Steve said.

Lou recited Sarah's number and a few moments later heard ringing in his headset.

"Hello?" Sarah sounded unsure.

"Hey, there, Sarah, it's Lou."

"I didn't recognize the number."

"That's because I'm in a helicopter with Cap and Papa Steve, on our way to Dover Air Force Base. Are you okay?"

"Aside from having Detective Bryzinski try to kill us a little while ago, we're fine."

"Jesus. Where are you now?"

"Edith and I are in the car. Bryzinski is in the trunk."

"Does he fit?"

"Just barely. We're certain Hogarth has something

big on him—enough to put him up to murdering us. He was about to do it, silencer and all, when Edith shot him in the leg."

"Edith?"

"There's more to this woman than you think."

"I guess. What are you going to do with him?"

"His wound's not too bad. We're either going to give him to the police, drop him off at a hospital, or use him for some sort of bargaining chip with Hogarth. I'm leaning toward trying that first."

"I agree. I have some information that might help."

"What's this about Dover?"

Talking over the noise of the chopper, Lou quickly reviewed the frightening events at Mantis Base. When he was done, he felt the weight of Sarah's pause.

"You have the murder weapon?" she asked finally.

"Your ballistics expert will tell us for sure, but yes, we probably do. My pal Cap has it in the backseat."

"When is this Operation Talon taking off?"

"I suspect it won't be long."

Another hesitation. "I'll bet you think I'm furious because you've gone rogue again when you promised me you wouldn't."

"The thought was crossing my mind."

"Well, let it pass, please. From what I can tell, that was an incredibly brave thing you guys just did. I really feel like I owe you an apology for being so hard on you all this time. Edith and I nearly got ourselves killed by taking the same sort of risks you've taken."

"I can't believe what I'm hearing," Lou said. "I've been pardoned?"

"I'm done pushing you around."

"In that case, I'm done trying to stuff my feelings toward you. How's that?"

"I can handle it. See me when this is all over, Doc, and we have our acquittal. I'd love to set something up to thank you for all your help."

"Are you on speaker?"

"Yes, why?"

"Hey, there, Edith. I'm glad you can't hear my face turning red."

"You should be red, Doctor. She's a hell of a woman."

"So, tell me, did Bryzinski confess that Hogarth hired him?"

"I've asked him in polite and not-so-polite ways," Sarah replied, "but I think he needs a bit more time in the trunk to open up to us."

"Without Hogarth's cooperation, I don't know what we're going to do to get Brody to stop this Operation Talon. I thought you might be able to make that happen, but seeing as he tried to have you killed, I guess I'll need to go with my Plan B."

"What's Plan B?"

"Plan B is that we're going to Dover to stop him ourselves," Lou said.

"That's crazy. You'll get yourself killed. Listen, we can get to Hogarth."

"How?"

"We'll give him a new deal. We'll offer to bury Reddy Creek if he stops Operation Talon."

"Great plan," Lou said. "Maybe this time he'll hire someone less incompetent to kill you."

"And you think going up against Brody and his men is safer? Hogarth is power hungry and ambitious to the point where he is blinder than Edith. As long as he thinks Bryzinski is either dead or not safely with the authorities, he'll believe he can beat us. You've never met him, Lou. He's nuts."

"Let me run this past Papa Steve."

From the pilot's seat, Papa Steve gave Lou a thumbs-up.

Sarah sighed.

"Look, this is the man who arranged to have Edith killed and ended up blinding her. We don't have direct proof of that, but we have enough to get Hogarth to finger himself if we play our cards right. Believe me, if it comes down to Operation Talon or him, I know which way he'll go. He'll throw anyone or anything under the bus to save himself and his career. I want you to back off, Lou. Let us handle this. Edith deserves it. We can get to Hogarth. He doesn't know we have Bryzinski, so trust me on this. I've got a way."

"Fine, I trust you," Lou said. "But unless Papa Steve and Cap feel otherwise, we're still going in. If anything, maybe we can delay the mission launch until you get Hogarth to intervene."

"I don't want you to."

"Sarah, we need one another. We always did. Now, where are you?"

"If you think Hogarth is seeing the troops off at Dover, then I guess that's where we're headed."

"Given what's at stake, I'm sure of it," Lou said.

"Actually, I have his cell number. I can call him."

"Be careful, lady. I mean it."

"Same to you guys."

Lou could not bring himself to say good-bye.

After the call ended, Cap tapped Lou on the shoulder. "You know, you two sound like an old married couple."

"I would say more like we're inching up to the discovery phase. Do you think one of you would be willing to fill in for me with Officer Lemon?"

"You bet," the two men called out in near unison.

For ten minutes, the three flew in silence. Then Papa Steve dropped down to 250 feet and announced he was making a stop.

"What for?" Lou asked. "We've got to get there."

"We've also got to do something about that gun we worked so hard for."

Without any further explanation, Papa Steve landed effortlessly on the fairway of the ninth hole of a golf course Lou knew well—38.84783,-76.73744, the Sharpton Hills Golf Club. Using tools from an emergency repair kit under the pilot's seat, he quickly removed a piece from the passenger-side control panel and slid in the pistol that had probably been used to murder Elias Colston.

"Lou, do you have the number of your friend Sarah's office?"

"Right here in my wallet."

"Call and leave a message for the boss and one for Sarah, telling them where the gun can be found."

"Why didn't you just tell her while we were talking?"

Papa Steve's bittersweet expression answered the question. "You tell me," he said.

"You don't think we're going to survive this, do you."

"You want me to answer that? I was going to leave the gun with your friend Officer Lemon, but I don't know her well enough to trust her. And unfortunately, I do know Brody. Then I passed on just burying it here on the golf course. That would be time consuming and just plain sloppy to try in the dark, especially with the ground nearly frozen. So this is the best I can come up with."

"There is another option," Lou offered. "Cap, if you just say the word, we'll drop you off right here with the gun. You can make your way home and get it to someone you trust."

"Tell me what you would do if our situations were reversed. I'm stayin'."

"Up we go," Lou said. "I've got Sarah's office number right here."

"Make sure to leave a detailed message," Papa Steve said. "My best friend and the daddy of my godson was killed with this weapon. I'm not going to allow the man who pulled the trigger to walk away."

Lou replaced the repair kit as the Huey smoothly lifted off, and then made the call to Sarah's office. Papa Steve was right. The odds favored none of them surviving this night. He smiled ruefully, thinking about the irony of Gary McHugh being the only one to make it alive. It was dumb to try to stop Operation Talon—childish and naïve.

"Last chance, Cap," he said. "Just say the word and we'll set you down right here."

"I'm here to serve and protect, my friend. At the moment, there are only three guys I'm the sponsor for. It wouldn't look good for me to lose a third of them."

The next forty-five minutes were spent with each man lost in his own thoughts.

"Hey, gentlemen," Papa Steve suddenly announced, "we're approaching Dover. Make sure your seat straps are secured and your tray tables are in their upright and locked positions. And, oh yes, hold on tight."

"Do we have permission to land?" Lou asked.

Papa Steve lowered their altitude to 750 feet. Ahead of them, the dim lights of the airfield glowed like distant stars.

"Not yet," he said.

"So that's your plan?" Lou sounded concerned. "You're just going to wing it and see what happens?"

"I'm a fly-by-the-seat-of-my-pants type of guy."

"Or, more precisely, a get-shot-in-the-seat-of-your-pants type of guy."

As if on cue, the radio began to crackle. Then air traffic control took over and announced that they were being monitored and needed to turn around. Papa Steve handled the brief, tense communication smoothly and with class, keeping the copter flying slow and level.

"It's a no-go on landing," he said. "The air base is shut down to incoming traffic. Orders."

"Tell them to ask Brody for permission," Lou said quickly.

Papa Steve looked over at Lou, perplexed. "Not sure about this, Doc."

"Tell them to relay this exact message to Colonel Wyatt Brody, Mantis Company: Dr. Lou Welcome knows all about Manolo, and he's going to go public unless we get permission to land."

Papa Steve hesitated for a moment before sending the message back to the tower. A stream of chatter ensued. After a tense few minutes of waiting and circling, the helicopter made a sudden and rapid course change.

"Where are we going?" Lou asked.

"We're landing," Papa Steve said. "I guess your message worked. We'll be touchdown in a little over twenty minutes."

"Twenty minutes? Why do we have to circle for so long?" Lou asked.

"I guess they have to prepare the welcome wagon for our arrival. Brace yourself, boys, I think we're going to get more chop on the ground than we did in the air."

CHAPTER 46

Ten minutes after ending her call with Lou, Sarah drove over a pothole at forty and did not hear a sound from the trunk of her Mercedes. Not a cry. No shift in weight. Nothing. They had secured Bryzinski as best as they could. His handcuffs seemed too tight, so they went to clothesline, wrapped several times around his wrists and ankles. It seemed there was no way he could bang for attention. They left the gag on him, too, and crossed their fingers that he wouldn't vomit and choke to death.

It was time to find Hogarth.

Sarah called. The phone rang several times. She believed Hogarth would be at Dover, which was the direction in which she now was driving. If Operation Talon was as big as Lou had said, then Hogarth would want to see the fruits of his and Brody's labors take flight.

Three rings, and Sarah heard a satisfying click.

"Hello, who is this?"

"Secretary Hogarth, it's Sarah Cooper."

Hogarth's hesitation was long enough. Bryzinski had either failed or not made his move.

"Yes, Counselor."

"We need to talk."

Did she hear him suck down a nervous breath? It was hard to tell over the thrumming of her car tires and the spotty cell reception. But if Sarah ventured a guess, then Spencer Hogarth, for a fleeting moment at least, believed he was conversing with a ghost.

"Sarah, are you calling to thank me for the wine?"

"Not the wine, Mr. Secretary. I have a new deal to make."

"Talk to me now. You seem to have a way of getting my attention."

"No, this has to be done face-to-face."

"Now? I'm rather busy at the moment."

"Your choice. Meet me now or I'm going to begin a hatchet job on your career. You know I can do it, too."

"Well, when you put it that way, what choice do I really have?"

"None."

"In that case, I'm at Dover air base. Can you find it?"

"My car can."

"I'll meet you at the main gate. Call me when you're ten minutes out."

"See you soon." Sarah ended the call. "He's at Dover," she said to Edith.

"You knew he would be. Did he suspect anything?" Edith clutched her hands tightly in her lap, rubbing them together as she bit down at her lower lip.

"No," Sarah said. "And he can't. For our plan to work, Hogarth must believe that the killer cop he hired never made the hit—at least not yet. I'm sure he's calling Bryzinski right now."

"Will he hear him in the trunk?"

"Not the way we tied him down. But still, I'll pull over and double-check as soon as we see a safe place. Any peep from Bryzinski would give Hogarth enough reason to have us both killed on the spot."

"Or do it himself," Edith said.

Two hours later, Sarah arrived at the front gate to Dover air base. They had stopped twice and noted with relief that Bryzinski was lying on his side, breathing easily. The air base was an impenetrable fortress of barbed wire and tall fencing. Armed guards with rifles at the ready stepped in front of Sarah's car as she slowed to a stop.

Please don't open my trunk, she was thinking.

Sarah lowered her window as one of the guards approached. From high above, she heard the chop of a helicopter, its rotors whapping against the cold and windy air.

Lou, is that you up there? Is it you? Please be careful.

Another guard approached her car, this one shining a bright flashlight into Edith's face. The light, reflecting off Edith's dark glasses, evoked absolutely no response. The guard with the flashlight whistled for attention.

"She's blind," Sarah said.

Edith looked out Sarah's window. "Hey, I'm blind,"

she said, removing her dark glasses. "That explains a lot of things."

"Ma'am," the guard said to Sarah, "that's fine, but this is a restricted area. You'll need to back your vehicle away right now."

"I've got a meeting with Spencer Hogarth. He's supposed to be here."

"Secretary Hogarth? You know him?"

"Look, we don't want to make trouble for you guys, but he's expecting us. You can send us away without trying to reach him, but I promise it won't go well for you."

"The Americans with Disabilities people can be pretty tough adversaries," Edith added.

"One minute, please."

The guard left and two others took his place. They each carried powerful automatic weapons. Sarah took in a breath and held it. She didn't dare even to look up. At her girlfriends' insistence, she had gone on a few dates over recent years, but there was never any spark. Now there was a man who was getting to her, and he was up there. Getting ready, along with his friends, to risk his life to stop twenty young soldiers who were riding into their own Little Bighorn. He was totally maddening, but he was also totally good. And thoughts of him were gnawing at her chest.

The only person she knew who rivaled Lou's persistence was herself. Now, if she could not get Hogarth to turn on Brody, then Lou's life, and the lives of Cap Duncan and Papa Steve, would be in the gravest danger, to say nothing of Edith's and her own.

As if reading her thoughts, Edith reached across and

took her hand. "Hang in there, babe," she said, her jaw fiercely set. "We're going to do this."

The first guard returned, and for a moment—something about his eyes—Sarah thought they'd been denied entry.

"We need to check IDs first," he said, "then we'll escort you inside."

Sarah exhaled a relieved breath.

From above them, she again heard the steady thrum of a helicopter.

CHAPTER 47

A strong updraft wobbled the landing skids of the Huey, but Papa Steve, cool as ice on an igloo, adjusted the controls and brought the helicopter to a smooth touchdown on the helipad. He then cut the engines and waited until the persistent whapping of the rotors had come to a complete stop before announcing that it was okay to release their safety harnesses.

Cap came forward and joined the other two in the cockpit. His pistol dangled loosely in his hand. The rest of his knapsack lay on the metal floor, empty except for the tools he had used to break into Wyatt Brody's office and gun case. All three were looking out the front windshield into total darkness. No lights. No movement of any kind. Lou unbuckled his harness and rushed to the back of the helicopter, glancing out the rear windshields. Here he could see only runway lights. Otherwise, the surrounding grounds appeared to be completely deserted.

"What now?" Cap asked.

"Now we go outside," Lou said.

"I've got a bad feeling about this, pal," Cap said.

"I can't see a soul out there," Papa Steve said on his way from the cockpit to the cabin. "My gut says trap."

"Oh, they're out there, all right," Lou said.

"So, what's the plan?"

"The plan is we take our chances in the lion's den."

"Just my luck," Cap said with a frustrated sigh. "I get partnered with two guys who fly by the seat of their pants." He hung his head and made the sign of the cross.

"Um, Lou . . . I think—"

Before Papa Steve could finish his thought, Lou had the side door open and had jumped out of the cabin and onto the tarmac. Cap and Papa Steve followed. The trio stood in a tight circle, surveying the darkness, breathing in the quiet. A row of blue lights, shimmering like gas flames, stretched down the length of a long runway, casting a weak glow on the massive transport aircraft parked there. The airplane's engines rumbled at low volume like the snore of a sleeping giant.

In the distance, tower lights barely reached that remote section of the air base where air traffic control had directed Papa Steve to land. The shadows of a row of massive snowplows loomed like steel monsters. A steady, biting wind whipped at the men's faces.

Off to one side of the runway, Lou could see the three Chinook helicopters from Mantis, silent and dark. Maybe the men of Mantis Company were already aboard the transport aircraft. If so, it might be too late for anybody to stop Operation Talon.

"I'd like to up that bad feeling to a *really* bad feeling," Cap said.

As if on cue, blinding headlights from the snow-plows all came on at once. Lou and the others squinted and crouched low, shielding themselves from the glare. When they straightened up, they could see shapes—shadowy figures that had seemingly materialized from the night. Another blink, and the figures came into sharp focus. Soldiers from Mantis Company stood before them in a straight line, like a firing squad, their rifles at the ready. The men from Mantis, rigid as stone columns, appeared impervious to the cold. Their weapons were locked on the three intruders.

A man emerged from between two of the soldiers. He wore a thick down parka and hid his eyes beneath a broad-brimmed camouflage cap.

Brody.

Brody was followed by a taller officer in nearly identical dress, who Lou felt certain was Coon, the second in command he had heard at Mantis base. The two men entered the beams of the snowplows' headlamps as though they were stepping onto a Broadway stage.

"Dr. Welcome, how nice to see you again," he said. "I guess you've come to say your good-byes to our troops. I know the traitor next to you, who likes to blow things up, but this gentleman is new to me."

The three remained silent.

"It's over, Brody," Lou said finally. "We know who you are and what you've done, and soon these men will know, too. Operation Talon has to be stopped."

"Oh, I'm sorry," Brody said. "I didn't realize you were now in charge of matters of national security. I'll just let these guys know that rather than fight, they should just pack up and head on home. Or better still, how about I have them shoot you and your friends, here, for treason and for attempting to intervene with a military operation. Gentlemen, ready your weapons."

In an instant, twenty safety mechanisms were released. Lou raised his hands above his head. Cap and Papa Steve did the same, dropping their pistols onto the tarmac.

"We're unarmed," Lou said. "I'm a doctor. Cap, here, is a fighter who teaches inner city kids how to box. Papa Steve you know. Kill us, and you're killing Americans— you're killing what you all stand for."

"Enough!" Brody ordered. "Did you think mentioning Manolo's name would get you a free pass? I brought you in here so these men can see why they have accepted this mission—the forces that are constantly trying to stop us. Men, Manolo is in charge of making the drink we all share every day. The composition of that drink is a complex one, but he does a rather good job at it, don't you think? We pay him in cash and sometimes, when necessary, in weapons. Does that knowledge make a difference to any of you?"

"It should make a difference," Lou said. "You're being manipulated by this man like guinea pigs, being asked to sacrifice your lives so that he can prove a point. I've read his research. I know."

The soldiers remained in position.

"Game, set, and match, Welcome," Brody sang.

"Whatever it takes!" one of the men shouted.

The rest of Mantis Company echoed their battle cry.

"Whatever it takes!"

"No!" Lou pleaded. "Not whatever it takes. You are warriors. You do your best. You do what's right. You act with valor. But you don't knowingly and willingly enter a situation planning to take your own lives. That is above and beyond the call of duty. This mission must be stopped."

"Fire!" Brody cried. "Take them out! These men are a threat to our national security."

Papa Steve stepped in front of Lou. "Don't do it! Stand down, guys. Don't shoot!"

Brody pulled a pistol from a holster hidden underneath his parka. He aimed the weapon at Papa Steve. "I will shoot them myself if you men don't follow this order. Now, fire your weapons, dammit."

With feline grace and speed, Cap rushed Brody and, in virtually the same motion, landed a vicious right hook to the side of his nose, dropping the Mantis commander onto his butt.

Cap'n Crunch.

Brody's pistol skidded away. Blood spurted from both his nostrils. His eyes glazed. Lou tensed himself for the hail of bullets that would end his best friend's life. Instead, at that moment, there was only a loud pop. Cap went down like a flour sack, facedown on the cold asphalt, twitching and bucking.

"Coon, you stupid bastard!" Papa Steve shouted.

Lou kicked away the two filament wires attached to the Taser gun in Coon's outstretched hand and knelt beside Cap. The powerful darts had paralyzed him through his parka. Lou had treated enough Taser wounds to know quickly that Cap's situation was horribly unpleasant, but also temporary.

A click.

Lou heard a gun chamber loading and closed his eyes, bracing for the sting of steel and wondering how long he would feel the pain. A momentary flash, or would it be a lingering agony? His mind's eye saw blood, gallons of it, spewing out from holes in his chest. He pined for Emily in those final seconds, anticipating a sensation that never materialized. When he opened his eyes, one of the Mantis soldiers had stepped forward with his weapon pointed not at the three intruders, but at Brody, who was shakily on his feet, teeth bared, eyes still watering, clamping his bleeding nostrils shut with the fabric of his cap.

"We're not afraid to die, sir," the soldier said. "None of us. But that doesn't mean we murder innocent Americans. Don't touch your pistol, Major Coon."

Lou tried to rouse Cap, who was coming around but was still too dazed to stand.

"Staff Sergeant Morales, you'd best point that weapon where it's supposed to be pointed," Brody rasped.

"Morales is right," another man said, stepping out of line to aim his weapon at Coon. "We're not stupid. We know what you felt the ruby drink was doing to us, but not many of us believed it, or cared. We've always been ready to die for our country and our commanders."

Papa Steve stepped forward and faced them. "Your commander," he said, "this man who is ordering you to kill my friends and me, is a murderer himself. He shot

Elias Colston, Mark's father, in cold blood, because Colston knew the truth about Mantis. He didn't believe his son would have ever had the courage to act in battle the way he did unless he was acting under the influence of chemicals that altered his ability to experience fear."

"That's not so," Morales said.

"Ask Brody," Lou said. "I read his Ph.D. thesis cover to cover. Ask him if he thinks you men would undertake this mission if not for the drug combination he developed and fed you every day. Fear is a part of war, but Brody wanted to eliminate that factor, to bring you equal with the terrorists we are fighting. You men are true soldiers. Maybe you'll be killed in the line of duty. That's a risk every soldier takes. But let it be a risk and not the goal. Let it be something that happens to you and not something that you seek out."

Staff Sergeant Morales turned to Lou. "Doc, we appreciate what you're saying. But like it or not, we are going on our mission. Like you said, we're soldiers, Mantis marines, and we're trained to follow orders. No questions asked. No options accepted."

"You just chose not to commit the cold-blooded murder of innocent American civilians," Papa Steve said. "That's not following orders."

"Well, I guess you found the one line we're not willing to cross."

Brody had staunched the bleeding from his nose, and lowered his cap. Lou caught the sliver of a smile as it creased the corners of the commander's mouth. Fenton Morales lowered his gun, and the others did the same.

"Colonel Brody, sir, Major Coon," Morales said, "I

believe I am speaking for the group of us. Once these men have been taken into military custody, we are prepared to board the transport and complete our mission as ordered."

Lou read Wyatt Brody's eyes: *You're dead, Welcome.*

"I'll radio for the MPs," Brody said earnestly. "You men can watch from the transport as these three are escorted away. I'll even make certain this coward who sucker-punched me receives medical attention. Major Coon, supervise the securing of these men."

"Sir, yes, sir!" Coon said, saluting.

"Now, men, on that plane. You'll be airborne in fifteen minutes. First, though, let's take a minute together."

"Crimson is the color of courage, the color of blood spilled in battle, the color of valor. To justice. To country. To God. To Mantis."

"Whatever it takes!"

CHAPTER 48

The lights of an approaching sedan flashed several times. Sarah was driving at walking speed along an empty road inside the Dover air base. Two armed guards dressed for the cold flanked her car. The defogger was blasting on high, but the windshield kept misting up, giving her just a small porthole into the world outside.

The headlights flashed again and Sarah stopped. Twenty yards apart, the cars faced each other like a pair of jousters readying for a charge. Then the sedan's driver's-side door opened and Spencer Hogarth stepped out. He wore a long trench coat with the belt undone and dangling. The silver of his hair shone like snow under the glow of an isolated streetlight. He spoke to the guards, who checked his ID before heading back toward the gate. Then he rapped twice on Sarah's roof.

She lowered her window and studied the secretary of defense's hard-bitten face. In just over a day, his worry lines seemed to have deepened, the bags under his eyes become fuller.

Has the stress of ordering our murders taken such a big toll? she wanted to ask.

She imagined what Hogarth was thinking, *How are you alive? What in the hell happened to Bryzinski?*

"Follow me," he said.

"Where are we going?"

"Someplace I know where it's safe to talk."

Or someplace where it's easy to have us killed, Sarah thought.

Again, fear gripped her. She had her cards ready to play, and Edith's derringer loaded in her pocket for contingency, but this was a remorseless, power-hungry megalomaniac they were dealing with. There were probably countless ways for a man of his power and connections to get their bodies out of Dover undetected. The guards were out of sight now, leaving her and Edith alone. Timing was going to be everything. Her heart pounding, Sarah nodded that she would follow the man who was prepared to murder them both. The target for success was Hogarth's massive ego and belief that he could survive any situation.

As Hogarth headed back to his Cadillac, Sarah heard a loud thump from behind her.

Bryzinski!

Had his weight shifted? Were his hands now free? Could he hear what was going on outside the car?

Sarah's throat tightened as Hogarth stopped and turned slowly in the direction of the noise. He was focused on the trunk of the Mercedes, or so Sarah believed. She wrapped her hand around the derringer and waited for another rap. Maybe he was having a seizure of some sort?

"We don't have much time," Edith said to Hogarth, her voice brimming with anger and, Sarah felt, with confidence.

The outburst was enough to refocus Hogarth's attention. *Smart, smart girl,* Sarah was thinking.

"We get this over now, or we drive away," Edith added.

"Follow me," Hogarth said, turning back to his car.

When they were back in the Mercedes, Sarah put her hand on Edith's. "Nicely done."

"I hate that man so much. I'll do anything to make this work."

They followed Hogarth along a warren of empty streets that took them some distance from the gate. The Cadillac stopped in front of a closed hangar. Sarah parked as far away as she dared, and the two women quickly got out and moved toward where Hogarth was standing. There was no sound from the trunk. Sarah and Edith exhaled in unison.

One ominous sign: Hogarth hadn't checked either of them for a wire. He would do that after they were dead.

The trio stood six feet apart, tucked away in a quiet and seemingly abandoned section of the air base. Hogarth said nothing for a few tense seconds, then reached into his coat pocket. Instinctively, Sarah grasped the derringer but made no move to extract it.

"Okay, it's safe to talk here," Hogarth said. "What do you want from me?"

"Nothing has changed from the restaurant," Sarah said, her grip still on the gun. "We have enough information to bury your career if it becomes public."

Hogarth eyed her coldly. She was certain he had tried to reach Bryzinski, but he wasn't giving anything away.

"So, what are we doing here?" he asked. "I thought you had a new deal to offer."

"I do," Sarah said. "We bury Reddy Creek, for good and forever, we'll sign papers, whatever you need to feel confident that Reddy Creek and the other armory robberies never come to the surface."

"In exchange for Brody's confession to murder? I thought you said we had a new deal. That's the old one."

"No, we got Brody dead to rights on murder one," Sarah said. "We've got an alibi with Swiss cheese–sized holes in it, a compelling motive, and the weapon used to kill Elias Colston—a weapon that just happens to have come from Brody's gun collection."

For the first time, Hogarth's expression revealed his surprise. "How did that come to be?"

"Doesn't matter," Sarah said. "What matters is we've got the weapon."

"So what do you want from me? A confession for this woman's tragedy? That isn't going to happen, because I had nothing to do with it."

Hogarth withdrew his hand from his coat pocket. Sarah was about to pull out the derringer, or even shoot through her coat pocket, but something made her stop. The secretary's gloved hand came out empty.

"Nothing you can do will ever compensate me for my loss," Edith said.

"Then make your offer or I walk away."

"Okay. You need to put a stop to Operation Talon."

Hogarth's jaw came unhinged. "What?"

"We know," Sarah said. "We know all about Talon and your use of a psychotropic drug mixture to block out your soldiers' fear of death. We know these men are on nothing more than a massive suicide mission. Our terrorists versus their terrorists."

"Nothing doing. Even if unsubstantiated word got out, the American people will stand behind our troops."

That was it. Hogarth was almost certainly right, and he knew it.

It was time for the final card.

"We have Bryzinski," Sarah said simply.

"What?"

"The killer you hired made it as far as my condo, and we shot him."

Sarah passed over a plastic Baggie with the cop's silencer in it. If Hogarth put together this revelation and the noise that had come from the trunk, they were finished.

"That's bullshit!"

"Suit yourself. We have a recorded confession, including who paid him. I've left separate instructions with two of my partners as to how they can find both him and the recording."

Hogarth digested the revelation. At that instant, Sarah felt certain she heard more pounding from the trunk. It was all she could do to keep from looking back in that direction, or at Edith.

"I want proof he's alive," Hogarth said finally.

The bluff was running out of time.

"The proof is we're going to count to five," Sarah said with renewed force. "You agree to call Talon off and we'll tell you where your pudgy buddy can be found. If I get to zero, we leave. Killing us won't do you any good now. By morning, the police and the media will have all they need to put you out of business and in prison."

"Wait a min—"

"Five," Edith said.

"This is . . . bigger than you realize," Hogarth stammered. "There are reasons for what we're doing."

"Four."

"I can't just stop it. Do you understand what you're doing? How much planning and preparation has gone into this? You're putting American lives at risk."

"Three."

"Jesus! Give me a second!"

"Two."

Edith took Sarah by the arm and turned her toward where the Mercedes waited.

"Okay! Okay! I'll do it! I'll stop it. Jesus, I'll stop it. You two get back in your car and follow me."

CHAPTER 49

Lou watched the somber processional of Mantis marines ascend the portable staircase into the transport. He was desperate to try to stop them but, in his current situation, incapable of doing so. Along with Cap and Papa Steve, he'd had his hands secured behind his back with plastic cuffs by two marines he assumed were Palace Guards, and he was forced to a kneeling position on the cold tarmac. The men of Operation Talon had then waited until a call was placed to the Air Force security before turning their backs and boarding the plane.

Floodlights gave Lou a view of the orderly departure. Weapons and other provisions were efficiently being loaded into the cargo hold of the massive twin-engine jet. Members of Operation Talon, dressed in military fatigues and dark combat boots, vanished one by one through the plane's open cabin door. As the last of them disappeared into the cabin, kneeling there in the darkness and the cold, Lou quietly wept.

Cap, who had fully recovered from the Taser shock, knelt between Papa Steve and Lou. "They could be boarding a flight to Disney or something," he said. "Just a regular ol' plane ride. What is that, anyway?"

"It's a Boeing C-40 Clipper, the military version of a 737," Papa Steve explained. "The Navy uses them for logistic support."

"Logistic support, my ass," Cap said. "Do you think the pilots know that every one of their passengers is going to die before this mission is done?"

"It's not like that, my friend," Papa Steve said. "Soldiers are trained to follow orders. These men are doing their jobs—what they believe is right."

Lou's thoughts were focused elsewhere. "I didn't give Sarah enough time to deal with Hogarth," he said. "This screwup is my fault."

Papa Steve turned and made eye contact. "Doc, we've got Brody nailed for murder. I wouldn't exactly call that a screwup. I thought you AA people believe that you can only do what you can do."

"It's pretty sad, Welcome, when you have to be reminded about this stuff by an earth person," Cap said, using the AA phrase for a nonalcoholic. "As your sponsor, I hereby prescribe more meetings for you, and less time on the pity pot."

"There's still time," Papa Steve said. "Take it from an old experienced geezer," Papa Steve said, "so long as Brody doesn't just blow us away, anything can happen."

Lights from a pair of approaching vehicles appeared in the distance. *The MPs,* Lou thought. It appeared that, thanks to the men of Operation Talon, there was no longer a chance for Brody to do anything devious . . . at least for the moment. Just as the sound of the cars became audible over the rumble of the jet, the lead one began blaring its horn and flashing its lights. Sanctuary. The military police vehicles were their escort to a detention center somewhere on the air base—somewhere away from Wyatt Brody.

It was then Lou realized the vehicles were civilian, not military, the lead one a Mercedes. *Sarah!*

"Hey, if you're gonna be carted off to jail, might as well go in style," Cap said.

"I'm pretty sure that's not the MPs," Lou said.

Anything can happen, Papa Steve had said.

With a burst of acceleration, the second car, a black Escalade, zoomed ahead of the Mercedes and skidded to a stop several feet in front of the transport's staircase. The driver's-side door flew open, and Secretary Spencer Hogarth stumbled out, shouting. "Brody! Where's Brody, dammit! Somebody find me Brody!"

The Mercedes came to a hard stop thirty feet or so behind the Cadillac. A second later, Sarah jumped out, followed by a woman wearing dark sunglasses and a fur-lined jacket, brandishing a folding cane. *Edith!* Sarah's eyes met Lou's immediately. He could see triumph in them.

"Unlock these men right now!" Sarah shouted to the Mantis marines standing guard.

"Sorry, ma'am, these men are to be detained by the MPs. Colonel Brody's orders."

"We'll see about that. Are you guys all right?"

Ignoring the guards, she helped the three prisoners to their feet. Above them, the men of Operation Talon's faces were pressed to the portholes.

"Where is Brody, Lou? Hogarth is going ballistic. I told him that we had absolute proof Brody killed Elias Colston, and I thought his heart was going to stop. We made a deal I'll tell you about regarding Operation Talon, and then he went off the wall."

"I saw Brody board the plane a while ago," Cap said. "Maybe he decided to go on the mission after all, or maybe he was trying to do a repair job on the nose I busted."

"This mission isn't going on the mission," Sarah said. "Secretary Hogarth is about to see to that. Hang tight, guys. We'll get you out of those handcuffs. But we've got to find Brody first."

Several Talon marines had retraced their steps down the stairs to see what the commotion was about. Hogarth, meanwhile, continued to shout out Brody's name. Lou had seen explosive rage before, but mostly in the blackout drunks he and the orderlies and security staff at Eisenhower Memorial were too often forced to subdue. The anger Spencer Hogarth was exhibiting went beyond nearly anything Lou had experienced. It was as though the man who sat near the president's right hand had become detached from reason. He spun around in a series of frenetic circles, his overcoat flapping like a cape. Spittle shot from the snarling rictus of his mouth. His eyes were wild, his cheeks crimson.

"Wyatt Brody! You show yourself right now, you bastard—you murdering dumb-ass son of a bitch. Get out here. Do you hear me? Where is Brody?"

From the top of the transport stairs, there was movement. Mantis marines who were congregated at the base parted like the biblical Red Sea. Wyatt Brody, his parka unzipped, hands on hips, emerged from the cabin of the plane and had paused like the pope on his balcony. His nose was swollen and discolored. A storm cloud had settled across his glowering face and darkened as he connected with Hogarth. "What's the meaning of this?" he shouted. "What are you doing, Spencer?"

"What am I doing? I'm trying to do damage control because you went off plan."

Lou watched, fascinated, as Brody charged down the staircase to confront his mentor. Once on the runway, he and Hogarth stood red face to red face, two snarling alpha male wolves asserting themselves to retain control of the pack.

"What are you talking about, Spencer? This *is* the plan. With all due respect, you need to get a grip on your reality."

"If you didn't kill Elias Colston, none of this would have happened."

"I don't know what in the hell you're talking about. I never—"

"Enough! They know, Wyatt. They know all about Talon and Mantis. They know about the armories. We have to shut it down, and we have to go into damage control mode—effective immediately."

"Spencer, you need to take a step back and think about what you're saying. This mission can't just be rescheduled. We have ten high-value targets that are going down. Operation Talon is a go."

"Only with my blessing!" Hogarth bellowed. "I'm in charge of this mission, and I'm pulling the plug.

Civilians, Brody. Civilians know about what we're doing here. Do you understand what that means? Do you
grasp the ramifications?"

"I grasp that you are not sounding rational at the
moment. You're threatening years of planning and hard
work. My work, damn you! Now, I don't know what
this is all about, but I do know I'm not backing down."

"It's about you killing Elias Colston, you stupid ass!"
Hogarth shouted, spraying the Mantis commander. "And
because of that, we've got a massive security breach on
our hands. Colston was not a threat, Wyatt. He wasn't
going to blow the whistle on Mantis. You misread him,
and it's cost us all. Now, you stand down this instant.
Mantis is over. Operation Talon is over. Effective immediately."

"You're crazy!"

"That sort of insubordination will not be tolerated.
This mission is over."

"No! Nothing is over until I say it's over. Nothing!
Now, get ahold of yourself and back away, Spencer. I
mean it."

Lou and Sarah exchanged stunned looks.

Hogarth fell silent. But if anything, his eyes were
even wilder, his expression more deranged. "That's it.
I'm done with you," he said in a chillingly calm tone.
"I'm relieving you of your command. Effective immediately."

"Under whose authority?"

"Under whose authority?" Hogarth was incredulous.
"How about mine? I'm the secretary of defense, for chris-

sakes, and Operation Talon is my operation to run—and to cancel."

From his overcoat pocket, Hogarth drew a pistol and aimed it at Brody's midsection.

"You have cost this country a great deal, Wyatt. A great deal, indeed. Now, tell your men this mission is over."

"I'll do no such thing," Brody said.

"Tell them it's over! Do it now!"

"No! Men, you get back on that plane this instant. Spencer, give me that fucking gun. You and I will discuss this matter after departure. This mission is a go! I will not be denied!"

Fumbling for a pistol in his belt, Brody charged the older man. A pair of flashes burst from Hogarth's gun along with two whiplike cracks that became suspended in the December air.

Brody staggered several feet backwards, clutching at his abdomen. Blood soaked through his shirt and oozed between his fingers. He stared down in utter dismay at the source of his pain, then looked, eyes glazed, at Hogarth—a bewildered child surveying an abusive parent.

Why did you do this to me? Why?

Brody raised his pistol. Blood continued to drip briskly from his belly to the space between his feet. He tried to level his gun, but his hand began to shake violently.

"You brought this on yourself," Hogarth said. He fired once more.

Brody crumpled lifeless to the asphalt, blood pooling around his inert body.

The secretary of defense lowered his weapon and turned to the Mantis marines staring at him. "He was going to kill me," he said with no remorse. "You're all witnesses. He was going to kill me."

CHAPTER 50

Smoke from Spencer Hogarth's gun vanished on the night breeze. Holding up his hands without holstering his weapon, Hogarth circled several times, pleading his case for justified homicide to dozens of witnesses.

"You all saw that," he said. "Brody was going to kill me. I had no choice. Somebody call an ambulance. Now!"

His plea seemed to break the spell. Four Mantis marines rushed to Brody's side; one of them had procured a field medic kit, as if lifesaving were still a possibility. Numbly, Hogarth continued turning, until his gaze fell on Lou and the two others—not actually seeing them, Lou sensed, so much as assessing them.

Who are these men?

Why are they handcuffed?

Why are they even here at a top secret mission?

Is that one in the fatigues Mantis?

"Unlock these men," Hogarth ordered, as if testing whether or not his authority had survived.

For several moments, there was no response; then

two marines moved forward and cut away the manacles. Lou rubbed at his wrists. Cap and Papa Steve seemed steadier.

"Who are you, and what are you doing here?" Hogarth asked Papa Steve, as if the man he had just shot to death wasn't there at all.

"Sir, Captain Steve Papavassiliou, of Mantis Company, sir! These are my companions, Dr. Lou Welcome and Cap Duncan. Admiral Hogarth, sir, please put away the gun."

Hogarth ignored the request. He seemed to be looking straight through Papa Steve. His attention soon turned to Lou. "So where is the murder weapon?" the secretary asked. "The one Brody used to kill Elias Colston."

"It's safe," Lou said, not at all surprised that Hogarth had pieced together his involvement. "That's all I can say."

"I see." Hogarth continued to dangle his pistol loosely at his side.

Lou felt Cap tense and knew he was readying himself to charge, as he had done with Brody. "No, Cap. Wait him out," he said in a half whisper.

Lou was shaking. Not out of fear, but with rage. It was as if the man was standing in the center of a formal gathering without a stitch of clothing on, and acting as if it were situation normal. He wanted to leap on Hogarth himself, and beat him to within a breath of his disgraced and disgraceful life. This was the man who had blinded Edith and hired killers to remove those who stood against him. This was the man obsessed with power and control, who had orchestrated the combat deaths of any number of Marines. This was one half of the dual-headed beast known as Mantis.

The Mantis marines and Major Coon were on the radio, desperately calling for help.

"We seem to have a very serious problem, gentlemen," Hogarth went on, keeping his gaze fixed on Lou, "a problem that requires a great deal of discretion from all of you."

"No disrespect, pal," Cap said, taking a half step forward, "but I think you've got bigger issues on your plate than what we say or don't say."

Looking utterly shocked, Hogarth glared at Cap. "You don't have a clue what you're talking about, you . . . vermin. What you've just heard, what you've seen here, what you know, cannot be made public. Not now, not ever. You have been exposed to highly classified information. This is a CIA, military black op. Top secret. You are this far from being charged with treason. Perhaps if you're willing to cooperate by keeping your silence, we—and by 'we' I mean the government of the United States of America—would be willing to negotiate."

"I do appreciate the offer from such a fine, upstanding man as yourself," Cap said, moving another inch forward. "Honest, I do. But when I said you've got bigger issues on your plate, I wasn't talking about the guy you killed, lying over there by the staircase."

Hogarth appeared confused.

"Turn around, Mr. Secretary," Lou said, "and I think you'll see what my friend, here, is getting at."

Hogarth spun around. Sarah and Edith, propping a very wobbly Chris Bryzinski between them, stood in front of the Mercedes. Bryzinski's hands were tied behind his back, and blood had soaked through a makeshift tourniquet wrapped tightly around his meaty leg. He was bearing most of his weight on the other.

Hogarth stared at the detective, then at Sarah. "We had a deal," he said. "Goddamn it, we had a deal."

Sarah mocked him with her eyes and spread her hands. "So sue me," she said.

Hogarth whirled frantically, searching every person for a way out.

"It's over," Lou said. "You've taken this as far as it can go. It's over."

For the first time, Hogarth seemed to realize that he was still holding his gun. From ten feet away, hand shaking, he pointed the weapon at Lou. "Back away," he said. "Let me out of here."

"To go where?" Lou asked. "You've contracted men to kill innocent civilians, you've stolen from our country, sanctioned suicidal missions. Where are you going to run?"

Hogarth backed away, swinging his pistol from one person to the next. "You think I did this for glory? For power?" he shouted, turning as though he were onstage in a theater-in-the-round production. "I did this to win the war against terrorism. I did this to save lives! Our enemies do not fear death. They welcome it. They beg for it, for God's sake. We're at a disadvantage to them. Can't you see it? We need to fight fire with fire. That is our mission here. And we are doing it, too. Mantis is making our country stronger. Damn you, Cooper, we had a deal!"

Hogarth raised his gun and pointed it toward Sarah. Lou and Cap had seen enough. The sparring partners charged shoulder to shoulder and lunged at the man. But at the instant they reached him, Hogarth took a quick, purposeful step back and jammed the gun barrel into his mouth, pulling the trigger in the same motion. The shot was surprisingly muffled, but no less deadly. Bone exploded outward like crimson snowflakes from the back of his skull. His arms went limp, and his knees folded almost balletically.

He crumpled to the ground, just a few feet from his protégé, his overcoat splayed open beneath him like the wings of a giant mantis ready to take flight.

CHAPTER 51

Blinking strobe lights on the wings of the Boeing C-40 Clipper painted the wintry night with a continual flash of color. To Lou, it looked like a last gasp, a final weak breath from a living behemoth that once could fly. A small cluster of grim men stood some distance from where Hogarth and Brody now lay. The MPs had arrived and had radioed for their superiors and for the medics.

The group included everybody connected with Operation Talon. Just before the MPs drove up, Lou had finished giving an impassioned speech and now looked to each man for confirmation. *Will you go along with this plan?*

Sarah stood by the Mercedes, along with Edith, Papa Steve, and Cap. Bryzinski was in the backseat. Lou could see the tension on each of their faces. At his request, none of them had heard what he said to the men. Had Lou won them over? Each passing second raised doubts before the answer finally came from the men.

"Whatever it takes! . . . Mantis, whatever it takes!"

Lou nodded. "Whatever it takes," he echoed.

As the first wave of help arrived, the circle parted and Lou headed toward the others. He zippered his parka jacket to fight off a sudden burst of cold air.

"We started laying the groundwork for everything that's going to follow. Listen, if it's okay with the others, how about you and I take a walk?"

"Sure. Sure thing, Lou."

Lou placed an arm around Papa Steve's burly shoulders as he led him away. They walked until they reached a secluded area behind a stack of empty pallets. Their gaunt, haggard faces were eerily lit by the yellowish glow of a floodlight mounted to a large steel hangar.

"Coon will organize the response," Lou said. "He's the ranking officer on the scene. He's going to get some military investigators over here, now that we've got our consensus."

"And what consensus did we reach?" Papa Steve asked.

Something about his expression put a knot in Lou's chest. "The mission will remain a secret," Lou said. "Along with other things."

"By other things, do you mean—?"

"Mantis. As of this moment, Operation Talon doesn't exist. Neither does Manolo, the cartel, or the Mantis drink, for that matter. It's all gone. Buried. Coon and the CIA will take care of Manolo. There can be no loose ends here."

"I think that's really for the best. You did a hell of a

job today, my friend. A hell of a job. Cap, too. He's an amazing piece of work."

"That's an understatement."

"Thanks for speaking to the men. I watched their faces. I'm glad they took the advice of a civilian. No offense."

"None taken. Even a broken clock is right twice a day."

"What now?" Papa Steve asked.

"Now," Lou said, "we talk."

"About?"

"About your friends."

"My friends?"

"Cap isn't the only piece of work around here. You're one of them yourself, and your friends are a testament to that. You have a lot of them. Very useful they are, too."

"What are you getting at, Lou?"

"From the first time we met, I've been impressed that whenever you need help, one of your friends is there. The police officer that gave me a ticket, the guy who lent you a helicopter to meet me at the golf course, your buddy at the restaurant. That's a terrific credit to the kind of person you are. But one of those friends was even more impressive than the others—the one who knew so much about guns and ballistics."

"Well, I guess you might say I'm a very lucky guy."

Lou watched the man closely, marveling at his ability to stay composed. "A couple of days ago," Lou went on, "I flew out to Minnesota to see Dr. Sherwood, the director of the Pine Grove Clinic. Turns out, he and Elias were fraternity brothers at the University of Virginia. That's why Elias went to see him. Initially, he was freaked about violating confidentiality, and wouldn't tell me anything. But later, after he thought about what was at stake for McHugh, he had a slight change of heart and had his assistant call and tell me that Elias was in fact a patient of his. After I got back to D.C., he called me himself with some more information. Elias was dying from chronic myeloid leukemia. It's a type with what's called a Philadelphia chromosome—almost impossible to treat successfully. Six months, maybe a little more, with what would have been pretty painful therapy."

"Go on."

"Does the name James Styles mean anything to you?"

"Should it?"

"It's the name Elias is known by at the clinic. Dr. Sherwood communicated with him through a post office box in Bowie, Maryland."

"You've learned an amazing amount in a short time," Papa Steve said. "No wonder I'm so impressed with you."

"I don't think anyone knew Elias was dying—maybe not even Jeannine. No one, that is, except you."

"Lou, I don't—"

Lou reached out and gently placed his hands on Papa Steve's shoulders. "No more games, Steve," he said without rancor. "I understand what you did, and I understand why."

For a time there was only silence.

"I was hoping things would just pass," Papa Steve said finally. "How long have you known?"

"I began having suspicions when you told me you couldn't tail Brody, because of the Palace Guards. You just seemed too resourceful to be stopped by them. So I began to wonder why you wanted to protect the secret of where he was going. It was Mark Colston. You were protecting your godson. You never meant for me to find that CD, did you?"

"Of course not. The police were supposed to find it. I made it as easy as I could for them. It was the only picture in the whole damn office that was turned around. I did everything but hang an arrow from the ceiling pointing down to it. That buffoon Bryzinski and his cops should have found it, and after they listened to it, marched straight to Brody's front door."

"The investigation of a murdered congressman would have been intense, and the pressure on Brody massive—especially with your ballistics friend on the job."

"Except that Elias didn't know Jeannine was having an affair with your pal Gary," Papa Steve said, finishing Lou's thought. "The moment Bryzinski had a prime suspect, the investigation went south. The police did a half-baked job searching Elias's office because they already had their man in custody."

"Then I showed up," Lou said.

"Enter Lou Welcome."

"I became the police by proxy—the guy you fed just enough information to keep me on Brody's trail."

"That's it. All I wanted you to do was to get the police away from Gary and back on Brody. And you did a lot more than I bargained for."

"By that, you mean I followed Brody and found out about the drugs and the Mantis juice."

"All I wanted you to do was get the murder weapon."

"Because you didn't want me to know the truth about Mantis."

"The motive for Elias's murder was supposed to be his knowledge of Reddy Creek," Papa Steve said. "Brody was stealing weapons because of budget cuts, and Elias was on to him. That's what the prosecutors would have said, anyway, if the police had found the CD, and had done their job by following the trail to its logical endpoint."

"It's a weak case if you don't have the murder weapon, though," Lou said. "Good thing I got you that ballistics report."

"Elias came across a battalion supply sergeant who was willing to testify against Brody. He would have provided circumstantial evidence linking Brody and Hogarth to armory thefts up and down the East Coast. Still, we needed that weapon. I couldn't very well have waltzed into a police station and said, 'Here, I think this is the gun used to kill Elias Colston.' I needed another way to get the gun into the right person's hands."

"It had to have been terrible for you," Lou said.

"Shooting Elias? Killing my best friend? Yeah, Lou, it was worse than terrible. It was the hardest damn thing I've ever had to do. I refused again and again, but Elias wouldn't let up. He was like a terrier on a rat." Papa Steve looked away and rubbed at his eyes with the back of his hand.

"Eventually you caved in."

"Imagine if Cap asked you to kill him," Papa Steve said. "And you knew it was the right thing to do. You knew in your gut that it had to go down that way. Brody needed to be stopped."

"That's why you transferred to Mantis," Lou said.

"It was before Elias became ill, of course. He had his suspicions about Mantis and Brody. Mark's uncharacteristically heroic death, Brody's Ph.D. thesis, the Reddy Creek incident, and the missing reporter's blog. But he didn't have solid proof."

"You got yourself embedded with Mantis so you could follow Brody. That's how you found out about the Mantis drug. You knew all along."

"Mark and the others had died with incredible valor. Elias and I would never do anything to taint that. We had to eliminate Brody without having anyone learn about the chemicals the men were getting every day."

Lou could not stand back any longer. He put his arms around Papa Steve and made no attempt to stem his own tears. The real hero in the piece was the man there with him. "I'm so fucking proud to know you," Lou said.

"Once you found that CD, all I wanted was your help getting the gun to the right people. End of story."

"In the end, nobody was supposed to learn about Mantis," Lou said.

Papa Steve nodded. "That's what Elias wanted. That's what he died for."

"With Brody gone, Mantis would be gone," Lou said.

"And so would its secret. We needed to take down Brody without having to expose the world to the truth, without having to leave a black mark on the graves of those heroic young men. They would forever be associated with one of the most horrific examples of human experimentation since the Nazis. That would have been their legacy. For Mark, for the others, I did what had to be done."

"Whatever it takes," Lou said. "You picked the day because you knew Brody went to see Manolo each and every Wednesday. You knew he wouldn't have an alibi that would hold up. He'd say he was at the military parade because he couldn't very well confess to where he really went."

"Elias must have said something to Jeannine," Papa Steve added. "Of course, she wouldn't have known it was his final good-bye. But I'm sure he spoke from the heart, because even though he didn't pay as much attention to her as he might have, he loved Jeannine to pieces."

"It was a kiss," Lou said, remembering her description. "A very special kiss."

"Well, whatever he said or did, I'm sure it made her realize the mistake she was making with Gary, so she ended the relationship."

"And Gary showed up at the Colstons' place, drunk and despondent. Wrong place, wrong time."

"He must have got there just after I left," Papa Steve said.

Silence.

"What happened out there with the men, Lou?" Papa Steve eventually asked. "What are we going to tell the world?"

"Wyatt Brody and Spencer Hogarth were involved in a massive weapons-theft scheme as a way to circumvent congressional budget cuts and keep Mantis fully operational," Lou said. "Mantis was Hogarth's baby, Brody's, too. It made sense they'd do anything to protect it. Elias found out about Reddy Creek, and for that Wyatt Brody killed him on a Wednesday morning. There's video evidence showing Brody leaving a military parade on the day Colston was murdered.

"As for the murder weapon, I showed you the ballistics report at your request. You know a lot about guns. You suggested to me that the weapon used to kill Elias might be an antique Colt military pistol from Brody's substantial gun collection. A pistol that just so happens to leave a six left rifling mark. You got the gun—how, I don't know—and gave it to me. We got it tested and it came back a match. Brody was going to go public because he knew the walls were closing in. Hogarth wouldn't stand for it, so he killed Brody in front of dozens of witnesses. Once Hogarth realized he had no way out, he decided to take his own life. End of story. That's what happened here. And everybody from Mantis, Coon included, agrees."

"Anybody ever tell you that you're a piece of work?" Papa Steve asked.

CHAPTER 52

The third-floor courtroom, nestled within the labyrinth that was the circuit court for Baltimore County, would have been standing room only had the press known of Sarah's emergency motion for dismissal of the charges against Dr. Gary McHugh. Though the trial date had yet to be set, the state's case against him, thanks in part to the high-powered players, the sordid love triangle, and a *Dateline* special, was still very fresh in the minds of the public. It remained hungry for any new developments, and Sarah Cooper was just moments away from dropping a bombshell.

Lou and Cap were among the dozen or so observers seated in the gallery. On the bench in front of them, Judge Sandra Griffey, a stern-looking black woman with a reputation for fairness and an unparalleled legal mind, looked over the motion Sarah had filed just days before. The court clerk and court reporter were seated at their respective desks, awaiting the outcome of what Lou expected would be a stunning turn of events. The lawyers for the plaintiff, in this case the State of

Maryland, were grim faced and sullen. In stark contrast to them, Sarah and Grayson Devlin, flanking a stoic-looking Gary McHugh, exuded confidence.

Lou had thought Gary would be dressed in street clothes instead of the orange prison jumpsuit he wore. Before Judge Griffey entered the courtroom, Sarah had explained there was not enough time between her filing the motion and the hearing date to make the necessary arrangements. Gary was still a prisoner of the state and would remain so unless Sarah could change that outcome. To Lou's eyes, Gary looked gaunt, his skin stretched tight to the bone. Thank goodness Cap put Tiny on protective services duty, or Gary might have shown up to this hearing in far worse physical and emotional shape. Despite the quiet confidence of his attorneys, Gary wore the grave expression of a man still facing a potential death penalty.

Judge Griffey slammed her gavel with authority and brought the hearing to order. "It is my understanding that the attorneys for the defendant have filed a motion for dismissal. Are the attorneys for the prosecution aware of this motion?"

The lead prosecutor—a scarecrow of a man with a shaved head and graying goatee, sporting a crisply knotted bow tie—rose from his seat. "The prosecution is aware, Your Honor."

"The defense may present the motion," Judge Griffey instructed.

Sarah stood, smoothing out the fabric of her pleated wool skirt, and cleared her throat. Lou focused intently on everything she did. He tugged on the bottom of his crewneck sweater—a subconscious reaction that mimicked her movements. His finger got snagged on a small hole in the waistband, which he had failed to notice while getting dressed. Diversity's handiwork had followed him into court.

Nice kitty.

In the week since Hogarth took his life after ending Brody's, Sarah had vanished into what she warned Lou would be an all-consuming effort to get Gary out of jail. The motion to dismiss, she had explained, was an unusual legal step, but a necessary one to expedite the process. Now everything hinged on the prosecution's agreement that their case against McHugh was unwinnable.

"Thank you, Your Honor," Sarah said. "New and important developments have emerged since my client's arrest that I have outlined in the motion. Forensic tests, corroborated by the prosecution's own ballistics expert, have confirmed that the weapon used to murder Elias Colston, an antique Colt pistol, was registered to the late Colonel Wyatt Brody and was part of his extensive gun collection. It is impossible for my client to have procured this weapon from the highly secured military base where Colonel Brody kept his collection under alarmed lock and key. Also, there is no evidence that my client knew of or had ever come in contact with Colonel Brody. Therefore, it is reasonable to conclude that Gary McHugh could not have fired the weapon that killed Elias Colston."

Lou was enraptured by Sarah's commanding performance. Clearly, this was her game, her arena, and he could not have been more impressed with her poise and self-assurance. They'd been out for dinner once, in one of the rare moments when Sarah emerged from the confines of her office to take a breath of fresh air. Both she and Lou were acting cautiously. At some point, he thought, he might arrange a dinner with her and Emily—but not yet.

Sarah went on to detail other highlights from her motion, including the motive Wyatt Brody had for committing murder as well as the opportunity. Her presentation was flawless and her conclusions impossible to refute. When she was through, the prosecutors looked like a Little League team facing off against the pros.

"Does the prosecution have any objection to the motion to dismiss?" Judge Griffey asked.

"No, Your Honor. We accept the motion in full as presented."

"Very well," Judge Griffey said. "Dr. McHugh, please accept the court's sincere apology for the pain and suffering you've endured. We wish you only the very best. This case is now dismissed, and you are free to go."

Gary beamed as he hugged Sarah and then Grayson.

Then it was Lou's turn to give Gary a big embrace as soon as he entered the gallery. "We did it, buddy," Lou said. "We did it!"

"Thank you, Lou," Gary said, his eyes misting. "I still can't believe it's over."

"In some ways, it's just beginning. But for now, believe it. You're a free man. You heard the judge."

"Guess I better find some clothes to wear," Gary said, patting the pockets of his prison garb.

"Orange was never really your color."

"And I guess I'm going to need to find a place to live, too. Got any good hotel referrals for me?"

Lou grimaced at the implications. He had heard from Gary that Missy planned to file for divorce. Evidently, that plan had been set in motion. It certainly explained her absence from today's proceedings.

"I've actually given that some thought," Lou said.

"Yeah? What are you thinking? Four Seasons? Ritz?"

"More like the Hope House."

"Sounds a bit low rent for my tastes. I may not have a wife, but I've still got some money."

"Actually," Lou said, "it's a halfway house. That's where I lived after I got out of treatment. In fact, I sort of made a call and told them you might be coming later today to stay for a while. They're saving you a room. I can even provide you with a tried-and-true AA sponsor if you want." Lou thumbed behind him toward Cap. "But I've got to warn you—you're really going to have to toe the line with him. He's strict as he is bald."

"That's pretty strict."

"This will be good for you, Gary."

"Okay. If it's what I need to do. I'll try my best."

"Your medical license has been suspended, not permanently revoked. It's not all that matters. You're ready to return to being a doctor as soon as you don't have to."

"I understand. I really do. Thanks, Lou. For everything."

"Whatever it takes," Lou said.

Gary eyed Lou with amused curiosity. "What does that mean?"

"It means from now on, it's got to be a day at a time for you."

Sarah called out Gary's name. "There's paperwork to sign," she said. "Let's get this done."

"I've gotta run. I'll see you on the outside, buddy," Gary said.

Sarah waved at Lou in a way that said she would catch up with him later. Lou gave Sarah a thumbs-up and she returned one of her own.

Lou and Cap headed out of the courtroom together.

"Helluva show she put on in there," Cap said. "Helluva show."

"If you're ever in trouble, I know a great lawyer."

"So far, I've been able to settle all my disputes in the ring. I'm going to look after your buddy Gary, just like I looked after you."

"Then I know he's going to be all right," Lou said.

Stepping outside, Lou shielded his eyes from the glare of the midday sun. It took him a moment to make out the West Virginia highway patrol car parked out front. Judy Lemon leaned up against her car, arms folded, resplendent in her uniform. Her smile brightened the day. Papa Steve stood beside her, wearing jeans, a parka, and a broad-rimmed black leather cowboy hat.

"How'd it go in there?" Papa Steve asked.

"He's a free man," Lou said. "Case closed. It's great to see you both."

Hugs were exchanged. The four shared a unique bond—a closeness they would forever be reminded of anytime the "1812 Overture" happened to play.

"Great to see you, too," Papa Steve said. "Thanks for letting me know about the hearing. I'm sorry I couldn't have gotten here sooner, but I'm glad for your friend Gary. He'd still be in jail if it wasn't for you and Cap."

"And you and Officer Judy," Cap added.

"I thought you'd like to know that they've got confessions from the two Palace Guards who killed Hector," Papa Steve said. "He's going to be buried in Arlington Cemetery, and his family will receive the full military death benefit. It's the only positive outcome from a truly tragic event."

"That is great news," Lou said. "I've had a heavy heart about Hector. I'm glad to know Gary isn't the only one for whom justice was served."

"I also came here to say good-bye," Papa Steve said, "at least for now. I've put in my papers and I'm officially retiring from the Corps. I figured I'd do a little bit of traveling before my bones get too creaky for the road."

Lou shot Papa Steve and Judy a questioning glance. "So are you two—?"

"Happy, healthy, and headed out West," Judy said, preempting the need to supply any more details.

"What's with the hat?" Cap asked Papa Steve.

"We've got a reservation at a dude ranch in Arizona,"

Papa Steve said. "Saddle sores and hot tubs. I figured a fine Stetson hat will help me get into character."

"And don't tell me," Lou said. "You happen to have a friend who owns a fine hat store."

Papa Steve took Lou's right hand in both of his. "How'd you guess?" he said.

EPILOGUE

The Caribou Laundromat seldom needed air-conditioning, which was a good thing most warm days, because it had none. Summer days, like this eighty-degree beauty in late June, the breeze off Belmore Bay entered from the water through the rear door, swept through the place, and exited onto Maine Street, ending against the plate glass front of the *Belmore Current* newspaper. The Laundromat was empty this noon hour, except for Edith Harmon and a handsome young man in his early twenties, who was helping her fold.

"You know, Ma," Ian Harmon said, "I'll be happy to do this. Aunt Alice and Uncle Bill made me do all my own laundry, and I grew to sort of like it."

"Did it ever occur to you that I might like doing it, too?"

Ian, over six feet and rail thin, bent down and kissed his mother on the forehead. "It's good to be home," he said, "even though I'd never been here before Christmas."

"It's good to *have* you home, sweetie," Edith said.

"I'll take the real you over the Skype you any day. You've been a heck of an addition to the newspaper, too. I'm not sure I want to ship you off to U of Maine for your last year, even though it *is* in journalism."

"I've already learned more from a few months working with you than I did during three years of college in South Dakota. Maybe I shouldn't bother with the transfer just for my last year."

"Talk like that will get you smack-dab on my wild side, a place you don't ever want to be, even though I don't carry my derringer anymore." Edith cocked her head to one side. "Ian, is there someone outside?"

"How did you—? Sorry, by now I should know better than to ask. Across the street, a man and a woman just got off bicycles and are peering into the office."

"Describe them."

"She's got brown hair pulled back, and a pretty good body. No, make that a very good body, especially in spandex."

"Ian, you're a journalist. Is that the best you can do? She's got a very good body?"

"He's sort of tall, broad shoulders, dark hair flattened because he was wearing a helmet. Looks to be in shape. Great guns, actually. Maybe a weight lifter. No tattoos that I can see. They're coming over here. Did I say that she has a terrific body?"

Edith was already dashing toward the front door as if she could see perfectly, using her darting hands as antennas.

"Sarah! Lou!" she cried out the open door. "I didn't expect you until tomorrow."

"Turns out we're in better shape than we thought we'd be in," Sarah said, hurrying over to embrace her friend. "Sleeping in campgrounds, we're up at dawn, and five days on these hills has added like five miles an hour to our speed.

"You're not supposed to speed through Maine."

A hug for Lou and introductions to Ian, and the four of them left the laundry behind and crossed the street to the *Belmore Current* office. Edith and Sarah had stayed in touch, so it was no real surprise to learn that Sarah had made partner, and had decided to take down a wall or two with Lou. This no-particular-place-to-go trip to Maine was a big deal, but Edith could tell after just a short while that it was so far, so good.

Once in the busy little office, Ian became a charming, droll, and intelligent host, serving tea and discussing the events of the world to a depth that belied his years. Sarah ached at the notion of how painful it must have been for her friend to be blinded, and then to have to send him away.

"So," Edith said after a time, "Ian and I have some news to discuss with you two, but first fill me in. How's Gary McHugh doing?"

"Believe it or not, pretty good," Lou said. "On one of my visits to see him in jail, in what I suspect was a weak moment, he swore that he would be happy to have his medical license taken away if it meant he could get out of there. He's getting the chance to prove it. Right now he's still in the halfway house I was in, and get this, he's working in Dimitri's Pizza right below my apartment. He likes it, too. The Costa Brothers, who own the place, tell me that he's become something of a savant at spinning and flipping dough. An A-plus student, they called him. Gary claims they've actually named a toss after him."

Sarah said, "Once a doctor, always a doctor."

"I would think another six months of hard work and meetings," Lou said, "and he could apply to get his medical license returned. It's a great sign that he never talks about it."

"And I have some news," Sarah said. "Bryzinski and the AG just agreed on a plea bargain. Nine years for attempted murder. No parole. I'm not sure yet what will happen regarding the teen he allegedly killed. The best thing he'll end up with down the road may be a job like Gary has."

"Death by pizza," Edith said. "I've always felt it was a gift directly from God that we were able to smush him into the trunk of your car."

"So, what have you got for us?" Lou asked.

Ian opened the top drawer of a cabinet, retrieved a thin file, and opened it on the table. It contained some pink phone messages, pages of handwritten notes and printouts, and a couple of newspaper articles, including one in Hebrew.

"Mom has told me pretty much everything that happened at Reddy Creek, and this past Christmastime at the Dover air base," he said. "I'm the paper's vice president and associate editor in charge of research, right, Mom? Well, two weeks ago, I came across a small piece about the leader of the Palestinian terrorist group known as al-Aqsa Martyr's Brigade being killed in Beirut by a suicide bomber. That seemed a little queer to me because usually it's the terrorists who are doing the suicide bombing, not having it done to them. So, with the help of some of Mom's connections, I started to try to figure out who was taking credit or being blamed for this."

Lou and Sarah were already exchanging concerned glances.

"Go on, Ian," Sarah said.

"Well, so far, nobody has admitted to doing it. Nobody. That was strange, too. Usually people jump to take credit for this sort of thing. Then, the day before yesterday, I got a call from a man in Israel named Jacob. Mom?"

"Jacob is Mossad," Edith said, "a spy and counterterrorist now living just outside Jerusalem. Eight or nine years ago, I was researching a piece on the suicide of an important, Iraqi-born atomic scientist in the research triangle in North Carolina. I came across enough information to believe the man was spying for Iran and had been assassinated by the Mossad. Jacob paid me a little visit and asked me to drop the story. He refused to tell me why, but he said if I didn't, things would not go well for me or Ian. In exchange, he would make certain I was first in line for a number of other stories. Over the years, he's kept his part of the bargain."

"So I e-mailed him, asking about this assassination," Ian went on. "He called Mom and told her that a secret unit of the Mossad had been put together expressly to perform hits such as this one. He said that even members of his unit were being kept in the dark about it, but that he had learned it was connected in some way with research the Americans had perfected dealing with the basis of fear."

"Did this Jacob happen to know which Americans?" Lou asked, barely able to hold his cup steady.

"Not at the moment," Edith said. "But he said he'll keep me posted. You two want me to keep you in the loop?"

Sarah and Lou again exchanged grim looks.

"We'll let you know," they answered.

Read on for an excerpt from Michael Palmer's next book

RESISTANT

Available in hardcover May 2014 from St. Martin's Press

PROLOGUE

A heavy pall had settled over Boston's White Memorial Hospital.

Becca Seabury's condition was deteriorating.

The hospital grapevine was operating at warp speed, sending the latest rumors through the wards and offices of the iconic institution, chosen two years in a row as the number-one general hospital in the country. This morning, in all likelihood, the decision would be made—a decision that almost everyone associated with White Memorial, from housekeeping to the laboratories to the administration—was taking personally.

Before long, the team of specialists—orthopedic, medical, and infectious disease—would either choose to continue battling the bacteria that the press and others had begun calling the Doomsday Germ, or they would opt to capitulate and amputate the teen's right arm just below the shoulder.

In room 837 of the Landrew Building, a group of

carefully selected physicians and nurses had been assembled. At the doorway to the room, as well as at every elevator and stairway, security was keeping the media at bay, along with any but essential personnel.

From the day more than two weeks ago, when Becca was operated on to clean out infection from the site of her elbow repair, she had been front page news.

FLESH EATING BACTERIA COMPLICATING
CHEERLEADER'S HEALING

The seventeen-year-old captain of her school's championship team had shattered her elbow in a spectacular fall during the state finals. The violent injury was chronicled on YouTube, and immediately went viral, making Becca something of a household name around the globe. After a successful reconstruction by Dr. Chandler Beebe, the chief of orthopedics, followed by several days of IV antibiotics, the conservative decision was made to wait one more day and discharge.

That was when Becca Seabury's fevers began.

The Landrew Building, less than two years old, was the latest jewel in the expanding crown of White Memorial. The eighth floor featured four negative pressure isolation rooms—airtight spaces except for a gap beneath the door, with a ventilation system that brought more air into the room than it allowed out. By the time a nurse escorted Becca's family to the waiting area, there were seven in gloves, gowns, and hoods in the spacious room.

Chandler Beebe, six-foot-six, towered over the rest.

Nearly lost among them, motionless on her back, was a pale, fair-skinned young woman, with hair the color of spun gold. Her lips were dry and cracked, and the flush in her cheeks looked anything but healthy. An IV with a piggy-backed plastic bag of meds was draining into her good arm. The temperature reading on her chart was 102.5 degrees. It had been as high as 104. Her blood pressure was 85/50.

Chandler Beebe, once a guard for the Harvard University basketball team, was generally unflappable. Now, beneath his mask and hood, he was nearly as pale as his patient. It was the smell, he knew, that was getting to him. Despite his years operating in war zones and medical missions to third-world countries, he had never been fully able to accustom himself to the odor of pus and of rotting flesh. Glancing at the monitor, with a nurse holding Becca's arm up, he began unwrapping the gauze he had placed around it eight hours before. Beebe had two teenagers himself, a boy and a girl, both athletes and excellent students, and as brave and well-adjusted as this girl. But he couldn't get his mind around the image of either of them being at the crossroads of decisions like this one.

The progressive layers of bandages, as they were removed, were first damp with bloody drainage, then soaked. The ooze, from eight inches of filleted incision, reeked of untreated bacterial growth. The color of the flesh had darkened. Twelve days before, Beebe and a surgical colleague had reopened the incision he had made when he did the initial, meticulous reconstruction. The infection had come on with the speed and ferocity of a Panzer attack. Fever, shaking chills, new swelling, intense pain, dehydration, blood pressure drop. Signs of infection in an enclosed space. There was no choice that day. The incision had to be opened, debrided, irrigated, and drained.

Now, it was time for another decision.

Becca Seabury's antecubital space—the inside of her elbow—looked like ground beef that had been left in the sun. Muscle fibers, tendons, ligaments, all basted in thick, greenish purulence, glinted beneath the portable saucer light overhead. Beebe heard his brilliant chief resident inhale sharply, and vowed to reprimand her for the audible reaction as soon as it was appropriate. In the next moment, he decided not to mention it.

"Becca, it's Dr. Beebe. Can you hear me?"

There was little response except a fitful moan. Beebe, his jaw set, looked across the bed at the chief of infectious disease.

"Sid?" he asked

Sidney Fleishman shrugged and shook his head. "As you can see, she's still toxic. No change in the bug, and no effect from every antibiotic in our arsenal. Her white count has dipped a bit, but there are no other signs that we're winning. We've gotten permission to try one of the most promising experimental drugs that is being tested on strep and MRSA— but this doomsday g—this *bacteria*—is like nothing we've seen. Strep, but not really strep, resistant to methicillin and vancomycin, and carbapenem."

"Conclusion?"

"I think we have some time. Not much, but some—especially with the infection still limited to her elbow."

Beebe inhaled deeply and exhaled slowly. Fleishman, as bright as anyone at White Memorial, was advocating a continued conservative approach with the addition of a new, experimental drug, which was showing effectiveness against methicillin-resistant staph aureus.

How much time do you think? Beebe was about to ask when Jennifer Lowe, Becca's nurse, standing at the foot of the bed, cleared her throat by way of interruption. She had been massaging lotion onto Becca's left foot and now had turned her attention to the right one.

"Dr. Beebe, I think you'd better have a look at this," she said. "I didn't see anything here an hour ago."

She gently folded back the sheet and gestured to the foot. All five toes were reddened, and swelling extended two inches toward the ankle.

Beebe stepped to his right and inspected this new development—first with his eyes, then with his gloved hands.

"Sid?"

Fleishman studied the foot, then checked for swollen lymph nodes in their patient's right groin—often a sign of expanding infection.

"Nothing yet," he said, "but this is clearly new infection, probably seeded from her arm."

Chandler Beebe ran his tongue across his lips and took one more breath.

"Jennifer, is the OR ready?" he asked.

"It is."

"Call down and tell them we're bringing Becca Sea-bury down for removal of a septic right arm. I'll speak to her family. Thank you for your efforts, everyone. My team, go ahead. I'll meet you in the OR. Oh, and Jennifer, call pathology, please, and tell them we'll be sending down a specimen."

The room emptied quickly and silently. These were medical professionals—the best of the best. But every one of them was badly shaken.

Jennifer Lowe, thirty, and a veteran of half a dozen missions to villages in the Congo, bent over her patient. Lowe, her marriage to a physical therapist just six months away, was a sparkplug of a woman, the daughter and granddaughter of nurses.

"Be strong, baby," she whispered. "We're going to get through this. Just be strong."

It was at that moment she felt an irritation—an itch—between the middle and ring fingers of her left hand. While she was at work, her modest engagement ring hung on a sturdy chain around her neck. She had eczema, but never bad and never in that particular spot.

Not all that concerned, she moved over to the sink and stripped off her latex gloves. The skin between the fingers was reddened and cracked.

CHAPTER 1

Liberty is worth more than every pearl
in the ocean, every ounce of gold ever mined.
It is as precious to man as air, as necessary
to survival as a beating heart.
—Lancaster R. Hill; A Secret Worth Keeping;
Sawyer River Books, 1937; p. 12

"Two-hundred-six . . . two-oh-seven . . . two-oh-eight. . . ."

"Come on, Big Lou. It hurts so good. Say it!"

"Okay, okay," Lou Welcome groaned. "Two-oh-nine. . . . It hurts so good. . . . Two-ten. . . . It hurts so good. . . . Oh, it just frigging hurts! My . . . stomach's . . . gonna . . . tear . . . open. . . . Two-twelve. . . ."

Lou was doing sit-ups on the carpet between the beds in room 177 of what had to be one of the bargain rooms at the venerable Chattahoochee Lodge. Cap Duncan, shirtless and already in his running shorts, was kneeling by Lou's feet, holding down his ankles. Cap's shaved pate was glistening. His grin, as usual, was like a star going nova. He had done three hundred crunches before Lou was even out of the sack, and looked like he could easily have ripped off three hundred more.

Every inch a man's man.

Lou's best friend, and for ten years his AA sponsor, was a fifty-two-year-old Bahamian, with a physique that looked like it had been chiseled by one of Michelangelo's descendants. He had earned his nickname, Cap'n Crunch, from his days as a professional boxer, specifically the sound noses made when he hit them.

It was April the 14th—a Thursday. Lou's trip to Georgia had been ordered by Walter Filstrup, the bombastic head of the Washington D.C. Physician Wellness Office, a position that made the psychiatrist Lou's boss.

Filstrup's sweet wife, Marjory, a polar opposite of her husband, was in the ICU of a Maryland hospital, with an irregular heartbeat which had not responded to electrical cardioversion. But as one of two candidates for the presidency of the National Federation of Physician Health Programs, Filstrup was scheduled to address the annual meeting being held this year at the lodge in the mountains north of Atlanta.

Wife in ICU versus speech in Georgia. Let . . . me . . . think.

Not surprisingly to Lou, Filstrup had actually wrestled mightily with the choice. It wasn't until Marjory had an allergic reaction to one of the cardiac meds that the man turned his speech over to Lou along with his conference registration, and an expense account that would cover all Lou's meals, providing he only ate once a day.

Whoopee.

"You're slowing down, Welcome," Cap said. "You're not going to get to three hundred that way."

"I'm not going to get . . . to three hundred *any* way."

Cap, his competitive fire seldom dimmed, delighted in saying that most people's workout was his warm-up. Lou, nine years younger, and at six feet, an inch or so taller, never had any problem believing that. Their connection began the day Lou was checked into Harbor House, a sober halfway house in one of the grittier sections of D.C. Cap, given name Hank, was working as a group leader there while he cajoled one bank after another, trying to scrape together enough bread for his own training center. Twelve months after that, Lou was living on his own, the Stick and Move Gym had become a reality, and the two friends, one black as a moonless night, and the other a blue-eyed rock-jaw with the determination of a Rottweiler, and roots that may have gone back to the Pilgrims, were sparring three times a week.

A year or so after that, following a zillion recovery meetings and the development of a new, infinitely mellower philosophy of living, the suspension of Lou's medical license was lifted, and he was back in the game.

"Okay, then," Cap said, "do what you can. It's no crime to lower your expectations. Only not too far."

"Does everything . . . we do together . . . have to be . . . some sort of competition? . . . Two-twenty . . . two-twenty-one . . ."

"I assume we're going to have breakfast after our run and I don't believe in competitive eating, if that helps any."

"Of course. It would be the one area I could kick your butt."

The Chattahoochee Lodge had been built in the twenties for hunters and had been enlarged and renovated in 1957, the same year Elvis purchased Graceland. A sprawling, rustic complex, the main building was perched in the mountainous forest, high above the banks of the fast-flowing Chattahoochee River. As ecotourism boomed in the early 1990s, the place became a major destination for leisure travelers, birders, hikers, and convention-goers, with rooms often booked a year in advance.

Lou, board-certified in both Internal and Emergency Medicine, had never particularly enjoyed medical conferences of any kind, so it was a godsend when he whined about the impending trip to Cap and learned that his friend's only living relative was an aging aunt, living just outside of Atlanta. Working full time in the E.R. at Eisenhower Memorial Hospital, and part time with the PWO, Lou had more than enough in his small war chest for another ticket south. The quite reasonable rent for his second-floor, two-bedroom apartment down the street from the gym and just above Dimitri's Pizza, helped make a loan to his sponsor even more painless.

Proof that the idea was a solid one was that Cap haggled surprisingly little over the bartering agreement Lou proposed—two months of weekly sessions in the ring for him, plus an additional four lessons for his precocious fourteen-year-old daughter, Emily. Cap would get the window seat.

Having to put up with Filstrup notwithstanding, Lou

loved his job at the PWO. The pay was lousy, but for him the irony of going from being a client to being an associate director was huge. The organization provided support and monitoring services for doctors with mental illness, physical illness, substance abuse, sexual boundary violations, and behavioral problems. Most new PWO contracts required the troubled physician to enter some sort of treatment program or inpatient rehab, followed by regular meetings with their assigned PWO associate director, along with frequent random urine screens for alcohol and other drugs of abuse.

Lou was hardly averse to counseling and psychotherapy for certain docs, but he strongly believed that, physician or not, addiction was a medical illness and not a moral issue. Walter Filstrup disagreed.

When Filstrup finally handed over his carefully typed speech and the conference program, the trip got even better. Not only would Lou and Cap have time for some training runs together in the mountains, but while Cap was visiting his aunt, Lou would be able to take a conference-sponsored guided tour of the Centers for Disease Control—the CDC.

More irony.

Lou had spent nearly ten months of his life in Atlanta and had never even been close to the world-renowned institute. The last time he was in the city, nine years before, was for the one-year reunion of his treatment group at the Templeton Drug Rehab Center.

It was time to complete some circles.